KT-153-487

She had a body made to be touched by a man's hands.

The skin of her face was creamy, glowing, a soft flush highlighting perfect cheekbones. Her lips were moist and the shade of coral that lay on the bottom of tropical seas, her eyes large and framed by sweeping dark lashes, her hair a warm shade of honey-gold, thick and gently curling.

He moved slowly forward to stand before her, his eyes never leaving hers for an instant. Who was she? Her lovely features, mirroring her thoughts, were clouded with undisguised resentment. What had he done to deserve her ire?

'Is there something about me that you find distasteful?' he asked.

His voice came smooth and deep to Eleanor's ears, yet there was an amused mockery that seemed to scorn everything about the occasion and the people present.

'Indeed, I have heard nothing to recommend you, sir.'

His wry smile indicated his surroundings. 'You are not alone in that.'

Dear Reader

Mills & Boon—the very byword for romance—will be celebrating its centenary in 2008. The company has been reflecting ever-changing romantic and social attitudes, fanning the flames of passion for the past one hundred years, frequently launching brand-new looks featuring new logos and vibrant cover designs. The high reputation and quality of their books rests at the core of Mills & Boon's success, and when it comes to romance there is none better—which is why I feel privileged to write for a publishing company that launched such great names as Georgette Heyer and P.G. Wodehouse.

I have always enjoyed reading romance, which is my favourite form of escapism. At first I was content to read other people's work, to absorb myself in their stories and feel a sense of discovery with each new book, but eventually I wanted to create adventures of my own, to write my own stories and bring my own characters to life—which I did. I began writing as a hobby, with no set pattern, fitting in with house and children, but it soon became compulsory. It gives me an indescribable thrill to witness a story of my own creation unfold before my eyes. Writing gives me enjoyment which is both intense and real. I am passionate about history—whatever the period—and my novels are historical romances.

I shall never forget the excitement of having my first book accepted, meeting my editor for the first time, and the wonderful sense of achievement at seeing my books in the shops. I also enjoy attending the author parties, which give me the opportunity to meet and chat with other Mills & Boon authors. I remember my first Mills & Boon get-together very well, and my apprehension—which increased dramatically when I found myself seated next to Mr Alan Boon—but I needn't have worried. He was so interesting and easy to talk to—a true gentleman in every sense.

FORBIDDEN LORD is my first Elizabethan novel. I hope you enjoy reading it as much as I enjoyed writing it.

Helen

FORBIDDEN LORD

Helen Dickson

⊚™ MILLS & BOON®

Pure reading pleasure

DID YOU PURCHASE THIS BOOK WITHOUT A COVER?

If you did, you should be aware it is **stolen property** as it was reported *unsold and destroyed* by a retailer. Neither the author nor the publisher has received any payment for this book.

All the characters in this book have no existence outside the imagination of the author, and have no relation whatsoever to anyone bearing the same name or names. They are not even distantly inspired by any individual known or unknown to the author, and all the incidents are pure invention.

All Rights Reserved including the right of reproduction in whole or in part in any form. This edition is published by arrangement with Harlequin Enterprises II BV/S.à.r.l. The text of this publication or any part thereof may not be reproduced or transmitted in any form or by any means, electronic or mechanical, including photocopying, recording, storage in an information retrieval system, or otherwise, without the written permission of the publisher.

This book is sold subject to the condition that it shall not, by way of trade or otherwise, be lent, resold, hired out or otherwise circulated without the prior consent of the publisher in any form of binding or cover other than that in which it is published and without a similar condition including this condition being imposed on the subsequent purchaser.

® and TM are trademarks owned and used by the trademark owner and/or its licensee. Trademarks marked with ® are registered with the United Kingdom Patent Office and/or the Office for Harmonisation in the Internal Market and in other countries.

First published in Great Britain 2008
Harlequin Mills & Boon Limited,
Eton House, 18-24 Paradise Road, Richmond, Surrey TW9 1SR

© Helen Dickson 2008

ISBN: 978 0 263 86254 6

Set in Times Roman 10½ on 12¼ pt.
04-0408-89981

Printed and bound in Spain
by Litografia Rosés S.A., Barcelona

Helen Dickson was born and still lives in South Yorkshire, with her husband, on a busy arable farm, where she combines writing with keeping a chaotic farmhouse. An incurable romantic, she writes for pleasure, owing much of her inspiration to the beauty of the surrounding countryside. She enjoys reading and music. History has always captivated her, and she likes travel and visiting ancient buildings.

Recent novels by the same author:

JEWEL OF THE NIGHT
HIGHWAYMAN HUSBAND
THE PIRATE'S DAUGHTER
BELHAVEN BRIDE
THE EARL AND THE PICKPOCKET
HIS REBEL BRIDE
THE DEFIANT DEBUTANTE
ROGUE'S WIDOW, GENTLEMAN'S WIFE
TRAITOR OR TEMPTRESS
A SCOUNDREL OF CONSEQUENCE
WICKED PLEASURES
   (part of *Christmas by Candlelight*)

Prologue

The waiting woman stood in the doorway to the solar, breathless after running up the long flight of stairs.

Eleanor sprang to her feet. Seeing the ashen colour of the woman's skin and the anguished expression on her face, she felt her own face blanch in sudden terror.

'It's—it's my lady. She's sinking fast and is asking for you.'

Eleanor's blood seemed to chill in her veins as the awful truth dawned on her. Her beloved mother was dying. Following a difficult labour in which she had given birth to a stillborn daughter, the midwife had been unable to staunch the flow of blood. No one was in any doubt that the mother would follow the child. The child was Eleanor's half sister, and she had watched with a heavy heart as the lifeless baby had been wrapped up like a parcel in white linen and carried off to the still room to be dealt with later.

Marian Collingwood was lying in the big canopied bed she had shared with her husband of three years—Eleanor's stepfather, Sir Frederick Atwood. With her face drawn and haggard from long suffering, and her eyes sunk in dark sockets, there seemed little life left in her. She turned them to Eleanor as she stumbled into the bedchamber.

The room was fetid and airless and as hot as an oven. Knowing there was nothing more she could do to save Lady Marian, the perspiring midwife was clearing away her ointments, cloths and water basin and the birth-stool with its cut-out seat. The wooden cradle stood empty in a corner. On the periphery of her vision Eleanor was aware that two of her mother's waiting women were watching what was happening with tense, anxious faces.

Crossing quickly to the bed, she took hold of one of her mother's hands, which lay on the snow-white sheet, and gently gave it a squeeze, willing her mother's own tenacious strength into the ailing woman, but her damaged heart was slowing tiredly and irrevocably to its final beat. Stooping, Eleanor kissed her forehead.

'I'm here, Mother—your Eleanor,' she whispered, fighting back her tears.

'Bless you, my darling…' Her voice was a thread but her blue-tinged lips turned up at the corners in a small, loving smile. 'Don't be sad for me… It's what I want since your father… I'm sorry the child was stillborn… I did so want to give you a sister.' She sighed resignedly. 'What's done is done. It is God's will.'

'Please try not to talk. Save your strength. Go to sleep and I'll be here when you wake.'

'It's too late, Eleanor. Death is staking its claim…and I welcome it. I'm glad to be going to your father. How wretched my life has been in this house.' Bitterness thinned her lips and a hard gleam added new life to her dull eyes. 'When I married Frederick…I—I thought we would be protected…' She paused momentarily. 'I should have heeded my sister and never married him. But had your father not been taken from me…from us both in such a cruel manner—betrayed by the man he trusted, that traitor, Lord William Marston—then we would still be living at Hollymead.'

Eleanor stood beside the bed, looking down at the pale, stricken face, bitterly aware that it was Lord William Marston's act of betrayal that had sent her father to the scaffold and brought them to this, that he had played a major part in her mother's destruction. Nothing would ever lessen the deep bitterness she felt towards that man for what he had done. It was a bitterness that burned inside her with an all-consuming intensity.

But at that moment her thoughts and her sorrows were for her mother alone. She felt numbed. It was impossible to imagine a world in which this gracious woman had no place. But one day she vowed Lord William Marston would pay for this. One day he would answer to her for what he had done.

Eleanor sat by her mother, holding her hand. Marian's eyes were closed, and just before dawn she died.

The day in January 1560 as the *George* sailed towards England dragged out interminably, a matter William Marston—self-appointed captain of the galleon following a bloody mutiny off Panama—could do nothing about but await the wind to fill the sails.

A full growth of beard covered his face—not until he put to shore would he shave it off. In his ragged garments, with a couple of daggers shoved into his broad leather belt about his hips, a sword by his side and his dark brown hair uneven and wildly tossed about his head, he presented a fearsome appearance. His eyes, silver-grey, hard and as cold as winter, were bitter with memory and filled with alert awareness. They were fixed on the line where the sea met the sky.

Fair, crisp weather graced the afternoon as he restlessly paced the heaving deck as the ship was tossed about on the high seas. The shadow of the dark early days aboard the *George*, the fear and the pain that had come close to breaking him, were for ever in his tortured mind. Just to see England's shores after three years' enforced absence would be a heady draught and would go a long way to restoring his spirit.

And so he paced, his eyes searched the horizon, he waited—for the day that would eventually come when he would confront the men who had condemned him to three years of hell.

He turned and looked at his friend, Godfrey.

Meeting William's stare, Godfrey felt a strange chill crawl down his spine and shuddered. Beneath the beard William's face was blank, his eyes ice cold, shining with a light that seemed to come from somewhere in the very depths of them. Godfrey was certain that, if he didn't shift his stare, William would suck the very life from him. He reconsidered praying to the Almighty fervently, which he hadn't done since he was a child—and God help the man on whom William had sworn revenge, for there would be no mercy in his unforgiving heart.

Chapter One

It was pitch-black behind the curtains of the high bed. Eleanor woke, turning her head this way and that, like a trapped animal looking for a way out. Some instinct seemed to be telling her, warning her, that there was danger, that she was not alone. She lay absolutely still, terror holding her in frozen shock.

Then she heard him, heard his breathing as he edged closer to the bed. She could feel the sweat, ice cold on her flesh. If he reached her, she would die. If she didn't make a sound, if she stopped breathing and her heart ceased its infernal pounding, if he didn't smell her fear, her rage, perhaps he would go away and she would be safe.

Inching her way slowly up the bed, she peered through a crack in the curtains. The faint glow from the remaining embers of the fire showed the huge, dark figure of her step-father not six feet from the bed. The light was behind him so she could not see his face, but she could imagine his eyes—slits of reddened lust—and his slack lips.

Suddenly Frederick Atwood reached out and, whipping the curtains apart, stood looking down at the girl cowering beneath the covers. 'Don't move.' He was excited, inflamed by his own lust. His claw-like hand gripped her, pushing her back, bending over her. He held her firm, a sadistic thrill running through him when he felt her tremble.

Eleanor could smell his rank breath, felt his mouth wet against her shrinking flesh. A scream rose to her lips, but it was cut off when his hand clamped over her mouth. Flinging her arms wide his fingers began tearing at her nightdress. Feeling his weight upon her, pinning her to the bed, for a second she was so dumbfounded she could do nothing when she felt his hand slide up her inner thigh. And then her spirit rose to the fore, exploding within her, and she was fighting the vile creature whose intent it was to ravish her. With a cry of revulsion and with all the strength she could muster she forced her knee upwards.

Eleanor's assailant grunted and groaned and fell away from her. Springing from the bed, trembling—not with fear, but with disgust, repugnance, humiliation and fury—she glared at him. In her mind she wanted to run from the room, to find someone, anyone, to tell the world what a vile lecher her stepfather was, but she knew no one would believe the word of a hysterical eighteen-year-old girl over that of the powerful Frederick Atwood, an alderman and influential and powerful merchant in the City—who aspired to one day becoming Lord Mayor of London, a man convinced of his own invincibility.

As though he had read her thoughts, his voice came to her from the gloom at the other side of the bed. 'Don't think you can run from me or hide from me, girl,' he spoke with terrifying authority as she scurried towards the door. 'If you have a mind to run to the servants, then I advise you to think again. They will not dare have the temerity to interfere lest they find themselves out on their ear. I am the master here. My authority is absolute and my word is law,' he said, with that arrogant indifference of his position to those beneath him.

Breathing hard, Eleanor swung round and faced his shadowy figure, her eyes blazing like hot coals in her white face, her small chin jutting out at a truculent angle. As her stepfather struggled to his feet, it was evident he was experiencing great discomfort.

'You beast!' she raved. 'You lecherous beast! You killed my mother with your perversions, even if it did take you almost three years to do it, and now you have transferred your attentions to me. Now you think to dominate me as you did her, to grind me down too, but I tell you now, Frederick Atwood, you will not.'

'I always achieve whatever it is I want, and one way or another I shall have you. However long it takes, I will succeed.' His voice slithered over the trembling girl, menacing and dangerous, but she was not afraid of him. It was one of the reasons why he wanted her so much, he would enjoy taming that wildness, crushing that audacious spirit like a cockroach beneath his shoe.

'Never. I am not my mother. I am tougher than she was—stronger. Like a cat I have a way of surviving in the most dire circumstances and you will not defeat me.' Without more ado she flung the door open and rushed out.

The great house was silent as Eleanor tumbled behind the heavy curtains into one of the window embrasures in the great hall. Leaning her head against the stone mullion, she drew up her knees, so depressed and weary that she could not think. In February Fryston Hall was cold, damp, dreary; tonight, with the fire in the central hearth having gone out, it was doubly so.

When her mother had been alive, the way her stepfather had always looked at her had made her suspect him of unspeakable things. But though he watched her, he had never laid a hand on her in that way—until now. Suddenly Fryston Hall had become a prison that fostered in her a desperate need to escape. While ever she remained she was a prisoner of her gender and her stepfather's wicked intent.

She could not believe she had said those things to him. As a child she had been brought up to show respect, to speak when spoken to and accept what she was told by her elders, but all that had been forgotten in the heat of the moment. She had never lacked courage, but sometimes it was hard to maintain cheerfulness in the face of despair.

If only she could go back to Hollymead—if only her mother and father were alive. Never had she needed them as much as she did then. Hollymead had been a warm place, a place of laughter, as serene and beautiful as a benediction. Her eyes bespoke the sadness of its passing, of the memories that would never again return to life, and she could not stop the welling tears. It had ended when her father, Sir Edgar Collingwood, a knight of the realm and Frederic Atwood's cousin, had been executed for conspiring against Queen Mary, bringing disgrace, devastation and heartbreak to the entire family.

Taking advantage of the widow's plight and secretly coveting her wealth—Marian's own private fortune that had come to her on her father's demise at the time of Edgar's execution had not been stripped from her, unlike her husband's and along with all his properties when the court had passed sentence—Frederick Atwood had befriended her and married her.

Just as though the image of her parents had brought sanity, a calm reason took over Eleanor. She would return to York, to Hollymead, where her Uncle John now lived, her father's brother. Sir John Collingwood, a widower with one son, was a proud man, a man of intellect, a scholar; he had been deeply affected and shamed by his brother's treasonable scheming to prevent the Queen's marriage to Philip, the Catholic Prince of Spain, soon to be king. There had been no contact between Sir John and Edgar's widow and daughter since that dreadful day of Edgar's execution and Eleanor had no idea how he would receive her, but he had always shown a fondness for her and been keen to tutor her in her lessons.

Of course she could always go to her Aunt Matilda at Cantly Manor in Kensington, but she was in France visiting friends and was not expected back for several weeks. Unfortunately Cantly Manor was too close to Fryston Hall and it would be the first place her stepfather would go to look for her, and without her aunt's protection he would bring her back.

And so her decision was made without impediment. Her mind was calm and clear for the first time since her mother had died, her heart alive with elation and hope. She considered the many dangers that could beset her on the long journey north, but she dismissed them in her eagerness to get away. How she would like to leave right now, before daybreak, but it was Catherine's wedding day and Eleanor was to prepare her for the event.

Catherine, who was five years Eleanor's senior, was her stepsister and the reason why Eleanor had not gone to live with her aunt when her mother had died. Catherine always managed to maintain a calm poise throughout her father's blusterings and firmly believed he had absolute authority over her. Like Eleanor, she was an only child; when Eleanor had come to live at Fryston Hall she had looked up to her. She had strived to form a close relationship with the older girl, but Catherine's nature did not encourage closeness—which Eleanor attributed to her father's harsh, unloving treatment throughout her life, although Catherine's sympathy and presence had been a comfort to her when her mother had died.

Eleanor attended Catherine into her bridal finery assisted by two of her ladies. Catherine insisted on her ladies, who dressed her and saw to her every need, being within calling distance at all times. The most favoured of her ladies even slept in her chamber at night, when a pallet and rolled-up straw mattress would be pulled out.

Catherine did not display the happiness usually found in a bride. Her face was submissive and she submitted to the ministerings with a quiet dignity as she sat at the *toilette* table. With her lips set in a thin line, she was holding a hand mirror in one hand, gazing at her reflection, while the other idly stroked the silken ears of her small pet spaniel in her lap.

Eleanor was sentimental about marriage and felt sympathy for her stepsister, which she didn't do very often, for Catherine was a prickly female. She was to marry Sir Henry Wheeler, a merchant of considerable wealth and influence in the city, which suited Frederick Atwood's ambitious bent.

Gilded with a fairness and cold serenity, Catherine seemed without any flaw or imperfection. Accepting that any hope of a union between her and the handsome Lord Marston was futile, she had dutifully and without complaint agreed to marry Sir Henry Wheeler with a dignity that had made Eleanor want to cry, but deep within Catherine lay a part of her that had loved Lord William Marston, and maybe still did.

Having tried and failed to convince Catherine that Sir William was a traitor and a rebel, and that even if he should appear after so long a time he would refuse to consider his suit for his daughter's hand, out of greed and self-satisfaction Frederic had entered into the agreement with Sir Henry Wheeler. But whereas Sir Henry was already enamoured of the fair Catherine and assured theirs would be a happy marriage despite her acerbic tongue, to Frederick it was a business arrangement.

'You look lovely, Catherine,' Eleanor said, shooing the two tiring maids away as she secured the French hood decorated with jewels to the bride's head. Her gown was of richly embroidered ivory satin with a standing collar and hanging sleeves. 'Sir Henry will be quite dazzled by your beauty.' Glancing at the mirror, she noticed Catherine's frown. 'I hope you haven't developed an aversion to the gentleman?'

'No, of course I haven't,' Catherine replied, her tone waspish as she irritatingly shoved the spaniel from her knee. 'Henry may not be as young or as handsome as…' she faltered, biting her lower lip '…but he is not unattractive. He is kind and attentive and to my liking. Father holds him in high regard, and I am convinced of his sincerity to me.'

'But you continue to think of that other,' Eleanor dared to say quietly, glancing round to make sure they were alone. Though the memory of William Marston was still strong in Catherine's heart and mind, she had long since begun to accept that he had gone and was not coming back. 'It is three years since he fled—to the Americas, your father said—and never a word to you. The man is not worthy of your thoughts. Now you have a good life before you—away from Fryston Hall. You must put him from your mind.'

'You are right, Eleanor, and that is what I intend to do. I will be a good wife to Henry, but William was so handsome— so gallant.' Catherine's eyes softened and misted over with remembrance. 'He was rich—although not as rich as Henry, and he was tall—taller than any man I have seen.'

'And a traitor,' Eleanor reminded her coldly, 'if what your father told you is to be believed—and, as you know, he is never wrong.' Her voice was heavily laden with sarcasm.

Catherine's kohl-ringed eyes meeting her stepsister's in the mirror were narrowed and suddenly dagger sharp. 'Why you insist on thinking ill of William, Eleanor, when nothing was ever proven, amazes me. William was guilty of association with the conspirators and that is all. There were those at Court envious of his success and determined to destroy his reputation and prestige with Queen Mary. Thus she was led to suspect his guilt in trying to prevent her marriage to Philip. If he had not fled the country—'

'After betraying my father and fellow conspirators. Do not forget that it was Lord Marston who divulged my own father's involvement in the plot.'

'That is circumspection, Eleanor, but if he had not gone away—'

'Run away more like,' Eleanor retorted scornfully.

Catherine shot her an annoying look. 'Think what you like. You are entitled to your opinion, but I suppose if William had stayed then he, too, would have been apprehended and probably executed. But why did he go so far—and without a word to me?'

'I don't know, Catherine.'

Eleanor had heard many things about the dashing Lord Marston, yet none of them endeared him to her. When life at Court had palled he'd escaped abroad and sought fame as a soldier, winning the esteem of a brilliant man of war. Honours came easily, for he possessed all the qualities that favoured a young man of spirit and adventure.

She could not fault Catherine for her loyalty and her rejection of the evidence her father had produced of Lord Marston's involvement in the conspiracy that had been responsible for sending her own father to the block, but after the despicable manner in which he had denounced her father and fellow conspirators and cast Catherine from his life, she was not persuaded that he was deserving of such devotion.

'Nevertheless, he was lucky to escape with his head intact,' Eleanor remarked, not without bitterness, as she felt the pain of memory. 'The same cannot be said of my father, who confessed his guilt. He could not accept the Catholic, Spanish Philip as Queen Mary's husband. He remained a true Protestant to the end.'

Seeing Eleanor's pained and sad expression, Catherine turned and looked at her. 'Along with many more, Eleanor. At that time England was a tense country of continual suspicion and pretend friendships. The violence and uncertainty of Mary's reign influenced many lives—even my father's, in a way, and it made me see him for the kind of man he is.'

'What are you saying?'

A bitterness entered Catherine's eyes. 'That he is a coward at heart and he can change his coat in a moment. He has always been of the Protestant faith, but if it came to recanting that faith in exchange for his life, then I have no doubt that he would do so—unlike the brave ecclesiastics who were tried and condemned and burned in those horrible fires at Smithfield.

'I remember Father called them fools. It made me ashamed. And I shall never forget that it ended disastrously for you too, Eleanor, and your mother—but, contrary to what you were told, I will never believe William had any part in it.'

'Perhaps we will never know the truth of it. Being just fifteen years old at the time, I never did fully understand what was happening. But I did know that the brutal manner of his execution, of being separated from him, broke my mother's heart.'

'I knew she was unhappy married to my father,' Catherine conceded half-heartedly, dabbing rose water on the exposed flesh above the stiffened bodice of her bridal gown. 'He—is not always considerate to those around him.'

'No—no, he is not.' Eleanor had never made any attempt to hide from Catherine how much she despised her father; she wondered how Catherine would react were she to tell her he was an evil old lecher who wanted her in his bed.

Guests—over three hundred people from the city and far and wide, had arrived at Fryston Hall for the wedding feast.

It was a lavish affair, intended to impress, with no expense spared, the well-laden tables in the brightly lit banqueting hall demonstrating Frederick Atwood's wealth.

The nuptials spoken, after a short prayer was said thanking God for the food, there followed a prolonged banquet of countless dishes: mutton and venison, capons, larks and duckling, and boars' heads on beds of apples. The *pièce de résistance* was a peacock royal—a bird that had been carefully skinned, cooked and then placed back inside its feathered skin.

This was followed by desserts of every size, description and flavour, from preserved fruits, jellies, tarts and cakes. Eleanor's favourite were the impressive-looking sweets made from marchpane—a mixture of ground almonds, sugar and rose water. They were brightly coloured, using vegetable dyes and then shaped into models of ships, fruits, flowers and anything else that took Cook's fancy.

Even Frederick Atwood had to admit that the three cooks at Fryston Hall had surpassed themselves. Jack, who was in charge of the roasting and the boiling of meat, Mrs Grimshaw, whose speciality was making rich, spicy sauces to go with the meat, and Bessie, the pastry cook, who made pies and baked bread in the big brick ovens in the pantry.

Wine flowed with abandon. Festive entertainment followed to impress his daughter's new in-laws—jesters, acrobats and jugglers cavorting for the guests—while harassed servants rushed to and fro. Every room of the rambling fourteenth-century manor house, from the great hall to the kitchens, was covered with cavorting revellers.

To the left of Eleanor's stepfather was his nephew and heir, Sir Richard Grey, lounging in his chair with a lazy indolence. His clothes were ostentatiously rich—a blaze of purple-and-scarlet velvet, satin and lace embellished with silver thread. With gold and jewelled rings on his fingers and a huge ruby at his throat, his whole person exuded pride and prosperity—false prosperity, since most of what he had came from his uncle.

Tall and sinewy, he was a fancy, good-looking fair-haired popinjay, a slippery character, stuffed full of himself and his own importance. In fact, he would have been an impressive figure but for his disagreeably cunning expression. Eleanor had no particular liking for him and always avoided him when he was at Fryston Hall.

Outside the storm that had been threatening all day finally broke, whipping itself into a frenzy. Returning from the garde-robe, Eleanor shuddered. It was hardly the sort of night to be abroad, but when she looked at her stepfather sitting smug and confident and saw how he was watching her through hooded lids, she felt that anything was better than staying at Fryston Hall one more night. Come what may, she would leave just as soon as the bridal couple had been put to bed.

Swathed in a tight-waisted gown of garnet silk, the chemise and Spanish farthingale making the skirts stand out and fall in a shimmering cascade to her feet, and her square-toed matching velvet shoes, she looked dramatic and arresting. Eleanor knew that she looked no less beautiful than the bride as she danced at the wedding feast with a buoyancy that belied the rising tension inside her as the hour for her departure approached.

The music swelled as people took to the floor for a courante, a pantomimic dance suggesting courtship. It was quite fast in tempo and who better for Eleanor to dance it with than Martin Taverner, a bright, intelligent young man who had been seated next to Sir Richard Grey throughout the evening. Martin was no stranger to her and he was extremely nimble on his feet. He also had a tendency to stutter, which many of his friends found annoying but which didn't bother Eleanor.

'Are you having a pleasant evening, Martin?' she asked,

bestowing on him a dazzling smile as he led her out on to the floor, thinking how fine he looked in a sky-blue jerkin and matching cap and a light grey doublet with slashed sleeves.

'Immensely, and l-looking forward to d-dancing with the fairest lady in the r-room.'

She laughed lightly, enjoying the sound of the music. 'Your flattery is misplaced, Martin. I think you spend too much time writing poems. Surely the bride is the fairest lady here tonight.'

'Mistress C-Catherine is very lovely, I g-grant you,' he replied, 'b-but you outshine them all, Eleanor.'

With a shock of bright blond curls and bright blue eyes, Martin was good looking, slight and fine boned; in fact, some would call his boyish features pretty and effeminate. He was for ever scratching away with his quill writing poetry, which Eleanor always found both interesting and entertaining in content.

Nobody could understand all the things she liked about Martin—the way he listened to her and was all consideration and gentleness. He was always amiable towards her and considered her his friend—it was a friendship both his father and her Aunt Matilda would like to nurture and steer towards marriage. Affected by the spectacle of her mother's sufferings before her death, Eleanor always avoided the issue through a personal wish to remain single for as long as possible, but she knew she would have to consider the matter when her aunt returned from France.

As she danced her eyes were caught by Sir Richard, who was lounging indolently in his chair, watching them with his peculiar intentness—in particular Martin—over the rim of his goblet until his scrutiny made Eleanor feel uncomfortable and intensely irritated. She saw his hand reach out and surreptitiously caress the rump of a young page, whilst keeping his gaze on Martin with every indication of interest.

The young page flinched and glanced at Sir Richard, startled, but Sir Richard seemed totally unaware of him as he continued to stare at Martin. Curiously troubled by the act, Eleanor frowned as she watched the page scurry away out of reach.

'None of the men can keep their eyes off you,' Catherine remarked pettishly during a lull in the dancing as they listened to Harry, the fool, strumming his lute and baring his soul in a troubadour's song.

Catherine hadn't been too disturbed until lately by her stepsister's popularity with the opposite sex as she had grown to young womanhood, but now, as she had observed the fresh-skinned, laughing dancing girl pirouetting with first this adoring partner, and then that, her amber eyes shining like lustrous candles and her honey-gold hair, which she wore loose beneath her hood as if to flaunt her youth and maiden-hood, bouncing down her slender spine, a surge of jealousy chilled her blood.

'You are old enough to marry, Eleanor. I suspect Father will be looking to one of them for a husband before the winter's out.'

Hearing the barb that curled behind Catherine's words, though her tone was pleasant enough, while sipping spiced wine from a pewter cup, Eleanor put it down and looked at her squarely. 'Your father and Aunt Matilda both. When the time comes it will be a convenient arrangement—like yours to Henry, and I hope I will be given a say over my own marriage partner.'

How smug and confident Eleanor sounded, Catherine thought with annoyance. 'How childish you are, Eleanor, to think you are strong enough to stand against my father. When he finds you a husband, the marriage will go ahead whatever your whims and fancies, so you'd best resign yourself to it.'

'My feelings must be regarded—I shall insist on it, and before any marriage is contracted, my aunt will have to be consulted.'

'Say what you like,' Catherine uttered with an inward snigger, 'but my father will not be overruled.'

Despite her harsh words it was a source of irritation that Catherine was forced to admire her stepsister's striking looks and the proud set of her face, which was a defiant gesture and not in the least childish.

When the dancing was about to resume, no one heard the sound of clattering hooves from the courtyard in front of the house. A few moments later the door was flung open to admit two newcomers, travel stained from riding far.

One of the men paused to carefully assess his surroundings. Ignoring the servant who approached to enquire his business, with his gloved hand on the hilt of his sword and his sodden cloak swept back over his broad shoulders, he climbed the cantilevered shallow staircase to the great hall followed by his companion. The music and loud laughter streamed forth, drowning out the sound his close-fitting leather thigh boots made on the wooden stairs.

In the entrance to the hall he paused and calmly surveyed the scene. It was lively and colourful, packed tight as any barrel of herrings, with liveried servants bearing great platters of steaming food. Hundreds of candles flared and wavered and smoked. Lords and ladies slouched or sprawled at tables littered with food and flagons and goblets of wine and spilled ale. Wolfhounds and deerhounds scavenged beneath the tables, while minstrels in the gallery strummed their guitars and played their lutes, trying to make themselves heard above the din of voices.

The man's hard gaze swept the throng, coming to rest on Frederick Atwood. He was seated at the long table on the raised dais—an elevated position for the lord of the manor and his family.

Frederick halted his conversation with the lady next to him as he caught sight of the black-garbed figure striding purposefully towards the dais. Their eyes met. Frederick rose, grim faced.

'Marston!'

His voice came out as a hiss, but its mere sound attracted attention, and then an ominous silence swept over the hall as the musicians ceased to play and every eye became riveted on the newcomer in fuddled disbelief. The very name scalded Elcanor's being with hot indignation. Tall and powerfully built, this intruder, who looked as if he could claim the ground on which he walked on, emanated a wrath so forceful that every man and woman shrank in their seats.

William Marston, a man whose features were chiselled to perfection, had once been one of the most audacious, imperious gentlemen of the Court. The ladies and general public had adored him, and he had taken a charter of their hearts to the Americas, which was never cancelled. He had been a great courtier of the realm, a great swordsman. Dressed in sombre black, his wide-brimmed hat dripping water on to the floor, he was a shock to the beholder.

Frederick thrust his chair back so violently that it scraped harshly on the floorboards. He started up, his hands supported on the table. There was an expression of outrage on his face, his colour choleric. 'So you are back.'

'As you see, Atwood. Back to wreak vengeance on those who conspired against me—and others, men who were not as fortunate as I.'

The deep timbre of his voice reverberated around the hall.

'How the devil did you get in? Had I foreknowledge of your visit, you would have found my doors barred.'

'It wasn't difficult gaining entrance—your watchmen were not at their posts—but worry not,' William said drily, 'I'm not staying. I find being in this house distasteful to say the least. This is an unappealing but necessary visit. I wanted you to be the first to know I have returned to England from foreign parts.'

'But this is an outrage—to come bursting into my house without invitation,' Frederick declared forcefully, his long, thin face suffused an angry crimson.

The air between them was filled with tension, hostility and hatred.

William's gaze passed along the rows of diners and came to rest on an empty chair, where it dwelt for a moment and then shifted to the swaying tapestry behind the chair, before coming back to Atwood. 'Your nephew, Sir Richard Grey, is absent, I see.' He smiled knowingly. 'Perhaps he saw me coming and crept away to hide his cowardly carcass,' he drawled, a razor-edge of sarcasm in his voice. 'Not that it matters. I'm in no hurry. If my suspicions about him are proven, I'll catch up with him in my own time.'

William laughed in derision, the silver-grey eyes taking on a steely hardness. 'You hoped to see me dead, Atwood. Come, admit it. You worked your mischief, I know it, and the reason why does not elude me. Disgraced for standing against the marriage of Mary Tudor to Philip of Spain and dispossessed of my family's wealth and property, I was a pauper. You did not merit me as suitable a husband for your daughter's hand as Sir Henry Wheeler,' he said, knowing all there was to know about the highly respected and influential City merchant, 'and your decision to get rid of me was not only out of fear at what I would do, but greed-inspired—taking into account that Sir Henry's wealth far outshone my own.'

'Believe what you like. 'Tis of no consequence to me. It offends me beyond measure to have you strut into my hall when I am entertaining my guests.'

'The occasion being?'

'My daughter's wedding day,' Frederick flung at him smugly. A slight narrowing of his eyes was William's only reaction. What went on behind his cold visage Frederick could only guess at.

Understanding dawned on William. 'Ah! So that is the reason for the celebration.' He shifted his gaze to Catherine, who was staring at him with an expression of stunned disbelief and was as white as a sheet. She was still holding the loving cup she had just shared with Henry. He smiled broadly and, removing his dripping hat, bowed his dark head politely.

'I always knew you would make a beautiful bride, Catherine I remember telling you so but a marriage between us was not to be. I rejoice to see you well, and may I take this opportunity to congratulate you.' His gaze took in the man at her side. 'Both of you. I wish you every happiness.'

From where Eleanor sat, her gaze encompassed her stepfather and the intruder. The strange atmosphere that threaded these two people together made her uneasy. It was as tangible as the air she breathed, and as mysterious as the strange gleam in Lord Marston's eye. As he moved closer to her stepfather, entirely assured, he emanated an angry vigour. There was arrogance and a certain insolence in the lift of his head and in the relaxed way in which he moved.

He was a man of impressive stature, tall and lean and as straight as an arrow with a whipcord strength that promised toughness, and, even in her predicament, she could not help but admire the fine figure he made. His curly dark brown hair sprang thickly, vibrantly, from his head and curled about his neck, a few threads of silver gracing his temples. He was clean-shaven, his dark-complexioned face slashed with two black brows. His chin was juttingly arrogant and hard, his mouth firm, hinting at stubbornness that could, she thought, prove dangerous, making him a difficult opponent if pushed too far. Yet there were laughter lines at the corners that bespoke humour. But it was his eyes that held Eleanor. They were compelling, silver-grey and vibrant in the midst of so much uncompromising darkness, and they were settled on her stepfather, watchful and mocking.

'Have a care what you accuse me of, Marston,' Frederick uttered, his face hardened into a mask of icy wrath. 'You are a traitor and deserved to die along with the rest, and should you have returned from wherever it is you've been hiding these past three years before Queen Mary's demise, then your disobedience might have resulted in a long term of imprisonment in the Tower or the removal of your head.' His righteous display of anger fairly bounced off the walls.

The guests listened and stared in unbridled curiosity, leaning their heads together as they exchanged whispered comments. All eyes were on William, the gentlemen wondering how he had the audacity to come back so cocksure of himself after so long an absence, the ladies thanking God for the return of his handsome face. He didn't look worried; if anything, he looked supremely confident.

William's firm lips curved in a lopsided grin. 'I doubt Queen Elizabeth will call for my blood.'

'Aye, the Queen has a penchant for attractive young men,' Frederick uttered with scathing sarcasm. 'Your sort will always find favour at the Court of Elizabeth—where, I suspect, you will idle your days dancing attendance on her, for it is only at Court where position is to be granted, offices to be won, and money to be made.'

'The pursuit of wealth and position is a weakness in a man, which you should know all about, being prey to it yourself.'

Seeing the vivid alarm showing in Catherine's eyes and startled by the flood of emotion on her face, bristling with resentment and pushed beyond the boundary of reason and caution by this man's sudden appearance and used to speaking her mind, Eleanor stood up, emboldened by the wine.

'Can you not be satisfied that you escaped with your life, when others, good men, all of them, went to the block at Queen Mary's command?' Her voice rang out, clear and vibrant.

With considerable surprise, William turned. The piercing amber gaze from the girl's eyes almost knocked him back on his feet. A spark of desire was sent coursing through his body, and for a moment he was rendered speechless. What irresistible charms did Atwood have at Fryston Hall?

Attired in garnet silk with a stiffened belt of gold fastened round her tiny waist, she was quite tall and lithe, with rounded breasts—a body made to be touched by a man's hands. The skin of her face was creamy, glowing, a soft flush highlighting perfect cheekbones. Her lips were moist and the shade of coral that lay on the bottom of tropical seas, her eyes large and framed by sweeping dark lashes, her hair a warm shade of honey gold, thick and gently curling down her spine from beneath her bejewelled headdress.

His attention full on her, he moved slowly forward to stand before her, his eyes never leaving hers for an instant. They assessed her speculatively with that look that the male assumes when presented with an attractive woman. She was perfect, exquisite, and she reminded him of a young warrior queen, proud and unyielding. Who was she? Her lovely features, mirroring her thoughts, were clouded with undisguised resentment. For some unknown reason she was angry with him. What had he done to deserve her ire?

'Is there something about me that you find distasteful?' he asked.

His voice came smooth and deep to Eleanor's ears, yet there was an amused mockery that seemed to scorn everything about the occasion and the people present. At the moment he seemed relaxed and at ease, but she sensed that he was aware of everything that transpired around him.

'Indeed, I have heard nothing to recommend you, sir.'

His wry smile indicated his surroundings. 'You are not alone in that.'

Eleanor saw admiration in his perusal of her face and her breath caught in her throat, for he stood a head taller than any man present. She had the kind of beauty that drew men's eyes, and she knew it. Any visitor to Fryston Hall was quick to pay her compliments, especially the men.

William turned and arched a dark brow towards Atwood. 'What lady is this,' he enquired, 'who speaks so freely?' The silver-grey eyes settled on Eleanor's once more, capturing them with a calm coolness.

'She is Mistress Collingwood,' Frederick provided with caustic venom, resenting the appraisal he had seen in Marston's eyes when he had looked at Eleanor. The mere thought that some other man might take what he coveted was enough to turn his mind, and if that man happened to be William Marston it could not be borne. 'Her father was Edgar Collingwood—one of your fellow conspirators.'

Eleanor saw Lord Marston's brows lift and he could not hide his amazement, his bewilderment, but suddenly his expression cleared as though a candle had been lit in his mind, revealing the answer to the puzzle. Shock and dismay were mirrored in his look and his features softened. As he looked at Frederick Atwood there was cold hatred in his eyes.

'So, you got what you wanted after all, Atwood, after all your scheming.' Turning to the irate young woman, he inclined his head with some modicum of respect. 'My apologies, Mistress Eleanor. I didn't recognise you after all this time—all grown up and lovely to look at.'

Hearing him speak her name with a familiarity that

bemused her caused Eleanor's composure to falter slightly. She might have seen him some time, possibly as a child, but so many people had come to Hollymead she couldn't remember—although she could not imagine anyone forgetting meeting a man as striking as Lord Marston.

She checked herself, reminding herself that this man had been the cause of her father's downfall. He, too, had been arrested, and as a concession for betraying the names of his fellow conspirators he had been granted his freedom—although his properties were stripped from him. Afterwards, so word would have it, he had fled England to save his own skin. This injustice caused the softening of her features to yield beneath the onslaught of pure rage as her pride ached for revenge.

'It is Mistress Collingwood to you, sir.'

William laughed softly, his teeth sparkling white in his tanned face. 'I beg your pardon. Mistress Collingwood it is—until I know you better.' Now he knew who she was, he summed her antagonism up in a moment. Both he and her father had been involved in the same conspiracy, and she must resent the fact that he was alive, her father dead. He turned his attention back to Frederick. 'I'm astonished to find Mistress Collingwood here beneath your roof. Your stepdaughter, is she?' He cast Frederick a look of frozen contempt. 'You made Edgar Collingwood's widow your wife?'

'That is my affair.'

'So, you got what you planned all along. I congratulate you, Atwood. You are a connoisseur of manipulation and deceit. But, if Marian is now your wife, I find it strange not to see her seated beside you at your daughter's wedding.'

'My mother is dead.' Eleanor's voice shook with the passion of remembrance, as if she wanted to dredge the bitterness and hurt from within her and cast it at this man's feet.

William met her gaze, understanding more than she realised. For a split second the intensity of his eyes seemed to explode and an expression Eleanor did not understand flashed through them, then it was gone. The mere thought of Atwood touching Marian Collingwood sickened him. His brows knit together in a query.

'I'm sorry to hear that. She was a fine lady. How long?'

'October last year. Just four months.'

William digested this calmly. He knew Marian had been out of her mind when Edgar was executed. She had been a lovely woman, with a gentleness and unworldliness combined with a look of innocent sensuality. Being totally devoted to her husband and daughter, she had rarely come to London, much preferring to spend her days at Hollymead. She had been protected by her husband, and when she was at her most defenceless, when her mind was sorely wounded, she had fallen prey to Frederick Atwood, a man whose reputation was one of dissipation and debauchery—a man her husband had despised.

'Tomorrow I travel to my home in the north—it was restored to my family when Queen Elizabeth came to the throne. I intend calling on Sir John Collingwood, your uncle, at Hollymead, since it was his petition that brought the matter to her Majesty's attention. I shall tell him I have seen you and found you in good health.'

'Enough, Marston,' Frederick fumed. 'Mistress Collingwood is none of your concern. Your presence in my house offends me, so get out. 'Tis a brave man who barges into my home uninvited.'

'I am a cautious man, Atwood—as you can see,' William said with a slowly spreading sardonic smile, turning slightly to indicate his companion standing back in the doorway, a heavy crossbow held in massive fists directed at Frederick. 'I come well prepared. May I present Godfrey, my loyal companion.'

Godfrey was a huge golden oak tree of a man, with a shaggy head the colour of a lion's pelt and his granite face half-covered by a curling beard. Every eye, as if drawn by a magnet, became riveted on this terrifying apparition with his feet braced wide apart. The wooden floorboards seemed to strain and creek as he moved forward, each stride twice that of an average man's.

William looked at Frederick, seeing how his face had tightened and paled, his brow dewed with sweat. He smiled. 'Be wary of him, Atwood. Only a fool would court risk when he doesn't have to. Could I shoot the way my friend does, I'd never again pick up a sword.'

'The devil he does,' Frederick hissed.

'Godfrey obeys my orders to the letter. Providing he is given proper respect, left alone he is really quite placid—though I'm afraid he is not very refined. He is a master when it comes to his fists and with weapons—none finer—and, should any man feel inclined to test his skill and raise his sword against me, his arrow will pierce your heart before you can blink. So you see, Atwood, his foe might just as well commend his soul to the Almighty, for he is already dead.'

Frederick drew himself up in outraged disbelief. 'You wouldn't dare threaten me.'

'Try me,' William responded, his voice silky smooth, his eyes chips of ice. He moved closer. 'I bid you farewell, Atwood, but heed me and heed me well.' Bracing his hands on the table and leaning forward so that his face was only inches from Atwood's, the words he next uttered were for him alone, but heard by those in close proximity, including Eleanor.

'I shall pay you back in full measure for the harm you have done me and my family. I did not leave these shores by choice—as well you know. You made a serious error in crossing me—you made an even more serious one when you embarked on your crusade and chose me as the focus of your ill will. I am going to crush you. Not necessarily at once—there is no limit to my patience and determination. But I will do it. Before God I will. That I swear.'

Turning on his heel, he strode out, followed by Godfrey. Those who had witnessed the bitter altercation between the alderman and William Marston listened to the retreating footsteps until they could be heard no more, then there was a collective sigh of withheld breath and everyone began to talk at once, but there was no denying that his appearance had cast a mocking shadow over the festivities.

Chapter Two

No one noticed when Eleanor, with a sense of abandoning herself to her fate, slipped out of the hall and ran in hot pursuit of Lord Marston.

She felt a twinge of doubt at what she was doing, as if she was about to make a decision that would have far-reaching consequences, but she refused to be deterred. With long, purposeful strides, Lord Marston and his companion were crossing to the outer door.

'Lord Marston, wait—please wait,' she cried, glancing at the servants scurrying to and fro, too busy to dwell on Mistress Collingwood conversing with the intruder.

On hearing someone call his name, he spun round, his black cloak flaring from his broad shoulders like a bat's wings. He was unprepared for the impact of Mistress Collingwood's eyes as she steadily looked up into his face. They were an incredible shade of warm amber, framed in a thick spiked fan of dark lashes. They were quite glorious, but filled with a wary expression he'd once seen in a cornered feral cat.

Surprise registered on his stern features and then he

smiled slightly and bowed his head. 'At your service, Mistress Collingwood.'

'Sir, I have need of your assistance.' Eleanor could sense he was wary, that his guard was up. His face was expressionless, as were his eyes. This was a man who could hide his thoughts, whose thoughts could conspire to hide his emotions. The startling grey eyes rested on her ironically.

William turned to his companion. 'Wait for me outside, Godfrey. Whatever it is Mistress Collingwood has to say won't take long.' Focusing his gaze on Eleanor, a muscle twitched in his cheek. 'My curiosity is aroused. Of what help could I possibly be to you?'

'Was it right what you said—that you are to go to York on the morrow?'

'What of it?'

'Will you take me with you?' she uttered quickly, quietly, lest she be overheard. She paused, watching him, waiting for his reaction. His brows lifted and his mocking silver eyes gazed right back.

Mistress Collingwood's earlier hostility and having found Catherine married to another made William brutal. 'Well, I'll be damned! What makes you think I would want you or your company, Mistress Collingwood?'

Eleanor paled but she stood up to him and took a deliberate step closer. 'Because you owe me.'

His eyes became wary. 'I do? What I find odd,' he said with a tone of frosty disapproval, 'is that I evoke such animosity in you—a man who is a stranger to you. It is clear you are embittered about something.'

'Yes, and don't plead ignorance. You must know why.'

'That is an interesting assertion.'

'I am claiming a debt. Like I said, you owe me.'

William's eyes hardened and he moved closer to her so that

they stood only inches apart. His jaw was rigid and a muscle was beginning to twitch dangerously in the side of his neck. 'Be damned I do! I owe you nothing.'

Eleanor's face became flushed with ire and there was a thrust to her chin that told William she was ready for a fight. 'It was you who deprived me of my father,' she accused bitingly, 'or was it so long ago that you don't remember how you betrayed him and others before fleeing? You alone were responsible for sending him to the block, as bad a death as any, and I, of all people, having witnessed the wretchedness a beheading can cause, know how bad that was.'

William looked at her upturned face long and hard. 'It would appear you have me hanged, drawn and quartered without granting me a fair trial, Mistress Collingwood,' he remarked drily.

'And why should I grant you such a luxury? My father's trial was anything but fair.'

'And you would know that?'

'Yes. Yes, I do. He went to the scaffold bravely, repenting his sins, but he would not repent of his principles or his fidelity for the chance of forgiveness.'

William raised a sceptical brow. 'If you believe I was the one responsible for betraying him and his fellow conspirators, if I am such a cold-hearted villain, then how do you know I won't balk at killing you also?'

Eleanor met his eyes without flinching, then dropped her gaze to the sword at his side. 'I don't,' she said calmly, her anger beginning to diminish, 'but I am so desperate to leave this place that I will take that risk. I would travel alone, which is what I intended anyway, but York is a long way and it is almost impossible for a woman to travel without an escort.'

'So you claim I owe you some recompense and think to collect. And what do you think will happen when your stepfather discovers you have fled? He will hunt you down, that's certain. Besides, I am in a hurry. I cannot afford to have a woman hold me back.'

Eleanor eyed him with scorn. 'You can afford anything you like if you wish to,' she said coldly.

'The way I see it, what you need is a male escort to lend you protection and a certain respectability. Whilst I can give you both, I grant you, you will be a hindrance to me.'

'But you go to my uncle at Hollymead. You say you wish to thank him for petitioning the Queen on your behalf to have your property restored to you. That is your business—but would you be comfortable on your journey knowing I would be close on your heels?'

William wanted to tell her to forget it, but he was strongly attracted by the delicate pride in this young woman's bearing. There was also something about her stance, a vulnerable part of her behind the stubborn facade, that ignited a spark of sympathy. 'It would seem you have the measure of me, Mistress Collingwood. And your stepfather?'

Eleanor moved to stand closer still to lend strength to her words. 'My stepfather is the weight of my problem. He knows nothing of this. It concerns only me. If he should find out what I intend doing, he will draw and quarter me for sure. It's imperative that I leave. I beg your discretion.'

William peered at her. Her flesh gleamed rich and warm and his head was filled with the delicious scent of her. Something quickened that had lain dormant for a long time. It was a good feeling, but he did not intend nourishing it lest it weakened him.

Eleanor stood still, feeling suffocated by his nearness. He watched every line of her face as he considered her request, every fleeting expression. Nothing escaped those bright eyes. It pricked sorely that she had to wait, and had the cause been less dire she would have stormed off in disgust.

'Earlier you spoke of my mother with kindness and I believed you to be sincere. Is this not the least you can do for her daughter? I promise you I will give you no trouble,' she hastened to assure him. 'You won't even know I'm there.'

The silver eyes glinted and William's white teeth flashed as he laughed mockingly, thinking she would be hard to ignore at any time. 'Not so haughty when you want something, are you, Mistress Collingwood? Not so proud to seek my protection—and my company, I would like to think.'

She stiffened. 'Your protection will do, sir. You can keep your company to yourself.'

'What you ask is both reckless and foolhardy—and I would be a fool to agree to your request.'

'Believe me, it is costing me a great deal to ask this of you. I am perfectly serious.'

'I know you are. And if I refuse to take you?'

'Then I shall go by myself—which I had planned to do anyway—tonight. I have everything prepared.'

His expression became serious. 'So, you are that desperate.'

'I am.' Her eyes hardened and her small chin tightened. 'The years I have been at Fryston Hall have been like a lifetime. Everything that I had was lost to me, and while ever Mary Tudor remained on the throne my name was attainted by treason. Now Mary is dead, everything is different. I am a pauper here in my stepfather's house, so I may just as well be a pauper in my uncle's house. I will go back to Hollymead, even if I do have to depend on Uncle John's charity when I get there.'

'And be humbled?'

'Yes, that too. Yet I am still a Collingwood and very much my father's daughter. I would rather be dead than live here a moment longer. Now more than ever I have to escape this monstrous place—and the monster within it. You don't understand what it's like. I only ask that you believe me.'

'I understand more than you realise. I know what it's like to be a prisoner and in fear of your life,' he said in a low voice, something dark and sinister belying his words that was not lost on Eleanor. 'Are you not afraid of Atwood?'

'I am afraid of no one.' Her clenched fists, flushed cheeks and the brilliance of her eyes told William so. 'He keeps everyone under his control. He destroyed my mother's pride, her confidence and all belief in herself. I am willful; because of this he treats me with a firmer discipline than he does his own daughter—and he will not be satisfied until he has replaced my mother with me. I hate him and I will leave here with or without your help.'

William drew a deep breath and by extreme effort of will replied casually, 'There is much to consider.'

Eleanor felt a wave of desperation as she strove for control and to calm her mounting fears that he would refuse her request. 'Normally I would not ask for your help for any reason whatsoever.' Damn him, she thought, her temper rolling over restlessly. He was enjoying every moment of her discomfort, of having her plead with him. 'Well? Make up your mind,' she retorted sharply. 'Will you take me?'

William had already made up his mind to let her travel with them. Despite his earlier resolution not to give a damn what her problems were, he was a little unnerved by Atwood's treatment of her and the threat he posed. He had no wish to be the cause of her stepfather ill treating her. Eleanor Collingwood looked harmless enough, but she'd be trouble, he just knew it. She needed protecting, he decided—and it was the least he could do for Edgar and Marian Collingwood, to see their daughter safe.

With surprise Eleanor was conscious that he was studying her with a different interest. His expression remained unreadable, and yet she felt the air between them reaching to her, drawing her towards him by some irresistible force. For all her aversion to him, there was an indefinable quality about him that communicated itself to her.

As he cocked an eye at her, his smile broadened, his face lighting up with such radiance that Eleanor was startled. Hope sprang into her heart. 'Do you agree to let me travel with you?'

He laughed and there was a devilish glint in his eyes. 'Common sense tells me you spell trouble, a heap of it, but knowing how furious Atwood will be when he finds you gone will be worth it. There will be no company of horse and standard bearer, but you can ride with us. We are staying at the White Swan. We'll wait for you—but don't delay. I want to be on the road by sun up. We also travel light.'

Eleanor was so overwhelmed she suppressed the urge to twirl around with relief. Meeting his eyes, in the depth of her wretchedness she felt a small spasm of warmth and gratitude. She did not know this man or even why he was at war with her stepfather, but he had agreed to give her his protection.

'So do I. I will be there—and I won't hinder you.'

She watched him leave before returning to the festivities. Lord William Marston had preyed on her mind for a long time; now she had seen him and spoken to him she was uncomfortable. For some inexplicable reason there was something about him that got under her skin and she was not looking forward to the journey to York with him and his fearsome companion, but anything was preferable to travelling alone—and worse, to remaining at Fryston Hall.

With her women laughing and fussing round her as they stripped off her wedding gown and prepared her for her marriage bed, Catherine turned and her eyes sought out Eleanor as a flimsy nightgown was pulled over her head. Irately she shooed her ladies away and, standing straight as a spear, her shoulders drawn back and her eyes gleaming in a rigid white face, she confronted her stepsister.

'Well, Eleanor, what a turn out this is.'

Warned by something in her voice, Eleanor was instantly on her guard. There was a spark of malice in Catherine's eyes, and something else that Eleanor couldn't decipher.

'You know what I'm talking about, so don't pretend you don't. William appeared to be very interested in you. I saw him look at you as if you were a kingdom he planned to conquer.'

'Don't be dramatic, Catherine,' Eleanor reproached, trying to remain calm, going to the bed and beginning to turn the violet-scented sheets back. Catherine's voice reminded her of a sulky child.

'Dramatic? He barely noticed me. I am well and truly heartlessly discarded in his eyes and now he hankers after my stepsister. But you will not have him, Eleanor. I will not let you.'

Catherine was in full spate and was clearly going to brook no argument. Eleanor stared at the demented, venomous woman and did not know her. Such malevolence sparked in her eyes that Eleanor involuntarily shivered. Why, she thought, she looks just like her father. Why had she not seen it before? Disturbed by her behaviour, Eleanor stared at her, unable to believe what Catherine was saying.

'Please don't say such things,' she flared, angry and indignant. It was most unlike Catherine, but then tonight some perversity had her in its grip. 'You know full well how much I detest William Marston and why.'

Stark emotion darkened Catherine's eyes. How could she tell anyone how she had felt when William appeared—on her wedding day of all days—that the mere sight of him had stirred all the old feelings of want and need and desire for this man, the man she would have married, and how angry she was to find herself married to another not of her choosing.

Cheated! That was how she now felt, cheated. Vicious rage welled up within her when she remembered the way he had looked at Eleanor, the interest and admiration that had kindled in his eyes. It was not to be borne.

'William is a man with a man's appetites, Eleanor—some of them base. I did not like the way you claimed his attention. You were brazen, speaking out as you did. You made him notice you.'

Eleanor raised her brows and bit back a sharp retort. She did not want to be at odds with Catherine over this. She would soon be gone from this dark house, and for now her only weapon against Catherine was her pride. But how she wished things could have been different between them. Somehow she forced a smile to her lips.

'Come, Catherine,' she said gently, taking her hand and leading her to the *toilette* table, sitting her down and beginning to brush her hair, which always had a soothing effect on her. 'We'll speak no more of Lord Marston. He's of no consequence.'

'How easy that is for you to say. Doing so is another matter entirely.'

Closing her eyes, Catherine gave herself up to the soothing brush strokes. Strangely, when she considered the moment when she had first become aware of William's presence, her gaze had been drawn to his servant. Over the top of her goblet her narrowed eyes had focused on the shaggy-haired giant. As if he had felt her eyes on him, he had met her gaze head-on. His look had been bold, rude, without the respect she was entitled to as Frederick Atwood's daughter and Henry Wheeler's wife. But there had also been admiration in his insolent stare and she enjoyed being able to wield that kind of power over a man—any man, including that uncouth, unkempt giant.

'You are Lady Wheeler,' Eleanor said softly, 'married to

one of the wealthiest merchants in London. He is a good man who will make you a good husband, and you must try and take pride in that, for you cannot go back to being Catherine Atwood. The day when you would have married William Marston is gone. Put him from your mind, Catherine, otherwise it will eat away at you and you will become embittered. This is your wedding night and your husband is impatient for your ladies to put you to bed and be gone.'

'Yes, yes, you're right—and thank goodness Henry agreed to forgo the bedding ritual and I don't have to suffer the indignity of having an audience to watch us consummate our marriage. But wherever William has been these past three years, whatever his desires, it was wrong of him to treat me so abominably.'

This was the first time Eleanor had heard Catherine utter angry, reproachful words against William Marston. Catherine had hoped for loyalty and some degree of affection from him, but she had received neither. The man truly was a monster, and she had willingly placed herself in his hands for the time it would take them to reach Hollymead.

Eleanor could not control the apprehension in her heart, or her sense of dark foreboding, when, just before dawn when the house still slept, with her heart racing, carrying her bag and her father's sword, she made her way down the long cold stairway at the back of the house. Servants were sleeping all over the place. The upper servants had their own rooms while the lower servants bedded down more indiscriminately on landings, in the scullery, the hall, anywhere.

Intending to leave by the kitchen, slipping inside she glanced around the candle-lit interior. Two young scullions were curled up under blankets on the kitchen floor. Having washed all the silver and pewter plates and wooden trenchers from the banquet, exhausted, they had fallen to sleep, warmed by the dying embers of the fire in the great hearth of the big arched fireplace.

She was about to cross to the door to the outer yard between the buttery and the brewhouse when a man's hand came from behind her and clamped itself round her upper arm. She spun round.

'Well, well, well. Now where do you think you're creeping off to at this hour?' Sir Richard's hard eyes raked over her, taking in her male attire, her leather bag in one hand and the sword in the other, ticking off each damning piece of evidence against her.

Eleanor quailed. He knew! Somehow he had found out, and she was experienced enough to realise she would be foolish to pretend otherwise. Tiny shards of fear pricked her spine while a coldness congealed in the pit of her stomach.

'So, you're running away, Mistress Collingwood,' he said smoothly, 'sneaking away like a thief before cock crow to meet Lord Marston. Did you think when he mentioned he was going north that I wouldn't know what was in your head— that you're so desperate to get away from here that you'd forget he was the one responsible for sending your father to the block? I may have vacated my chair, but I heard every word Marston said. So did my uncle, and I believe if you don't leave now you will have him to contend with.'

Taken off guard by the hectoring tone, Eleanor felt her heart almost ceased to beat. She was aware of the power of the man the voice belonged to, could feel it closing around her like the sharp metal teeth of an animal trap.

'I haven't forgotten. I'll never forget,' Eleanor replied, breathing deep with anger as she pulled herself together, 'and you're right, I am so desperate to get away from here, from my stepfather and his warped mind, that I'd do anything to achieve that—even if it means swallowing my pride and re-sentment and asking Lord Marston to help me. Yes, I hate him, but I hate my stepfather more.'

'I know you do—I always thought so—and you'd do well to fear him if you know what's good for you. But how long will it be before you fall for that arrogant lord like any other smitten virgin? 'Tis true he's a handsome devil, but to those who know him he's a cold one. A man can see it in his eyes.'

Eleanor remembered the vibrancy of those crystal-clear orbs, filled with an intensity that no one could deny, and they had been anything but cold.

'Did Marston agree to take you with him when you asked him so prettily?' Sir Richard laughed low in his throat. 'It's as well I returned to my seat as he was leaving. I was watching you, knowing I would only have to bide my time before you tried to sneak away.'

Driven by self-preservation and a determination to escape, Eleanor stepped away from him. 'What's it to you, Sir Richard? I am leaving this place. Do not try to stop me.'

'I have no intention of stopping you, Mistress Colling-wood, in fact it's in my own interest that you go—I'd even go so far as to encourage it, since you get in the way of what I want. Although no matter how brave you feel, you cannot escape my uncle, you know.'

'You're damn right she can't,' came a low, angry voice behind Sir Richard.

Suddenly a dishevelled Frederick Atwood stumbled towards Eleanor and grasped her arm, causing her to drop her possessions. She didn't know what warped conceits made this man what he was, but she knew that the rebuff she had given him two nights ago must have festered in his head. 'Damn your eyes! You let me go,' she flared.

'Never—you, a lass who fancies herself stronger than me

and shows it. Well, permit me to tell you something,' he hissed, thrusting his face close to hers, his breath reeking of stale ale and his cocksure smile having acquired a malevolent twist. 'I'm a man who doesn't hold on being put down by a girl—although I'll admit that's part of your charm that attracts me.'

Even though Frederick was still affected by the immense quantities of liquor he had consumed at the wedding feast, and angered by the knowledge that she was sneaking away from Fryston Hall, his lustful cravings were sharpened by the sight of her shapely figure outlined in male attire.

Writhing this way and that, Eleanor managed to wrench herself away from him. His face flushed crimson as his rage showed white around his hard, glittering eyes. He followed her as she danced this way and that to avoid his hands, big, grasping hands.

'Stay away from me,' she warned, incensed, throwing a ladle at him—it sailed over his shoulder and clattered on the stone floor at an amused Sir Richard's feet. Her stepfather advanced on her and she heaved a crock off the table. It hit the floor in front of him and exploded in a shower of pot and flour. 'You're a pitiful excuse for a man, Frederick Atwood. You revolt and disgust me and I want none of you.'

'Such cruelty, Eleanor, such ingratitude. Have I not given you my protection and a home? I gave a service and I never give anything without a service being rendered in return.'

His arrogance fuelled Eleanor's fury. 'Have you no honour, no decency? Have you no shame? For shame it would bring Catherine if she knew her lecherous father was lusting after her stepsister.'

His arching gaze turned to a leer that mentally stripped Eleanor of her clothing. It turned her blood to ice.

'Catherine is abed with her husband—as every dutiful wife should be. Let's hope she proves to be more fruitful than her mother,' he growled, having resented his first wife for not giving him a healthy son, only dead ones. He advanced towards Eleanor on stumbling, drunken legs as she edged towards the door.

Catching her arm roughly, he threw her away from the door. Losing her balance, she fell, hitting her shoulder heavily on the edge of one of the two huge oak tables necessary in a kitchen of that size. Recovering herself quickly, she hauled herself up, set her jaw and flared her hatred through the sudden fear that threatened to engulf her as they circled the kitchen like two wild animals, half-crouched. He had her cornered, his teeth showing in a ragged snarl as he bore down on her, and then suddenly he slumped at her feet when Sir Richard hit him on the back of the head with a heavy candlestick.

Eleanor stared at Sir Richard in startled amazement. 'Why did you do that?'

'I told you, I want you out of this house, out of London, and I think York is far enough away. But have a care,' he said, placing the candlestick on the table and looking down at his uncle's crumpled form with a baleful eye. 'He'll not let it rest at this. He has no idea it was me who rendered him sense-less—being addled with drink, he'll assume it was you.' With a smirk on his lips he turned and sauntered towards the door, where he turned and looked back at her. 'Have a good journey, Mistress Collingwood. You are going to need all the luck you can get if you are to survive my uncle's vengeance.'

Paying scant notice to the two scullions, who had been rudely wakened when the crock hit the floor, their eyes as wide as plates as they gaped at their master's inert form, Eleanor grasped the bag and her father's sword, which she had dropped when her stepfather had brutally taken hold of her.

With her heart in her mouth and a prayer on her lips, with one last look at her stepfather—feeling no remorse, only a weary sense of satisfaction—Eleanor lifted the wooden latch of the heavy door. Stepping outside, she was a slight shadow in a world of shadows. Pulling the brim of her hat down to shield her face from the driving rain and drawing her thick-lined cloak tightly against her, she sped across the courtyard.

Reaching the stables, she slipped inside, straining her eyes in the dim light as the familiar smells of horses, hay and dung assailed her nostrils. Loud snoring came from the loft, where grooms and stable boys were sleeping off the effects of the festivities. When she had quickly saddled her beloved horse Tilda with the rain lashing the walls of the house she was soon away and galloping into the darkness.

There was danger in her flight from Fryston Hall, but despite the pain in her injured shoulder Eleanor felt her spirits soar at her freedom. She didn't look back.

When she rode into the yard of the White Swan the rain had ceased to fall, but the wind was still strong. A sign above the portal squeaked and swung wildly and straw blew fren-ziedly about the puddle-laden cobbled yard. Horses were being harnessed and yoked up to carriages, and ostlers and stable boys all went about their work.

Dressed in thigh-length boots and leather jerkin, Lord Marston was getting ready to leave. With his back to her and unaware that he was being observed, Eleanor paused. His dark head was slightly bent as he secured the saddle girth. Beneath his leather jerkin his muscles flexed as he worked. Her gaze took in the sheer male power of his wide, muscular shoulders, his broad back and narrow waist.

'Good morning,' she greeted quietly, dismounting, knowing she would have to set the hostility she felt for this man aside for the time they would be on the road, which would be no easy matter.

William turned his head and his eyes swept over her. Surprise registered in their depths at the picture she presented. It was quickly concealed and he returned to his task. 'You're late.'

'I don't think so.' Her tone was truculent. 'I have gone to a great deal of trouble to get here early, in case you thought to slip off without me.'

'I have no doubt at all, Mistress Collingwood, that if we had you would have soon caught up with us.' Straightening and resting one arm on his horse's back, he cocked an eye at her. 'I hope your temper has improved from last night— although you do look somewhat jaded.'

Eleanor's eyes struck sparks of indignation. 'That's because I haven't been to bed.'

His eyes sharpened, going over her outlandish short-cropped coat beneath her cloak and thick black hose, which outlined her long legs above soft knee-high boots—the clothes she hoped would disguise her gender. 'Have you any idea what you look like?' He eyed her shapely legs in the most insolent manner as he shoved himself away from his horse and circled her like a predator.

'A youth, I hope.' His insolent perusal brought an indignant scowl to her face.

'Never have I seen a youth who looks less like a youth than you do, Mistress Collingwood.'

The deep sound of his voice curled around her name with a soft intimacy that caused heat to rise in Eleanor's face.

'I suppose some poor devil will be missing his clothes.'

'I found them in a trunk some time ago. I don't know who they belonged to, but they're near enough my size to be serviceable. As long as this wretched wind doesn't blow my hat off, everyone will think I'm a lad. Oh, and I have some money, so I can pay my way.'

William cocked a brow at the sight of a pistol and dagger

in the black sash about her slender waist and a sword attached to a baldric across her chest. 'You also come armed to the teeth, I see,' he remarked drily. 'You can use them, I hope, otherwise 'tis pointless carrying them— and you're in danger of tripping over your sword.'

Eleanor saw his eyes darken, but not even an eyelash flickered to betray that the sight of her weapons alarmed him. He raised a dark eyebrow with a mocking amusement that exasperated her and brought her chin up with a proud hauteur. 'I am accomplished with the use of all three, should the need arise— besides, the sword was my father's and I refuse to part with it.'

'It's not too late to go back.'

'I'll never go back,' she said vehemently. 'Better to be set upon by a band of cutthroats than to go crawling back like a whipped dog to Frederick Atwood. If we are accosted and it's a fight they want, they shall have one. My weapons are just proof that I can take care of myself.'

William's expression told her he was unconvinced, but faced with her courage and lack of fear he was prepared to give her the benefit of the doubt. Dressed as she was with her long, elegantly turned legs outlined in hose, his grin was audacious. 'You speak brave words, Mistress Collingwood; however, the hat may hide your hair, but, despite your male garb, the rest of you is a bit of a giveaway.'

'I don't think so. I've gone to a great deal of trouble to make myself inconspicuous. Dressed like this I am not an object of curiosity and will be able to ride to York very much as I like.' With her hat pulled well down and only her amber eyes glowing beneath the brim, she was certain no one would recognise her for what she was.

'I seem to recall your mother's sister lives in Kensington or some place close by. Wouldn't it save a whole lot of trouble if you went to her instead of going all the way to York?'

Eleanor's chin lifted haughtily and her lips twisted with distaste. 'Aunt Matilda! She is in France visiting friends and not expected back for several weeks. If I were to go to her house while she is away, my stepfather would find me and bring me back, which is why I must go to Hollymead. Besides, it would be no easy matter living on my aunt's charity. She never hid the fact that she hated my father and was always taunting my mother, telling her that he was a good for nothing and their marriage a mistake from start to finish.'

'Don't you think that with your mother's death she may have softened in her attitude?'

Eleanor looked at him as if he'd taken leave of his senses. 'Aunt Matilda? Never. She has no kindness in her. Her poor husband was so hen-pecked I'm surprised there was anything left of him when he died. After Father was executed I spent only six months in her house and those months were a lifetime. It was like wearing shoes that were too tight every day. At a time when my mother and I were grieving for the loss of my father, she never let us forget that she was keeping us for nothing, delighting in our humility. I have no desire to enter her house again in a hurry.'

'Then I can understand why you want to go to Hollymead,' William said, his voice surprisingly gentle with understanding. 'Did you manage to leave Fryston Hall unseen?'

'No—no, unfortunately I didn't,' she said haltingly. 'Sir Richard Grey, my stepfather's nephew, knew what I had in mind and was waiting for me. I confess to being confused by his manner.'

'You were? Why is that?'

'He wanted me gone. The reason why I found impossible to fathom.' She frowned, genuinely puzzled by Sir Richard's odd behaviour and unable to make any sense of it. 'Why he wanted me away from Fryston Hall I cannot imagine. Are you acquainted with him?'

Apart from a slight narrowing of his eyes, William's expression remained inscrutable. 'We are acquainted. The man's a ne'er-do-well—and, like his uncle, blinded by his own ambition. Since he inherited a title and nothing else, he's devoted his life to spending the money of those rich relatives who'll have anything to do with him. He's Atwood's heir, so no doubt he will hurry his demise if he can.'

'My—stepfather also accosted me. According to Sir Richard, he saw me talking to you. He knows how much I want to return to Hollymead and when you said you were to travel north to York, he knew I would want to go with you.'

'Despite holding me to account for your father's death.'

The hint of sarcasm in his tone did not go unnoticed by Eleanor. Her face gave no sign of softening and there was a coldness in her amber eyes as she pushed her woollen cloak back over one shoulder.

'What you did cannot easily be put aside. I will never do that. The harm you have done my family will always stand between us. My mother suffered greatly because of your traitorous deed, and when she died, with each passing day my own lot grew more desperate the longer I remained in my stepfather's house—that, too, was because of you.'

William considered her apace. His eyes narrowed as he looked at her. There was something hidden there, some regret or sorrow, but he simply slipped his hat onto his head and said, 'You set your verdict against me before I could voice a plea. So be it. There is no argument against a closed mind. And so, did Atwood simply let you walk out of the house without trying to stop you?'

'No. It—it wasn't that simple.'

William glanced at her questioningly. 'No? Did he try to prevent you leaving?'

'Yes.'

'Was he violent?'

She nodded. 'But I still managed to get away.'

'How? Atwood is a big strong man—too powerful for a defenceless girl.'

'Sir Richard hit him over the head, rendering him unconscious.'

William cocked an eye at her and his lips twisted in a wry smile. 'Did he now! He must have been desperate to see the back of you.'

'He was. Very.'

A wicked, knowing gleam entered his eyes, giving Eleanor cause to think he knew something about Sir Richard that she didn't. 'I can't for the life of me imagine why.'

Seeing Lord Marston was clearly at pains to control his humour caused by some private thought, Eleanor's glare was scathing. 'Don't mock me,' she flared, her amber eyes flashing fire. 'Don't underestimate me either. I don't fear the consequences of my actions—even though you provoke me with your mockery. Women may be regarded by everyone as being subordinate to men, but I own no man my superior—not you or Frederick Atwood.'

'I can see that.'

'I am not afraid of him. Nothing that he did could touch me. When my mother died I was a dutiful stepdaughter and accepted the hard lot fate dealt me, but I was determined I would be free of him—from his lust-filled glances.'

'Then I am surprised you chose to stay when she died.'

'I didn't choose to remain. At the time, I had nowhere else to go, and anyway, there were reasons why I had to stay, one of them being Catherine's wedding. There were many preparations to be made and she was relying on me. I—I was always uncomfortable about the way my stepfather looked at me,' she said, embarrassed to be talking to him of so intimate a matter and lowering her eyes, 'and it is only in recent days that he began making unwelcome advances, which made me realise that he covets me in a way that makes him dangerous.'

'The man has a fiendish temper. You can be sure he will come after you. Your leaving will have touched his pride, and his resolve to pay you back will harden more each day.'

'That I know, but I feel an overwhelming relief at having succeeded in escaping him at long last.'

'We have yet to reach York,' William grimly reminded her. 'Before you know it, his men will be hard on our heels.'

'Then we'd best get started.'

'If we are to be in each other's company for days, try to be more agreeable and summon more warmth. I will not endure a surly companion.'

Silently Eleanor seethed at his boldness, his rudeness. Inside she rebelled, but she knew she would have to accept his terms and compromise, and that was what he would have, and that unwillingly and without grace. But she dared not show too much animosity until her feet were safely on Hollymead's solid ground.

'Be assured that I shall endeavour to do my best,' she replied tightly. A silver flame in William's gaze kindled bright, burning her with its intensity.

'It would be appreciated. We'll stop after a time for something to eat. If you tire, tell me and we'll pause a while.'

'I am gratified by your consideration, but I require no special favours. I can ride as well as anyone and for as long,' Eleanor told him, her head held high and aloof. Seeing the giant Godfrey leading his horse across the yard towards them, his ruddy face above the golden beard devoid of any expression, she stiffened. 'Is your servant as fearsome as he looks?'

William watched Godfrey mount his horse, a huge chestnut warhorse with four identical white socks, and smiled. 'Don't be put off by the way he looks. He is from Glasgow, the son of a boat builder. We met on our travels two years ago. He's been with me ever since.'

'He seems very quiet. Does he speak English?'

'Very well, as a matter of fact, but he never utters more words than is absolutely necessary. Don't worry,' he said, chuckling softly when he saw her cast Godfrey a dubious look, 'he's quite harmless unless crossed. You'll get used to him.' As they rode out of the inn yard he turned and looked at her, his face relaxed. 'I salute your courage and your boldness, Mistress Collingwood. You are undeniably brave— and reckless, running away on some wild escapade with very little thought of the consequences. This is clearly your style and I admire such spirit in a woman.'

Surprised by his compliment, she stared at him and smiled broadly. 'Thank you. That means a lot—coming from you.'

It was cold and wet that early morning as the three of them set out on the road north. At Hollymead it would find Eleanor in an equally cold place, but better that than what was left of the winter in Frederick Atwood's house.

Frederick Atwood's face was twisted into an ugly expression. When he told Catherine how he had attempted to stop Eleanor running off with William Marston, the look of malevolence that was added to his bitterness was quite terrifying, and he meant to make her sorry for leaving Fryston Hall.

Catherine burned with indignation and her expression was fierce. Eleanor's courage to stand up to her father meant nothing to her, but the fact that she had left Fryston Hall with William did. She would never forget how Eleanor had humiliated her and she was shamed to have such a wanton for a stepsister. Seated beside Henry in the carriage taking her to her new home in the riverside village of Chelsea, inwardly she seethed. So much for Eleanor's hatred of William. She had somehow inveigled her way into his company, dazzling him in a way Catherine would never forgive. When Henry fumbled for her hand among the folds of her sapphire-blue velvet gown, she cringed and closed her eyes to hide the feral glitter in their depths, and her revulsion and disappointment in her new husband. Just twenty-four hours into her marriage and she was struck by a realisation that Henry was not, and never could be, William Marston.

Her heart was filled with a dreadful blackness that would grow as day followed day and night followed night, when she would have to endure the disgusting things Henry did to her body. Making Eleanor the object of her suffering, the hope of revenge would become the sweetest thing of hatred on earth— and yet her feelings were not as clear-cut as she would like.

The closer they got to Henry's house, for the first time in her life Catherine felt vulnerable, afraid and very lonely and she was surprised to feel tears prick the backs of her eyes. Behind everything there was a feeling of regret, of loss, for despite everything Eleanor was the closest she had come to having a sister.

Chapter Three

Why Eleanor's mother had married Frederick Atwood Eleanor would never understand. Of course a woman was brought up to be a wife and mother and not think of herself as a man's equal, and indeed she had more status as a married woman. When one of the partners died, both men and women frequently remarried with speed regardless of whether their previous marriage had been a success or not.

Unlike her mother, Eleanor had not been sent away to live in another household, where she attended the lady of the house and learned by watching her how to behave in polite society and was taught how to look after a house and bring up children. Eleanor had been educated at home by her mother and Uncle John, who taught her to read and write and also French and Latin.

When her mother had died and they had shut her away in the blackness of the Atwood family vault, the sun had gone out of Eleanor's life. But now she was going back to Hollymead— a safe haven in a dark world. A quiver of excitement raced through her and she felt Tilda respond as though she had trans-ferred her feeling to her mare. Freedom, that's what she wanted.

Freedom. Exultant, she wanted to take off her hat, throw it in the air and shout for joy, and it was only the grim faces of her two companions that kept her hat clamped on her head.

But William was not unaware of her change of mood. Slowing his horse he glanced sideways at her, cocking a handsome brow as he gave her a lengthy inspection. 'Why, Mistress Collingwood, I do believe you are smiling.'

Looking across at him, she was unable to prevent her happiness bubbling to her lips and letting her laughter flow free. 'You would, too, my lord, had you been under my stepfather's rule for almost four years. Free of his restrictions, I feel reborn and I'm already enjoying the adventure, which is stirring the life within me and I'm sure will carry me forward to some exciting future—what, I have no idea, but if it is up to me it will not be dull.'

Her enthusiasm brought a smile to William's lips and a gleam of admiration in his eyes. 'That is an extremely daring proclamation.'

'Prior to this, the most daring thing I have ever done is answer my stepfather back. My rebelliousness and disobedience almost made him have a seizure. This will probably kill him—God willing,' she cried joyously.

William's smile broadened at her exuberance, his teeth gleaming white from between parted lips. 'It will take more than the disobedience of an eighteen-year-old girl to kill Frederick Atwood.'

She looked at him curiously, thinking how incredibly handsome this man was. The tanned flesh of his face gleamed with the health of one who has enjoyed freedom in a tropical country. Where had he been, she wondered, these past three years, and why had he disappeared from Catherine's life so suddenly?

'How do you know how old I am?'

'You were five years old when my father took me to Hollymead. I was fifteen at the time—I remember because my father had presented me with a horse for my fifteenth birthday the week before. I rode it that day.'

'Your memory is better than mine. How strange it is that I don't remember.'

'Our meeting was brief and you were intent on playing a game of shuttlecock with your friends.' Falling silent, he continued to look at her. 'Were you really planning to travel to Hollymead alone?'

'Yes. That was what I intended.'

'Do you not understand what could happen to you? The bands of thieves and miscreants who roam the countryside would see you as easy prey.'

'Then it's fortunate for me that I am well armed and that you allowed me to accompany you, Lord Marston.'

'You needn't be so formal, Eleanor,' he teased with a devilishly wicked grin. 'You may call me William or Will as you please. 'Tis a good many miles to York, so it is better to be easy with each other. We got off to a poor start, but there is no reason why we cannot be civil to one another.'

Putting aside everything she held against him for the time being, Eleanor agreed—but only for the time it took them to reach their destination, she was quick to tell him. Men like William Marston found it easy to manipulate a woman's heart and she wanted nothing to do with any of that.

The journey would prove to be long and tiring and an entirely new experience for Eleanor. Two hours into the journey and her euphoria had diminished somewhat as her shoulder began to ache with grinding insistence, from which she could find no ease as she galloped along at a gruelling pace and struggled to keep up with her companions.

* * *

At midday they stopped for refreshment. Providing a reasonable standard of food and service, the coaching inn was not short of customers. They were from all walks of life, of every description and travelling in every direction. Eleanor's temper was on short rein as she ate her kidneys and beef, washed down with ale.

William observed her closely, studying her face as she shoved her food around her trencher. He had seen her wince as she had dismounted, holding her arm close to her chest, which told him she might be injured. She had told him that Frederick Atwood had been violent towards her when he'd found her leaving—how violent had he been?

On leaving the inn, he heard a muffled groan of pain escape her lips as she mounted her horse and her face was pale and drawn.

'Wait,' he said sharply, looking up at her as she was about to turn her horse in the direction of the road. 'You're hurt.'

'A mere twinge,' she lied. 'It's nothing, truly.'

William was determined. 'Get down.'

Eleanor's eyes struck sparks of indignation. 'What?'

'I said, get down.' Without waiting for her to obey, he reached up and clamped his hands tightly about her slender waist, and she was seized from the saddle as if she were a child. 'I can see your shoulder pains you. Before we go any further, I'll take a look.'

'You most certainly will not. The devil take my shoulder! Kindly let go of me and please don't fuss.'

Ignoring her remark and her glare of indignation, he grasped her elbow and marched her back inside the inn and into the privacy of a small room the landlord quickly put at his disposal.

'Show me,' he demanded.

'You want me to take my clothes off?' she retorted, shocked at the mere thought. 'I most certainly will not. This is quite outrageous.'

'I agree, but if you won't help yourself, then someone else must do it. We have only just embarked on an exceedingly long journey and I want to be assured that you're up to it before we go any further. Now, let me see your shoulder.'

Seeing he was deadly serious, on a sigh Eleanor removed her doublet and pushed the shirt and flimsy undergarment down off her shoulder, just short of uncovering her breast.

Seeing the ugly bruise that stained her delicate skin like spilled elderberry juice, William uttered a violent curse and his angry gaze settled on her face. The cold fire in his eyes bespoke the fury churning within him. He held himself on tight rein until the rage cooled. What was left was a gnawing wish to see Atwood dangling from the end of a rope. He was not a man, but a rabid beast with a twisted mind who had abused the daughter of Edgar Collingwood.

There was a silence for a while as deftly William's fingers began to examine Eleanor's shoulder. At first her skin began to prickle with outrage, yet at the same time she felt alarmingly vulnerable and exposed. Something stirred in her breast, making it suddenly difficult to take a breath. Every nerve in her body piqued at the feel of his touch, which was like a brand of fire against her skin, and a searing excitement shot through her breast. She felt overpowered by his nearness. Her whole body throbbed with an awareness of him, but she would not give any hint of her weakness.

His snug-fitting leather jerkin and high boots accentuated the long lines of his body, and she noticed again the incredible silver-grey eyes intent on her shoulder. It was impossible not to respond to this man as his masculine magnetism was dominant in the room. Little wonder Catherine had been enamoured of him and, Eleanor suspected, was still in love with him.

His face was creased with concentration, his fingers strong and soothing. His touch was impersonal, as if he were examining an object, yet it was gentle and Eleanor did not feel like an object—far from it. She felt cosseted. There was something agreeable in his touch, almost sensuous. Her whole body felt as if it were unwinding, growing weak with the pleasure of his ministering. Vividly conscious of her close proximity to him, she abruptly turned her thoughts away from this new and dangerous direction and averted her head, before he could realise just how much he affected her.

She had everything mapped out and did not want complications, especially not of this kind, and, she suspected, neither did he; she was almost ashamed to acknowledge her feelings as she watched him. What kind of man are you, William Marston? she wondered, and realised she had no idea at all.

'Catherine,' he murmured unexpectedly. 'Is she happy?'

Eleanor turned and looked at him as he continued to examine her shoulder. 'Is every bride not happy on her wedding day?'

His eyes were chilled. 'You prevaricate, Eleanor. I asked you if she is happy.'

Eleanor nodded, her gaze focused on his bent head. She felt the sudden urge to shove back the heavy lock of his hair that had fallen forward to better see his features. It was evident that Catherine mattered to him, which made her wonder at the depth of his feelings for the woman he had left. If he still loved Catherine, then she could only imagine how desperate he must be feeling, and that he was handling it the best way he knew how, but there really was no excuse for the pain he had caused her.

'I thought she was, before you arrived and disrupted the

wedding celebrations. Now I have no concept of how your re-appearance will have affected her. Henry Wheeler is a good man, but he was not her choice of husband. She—was to have married you. I can understand why you are concerned. Why did you leave without a word?'

As he towered over her, William's lean, hard face bore no hint of humour. His lips curled with bitterness and a coldness entered his eyes. 'For the answer to that question, Eleanor, you will have to ask your stepfather. He holds all the answers in his twisted mind. One thing I would like to know,' he said, holding her gaze steadily, 'is did he turn Catherine against me?'

'No,' she replied harshly. 'You did that all by yourself when you disappeared without a word to her. Why did you?'

William looked her squarely in the eye, his own glinting like hard metal. Anger roiled through him. What did she expect? For him to reveal all, to bare his soul to her? He may have agreed to take her to Hollymead, but he needed neither her respect nor her kind regard.

'Whatever poison Atwood has filled your head with, Eleanor, I never meant to hurt Catherine, so let that be the end of the matter,' he reproached curtly. 'I am not a man to start a quarrel with you, but I will give you this word of advice. If you persist in baiting me with your tongue, you'd best get on your horse and head right back to Fryston Hall. Your barbs are beginning to irritate me.'

Eleanor's eyes were blazing as if they had a fire behind them. 'I will not go back. I do not care for your company, but I am stuck with it and glad of your protection. Threaten me all you like, but do not think I am afraid of you.'

'Then you should be,' he mocked, his tone caustic. 'And perhaps you have cause. Where I have been for the past three years has frayed my courtly manners and I often forget how to behave like a gentleman should. So, if you are to continue to ride with us, do you agree to declare a truce for the time it takes us to reach Hollymead, where we will part company with good grace, I hope? Come, Eleanor, surely we can benefit from a surface friendship on the long journey north.'

The colour drained from Eleanor's cheeks as his words sank in. A light blazed briefly in his silver eyes, then was quickly extinguished. She was deeply conscious that his easy, mocking exterior hid the inner man, and as she gazed into those fathomless depths of his eyes, some instinct warned her that his offer of a truce could make him more dangerous to her as a friend than he had been as her enemy.

There was a withheld power to command in him that was as impressive as it was irritating. If she agreed to a truce, she was determined he would not get the better of her. She would not let him reach her, for by shielding her innermost self from the touch of another human being she would always be strong and complete and in control.

His brows lifted in mocking challenge. 'What do you say?'

Gnawing on her bottom lip as if she could not quite make up her mind, she nodded. 'Very well—but only for the time it takes us to reach Hollymead,' she was quick to add.

'Agreed. Now, as far as your shoulder is concerned, there is nothing broken—just badly sprained. I'll ask the landlord for some witch hazel to apply to the bruising—and it should be bound.'

'And you would know how to do that?'

'My years as a soldier taught me many things, one of them being that a soldier may owe his life to his knowledge of tending wounds.'

'I'd rather not have it strapped. I can't possibly ride with one arm.'

'Then we'll ride at a slower pace so you don't suffer unnecessary discomfort.'

'No. I don't want to hold you back.' She sighed with capitulation when she saw the determined gleam in his eyes. 'All
right. I'll ask for help when I think I need it, so there, does
that satisfy you?'

When he unexpectedly smiled broadly, Eleanor noticed
how white and strong his teeth were and how the tiny lines at
the sides of his sharp eyes creased up attractively. He really
was so handsome, so well made, so perfect to look at. Little
wonder the women of the Court pursued him.

For a moment she was confused and found herself striving
for normality. It was difficult to organise her thoughts when
those amazingly silver-grey eyes were focused on her so
intently. Before the rogue thoughts could progress further, she
lowered her eyes, quickly shaking off the strangeness of the
moment that had caught her unawares. What was she thinking
of? This man was practically unknown to her, and yet just for
a moment she had felt drawn to this handsome, desirable
stranger. Men like William Marston found it easy to manipulate a woman's heart and she wanted nothing to do with him.

Turning on his heel, William strode to the door. 'Perfectly.
I'll go and get some witch hazel and then we'll be on our way.'

Never had Eleanor spent so much time in the saddle. Her
thighs and bottom were sore and her back ached, but, trying
to ignore her discomfort, she rode on uncomplaining. When
they stopped for the night she looked and felt fit to drop,
although now she was out of the wind she rallied a little, but
not enough not to long for a bed.

'I can't eat anything,' she told William wearily. 'I must go
to bed, otherwise I shall fall asleep on my feet.'

'As you like. Just make sure you eat a good breakfast
before we set off in the morning.'

Eleanor followed a serving woman through the busy,

smoky taproom where men were drinking, playing dice and calling for more ale. They went up a narrow flight of stairs where the woman stepped aside for her to enter an extremely small chamber beneath the eaves. Unable to resist the little bed, she stripped off her clothes and slid naked beneath the coarse sheets, so tired she was insensitive as they chafed her flesh. Soon she would be at Hollymead, safe inside its strong walls, where there would be warm scented water to bathe in and smooth Holland sheets to lie between and rest her sore and weary body.

Arriving downstairs the following morning and finding Godfrey tucking into a hearty breakfast alone, after fifteen minutes and still no sign of Eleanor, William went to see what was keeping her.

When there was no answer to his knock, William went in and found her still snuggled deeply into the covers, with the sheets covering her nakedness, her hair tumbling about her, and her eyes closed in sleep. With the full tender curve of her mouth, her face softly flushed and naked, she looked like a child— young, vulnerable and defenceless.

Growing aware of a firm hand gently prodding her, struggling to open her eyes and clear the fuzz in her head, Eleanor glanced up and saw William standing over her. Resentful at being disturbed, sighing crossly, she turned her head away and pulled the covers up to her chin. 'Go away,' she mumbled sleepily. 'Leave me alone. It can't be time to get up yet.'

William chuckled softly. 'I didn't expect to see you still nestled in so cosily, Eleanor. I apologise for disturbing your sleep, but it's way past time to get up. Come. There's time for some breakfast before we leave. The food smells good. It will set you in good stead for the day.'

'All right,' she conceded with a deep sigh, pulling herself

up, pushing the heavy curtain of her hair off her face and rubbing her eyes. Realising that she was naked beneath the sheets, she kept tight hold of them. 'I feel as if my body has been tortured beyond endurance.' Looking with longing at the pillow her head had just parted from, she sighed. 'Don't let me keep you,' she murmured softly. 'Give me a few minutes and I'll join you.'

Seeing where her attention was directed and suspecting she would go back to sleep as soon as he left her, suppressing a smile and adopting a stern countenance at her, William leaned against the door and casually folded his arms across his chest. 'I'll leave when you're out of that bed and not before.'

With a sigh of irritation, Eleanor shuffled to the edge of the bed and stood up, careful to keep tight hold of the covers. Stretching her long limbs, she gave vent to a prodigious yawn. 'There. Are you satisfied now?'

William's smouldering gaze casually caressed her as if the bed covers did not exist, his eyes resting on the twin orbs of her breasts swelling above the top of the covers, and he could well imagine the softness of her flesh beneath the sheets. Surrounded by a frame of honey-gold tresses, vibrant and glorious, the harsh planes of her face retreated and her eyes grew soft, her cheeks taking on a fragility like hand-blown glass that could be easily shattered by a careless move.

In fact, she appeared remarkably younger. He hadn't expected that without her male attire and the loosening of her hair to change his perception of her to such a degree and an unexpected rampant desire speared him.

'Will you stop looking at me like that?' Eleanor whispered, feeling devoured by those burning eyes. She looked up into his face and for a long moment she could not look away again. It was something she was unable to name, but which her female body instantly recognised. As if her body were awash with feeling, alive with need, she felt like a caged creature bursting to be set free.

William's brow arched as he peered at her, his desire hard driven as he became preoccupied with her rosy mouth and pert nose. She was completely unaware that her hair tumbling about her shoulders was a hundred different shades and dazzling lights.

'I assure you, Eleanor, that a naked woman is most provocative at this time of the morning.'

'You are indeed the most unmannerly man I have ever met, William Marston,' she hissed, a storm brewing in her eyes.

He was quite undaunted; a dazzling smile broke the firm line of his mouth. 'I never pretended otherwise.'

Drawing the covers tighter about her, she flashed him an indignant look. 'If you must ogle somebody, William, go and seek out one of the servant girls. I'm sure they will be flattered to acquire the attention of a gentleman of your calibre.'

'It's not a servant girl I want.' An audacious smile began to curve his lips, his expression watchful and a knowing look in his eyes as his mind reminded him of all the delectable female attributes that lay within his reach—mentally he could feel the firm softness of her breasts filling his palms. 'You really are very lovely, Eleanor.'

Mesmerised, she stared into the fathomless silver eyes while his deep husky voice caressed her, pulling her under his spell. She was unprepared for the sheer force of the feelings that swept through her and she knew, with a kind of panic, that she was in grave danger, not from him, but from herself.

'Do not attempt to dazzle me with glib flattery, William Marston,' she retorted sharply, 'for you haven't a prayer for success.'

'I do have other skills to persuade you if I had a mind.' The sudden gleam that danced in his eyes was wicked.

'You're blushing,' he murmured, observing the familiar pink that stole over her cheeks that somehow reflected her innocence. Strange how he'd come to expect it—and stranger still was the warmth it stirred within him, the need to protect her that it brought to the fore. He smiled slowly, enjoying teasing her. 'And your eyes are far too eloquent to claim uninterest.'

Eleanor's lips trembled. He wrapped such carnality around the words that she almost fell back on to the bed. For a second she glimpsed a different face—lowered eyelids, a passionate gravity, a face from which all cynicism and irony had vanished under the surge of a single feeling.

'Please don't say these things to me,' she said, sighing wearily, beset with confusion on finding herself in a situation she had never been in before and not sure how to handle it. 'I think you've set your mind to torment me.'

For a long moment William's hungering eyes looked at her and then, pushing himself away from the door, he smiled. 'I apologise, Eleanor. I can see it takes more than flattery and a spot of teasing and cajoling words to move you to ardour.'

Her flush deepened as her eyes flared to life. 'It does, much more than that. Now please leave so I can get dressed. I'll be down in a moment.'

A heavy lock of hair caressed her temple and William had the urge to brush it away. Suddenly recollecting himself, he clenched his hands into fists to stop himself. Suddenly, touching Eleanor Collingwood did not seem like a good idea. A part of him wished he'd never instigated this moment, another part of him wanted to drag her into her arms and kiss those luscious lips that were parted and slightly trembling.

Turning from her, impatient to be away, he opened the door and said, 'Don't take long.'

Why had he behaved like that? he asked himself angrily as

he walked away. The fact was that flushed with sleep and wrapped in bed covers—which to William's observant eyes was more of an enticement than a covering—Eleanor had looked so delectable and desirable that he had wanted her with an aching need that seeped into the deepest parts of his body, had wanted her with a recklessness that was completely foreign to his nature, but it had been a momentary aberration, and now it had passed.

Eleanor had been heartened by a night of rest and good food, so the rattling harness and the ring of horses' hooves on the hard cobblestones as a coach full of refreshed passengers went out into the road and headed for London was like music to her ears. She was mounted and ready to leave when she saw Godfrey, with his cloak slung carelessly about his massive shoulders and broad, studded, leather belt about his hips, striding across the yard in the direction of the stables, crossing the path of her horse. His blond hair, unfashionably long, fell in heavy waves to his shoulders.

Initially she had been uneasy with William's servant. He rarely spoke to her, only to acknowledge her presence with an occasional greeting in a deep, guttural voice, but gradually she was becoming used to him.

He did not trouble to lower his gaze, which was amused and slid over her, but not in an insolent manner. Eleanor stared back at him, and when he smiled broadly she returned his smile. He was a stranger, a servant, but it was clear that William thought highly of him.

'You feel rested this morning, Mistress Collingwood?'

'Perfectly, thank you, Godfrey,' she answered. His voice was deep, quiet and compelling with a pronounced northern accent. 'William tells me you are from Scotland, Godfrey.'

'Aye, my father was a boat builder on the Clyde. He had a

thriving business, his vessels being sold all over England and sailing for ports the world over.'

'Then why is the son of a successful boat builder Lord Marston's servant?' she asked him curiously, hoping he would tell her something of what William had been doing for the past three years.

Godfrey looked at her for a long moment, considering whether to answer her question. Shrugging his enormous shoulders he smiled a secretive smile, and, shaking his head, started to walk away. 'Things changed for my father. He lost his fortune and died in debt. William is generous. We have an understanding—and,' he said, chuckling softly and giving her a playful wink, 'he pays me well.'

Eleanor watched him disappear into the stables for his horse, feeling strangely disappointed, which was foolish. Why should he tell her anything—and why should she care? But her curiosity about William was not appeased. There were rings in Godfrey's ears and rings on his fingers, gold rings that sparkled with jewels. Since when did a man's servant behave without subservience towards his master and flaunt a wealth his master did not? Godfrey was big and bold and, despite being William's servant, he was his own man.

But the question of the past three years of William's life nagged at her. Wherever he had been, he was keeping it locked away inside, as if it was some dark secret he didn't want to talk about. Whatever had happened to him, it was eating away at him, but he would not share it with her.

Coming into the yard, distractedly William paused to watch Eleanor ride towards the road. Her hat was set at a jaunty angle on her head and she sat her horse with a straight-backed, easy grace he admired. Godfrey sidled up to him, chuckling deep in his throat when he saw where William's gaze was directed.

'Am I to deduce, since you've been staring at our

charming companion for the best part of two minutes with
an inane grin on your face, that you are not finding her
company as objectionable as you feared you might?' he
taunted, provoking William to throw him a dark, though
smiling, look.

William took the bridle of his horse that Godfrey had
brought out of the stable. 'You are welcome to deduce
anything you wish, Godfrey,' he barked, his eyes twinkling
merrily at his servant, 'but she has made the journey less
tedious—as I'm sure you will agree, since I have noticed you
spend a good deal of time watching her yourself. You're be-
dazzled, Godfrey. Never have I seen you so smitten.'

'Nay, not smitten, William,' Godfrey said on a serious note.
'She made a courageous decision when she decided to leave
Fryston Hall. I'm merely concerned for the lassie and that's all.'

William frowned. 'So am I, Godfrey, so am I, and I doubt
she will be as safe from Atwood's machinations at Hollymead
as she expects to be.'

'Aye, well, she's out of his clutches for now—as is the fair
Lady Catherine'

William turned and met the other man's sky-blue eyes and
smiled. Godfrey was a connoisseur of women. Where they
were concerned he had the charm of the angels and the luck
of the devil. 'Catherine? She impressed you, did she, you old
reprobate?'

Godfrey's chuckle was like a low rumble. 'Reprobate I'm
happy to live with, but less of the old. Now the lady is wed
you'll be looking for a new bride with a lovely neck to hang
your family jewels around.'

'I'm in no hurry. Marriage is the last thing on my mind at
this time.'

'You will be when a list of eligible ladies has been drawn
up by the ladies of the Court.'

'Then I shall endeavour to keep well away from the place. Following my brief time at Court and the necessary visit to Fryston Hall, time spent with my family is what I need just now.'

'It wasn't the fair Catherine that drew you to Fryston Hall, but Atwood himself, wasn't it? And who could blame you after he consigned you to a living hell.'

William was not offended that Godfrey spoke plainly. Shaking the dust from his hat and placing it on his head, he swung himself up into the saddle. 'You always seem to know my secrets, Godfrey.' He paused, giving his friend a long, knowing look. 'Is it possible that if Catherine hadn't wed Henry Wheeler, you might fancy her for yourself?'

'And would you be angry if I did? She's a handsome woman.'

William gave a sudden laugh. 'Ye Gods, Godfrey, by no means! Catherine is in the past—and between you and me, I'm relieved she wasn't waiting for me. I've complications enough without having to find an excuse why I no longer wish to wed her.'

'If you wanted her, none of that would matter,' Godfrey remarked, hoisting himself on to his horse. 'Anyway, I don't think your lordship is the type she admires.'

William cocked a brow. 'And you are?'

Heading out of the yard, Godfrey gave a bark of laughter. 'Had I met her before that milksop she's married, I warrant she'd be willing enough.'

Godfrey was supremely confident that this was so—despite her scathing look when she had met his gaze and the way she had lifted her lovely head haughtily. The woman was beautiful in a different way to Mistress Collingwood, and one thing he had discerned was that she was indifferent to her new husband. His gaze swept to where Mistress Collingwood waited for them by the roadside, an impatient look on her face.

'But for now we have another young lady to contend with—all the way to York.'

The weather turned colder and the condition of the roads deteriorated as they travelled through the counties of Cambridgeshire, Nottinghamshire and at last into her beloved Yorkshire. The winter's rain had turned puddles into small lakes and roads into quagmires, but Eleanor was full of hope despite the weather.

Somehow, despite all her efforts to dislike William, Eleanor was unable to sustain her animosity and a genuine camaraderie had sprung up between them. The tense, stilted journey she had feared had turned out differently and she had enjoyed the casual banter between her companions.

Eleanor and William were riding two abreast, Tilda stepping out to keep pace with the bigger horse, Godfrey several yards in front. They had been riding in silence at a steady pace for several miles. For once the sun was shining and the sky was a pale blue with wisps of cloud. The view on either side was picturesque, with grassy hills dotted with woolly sheep and water meadows where plump cattle grazed.

Skilfully riding his prancing stallion, William looked at his companion, becoming distracted with the delicate curve of her cheek and mouth, the slight swell of her bottom lip and the gentle arch of her brows. He enjoyed riding beside her. She sat her horse with an ease that came with knowing how to.

'You ride well, Eleanor,' he commented softly.

His eyes went over her figure in her hose and doublet, the padded fabric pulling over her breasts. Her cloak was thrown back over her shoulders and a jaunty brown feather curled in her hat. She was exquisitely lovely, sensual and complex and with none of the pampered softness of so many women he had known. She was standing up to the hard journey admirably, but she was weary and saddle sore and straining to reach Hollymead. Thankfully the pain in her shoulder had eased.

Eleanor smiled carelessly, enjoying the feel of the sun on her face. 'I've had plenty of practice at Hollymead and at Fryston Hall—at least my stepfather didn't begrudge me that, and Tilda's been mine ever since I went to live there.'

'She's a fine mare,' William remarked, keen to engage her in conversation; despite having spent a good deal of time together, he knew little about her. But he was beginning to decipher her moods. She was strong, confident, spirited and determined one minute, and vulnerable and unsure of herself the next.

'She has a sweet nature and handles well. She also has stamina—which you will have seen for yourself, although she's not up to your splendid animal.'

'He is rather fine. I bought him off a dealer when I arrived in London a week ago. Savage, he was—thought he'd kick the stable door down, but he's beginning to know who's his master.' Chuckling low, he leaned forward and slapped his horse's neck affectionately when it pricked its ears and snorted, the clever beast knowing it was being discussed. After a while he gave Eleanor a sideways glance. 'What do you really think of me, Eleanor?' he asked before he could stop himself, but he was curious to know her opinion of him.

She gave him a pointed look, an impish smile playing on her lips. 'I think you would trouble a woman, Lord Marston—not dressed as a boy, that is.'

William laughed out loud at that. 'Then think yourself fortunate that you are wearing hose.'

She laughed back at him. She could not help herself.

They rode for a few moments in silence. William turned his head and found Eleanor looking at him. He looked into her eyes, enormous, captivating eyes, amazing eyes, of a deep rich amber that made him think of copper and liquid honey and burnished gold—candid and expressive, with long dark lashes. The silver flame in his gaze kindled brighter, burning her with its intensity. Raising his eyebrows a fraction, he grinned suddenly, the change lessening the tension of the moment.

'I can imagine how eager you are to reach Hollymead,' William remarked. 'I trust you will find your uncle in good health.'

'So do I. I haven't seen him for a long time. What will you do when you have spoken to him? Will you remain in York?'

He shook his head. 'I shall go home to Staxton Hall—just a few miles north of York. I've been away a long time. I'm eager to see my family—my mother and my sisters.'

'They are expecting you?'

'I wrote to my mother from London.'

'And how many sisters have you?'

'Two. Anne and Jane are twins and still at home.'

Her look was one of envy. 'You're lucky. I would have liked a sister.'

'You have Catherine.'

Eleanor's eyes clouded with regret. 'Catherine and I never enjoyed the close relationship that real sisters share with each other, and we rarely confided in each other.'

'I'm sorry to hear that. Catherine was often moody, her temper volatile, but she had a gentle side to her nature—and she was also a victim of her father's harshness and, at times, indifference.'

Eleanor glanced at him, wondering if he still loved Catherine. The blankness of his expression showed her he was desperately trying to hide what he still felt for her; in fact, his seeming lack of concern was not convincing, for a man who has loved a woman cannot help but hold on to the memory of that love, even if it is no more.

'You—have been to the Court since returning to London?' she asked, having no desire to discuss her temperamental stepsister.

'Briefly.'

'And is Queen Elizabeth as beautiful as everyone says she is? And is it as exciting as I have heard?'

William seemed amused as he studied her. Eleanor saw a twinkle in his eye and a twist of humour about his attractive mouth.

'Each to his own. There are better things to do than to idle away one's time at Court. It all appears civilised on the surface, made up of civilised human beings, but there runs many dangerous and treacherous undercurrents as ambitious courtiers court the Queen's favour and scheme to better their position and fill their family coffers.'

'And are you too not ambitious? I—am aware that your own scheming resulted in the confiscation of your home,' she said haltingly.

'No,' he said decidedly. 'Besides, my home has been restored to me—and for that I have to thank your uncle, since he petitioned the Queen on my behalf. Thankfully Elizabeth knows who her friends are. She knows who stood by her through the years of her troubles and rewards them well for it now she has the power to do so.'

'I did not realise my uncle was influential in Court matters, never having sought favour.'

'The Queen met him several years ago when she was at Hatfield Palace and she admired his intellectual mind. But where the Court is concerned, believe me, Eleanor, it can be a dreadful place. There is also much warmongering among the ladies who surround the Queen, with their petty jealousies and intrigues, weaving webs of deceit. And the men are equally as bad, with their love of corruption, of besting the next man in the frequent tournaments—jousting, pageants and masques put on for the Queen's entertainment.'

'They say she is much admired by the gentlemen of the Court.'

'She is the Queen. It flatters her vanity to be surrounded by men, and she is not averse to a handsome face.'

'And do you not aspire to be one of them? There was a time when you dazzled the ladies of the Court of King Edward and did not lack for female companionship—and I know all about your spirit of adventure that took you to foreign parts.'

A cloud seemed to cross his face. Elizabeth's Court was livelier than the Court of the young King Edward, of which he had been an integral part, where nobles had seen him as an astute friend or a man to be wary of if they were involved in anything detrimental towards the King.

'Those days are gone. The Queen's Court holds no attraction for me, and much less the Queen herself. Besides, she is enamoured of Lord Robert Dudley—and he of her.'

'I have heard the gossip—' she shot him a little smile '—who has not? But there are those who say it is scurrilous and untrue.'

'I assure you, Eleanor, that the rumour is not unfounded. They cannot keep their eyes off each other.'

'But Lord Robert is a married man so nothing can come of it. A wife cannot be set aside.'

'She can if the lady who wants a wife set aside happens to be the Queen of England and supreme governor of the church. As such she has the power to do so, and do not forget that her father did just that in his desire to wed Elizabeth's mother and later to divorce Anne of Cleves. Unfortunately Elizabeth has inherited a bankrupt and rebellious country from her sister, and considerable debt abroad.

'Her advisors have warned her that she will only survive it if she marries a strong prince. There are several being talked of and

Robert Dudley is definitely not one of them. However, he thinks very highly of himself and is ambitious, certain he can reclaim his destiny at Elizabeth's side, but his enemies are many. If he does not return to his wife, he will have to watch his back.'

'I have much in common with Robert Dudley. Both our fathers were beheaded under Queen Mary.'

William's face turned hard. 'A tragic situation that you have laid at my door.'

The mood between them had changed. All at once the ugly reality had invaded the false, easy atmosphere of the journey, and Eleanor rounded on the man, knowing him for what he truly was, and before she could help herself, accusingly, she said, 'Yes, and with good reason.' Her eyes saw the changing expression on his face—a look that at once seemed to warn her and to shut her out.

'Good reason indeed,' he remarked brusquely.

Eleanor lifted her chin. 'That's the way it is. I'm in no position to judge.'

Anger ignited in his eyes. 'No, you're not.'

With nothing else to say, in one swift motion William kicked his horse forwards.

Becoming lost in her thoughts, Eleanor rode on in silence. Throughout the days she had been with William they had become not exactly friends, because what she knew to be his betrayal of her father had placed too great a divide between them, but they got on well enough. Moreover, she found in him a sensitivity that made him capable of perceiving her need for understanding. He was also the only man who had told her he admired her spirit, instead of condemning her for it.

Why had William disappeared from Catherine's life so suddenly, she wondered yet again, and where had he been for the past three years? The very fact that he refused to speak of it told her that whatever had befallen him had left scars, as yet unhealed. What treachery could have hardened his heart?

There were so many questions she wanted answers for. What was the cause of the enmity between William and her stepfather? Was Catherine at the root of it, or was it something more sinister than that?

Chapter Four

⸻

They were to spend the night at an inn beneath the grim, massive ramparts of Pontefract Castle, an impressive, impregnable structure built by a Norman upon a rock, in an area that was an established centre of the cloth industry.

The next day they would reach York. Darkness was falling and it had been raining for the best part of the day. Welcome lights shone from the inn's windows and smoke twisted up from its chimneys. Eleanor slid from her horse and ducked her head as a gust of wind buffeted her.

Camaraderie restored between them, half-smiling, William looked at her, knowing how relieved she was that this was to be their last night on the road, but she was staring straight ahead, her face ashen. Following her gaze, he saw two men taking to the road. They hadn't seen the new arrivals and they looked in a hurry. Both men were shrouded in black cloaks, their hats pulled down and partly shielding their faces from the buffeting wind, but they were familiar to Eleanor.

She became still as she puzzled over the familiarity of the men, looking at the gate through which they had disappeared, then shook her head.

'Why do you frown?' William enquired.

'Those two men who just rode out were familiar to me,' she replied quietly.

'Your stepfather's men?'

'Yes. It isn't my imagination.'

'No,' William agreed, his expression one of grim concern. 'It's not your imagination and nor do I think it's a coincidence. I knew Atwood would lose no time in dispatching his henchmen after us.'

'I don't think they saw us.'

'Neither do I. They must have passed us somewhere along the way without knowing and think we are ahead of them. Why did they not stay the night at the inn? Why the haste?' His dark brows were drawn together in a frown. 'I'm curious to know what they're up to.'

Eleanor's heart was filled with dismay and a cold shiver ran down her spine. 'I am afraid,' she whispered.

'Your fears are not without foundation. Anyone as ruthless and determined as Frederick Atwood will wreak his vengeance no matter what he has to do. We must be extra-vigilant from now on.'

'Do you think we should ride on a bit farther? Wouldn't you rather put some more miles behind us? We could reach Tad caster in a few hours.'

'It will soon be dark. Besides, given the choice of riding in the rain after a couple of Atwood's ruffians rather than enjoying a hot supper and sitting in comfort before a blazing fire with a lovely young woman,' he murmured, his eyes twinkling roguishly and a smile curving his lips as he attempted to relieve the tension of the moment, 'well—a man would have to be out of his mind not to choose the latter.'

Eleanor cocked her head on one side and smiled up at him. 'Are you flirting with me by any chance, William Marston?'

Throwing back his head, he laughed out loud, his white teeth flashing against his bronze skin. 'Heaven forbid I should feel romantically inclined to the one who has branded me a traitor, Mistress Collingwood, but,' he said, his laughter fading and his eyes coming to rest warmly on hers, 'I could be persuaded.'

Eleanor could barely speak, for at that moment there was nothing she wanted more than to persuade him. The proud set of his head and the way his dark hair curled over his collar, the lift of his brows and the curl of his lips made her heart heavy, for though she had made it plain to herself from the outset that she would avoid any advances he might make towards her like the plague, she had not bargained for the ache that had pestered her night and day since.

As she followed him inside the inn, it suddenly dawned on her that they'd be parting soon, perhaps tomorrow, and the re-alisation pierced her with unexpected poignancy. However, one thing was clear. Something had been lit between them, something that made her heart sing—and Eleanor did not have a clue what to do about it.

It wasn't one of the best inns they had stayed at, being dirty and dim, and yet it was lively enough and warm. It had been market day in Pontefract and it was crammed with local traders and farmers, their dirty boots stinking of the farm yard. There was much laughter and drinking and as the three of them, sitting as close to the fire as they could get, ate their meal and drank their ale, for the first time since leaving London Eleanor began to relax.

They were in her beloved Yorkshire and her journey was almost over. The two men her stepfather had sent in pursuit had unnerved her, but she wasn't unduly worried since she felt safe enough with William and Godfrey. She did not doubt William's prowess as a fighter, but anyone would have to be a fool to provoke Godfrey, and tomorrow she would be safe at Hollymead in her uncle's care.

Godfrey had a natural tendency after they had eaten to disappear to wherever it was he had a bed, but that evening, well fortified with ale and flattered by the open attention of the hostess, he was in no hurry to depart. Molly Brown, enormously well endowed in all the right places, was spurred into immediate action the minute he stepped through the door, for in Pontefract, men of Godfrey's splendid size and presence were as rare as hen's teeth.

William and Eleanor watched with great amusement as she served him brandy, and as she served it she leaned so far over that her loosely fastened blouse dipped down to reveal more of a rather splendid pair of mammary appendages than was decent, causing heat to warm Eleanor's face with embarrassment, for she was certain that if the woman's blouse gaped any lower her umbilicus would have been visible.

Godfrey couldn't take his eyes off the fine orbs and he grinned appreciatively. 'Nice view you have there, sweetheart.'

Molly grinned back and nudged him playfully with her elbow. 'Nice of you to say so, love.' Her eyes twinkled. 'Lonely, are you?'

'I might be.'

'Then we'll have to see what we can do about that, won't we?' she said, laughing suggestively. 'Though if you're staying we only have two empty rooms, one small, the other a bit bigger.' Her eyes devoured Godfrey unashamedly. 'I'll wager you, big fella, can fit in the small one well enough and these two gentlemen can share the other.' Only having glanced at Eleanor in passing, she was completely ignorant as to her gender, which only served to intensify Eleanor's and William's amusement. They had to struggle to keep themselves from laughing out loud.

Molly smiled cheekily at William. 'Very comfy it is—double bed, soft mattress. You'll have no complaints.' Placing her hands on her hips she chuckled, her more than ample body shaking as she winked at Eleanor. 'Why so coy, laddie? A handsome youth should not be shy with his friends, eh, sir,' she said, nudging William knowingly and laughing louder when Eleanor flushed scarlet by her casually thrown suggestion. 'Hot water for washing and the bed warmed will be extra.'

William cocked an eyebrow at Eleanor. 'That sounds perfectly agreeable to me. We'll have the extras.' His eyes passed over Eleanor lightly, contemplating her flushed cheeks. 'Very cosy,' he murmured as Molly sauntered away with a wink at Godfrey.

'Not as cosy as you'd like to think—so get rid of the twinkle in your eyes, Lord Marston.' Eleanor was quick to put him in his place, but she was not unmoved. His voice and his outrageous suggestion came as a soft caress and sent an eddy of sensations spiralling down through the core of her being, but she was not to be drawn. 'I'm unaccustomed to sharing my bed with anyone and I am not about to begin now—and you should know better than to think I would.'

William's laughter gave evidence of his amusement as Eleanor glowered mockingly at him. 'The male garb you wear is not unbecoming, Eleanor, but it does tend to overshadow what's beneath with gloom.'

'Which it will continue to do.' She smiled sweetly at Godfrey. 'I'm sorry to disappoint you, Godfrey, but I shall take the small room.'

'What Eleanor really means, Godfrey, is that you and I shall share the double bed.'

Still grinning, Godfrey shook his shaggy head, his eyes still fastened on the swaying rump of the fair and buxom Molly.

'You two go up to bed,' he said, folding his arms across his massive chest. 'I'll find my own place to rest.'

'That suits me fine,' William murmured, standing up and stretching his long frame.

'In which case,' Eleanor said, also getting up and moving round the table to William, 'I shall have the soft bed and you can sleep in the other room, William.' She smiled sweetly. 'I know you won't mind.'

'I won't?' he replied, leaving Godfrey to become better acquainted with Molly, who was clearly adept in satisfying her customers, being of that gallant breed of women who fornicate for fornication's own fine and pleasant sake, an art in which she evidently had sufficient practice. William had no doubt that his friend would feast upon her bountiful and vigorously abounding charms until he passed out in glorious bliss.

Escorting Eleanor to the foot of the stairs and envying his friend's busy, athletic night, he looked down at her. She had removed her jerkin and unfastened the neck of her shirt. It was parted in a V shape, exposing the velvety softness of the flesh of her neck and the upper part of her chest. His stomach clenched as he remembered how she had looked when he had entered her room two days earlier, finding her naked apart from the concealing bed covers. Godfrey wasn't the only one with an appetite.

He reached out to touch her cheek in a careless, intimate gesture. 'We could share the soft bed. There's absolutely nothing to be worried about,' he ensured, challenging her with a mocking grin. 'You'll be quite safe.'

Eleanor laughed with velvety softness, a light sound, her gentle humour infecting and warming William to such a degree that he wanted to snatch her into his arms and kiss her senseless.

'I know I will because you, my lord, will be next door.'

The expression in his eyes changed for a heartbeat and

then lightened again as he chuckled. 'I needn't be. I'd rather be in your bed.'

'That would make it a bit crowded; besides, you're mad if you think I'd agree to anything so outrageous,' she protested. She acknowledged that his suggestion was ludicrous, and yet if it was, why did her heart beat so hard in her chest, and why did she not want to move away from him? His looks and his nearness were seductive, but it reassured her to some degree that she'd so far managed to stand against him. 'I'd be a fool, an utter fool, to get involved with you.'

'Be a fool,' he prompted softly.

'I don't think so. We both know that would be a mistake.'

'Why, what is it you fear?'

'What should I fear?' she countered, pushing the hair from her face and beginning to climb the narrow stairs without giving him the chance to reply. 'Goodnight, William,' she said over her shoulder. 'Sleep well.'

Going in search of her room, Eleanor wondered what would have happened if she had agreed to his request. Heat poured through her. With the memory of his gaze touching her face as though it were a caress, she had wanted him to hold her, to kiss her, to tell her that he was glad she had travelled with them and that he would regret their parting on the morrow—and if there were to be no parting, how long, she wondered, would she be able to fight off the deep magnetic attraction she was beginning to feel for him? How long would she want to?

But come what may, she must. The last few years had made her distrustful and taught her to be on her guard against men's wiles, and she must never forget that this man was the architect of all her wretchedness.

When at last they neared Hollymead, a cold sheet of rain burst down from a sky the colour of mud, instantly soaking them.

William would have had them seek shelter until it had passed, but Eleanor was too impatient to reach her home to delay now.

An ache for the past came to her as she looked across the familiar rainswept landscape, seeing the Roman wall and bastions enclosing the city of York like a ribbon of white in the distance and the majestic twin towers of the Gothic minister—and despite the rain it seemed to her a wondrous fair sight. Her heart swelled with joy in her breast. York was the queen of cities to her mind and already she could hear the peal of church bells, which, she remembered, seemed to ring all the time—bells calling the hour and others summoning folk to meetings, and on All Souls Night they rang throughout the night.

Eager to reach Hollymead, Eleanor urged her horse to a faster pace, wiping the water from her face, knowing it would come within her sights at any minute—but it didn't. Panic coursed through her veins. Where was it? Had the trees grown so tall that its towers and chimneys were hidden from view? Had she really been gone that long?

The three of them fell silent as they peered ahead. William did not like the tension he felt in the air. It vibrated through the drenched landscape, through his body.

Eleanor did not turn and see William's face, but she felt his uneasiness, and her own discomfort grew. For half a mile they rode along the rough road, passing a huddle of cottages and a farmstead where a flock of hens scratted and a few pigs rooted around in the mud.

And then they came to what had once been Hollymead, that gracious, noble house where Eleanor had been born and had spent the happiest years of her life. The heavy gates stood wide open. Where were the gatehouse keeper and the stable boys? Where were the servants and Uncle John? Where was everybody? a voice screamed inside her head.

No one spoke as they rode into what had been the outer court, the building that reared in front of them with its broken leaded windows a blackened, tragic ruin. Not all of it had burned, only the older part built of wood, the stone of the newer section having withstood the flames.

Removing her hat and feeling the rain on her face, Eleanor looked about her dazedly, aware that several people were wandering about as if in a daze, but unable to focus her eyes on them. The fire had been recent, for smoke in places still curled up to the sky, yet the uncanny silence held. They dismounted and walked slowly forward to enter what remained of the great hall.

'My God,' William said in hushed tones. 'What has happened here?'

Eleanor halted on the threshold, thinking for an unbelievable moment that they must have lost their way and come to the wrong house, that they had somehow stumbled into a situation that had nothing to do with them and that this horrific sight was someone else's nightmare. Something deep and insistent mounted within her heart and cried out against it. The cry was building inside her, searching for a way to escape, so very painful to her, but the cry remained inside as her eyes took in the truly awful scene.

'Oh, no,' she moaned. 'Dear Lord, oh, Lord.' Her eyes wandered over the burned-out ruin, which bore no resemblance to the Hollymead she had known.

It was dark and smelled of scorched wood. The central hearth where the dogs used to lie was blackened, as was what was left of the trestles and benches and floorboards. Moving farther inside, Eleanor turned her head around to take it all in, remembering it as it had been in the days of her childhood— her mother and father at the long table, the smell of roasted meat and firelight and servants running hither and thither.

With a sob she slowly crumpled down to her knees. Nature cloaked her shock in mercy for she was unable to move, all thought having left her. She was very still, her heart dragging in pain. Her cloak was sodden, her hair hanging in soaked skeins down her back to her waist and clinging to her wet cheeks; it was a while before she realised that it was not the rain, but her own bitter tears.

Recalled to the present, she whispered, 'Hollymead was my lodestone, the centre of my being, the place reminding me of my origins, of who I am. Without it I am nothing. Who would dream of doing this?'

William could see the bleak agony on her face. 'I can think of one,' he said gently to her, taking her cold hand and raising her to her feet. Something in his chest gripped him, an urgent need to take her in his arms and comfort her, but, fearing she would push him away, he took a step back. However, his eyes studied her, gauging her, watching for every nuance of thought and emotion in her.

Eleanor fixed her tear-bright eyes on him. 'The two men we saw in Pontefract—my stepfather's henchmen. It was them, wasn't it? Little wonder they were in such a hurry. Dear God, William, this is only the beginning. I have only been gone from Fryston Hall five days and he has done this—struck straight at my heart. What wickedness will he undertake before he is done? I have paid a heavy price for thwarting him. And my uncle—where is he? Please, God, don't let him have perished in the blaze?'

'As to that, I can tell you he did not,' a voice said.

Eleanor spun round to face a man in middle age who had quietly come to stand behind her. She frowned for, despite his dishevelled and grimy appearance, he was soberly and decently attired and seemed familiar. 'And you are?'

'Thomas Walters, mistress—Sir John's steward. The

master barely escaped with his life, so badly burned he was and overcome with the smoke.'

Pale and stricken, Eleanor stared at him. 'Please—will you take me to him?'

'He isn't here, but I know he's safe—I took him myself to St Thomas's Hospital outside Micklegate Bar to be cared for. If you don't hurry, he may not be alive when you get there.'

Eleanor closed her eyes in agony. A sob rose in her throat. Destiny had struck her. Her uncle was dying. Someone had tried to kill him. How could such a thing happen? She felt enormous relief that he was safe, but was worried as to the extent of his injuries.

'I thank you, Thomas. I am Eleanor Collingwood, Sir John's niece. Perhaps you remember me, and my father, Edgar Collingwood.'

Thomas was weary and red eyed, but his soot-blackened features cracked beneath a smile. 'I know who you are, Mistress Collingwood. I remember you when you lived at Hollymead, when you were a child—and Sir Edgar and his gentle wife, your mother, God rest her.'

'What happened here?' William asked curtly. 'And what happened to the servants?'

Thomas turned his gaze on the taller man, whose compelling, intelligent and almost transparent eyes were colder than an icy winter sky and there was a thin, white line about his mouth. Speaking precisely and fluently, he said, 'It was no accident, that I do know, and what few servants there were— Sir John insisted on the absolute minimum at all times, got out—I have rooms at the opposite end of the house to Sir John, so I didn't hear the visitors arrive—from London, Sir John managed to tell me, who said they had been instructed to burn the house to the ground with him inside it.'

His words smashed into Eleanor's consciousness like an

axe blow. Feeling rage growing inside her like a rising storm, she reared up and turned her blazing eyes on William. 'We were right. It was my stepfather who ordered this. That he would order the house to be burned with my uncle inside is indeed the work of a monster.'

'I was in bed when I smelled the smoke,' Thomas went on. 'Sir John was already overcome with smoke and his night-shirt alight when I reached him. I managed to douse his clothes and get him outside, but there was nothing I or those who came to help could do to put out the fire. It was already out of control.'

On hearing this, in his fury William's first instinct was to throw himself on his horse and head straight back to London to slay the perpetrator, Frederick Atwood, to rage at him for the insanity of his power. The thought that he could burn down the home of his dead wife and with his elderly cousin inside filled him with anger. He wanted to destroy Atwood's arrogance, the wicked power-sated confidence of the man. That he should use his power, his remorseless will, against a target as young and vulnerable as Eleanor made him shake like an angry child at the strength of his feelings.

'You say my uncle is unlikely to survive,' Eleanor said quietly.

An intense pain descended on Thomas's features. Shaking his head slowly, he said, 'The wounds to his body are severe, but not life threatening, but the smoke damage to his lungs I fear will prove fatal.'

'Then I must go to him at once.'

'The men who did this?' William demanded. 'Did anyone see them—which way they were headed?'

'No, they disappeared.'

'And you, Thomas? Have you relatives you can go to?' Eleanor enquired concernedly.

'My brother is a cloth merchant in Petergate. I can go there when I have to, but there is work to be done here. But come, I will ride with you to the city and see how your uncle fares.'

Tears of fear and grief were forming in Eleanor's eyes. Shaking her head, she looked down, suddenly feeling weary and defeated. Focusing her eyes on a small object shining between the floorboards, she became distracted. Kneeling down, she picked it up and looked at it. It was a bead, a red, shiny bead. A shaft of light slanting through a shattered window high up in the wall penetrated the deep red mystery of the bead's inner fire and it winked and shone in a burst of colour in the palm of her hand. Perhaps it had been her mother's or even her own. She couldn't remember, but suddenly it seemed very precious to her. Closing her fingers around it she crushed it to her breast.

When they emerged into the open the sun came out in a sky streaked with the last remnants of cloud. It gave her no pleasure. It seemed that it had come out mock her, for she knew she had no power, no weaponry, against her uncle's vengeance. The future no longer seemed appealing or safe. Now everything was changed and she was no longer sure of anything. She was adrift.

As they rode away from Hollymead her face was whiter than death. She had herself under the tightest control. William saw her bite her lip to keep her tears at bay.

They rode to the city in silence, Eleanor, anxious about what she would find when they reached St Thomas's hospital, a little ahead of the others.

York was a pleasant and beautiful city. The countryside around it was rich, populous and fruitful and furnished with provisions of every kind, the river being so navigable and near the sea. It was a highway of great importance, not merely to York, but to the whole country and to the towns and territory farther north. The city was full of gentry and people of distinction who lived in houses in proportion to their quality.

On the outskirts the streets were mired in mud and smoke twisted from the timber-framed houses along the Mount. The closer they got to the walls an all-pervading, nauseous stench from the gutters assailed them. Nobody seemed to attach any importance to it and Eleanor herself breathed with indifference the foul, saturated air.

It was busy around St Thomas's Hospital, the streets full of noise and confusion as people went in and out of the city through Micklegate Bar, many folk pushing handcarts and crying out their wares.

Eleanor kept her eyes averted from the blind and rotting eyes in what was left of the heads stuck on poles above the gate. They were the heads of felons who had been hanged, drawn and quartered, the rest of their remains scattered. It was a gruesome sight for travellers to have to see as they passed through the gate to the city beyond.

Entering through an arched doorway with double-arched mullioned windows on either side, they went inside the infirmary and were taken to a small square room where the bandaged figure of Sir John Collingwood lay on a narrow bed. Two women tending him stood aside, but Eleanor paid no attention to them as she approached the bed.

Her uncle was almost unrecognisable, since his head and part of his face were covered. What she could see of his face was as pale as wax and two deep grey shadows ran from his nostrils down to the corners of his mouth. His chest rose and fell and his breath rasped in his throat as he struggled to breathe.

A great wretchedness dragged her down as she looked at this man whose life was so enriched with learning. The first two fingers on his right hand were permanently ink stained. He was a scholar, a thinker, a man to seek out the truth of what was written, a man who put great emphasis on education and had a great reverence for scholarship. The colleges where he taught in York appreciated the benefits his wide knowledge brought to the pupils and she knew that, should he die, he would be deeply mourned.

The doctor came to stand beside her. 'If I could, I would work a miracle that would save him—but, alas, my abilities are limited. Short of treating and dressing his wounds, I am powerless to do more. As you see, he fights for every breath. His condition has worsened since he was brought in.'

'You have done your best,' Eleanor whispered, 'and I thank you. The rest is in God's hands.'

'He—hasn't much time,' the doctor said.

There was silence around them. Stricken to the heart, Eleanor gently took her uncle's hand, trying not to think of the scorched flesh hidden beneath the bed covers. She had prepared herself for the ordeal of seeing him so close to death, and this dreadful weakness and helplessness she felt could only grow worse when this man she had depended on, placed all her hopes upon, was no more.

William knew her distress. Bending towards her, he whispered in a voice that was soft, 'Speak to him, Eleanor. He might hear you.'

Swallowing down the lump that had risen in her throat, she leaned forward. 'Uncle,' she said softly, 'it's Eleanor. Can you hear me?'

Slowly, with tremendous effort, her uncle opened his eyes. They moved about vaguely for a moment and then settled on his niece, uncomprehending. 'Eleanor?' His voice was low and hoarse and it pained him to speak.

As Eleanor gazed down at him, tears filled her eyes and a warm glow of affection spread through her body. When he smiled and gripped her hand, she held it close to her chest.

'Yes, Uncle John, it really is me.' A bleak smile crossed his parched lips. 'I am sorry you are so badly injured.'

'I—am going to die.'

'Don't say that,' Eleanor protested, then added affectionately, 'I will take care of you.'

'No. There is no point in fooling ourselves,' he said with difficulty. 'I know.'

What could Eleanor say when the vitality of his life was seeping out of him? His breathing was growing more laboured every minute and it was getting harder for him to speak. She had to bend her head to catch what he said.

'Hollymead? The fire? Why did he do it?'

'Who?' she whispered. 'Uncle John, do you know who did this?'

'My cousin—Frederick Atwood—sent men… But why would he want to burn Hollymead?'

'Because—because of me,' Eleanor confessed wretchedly, almost choking on the lump in her throat. 'I ran away from Fryston Hall—from my stepfather—and this is my punishment. I'm so, so sorry, Uncle—you will never know how much, how wretched this makes me feel. If I had known he would do this terrible thing, I would never have run away.'

'Atwood—he was not kind to you?' The panting breath came and went in the injured man's breast as his damaged lungs took in air with the greatest difficulty.

Eleanor shook her head. 'No—not since Mother died.'

'I—I was so very sorry to hear of her death. She was a good woman. Why did you not go to—Matilda?'

'Aunt Matilda is visiting friends abroad and will not be back for some time. Besides, I wanted to come home.' The words were spoken simply and from the heart.

Sir John smiled, understanding. 'Of course you did. And Hollymead is still your home, whatever happens. You must get word to Walter in the Netherlands. He—he is married now—with a child on the way. Hollymead needs a family again. When I am gone, the estate will be his. He must come home. It is a fine, prosperous estate and houses can be rebuilt.'

Eleanor bowed her head so he would not see her heart-break. 'I know, and I will get word to Walter and explain what has happened.' Her voice was barely audible.

'I always knew Atwood had an evil streak—like his father before him. Even as a boy—it did not take much for his anger to spill over into rage and violence. He would not forgive a transgression, imagined or otherwise—but that he should stoop to this… Marian, your dear mother, should never have married him.'

Sir John closed his eyes to absorb the pain. When he opened them again, they settled on William. Surprise registered and then he beckoned him closer. 'I haven't much time, William, I cannot talk much so I will not ask what you are doing here—although I suspect it has something to do with Staxton Hall being restored to you.'

'It has everything to do with that. I came to thank you, John, for all you did on my behalf—and my family.'

'Your father was a good friend of mine. I was happy to do what I could. How—is it that Eleanor is with you?'

'I have escorted her from London.'

'Thank you, but her coming here has presented a dilemma. There is now no one to care of her. Will you undertake to look after her—for me? After what Frederick has done, I fear she is in great danger.' He closed his eyes and his features began to take on a sinister rigidity. His lips moved, but the sound that came out of them was so faint that William and Eleanor had to lean closer to hear what he was saying. 'Promise me.' Sir John was a shrewd judge of character and he knew that Eleanor would be safe with William.

The knowledge that Sir John had requested such a thing made William feel anxious. He did not want to be anyone's guardian, and he certainly didn't want to keep watch over Eleanor, to have control over her—he knew just how strongly she would resent that. He was badly suited to such a position and he did not want the responsibility. And yet, did he not owe this man a great deal? Having taken it upon himself to petition the Queen on William's behalf to have Staxton Hall restored to him, William had much to be grateful for, to thank him for. The very least he could do was to agree to this one last thing that was important to the dying man, so he could die knowing Eleanor would be taken care of.

'I will do as you ask.'

Sir John nodded weakly and then, his hopeless and exhausting duel with death nearly over, he gave a last convulsive movement, and a noise that sounded like a death rattle, and then his body was still. Now that the laboured breathing had ceased, the silence that fell in the small room was terrible.

Eleanor knew it was all over for her uncle. Stifling a sob, she placed two fingers gently on his lids and closed his eyes for all eternity. As she gazed at the ravaged face, her throat ached with pain and grief. Bending forward, and with infinite tenderness, she pressed her lips to his dry cheek.

The look on her face and the silent tears falling slowly from her eyes were the most dreadful things William had ever seen. Eleanor had already suffered so much. He could not bring himself to contemplate the immensity of pain that this new tragedy would inflict on her. One thing he had to do was to get her out of the infirmary before her will and her strength deserted her altogether.

'Weep as long as you want, Eleanor. You cannot mourn too long for a man like that—but you are tired and hurting and there's nothing more to be done here.'

Eleanor whitened and swayed. William reached out an arm to support her. Never had his nearness been so welcome, the sound of his voice so comforting. His arm about her waist felt heavy and warm, giving her sympathy, assuring her without words of protection. In a daze she allowed him to lead her outside to where Godfrey and a sorrowful Thomas waited with the horses.

Giving William a wild stare, she saw compassion in the depths of his eyes. Confusion and grief and pain overwhelmed her. She felt lost, as if all feeling had frozen inside her. Never had she felt so alone, and she did not like it. Now she had nothing but memories to sustain her. She wiped her eyes. Tears would not avail her, as she knew now, beyond the mercy of a doubt, for this one terrible hurt there was no cure at all.

'This is my worst nightmare come true,' she whispered, feeling that the excruciating day's events seemed to have eaten into the deepest crannies of her mind. 'This is all my fault. It's because of me that my uncle is dead. But how could I have known when I left Fryston Hall that it would mean disaster for my uncle? My stepfather has done this to punish me.'

Looking down at her, William saw her lovely eyes were filled with pain and guilt. Eleanor truly did blame herself for this. 'You could not possibly have foreseen any of this, but this kind of malevolence from Atwood does not surprise me.' He turned towards his horse. 'Come, we must be on our way. We still have a long ride ahead of us. You will be safe at Staxton Hall, Eleanor.'

He spoke with a confidence he did not truly feel, for he feared greatly for his family and prayed Atwood's men had not wreaked the same devastation at Staxton Hall as they had at Hollymead.

When his words penetrated Eleanor's mind, she stared at him perplexedly. 'Staxton Hall? But—why should I go to Staxton Hall? There is nothing for me there.'

'And there is no longer anything for you here,' William countered. 'Your uncle has placed you in my care and I intend to honour his wish.'

'No, William,' she protested in anguish, shaking her head as she edged away from him. 'No, no, no! How can you ask that of me? I—I won't go. I don't want to; besides, I have no stomach to ride further—and neither has Tilda. She is quite worn out.'

A grim smile cast a disagreeable light over William's face. 'Whether you want to go or not is beside the point. This is not the moment to play at preferences. I have told you that you are going to Staxton Hall and such is my impatience to be on my way I am in no mood to argue the matter.'

Suspecting she was about to have a fight on her hands, Eleanor tried to steady the thunderous beating of her heart. Lifting her eyes, she saw there was a new tension in his body, a new tightness about his jaw. There was also a challenging glint in his eyes, but this was one aspect of their arrangement she would not give in on. She felt the dull ache in her chest grow as she contemplated the severe, determined expression on his face, and with trepidation slicing through her she felt her skin prickle.

'I shall go back to Hollymead,' she persisted determinedly, struggling to keep her voice steady. 'I know Walter will come to live there, but it's my home and I will not go anywhere else.'

'Give it up, Eleanor. You cannot go back to Hollymead. Surely you can see that.' There was cool reason in William's voice, despite his impatience to be away.

She shot him a dark look, annoyed by his high-handedness. 'I shall do just as I like. You knew we would separate when we reached York, and as far as I am concerned nothing has changed.'

'You're wrong. Everything is changed. There is nothing to go back to. There is nothing left.'

Eleanor could feel her own anger boiling up inside her.

How dare he feel he had the right to tell her what to do, as if he had a perfect right to do so? How dare he shout at her, order her about as though she were his to direct? She did her best to hold in her resentment, but it was hard and her expression was icy. Up until now he had been considerate, in fact what she would have done without his help she couldn't imagine, but that did not mean he could suddenly become responsible for her as he seemed to be doing.

'Do not start laying down the law and telling me what I should and should not do, William. I am quite capable of running my own life. Hollymead isn't burned down entirely. From what I saw, some of it is still habitable. In time it will be rebuilt, but in the meantime there is work to be done, land to be worked.'

William stared at her. So great was his astonishment and anger at her refusal to comply he could scarcely speak. 'By others, not by you. What are you going to do? Learn to wield a plough?'

Eleanor drew herself up haughtily and what might have been a snarl curled her top lip. She turned from William and stamped her foot, and even her hair seemed to swirl in defiance. 'If I have to. I will do anything I have to. I will go back to Hollymead,' she told him flatly. 'Please let that be the end of the matter.'

William grabbed her shoulders and spun her around, his voice like an angry whiplash. 'It is far from it,' he ground out. His face paled, the rush of furious blood beneath his skin ebbing away at the implication of her statement, her insufferable stubbornness. With clenched jaw and his fists balled at his sides, he towered over her, hating having to press her at a time like this—in fact, his heart went out to her—but he must be firm if they were to reach Staxton Hall before dark. He could not allow her to fall to pieces.

'William!' she flared wildly, her anxieties written in deep lines on her face. 'I have to stay here. This is my home. You don't understand,' she cried. 'How can you? You—who have a loving family waiting for you at Staxton Hall. I have no one. No one. I must reconcile myself to a life of desolation and learn to fend for myself.'

'With your family gone, then all the more reason for you to come with me. Do not pity yourself, Eleanor. You are above that. You cannot stay here. You cannot go back. So you must go forward. With me.'

'And if I've no desire to go to your home?' Her tone issued a definite, defiant challenge.

'If you want to remain safe, then I can see no alternative.'

'You can go to the devil, William Marston, and take your offer of a home with you.'

Reaching out and gripping her upper arms, he shook her hard. 'Will you stop it, Eleanor. Stop it at once.' His face was as maddened as hers. 'Prepare to leave or I will lift you on to that damn beast myself.'

'You would not dare.'

'Try me,' he stated icily, 'and you will see how much I would dare.'

She looked at him uncomprehendingly. His strong, handsome face had become stern and uncompromising. She was beginning to know that look. Its power was not to be underestimated. He was angry with her, and his words brought a pain to her heart that was sharper than a blade. But she kept it at bay—there would be time to feel later. Her flaring anger quelled under the silver stare and, lowering her eyes, she continued on a calmer note.

'But why must I go there? Why can I not go back to Hollymead? There are people there who were dependent on my uncle for their livelihood. What is to become of them?'

'Might I make a suggestion,' Thomas interrupted, stepping forward. 'You are right, Mistress Collingwood, there are dependents who will need taking care of. I could take care of things—as I have been doing for the past twenty years—until Sir John's son arrives. I can help find situations for those who need them—and see your uncle laid to rest. The ceremony will be in accordance with the instructions he passed on to me when I brought him here. I would be more than happy to remove the worry of such a matter from your mind. I will look after Hollymead.'

Having already made up his mind that Thomas was a man to be trusted, someone to be relied on, William gripped the older man's shoulder gratefully.

'Thank you, Thomas, that would be helpful. I'm sure Mistress Collingwood would appreciate that. You know where she will be if you need to contact her. When we reach Staxton Hall, I will send someone to assist with the formalities. I will write and notify Sir John's son about his father's death. But we have to leave now. I suspect the men Atwood sent to do this dastardly deed may have gone there. My mother and sisters are without male protection and may be in mortal danger.'

Eleanor's eyes flew to his. 'Danger? I don't understand.'

William's lips curled with irony. 'For an intelligent young woman, Eleanor, you are behaving irresponsibly, which outweighs all common sense. Where do you think those men have gone? Back to London?' He shook his head. 'I don't think so. If you will not think of yourself, then consider what this delay could mean for my family. Your dithering is putting them in danger.'

'But why? It's me my stepfather wants to avenge.'

'And me.'

'You? But why?'

'Because I took you away. Because I know too much about

him—and because he has an old score to settle. Now get on your horse and we'll get on our way. Sir John is dead and my family is alive and in danger. Good God, Eleanor, you know what Atwood is capable of. He will stop at nothing to achieve his ends. We must go to Staxton Hall. Time is pressing.'

Eleanor fingered the red bead in the pocket of her doublet as she faced him, and she could not restrain the tears that came into her eyes.

'Eleanor.' William's wrath ebbed as he confronted that misty gaze. He laid a hand on her shoulder in an attempt to console her. 'I can only imagine what you are going through, and please, God, I don't want to experience the same when I get to Staxton Hall.'

Suddenly ashamed, within his eyes Eleanor noticed something now she hadn't before—a profound fear. There was also an extreme anxiety, and a hint of something she had not seen before. Some terrible pain had him in its grip, and suddenly she realised his desperation to get to home and why. Of course he was anxious about his family, and she was beginning to realise he had reason. Bowing her head, she felt her shoulders slump in capitulation.

'Yes—yes, of course. You are right. It is selfish of me to think of myself when your entire family is in danger, but listen to me, William,' she said, raising her eyes to his, thinking that he looked older, the lines on his face seeming to have deepened. 'You may force me to go with you, if that is your desire, but you will not assume authority over me. Why you had to agree to such a ridiculous request is quite beyond me.'

Leaning forward until his face was only inches from her own, William looked directly into her eyes. 'Two reasons. One, because your uncle was dying and I wanted him to die with an easy mind, and, two, because I felt obligated.'

'You needn't,' she said coolly. 'You owe me nothing.'

'Not to you. Your uncle.'

'Of course. I'm sorry,' she whispered weakly, contrite. 'William, I don't mean to be difficult about this.'

'I know that. I do understand why you want to stay, believe me, but you must understand why I have to go to Staxton Hall and why I cannot leave you here alone. I am seriously concerned for your safety. Atwood wants you, Eleanor. Do you think he will give up?

She shook her head miserably.

'I want you to be safe,' he told her, feeling a need to protect her that he had never felt when he had thought of Catherine, 'and I see taking you home with me the only way to do it. I fear those men will have gone to Staxton Hall, but in truth I have no idea what they intend. It is possible they may still be in York, waiting for you to arrive at Hollymead. Without protection you will not stand a chance. They will take you straight back to Fryston Hall. I cannot abandon you to such a fate. Hollymead is no longer a safe haven, so there is only one place you can go. My mother will make you welcome, that I promise you.'

The veil that had descended before her eyes when she had first seen the devastation at Hollymead was clearing, lifting slowly. She put out a shaking hand to him and nodded. 'I'm sorry, William. You're right. This is no time for weakness. Come. Let's be on our way.'

Chapter Five

The mist was cold on the River Ouse when they rode out of York, heading north-east. Feeling as if her body was weighted down with heavy chains, Eleanor, aware of the blowing of the horses and the pounding of their hooves over the sodden ground, was also aware of William and Godfrey on either side of her, but they seemed far off, at another place, another time.

Eventually the countryside became more undulating, with fertile plains and woods clothing the gently sloping hills. It was beautiful, but Eleanor did not see it. A skylark rose up from a water meadow, rising higher and higher, its pleasant song causing William to look up and admire each rippling note, but Eleanor did not hear it.

Concerned by her silence and the fact that she looked straight ahead of her, seeing nothing and remarking on nothing, William glanced at her. He felt that behind her acceptance of what life brought to her were reserves of power, as well as an innate innocence that touched his heart. With the loss of everything she held dear, she was so pitifully alone—and her courage made him more ambitious to protect her.

* * *

Anxious to reach Staxton Hall before dark, William had kept up a gruelling pace. The land was swathed in a cloying mist and the moon already cast small light, but they could see the bulk of the great house and they all thanked the Lord that it was still standing.

Built in the fourteenth century, the stone-built house had a fortified wall around three sides and a moat across the fourth side. It had a drawbridge that could be raised and a portcullis above it that could be dropped down to seal the entrance. With a backdrop of dense woodland and fields it was a deceptively beautiful house that could none the less be held in a siege if necessary.

Eleanor was so cold she was almost frozen to the saddle. As soon as they clattered into the cobbled yard dogs began to bark clamorously from within the house and the heavy doors were flung open.

Lady Alice Marston, a tall, slender, graceful woman, came hurrying out to welcome her son home. She had been awaiting his arrival for days—indeed, the whole household had been waiting for the master's arrival. Behind her, their eyes round with excitement and apprehension, were William's sisters, seventeen-year-old twins, Anne and Jane, dark-haired, pretty girls, identical in looks. With her hands held out to her son, Lady Alice swept forward, her fine emerald skirts rippling.

Godfrey disappeared to see to the horses, leaving Eleanor standing looking very cold and sorry for herself. The reunion of son, mother and sisters was moving, a moment for them, and Eleanor stood back, watching, envious of this show of affection between people who loved each other, careful not to move lest she draw their attention and intruded. After a few moments William turned and held his hand out for Eleanor to step forward.

When Lady Alice looked at Eleanor Collingwood, whose face was pale and strained, she felt for a moment as if a shadow had fallen on the house and gave an involuntary shiver, as if the night had suddenly turned colder. Forcing a smile to her lips and thrusting any reservations she might have aside, she stepped forward to greet her.

Lady Alice looked the young woman over carefully. 'So you are Marian's child,' she remarked thoughtfully. 'I am happy to welcome you to our home.'

Eleanor found herself looking into a pair of light blue eyes, and, despite their warmth, she detected a hint of reticence in the dowager Lady Alice Marston. At fifty years of age she was still slim and supple, and except for a delicate tracery of lines around her eyes and her mouth, her face was timeless in its serene beauty. Eleanor would have curtsied, but considered she would appear comical in her male attire and with her hair hanging down her back like wet seaweed.

'You are most welcome, Eleanor. Your mother and I were friends—albeit a long time ago. We were both children in the household of Lady Barnett in Kent. They were happy days.'

Eleanor already knew this. Her mother had often spoken of that time. Most men and women of class sent their daughters away to be educated in a noble household. 'You are most kind, Lady Alice,' she said politely. 'I do not wish to put you out by being here.'

'How could you do that? You are William's guest and as such you will be treated. But, dear me, you look so cold. Please, come inside. After a glass of mulled wine in front of a good fire you'll soon feel better.'

Flanked by Anne and Jane, who were friendly and agreeable and eager to know all about her, Eleanor was led inside the house. Lady Alice hung back to speak to her son. She was a placid woman who helped the poor and needy wherever she could and lived her life through her children. She allowed them small indulgences and was happy if they were happy, but should anyone threaten them her placid, easy-going nature turned to steel and she would defend them like a tigress defending her cubs—but of all her children her first-born was most dear.

Eleanor Collingwood was the daughter of the man who had instigated that dreadful plot, drawing in William, which had led to his banishment and the confiscation of his home that had belonged to the Marstons for generations. To have that young woman under their roof would be a constant reminder, an embarrassment, but she was not about to anger William by voicing her thoughts when she had him home again.

But William was attuned to her thoughts and knew precisely what was going through her mind, so, taking her hand and tucking it into the crook of his arm, they walked together towards the house. 'Do not be hard on Eleanor, Mother. None of what happened was her fault. Do not forget that during those dark days of Queen Mary's rule, which affected us all in different ways, we were all of the same persuasion as Edgar Collingwood—and he paid for what he did with his life.'

'Maybe so,' Lady Alice remarked on a wry note, 'but some of us were quiet about it.'

William smiled when he thought of his mother's intolerance towards agitators, even though she more often than not agreed with them. What she could not tolerate was the disturbance it brought to her well-ordered running of things.

'When Mary Tudor came to the throne Edgar's voice was constantly raised in dissent, and when there was talk of her marrying Philip of Spain he could not countenance it. Following the dictates of his conscience, he stood against it. I cannot fault him for that.'

'I would not expect you to, but you cannot deny that his scheming brought misery to a lot of people.'

'Perhaps to Eleanor more than to anyone else. She was affected deeply by her father's execution—and she is still hurting,' William said, appealing to his mother's heart. 'She needs somewhere to live for a while, somewhere to lick her wounds. I didn't think you would mind if she came here. She's had a difficult time recently, losing her mother.' He went on to give her a brief account of how she had been affected by recent tragic events.

Lady Alice listened, her face white with shock when he told her what they had found at Hollymead. 'Sir John Collingwood is dead? But this is dreadful news, William. He was such a good man and we have much to be grateful to him for—'tis a pity the same cannot be said of his brother. And you say their cousin, Frederick Atwood, is responsible?'

'I am certain of it. I couldn't leave Eleanor at Hollymead without protection. There's something else. I suspect the men Atwood sent to destroy Hollymead will come here. Indeed, I feared they might be here already.'

Lady Alice stopped, frowning at him, a tiny wrinkle between her arching brows. 'But—William, why would they come here? Why would Frederick Atwood want to harm us?' Lady Alice glanced at her son. 'One thing I do not understand is why he would wish to harm you. I know it was expected that you would marry his daughter and that your banishment prevented that happening. Does he still hold that against you, or is he influenced by something else—a personal resentment, perhaps?'

William's jaw tightened and a hard light entered his eyes. 'I'll explain everything in good time, Mother,' he said, knowing she would press him for details, ask him questions he did not want to answer, force him to relive memories he did not want to face. It would be like opening a vein and being unable to stem the flow of blood.

'For him to attempt to do here what he did at Hollymead would be foolhardy,' Lady Alice went on, 'a thing bound to bring the wrath of Queen Elizabeth down on his head since she has so recently restored the estate to you. He cannot be allowed to work his spite on us all.'

'Do not underestimate him. Atwood is vicious, with a finger in every villainous pie. He is capable of anything, Mother, believe me. Besides, we know the men sent to destroy Hollymead were his men, but proving it is another matter.'

'We must do something.'

'I intend to. We have to be on our guard at all times. I'll set a watch—and—you will be kind to Eleanor, won't you?'

Lady Alice's features tightened. 'I would not be so discourteous as to show unkindness to a guest, William, and it offends me that you have to ask me. Her mother and I were friends, but I shall never forget that if it were not for that wretched plot we would have had you with us, here at Staxton Hall, which is where you belong. Now, come inside and get warm. Food is prepared, and I know you will want a hot bath.'

He smiled down at her. 'That would be most welcome. I'm as hungry as a hunter.'

Supper was a good meal of chicken broth, mutton steaks and roast ducks, and puddings to follow. The dining parlour with its walls hung with colourful tapestries glowed from the lighted candles and the huge log fire in the hearth. Eleanor, bathed and attired in clean hose and jerkin, which met with Lady Alice's quiet disapproval, was both tired and dispirited, and ate little. William chatted over the meal with his mother and sisters, eager to know all that had been happening in his absence with all the warmth that he genuinely felt for his family.

When Staxton Hall had been confiscated by Queen Mary, they had gone to live in his uncle's house in Pickering, little more than fifteen miles away. Staxton Hall meant a great deal to William—this grand estate had been bestowed upon one of his ancestors by the Crown for his acts of heroism and loyalty. Since his father had died, William had seen to it that this proud heritage was maintained in a manner that represented the grandeur his ancestor earned.

Lady Alice turned her attention on Eleanor, conspicuous by her silence, thinking how pale she looked and that she had hardly touched her food. 'You are quiet, Eleanor, although it is hardly surprising after the day you have had. You must be very tired after riding so far.'

'Yes—yes, I am. I think I should like to rest shortly.'

'And so you shall. I trust you find your chamber comfortable?'

'Yes, thank you, it is extremely comfortable.'

'Good. If I remember correctly, Eleanor, your mother had a sister—Lady Sandford?'

Eleanor paled and looked steadily at Lady Alice across from her. 'Yes. Aunt Matilda. She lives at Cantly Manor in Kensington.'

'When you decided to leave Fryston Hall, why did you not go to her?'

Lady Alice's tone was pleasant enough, but Eleanor caught the thread of determination that curled behind it. William's mother did not want her here. She could feel it. The feeling of panic sparked inside her and she cast William a look of appeal, but he merely cocked an eye at her and remained silent. 'I—wanted to go to Hollymead—to Uncle John. Aunt Matilda is in France visiting friends and is not expected back for some time.'

'I see. And did you write and notify your aunt of what you intended doing?'

'No. There was no time.'

'But surely, as your closest living relative, you have a duty to let her know where you are. It is only right. I am sure Lady Sandford is a very moral lady and wouldn't care to have her niece travelling in the company of two gentlemen—and looking as you do. Tomorrow I shall write and let her know that you are here. I shall address the letter to Cantly Manor and it will be waiting for her when she returns.' Holding Eleanor's gaze, she arched her eyebrows. 'You have no objection?'

Eleanor felt her whole body stiffen with resentment. She would rather Lady Alice didn't write to Aunt Matilda, but she had no wish to cross swords with William's mother. 'No, I have no objections.'

'Good. Then that's settled. Now, tell us about your life at Fryston Hall. I'm sure Jane and Anne would like to hear at first hand what London is like at this time.'

Eleanor doubted William would be pleased if she related all the details—honest and less than honest—of what her life had really been like at Fryston Hall. So, determined to omit the less savoury aspects, she embarked upon a doctored account of her life in her stepfather's house.

'It all sounds very interesting,' Lady Alice said when Eleanor had finished speaking. Once again her gaze took in her attire with distaste. 'You seem well at home in your clothes, Eleanor, and I am sure they were comfortable to travel in, but you can't possibly continue to go around dressed like that. We must see about finding you something to wear.'

'I do apologise for my appearance. I left Fryston Hall in haste and was forced to travel with just the bare necessities for the journey. I knew there were clothes at Hollymead, you see, so I didn't think it would be a problem. I do have a little money, so perhaps I could ride into York and purchase a couple of gowns—and perhaps go to Hollymead. Maybe some of my things escaped the fire—everything was so upsetting when we left that I didn't think to look.'

'You can return to Hollymead, but only when it's safe to do so,' William said sharply. He looked at his sisters, radiantly pretty in their matching blue brocade gowns and black velvet French hoods. 'I'm sure Anne and Jane will have something that can be made to fit you for the time being.'

'Oh, yes,' Jane piped up enthusiastically. 'We have several gowns and we are practically the same size—although I think Eleanor is more slender than either of us—but it won't be difficult, will it, Anne?' she said, looking to her sister for confirmation, which was always the case when decisions had to be made.

'Oh, no, and I have a lovely lemon that I have outgrown, but I'm sure it will fit you, Eleanor, and your blue will be perfect, Jane.'

Eleanor smiled from one to the other, touched by their generosity and their eagerness to make her feel at home and one of them, which was something she would never be. How different her life had been at Fryston Hall from the lives of these happy, chattering girls, and their closeness made her realise how much she had yearned for a closer relationship with Catherine.

When she had been growing up at Hollymead she had never been lonely. She had always known her parents loved her unequivocally, and there had always been local children of her own age to play with. Her home had possessed the same kind of warmth as Staxton Hall and her heart ached fit to break with the memories.

'Thank you. You are very kind. I should be glad of the loan of a gown, something simple, until I can get into York to purchase some of my own.'

'You're very pretty, Eleanor,' Jane said. 'Don't you think so, Anne?'

'Jane,' her mother admonished sharply, 'remember your manners.'

Jane tossed back her head and smiled at Eleanor. 'Well, I think she is, and I don't think it's unmannerly to say so.'

Eleanor laughed. 'Thank you for the compliment, Jane. You are also pretty, you and your sister—and I must say that I have difficulty telling you apart.'

'And so they are,' William agreed, smiling admiringly at each sister in turn. 'When I first saw you earlier your beauty startled me. I visualised you as the plump, over-boisterous fourteen-year-old girls I left behind. Now the plumpness has gone. You have changed in a way that both delights and fills me with anxiety for the future.' He winked at his mother. 'I think very soon we shall have adoring swains beating at the door, Mother.'

'Oh, William!' Anne giggled. 'How you exaggerate.' She shifted her gaze to Eleanor. 'Did you really ride all the way from London with William?'

Eleanor couldn't help glancing at William seated at the head of the table. 'Yes, I did—and Godfrey, so I was well protected.'

'Godfrey? That giant of a man you brought with you. As I understand it he is your servant, William—although I have to say he is the oddest kind of servant I have ever met. Is he someone you met on your travels?' Lady Alice asked, unable to quell her curiosity.

William nodded. 'He originates from Glasgow—I believe members of his family still live there.'

'And will he be returning to Glasgow?'

William shrugged, a twist of humour about his firm mouth. 'If he has a mind to. Godfrey is free to do what he wants.'

'Well, I can't tell you how good it is to have you home again, but when are you going to tell us where you have been all this time? When I received your letter informing me that you were coming home, you did not tell me anything that I wanted to know.'

William's expression tightened. 'Later, Mother,' he said, wanting to avoid the issue of his absence for as long as he could.

Lady Alice sat in thoughtful silence, as if considering the situation from every angle. 'William,' she persisted, 'I love you as a mother should and you know what I have suffered in your absence, not knowing where you were—if you were alive or dead. I have never endured such anxiety. Will you not tell me where you went when you were banished?'

'Not now, Mother.' He was breathing hard.

Eleanor watched him throw his napkin on to the table and get up. Turning sharply away from his mother's questioning eyes, he crossed the room to the hearth and stood looking down into the glowing embers. His shoulders were tense, the tendons in his neck corded, his back unyielding, as though under the force of some strong feelings. In fact, his very stance led her to believe he was on the verge of breaking in two.

Standing up, she went to him and placed her hand on his arm. 'William?' On hearing her soft voice, which was like a balm to his tortured mind, turning his head he met her eyes, and Eleanor saw beyond the silver-grey to something else— something dark and sinister she did not want to know about just then. His face twisted with pain, and it was almost unbearable. She wanted to tell him not to torment himself, that he did not have to explain anything he didn't want to.

And yet his unwillingness to speak of what had happened, of the demons that refused to let go of his mind, was as devastating as if he'd said what it was. Why Eleanor wanted to comfort this man who had wronged her, who seemed to look to the darkness of the time he had been away baffled her, but she did possess a strong desire to ease his torment.

'Whatever it is, there's no need to think of it now,' she said softly, 'not ever, if you don't want to. You are home and your anxieties unfounded.'

Lady Alice, touched and deeply moved by Eleanor's gesture to reassure her son, rose and moved to his side. Of an inquisitive nature and hating secrets, she wanted William to tell her everything. It was clear that she had revived painful memories for him, and she regretted her curiosity. Something had happened to him, something that went far deeper than his banishment. He was holding something back, as if he were looking inwards even as he laughed and teased his sisters. She knew her son too well to be deceived.

Whatever had happened to him, it was clear he did not want to share it with her, but, she thought, seeing how William's compelling gaze held that of the young woman by his side, what of Eleanor Collingwood? How much did she know?

'Eleanor is right, William.' She smiled and reaching up lightly kissed his cheek. 'I will question you no more. If you want to tell me, you will. Now, come and finish your meal—you, too, Eleanor—and then we will retire. It's been a long day for all of us.'

Tired as she was, Eleanor could not sleep that night. She lay on her back in the great four-poster bed, listening to the wind that had risen, blowing away the mist and moaning about the great house.

At three o'clock she rose and dressed herself quietly. The occasional candle lit the passage outside her room. It seemed to her that if she could walk a while in the night air, to feel the cold wind blow in her face, she might be eased of her heavy heart and she might understand the grief, the pain, the consuming guilt and remorse she felt over her uncle's death. The horror was stronger now than when she had actually lived through the horrendous day when she found her beloved home had gone and her uncle murdered.

Moving down the long shadowed corridor, past the dark,

draughty windows, seeing some ascending stone steps, on impulse she went up them and pushed open a heavy door. The wind hit her with such startling force that it snatched her breath. Stepping on to the moonlit, battlemented roof, she looked up. Stars blazed in the dark sky, like diamonds against black velvet. She moved slowly towards the parapet and stood breathing deep, filling her lungs with the cold air, feeling the wind catch hold of her hair and blow it free.

Sensing that she wasn't alone, she turned her head sideways. William stood a short distance away. He was little more than a silhouette in the night shadow, so still he could have been a statue. His masculine magnetism dominated the night. He was looking out over the moat towards the open fields.

Watching him throughout supper, she had been struck by the various emotions playing over his features. At times he'd seemed almost in awe of his mother and sisters, as though he was only just discovering they existed. At other times the love reflected in his eyes had caused her chest to ache. Eleanor had not known he was capable of such intense feeling and again she wondered about the years he had been absent from their lives.

Feeling like an intruder and not wishing to disturb him, she moved back towards the door, but he caught the movement from the corner of his eye and turned and saw her.

Although they'd spoken little since arriving at Staxton Hall, William had still managed to find some comfort in her presence. And earlier, when she had reached out to him, he had been unprepared for the warm pleasure that had flowed through him and the easing of the tension that had gripped him when his mother had questioned him about the past three years. Immediately he strode towards her.

The moon cast its glow over her and the wind caught strands of her hair and danced them wildly about her head. In her hose and jerkin she looked like no noble lady, yet she possessed a fierce pride that was apparent by the manner in which she held herself. For five days she had ridden hard by his side. She should have looked tired and worn and withered, yet she looked enticing and engaging.

'Eleanor? What are you doing out here?' he asked, his eyes not wavering from her upturned face. 'You should be in bed.'

'Forgive me,' she said, thinking how appealing he looked and very handsome. 'I have no wish to disturb you. I couldn't sleep.'

'You're not disturbing me. I couldn't sleep either.' Leaning against the parapet and folding his arms across his chest, he looked up at the clear sky. 'It's a better night. Thank goodness the mist has cleared.'

'Better to see any intruders. You're worried the same thing that happened at Hollymead will happen here, aren't you?'

He nodded. 'And with good reason.'

'Do you think those men will come?'

'If they do, they'll find it difficult getting past the guards. Their attack on Hollymead was a different matter. It was unexpected, the house undefended. Your uncle wouldn't have stood a chance.'

Eleanor peered down into the dark courtyard and the ghostly shapes of the outbuildings. 'I don't see any of the guards you have posted.'

'You won't, but rest assured they are there. If nothing happens after a week, you will be able to ride and roam outdoors, but until the time when it's safe for you to do so you must confine yourself to the house. Later, if you still wish to go to York, I'll take you.'

'And can I go to Hollymead? I would like to see how Thomas is managing. It can't be easy for him after all that's happened.'

William nodded. 'I'll send a couple of men first thing in the morning to be of help should he need it. I've already written a letter to Walter explaining all that's transpired.'

'Thank you. Walter was close to his father. I know he'll be deeply shocked. I do appreciate all you are doing for me, William. I owe you a great debt.'

'You don't owe me anything. I was happy to be of assistance.' Sitting on a lower section of the parapet, he looked up at her. 'I owe you an apology for what happened at supper. It was embarrassing for me and totally inappropriate under the circumstances.'

'You needn't apologise. It's only to be expected that your mother would voice her concern. You were gone three years. There is nothing wrong with her wanting to know where you have been. Any caring mother would.' She smiled when she observed how his face hardened and a guarded look entered his eyes. 'Don't worry. I am not about to pry. What happened is nobody's business but yours, and if you don't wish to speak of it then that too is your concern, so we will talk of something else.'

'What do you suggest?'

'Your delightful sisters. They have been very kind. They've made me feel so welcome here.'

'And Mother?'

'Your mother also—although…' She frowned, unable to put her thoughts into words without appearing rude.

William raised a questioning brow, with an amusing quirk to his lips. 'What?'

'I—sense she doesn't like me being here, that she resents my presence.' It hurt her to think she was here at Staxton Hall only because she had nowhere else to go. When William didn't contradict her, she said, 'There, I knew I wasn't mistaken.'

'If it's any comfort, it has nothing to do with you personally.'

'It hasn't? Then what?'

'She holds your father responsible for what happened to me.'

'Then it is quite wrong of her to blame my father,' she said, her voice shaking with indignation. 'Very wrong, and if the chivalrous feelings you have towards me are genuine, you can prove it very simply by telling her what really happened—that it was your betrayal that sent my father to the block. Do you think I could ever forget that? No, William, that memory will burn within me as long as I live.'

William's jaw tightened and a gleam of anger showed in his eyes. 'I know it will,' he said, making no attempt to defend himself. 'I promise I shall do my best to make my mother understand. Do not think badly of her. She may have a sharp tongue on her, but underneath she is kind and generous. I hope you don't mind her writing to your aunt, by the way.'

'I don't, although I expect that as soon as Aunt Matilda returns and reads the letter, she will order me to return to London.'

'Which is what one would expect under the circumstances?'

'She has long been determined to marry me to Lord Taverner's son, and since I have nothing of my own she will contribute generously to a settlement should I agree. Lord Taverner was a close friend of her husband, and he has remained her good friend. She will go to any lengths to please him. A union between the Sandfords and the Taverners is very important to her. What I feel is unimportant and that I should have feelings at all is incomprehensible. I'm merely a small piece in a large transaction. You will know Lord Taverner.'

William was unprepared for the jealousy that slammed into him. He stared at her, for once in his life lost for words. And, worse, a mixture of tense emotions twisted together like snakes inside his chest. Was one of them dread? And if so, why should he feel that?

Eleanor gave him a sharp, searching glance. 'William, why do you look at me like that?'

'I am astounded. Which one of Taverner's sons has she in mind? He has two sons—as I recall.'

'Martin—the eldest.'

'Good Lord! 'Tis all very well, Eleanor, but the man is seriously immature and feeble—too light in the head for you. He has an appalling stammer and he is ruled by his father, a ruthless, greedy man if my memory serves me well.'

Eleanor sighed. 'My feelings exactly. But Martin is different from his father. He is of a gentle nature and he is always polite and considerate and friendly towards me.'

'And would you object to the match between you?'

She shook her head. 'If I have to marry, then I can think of no one I else I would rather wed. Aunt Mildred could choose someone far more disagreeable than Martin.'

Standing with his back to her, staring out over the dark landscape unseeing, giving no indication of his thoughts, William asked, 'And does he want to marry you?'

'Yes—at least I think so. He has never been indifferent towards me. Mother and I lived with Aunt Matilda for a while—after Father...' She bit her lip, unable to finish what she was saying. 'Martin was a frequent visitor to Cantly Manor and we spent a great deal of time together.'

William turned and looked at her again, but this time there was in his eyes something like involuntary tenderness. 'Indifferent? What man in his right mind could be indifferent to you, Eleanor?'

Eleanor's eyes opened wide. 'Why, Lord Marston! Is that a compliment? And if so, do you mean it, I wonder?'

'You should know me well enough by now to know I never say anything I don't mean.'

The sudden warmth in his voice brought the heat creeping into her cheeks. 'No,' she said seriously. 'No, I don't know you really well. Remember, I first saw you as someone I distrusted and disliked—because you not only betrayed my father, but you hurt Catherine also—then as a—an acquaintance—and—and now as a...'

William's eyes flicked to hers and he said with a wicked grin, 'Saviour?'

She tilted her head to one side and considered the word carefully before answering. 'Yes. Yes, I suppose so—but only because you helped me escape from my stepfather's clutches. It would have been difficult for me to have made the journey north alone.'

'How does Lord Taverner feel about you marrying Martin?'

'He is as eager as Aunt Matilda. Martin is not unattractive and he does have a winsome look, I suppose, but he is too easily led by his father. If Aunt Matilda has her way, now I have left Fryston Hall and with the demise of Uncle John— for which I blame myself entirely,' she said quietly, 'she will do everything in her power to bring about our betrothal.'

'And you have already said you would not object to the match?'

'No, I don't suppose so. Opposing my aunt's authority would be hard—impossible. As an orphan I must consider myself fortunate. Beggars can't be choosers and I do like Martin.'

'You don't have to marry him. You could say no.' William was watching her closely, his eyes alert above the faintly smiling mouth.

Eleanor arched her brows and laughed. 'To Aunt Matilda? William, you do not know my Aunt Matilda.'

'No…' he chuckled, '…and I have no wish to. Does she not have a family of her own?'

'No. Her husband died leaving her childless—and very wealthy. Unlike many widows she never remarried, but I've always had a feeling that she is in love with Lord Taverner. There's a strange look in her eyes when he's present—almost a pleading look.'

'And if she insists that you go to Cantly Manor, what will you do?'

'What can I do? I must abide by her wishes. Hollymead belongs to Walter now. We were always close—but the reality of it is that with a wife and baby on the way he might not want me there. Besides, I can't go back there until it's safe for me to do so.'

'Don't think about it tonight—or tomorrow.' He stood up, towering over her, watching the crisp wind continue to flirt with her hair. Her dark lashes swept down over her expressive amber eyes. He caught his breath, wanting to draw her into his arms, to breathe in the scent of her flesh, to hold her close, to feel the softness of her body. But he could not. He dared not—but why not? he argued with himself. Where was the harm? They were both free, and she was young and ardent and willing to love. A kiss could hurt no one—could it?

Eleanor was vividly conscious of her proximity to him, his tall figure dark against the shadows of the parapet, and the warm trickle of a familiar sensation ran through her, a stirring she had felt once before when he had come into her room and found her in bed. Without warning his hand lifted and curved round her cheek. Gazing into those fathomless silver eyes, she felt a curious sharp thrill run through her as the force between them seemed to ignite.

More attracted to her by the moment, William wondered about her allure, for it was more than her face or her body that attracted him. Eleanor Collingwood had a gentleness that warmed him, and a fiery spirit that challenged him. He knew he was going to kiss her, finding the prospect infinitely appealing, even though on the morrow he would undoubtedly regret having taken things so far. On the other hand, if he was going to have regrets, he might as well have something substantial to regret.

'Tell me, Eleanor, have you ever been kissed?' he asked, his heavy-lidded gaze fixed on her lips.

Unnerved, and thoroughly confused at the way things were going, Eleanor shook her head. 'No, never,' she whispered.

'And I was of the mind that the times you've been kissed may be too numerous to count.'

'I've never met anyone that I wanted to kiss me.' At that moment she knew she wanted William to kiss her—and she also knew she should repulse him if he tried. She looked at him, entranced, hardly breathing. Strands of hair drifted over her face, and she thought his face bent over her was more beautiful than she had ever known. She saw the deepening light in his eyes and the thick, defined brows and wanted to touch him as one touches the soft flesh of a newborn babe.

And then, as if they had come to remind her, images of her mother and father passed before her eyes. Quickly she recollected herself. Vividly conscious of how close she was to William, she sharply turned away before he could realise how much he had affected her. But his hand shot out and grasped her arm, turning her to face him. Before she realised that he really meant to kiss her, his hand curved on her cheek and slowly snaked to the back of her head, drawing it firmly towards his.

'Then perhaps it's time you were kissed.' He smiled, his eyes twinkling bright. 'I believe I'm quite good at it—and afterwards you can judge for yourself.'

'How can I do that when I have nothing to compare it with?' she asked, breathing faster as his lips came close and she braced herself for some unknown sort of physical assault.

'Then you'll just have to take my word for it,' he murmured, his warm breath mingling with hers, his eyes locking on hers, which were frightened, beguiling. 'You're not afraid of being kissed, are you, Eleanor?'

Stunned into quiescence, Eleanor shook her head and remained completely still as his lips settled on hers. They were cool and surprisingly smooth as they brushed lightly against her closed mouth. A jolt slammed through her as they began to move on hers, thoroughly and possessively exploring every tender contour. With a feeling that this was all wrong, half-stifled, her head reeling, she found herself imprisoned in a grip of steel, pressed against his hard, muscular length, her breasts coming to rest against his chest, and there was little she could do to escape. Alternate waves seemed to run through her body, but there was also another far more disturbing sensation.

Without taking his lips from hers, William was thinking and behaving like a man intent on seduction. His lips increased their pressure, becoming coaxing as he slid the tip of his tongue into the warm sweetness of her mouth.

Eleanor gasped, totally innocent of the sort of warmth, the passion he was skilfully arousing in her, that poured through her veins with a shattering explosion of delight. It was a kiss like nothing she could have imagined, a kiss of exquisite restraint, and unable to think of anything but the exciting urgency of his mouth and the warmth of his breath, she felt herself falling slowly into a dizzying abyss of sensuality. His hands glided restlessly, possessively, up and down her spine and the nape of her neck, pressing her tightly to his hardened body.

Trailing her hands up the muscles of his chest and shoulders and sliding her fingers into the crisp curly hair at his nape, with a quiet moan of helpless surrender she clung to him, devastated by what he was doing to her, by the raw hunger of his passion. Inside her an emotion she had never experienced before began to sweetly unfold, before vibrantly bursting with a fierceness that made her tremble.

William's mouth left her lips and shifted across her cheek to her ear, his tongue flicking and exploring each sensitive crevice, then trailing back to her lips and claiming them once more. His kiss became more demanding, ardent, persuasive, a slow, erotic seduction, tender, wanting, his tongue sliding across her lips, urging them to part. Forcing himself to temporarily relinquish her mouth, he raised his head slightly. 'Kiss me, Eleanor,' he demanded thickly.

And Eleanor, lost in a wild and beautiful madness and with blood beating in her throat and temples that wiped out all reason and will, did. When she moaned softly beneath the sensual onslaught and opened her mouth and kissed him as deeply and as erotically as he was kissing her, he groaned with pleasure, the sweetness of her response causing desire to explode inside him.

When at last he lifted his mouth from hers, his breathing was harsh and rapid, and gazing up at him Eleanor felt as if she would melt beneath his scorching eyes. Slowly she brought one of her hands from behind his neck and her finger gently traced the outline of his cheek, following its angular line down to his jaw and neck.

'Well?' he asked, his voice low and husky, recovering more quickly than Eleanor. Her face was bemused, her eyes unfocused, her soft pink mouth partly open. 'Do you like being kissed?' When she did not reply immediately, he grinned and murmured, 'Surely I cannot have rendered you speechless,'

'It certainly took my breath, and, yes, I liked it very well,' she confessed, still drifting between total peace and a strange, delirious joy, while at the same time a feeling of disquiet was creeping over her as her mind came together from the nether regions of the universe where it had fled.

Then, in a split second, Eleanor realised full well what she had done. She! Herself! That much-loved daughter of Edgar Collingwood had brazenly yielded in the arms of the man who had betrayed him. William Marston. A rush of anguish tore through her. She had let him kiss her because of deeper feelings she hardly understood, and to her shame she thought of her parents and Catherine and felt like a traitor.

Releasing his hold on her, William gently cradled her chin in his hand. In the pale glow of the moon she was very lovely, with the dreamy, faraway look in her eyes and the passion his kiss had aroused in her softening her features. The metallic silver of his eyes was dim as, with passion still smouldering within their depths, they looked intently into hers.

'You have the body of a woman, Eleanor Collingwood, but in worldly experience you are still a child—and I thank God for it.'

'I'm not such a child that I don't know the difference between right and wrong,' she flared, drawing away from him, longing to respond to the look in his eyes, to feel his mouth on hers setting her skin tingling and her blood on fire. But the image of her parents and Catherine stood between them and always would. Nothing could ever erase that.

'Eleanor? What is it?'

'You should not have done that. Don't ever try it again,' she cried in a suffocated voice. In the light of the moon she saw his soft expression change as her words hit him.

'Eleanor,' he murmured, and Eleanor wanted to die because, even now, she loved the sound of her name of his lips.

'Don't say my name in that way,' she said hoarsely.

A light blazed briefly in his eyes, then was extinguished. 'Come now, Eleanor,' he managed to say smilingly, though he himself was shaken by the moment. 'It was only a kiss.'

'That should never have happened,' she said fiercely, wrapping her arms around herself. 'Don't you realise that? I regret it already—I shall always regret my behaviour just now, and if you are a gentleman you will forget all about it.'

William let out a long sigh and quietly and without emotion, he said, 'What you ask is impossible, Eleanor. It happened and neither of us can erase it from our minds. I think you should return to your chamber and go to bed. The hour is late. It's been a long day.'

In a daze of suspended yearning and confusion, Eleanor hesitated as his eyes held hers in one long, compelling look, holding all her frustrated longing, and unfulfilled desires, everything that was between them. That one kiss had been too much and too little, arousing deep feelings she did not fully understand. What had happened between them had been a sudden overwhelming passion, heightened by the intensity of the knowledge that it shouldn't be happening.

Turning abruptly, she started to walk away from him, but then she turned and looked back. 'I don't want a repeat of this, William. I do mean what I say. I have told you that I will never forgive you for what you did to my father, and besides, we have your mother's feelings to consider so there must be no outward show of intimacy between us. My position in your house is precarious, and to keep on the right side of your mother is important to me. She would be shocked if she knew what had just transpired.'

'I agree. You are right. It won't happen again. Goodnight, Eleanor.'

When Eleanor slipped between the sheets, sleep continued to elude her as she tried to understand the turbulent, consuming emotions William was able to arouse in her. With the taste of his kiss still warm on her lips, she was unable to think of anything else. What had happened between them had been a sudden overwhelming, irresistible passion. His gentleness and ardour towards her had shown her something of the man beneath the worldly, harsh surface, and melted her self-engendered resistance.

Within her bed she burrowed deep beneath the covers,

curled into a tight ball. She forced herself to suffocate all thoughts of the kiss and the feelings he had roused in her. It should not have happened and was something she preferred to forget, but, try as she might, she was unable to stop herself thinking of the way he had held her, of how it had felt when he had pressed her body to his own—even now it made her pulses race. So lost was she in her reflections that she didn't notice the moment when sleep claimed her.

Chapter Six

It was a subdued and nervous household that went about its business over the following days, but when a week had passed and nothing had happened, tension eased and they began to relax, but William insisted that a watch was to be kept at all times.

Eleanor felt herself to be in a state of waiting, not knowing how long she would stay at Staxton Hall, but she knew the time would come when there would be decisions to make, plans to consider.

The morning following her arrival she spent helping Anne and Jane alter one of Anne's gowns for her to wear. It was a subtle shade of yellow with a gossamer-fine green embroidery. The bodice was fitted and the skirt parted at the front to reveal an underskirt of pastel green. The lace on the collar and cuffs, tied with fine green ribbons, reproduced the pattern of the embroidery on the skirt. At her small waist was a belt of gold satin.

'Oh, yes,' Anne cried, when they had fitted it on Eleanor. 'I told you the colour is just perfect for you, and it looks so nice. It suits your colouring and your figure. Go and look in the mirror and tell us what you think.'

Eleanor padded across the floor in her stockinged feet and her reaction when she saw her reflection was all the twins could have asked for.

'Yes,' she gasped, laughing gaily, genuinely impressed, allowing herself the luxury of running her hands down the folds of the sumptuous skirt. It was cool to the touch and, looking down, she noted with delight that it was the right length. She knew that the gown was wonderfully becoming to her complexion and to her eyes. 'It's perfect. I feel as though I've been dressed like a youth for so long I've forgotten I have a feminine side.'

'I assure you no one else has.'

The deep, masculine voice caused Eleanor to spin round to find William on the threshold to her chamber, leaning casually against the door frame. Her heart gave a traitorous leap at the sight of his darkly handsome face. His crooked smile and the sparkle in his translucent eyes almost sapped the strength from her knees. She dropped her lashes in sudden confusion as his voice wound around her senses like a coil of dark silk. All at once her heart began to beat in thick, rapid strokes.

When she had got out of bed that morning, in the cold light of day, the kiss they had shared had been uppermost in her mind. Their camaraderie had suddenly changed to something else, something she was going to find hard to deal with while ever she remained in his home.

A slow smile of admiration swept across his face as he beheld the lovely vision in a yellow and green gown. His eyes unabashedly displayed his approval as his gaze ranged over the full length of her. Her glorious wealth of hair was parted down the centre and tumbled over her shoulders and down her spine in a shimmering, waving mass, framing her creamy-skinned visage. Her lips were soft and sensuous, her eyes a warm shade of amber, fringed by thick, dark lashes. Even with the undisguised fullness of womanhood, the features were unmistakably Eleanor's.

The remembrance of her being in his arms stirred him in a way he had never known before. He had felt he was holding the promise of something deep and untouched, something that eluded him for the present, but one day… Something in his chest gripped him—an urgent need to walk up to her, to reach out and take her in his arms, but he dare not, not in front of his sisters; if he were to do so, in all probability Eleanor would reprimand him and slap his face.

'She does look lovely,' Jane enthused, clasping her hands in delight. 'Don't you think so, William? Not a bit like the youth who accompanied you from London.'

'I am many things, Jane, but I am not blind—and it is not the first time I have seen Eleanor in a gown.' His gaze settled on her face and he moved to her side so as not to be overheard by his chattering sisters. 'So,' he breathed, 'you have put aside your tunic and hose and become a lady, Eleanor.'

'A woman,' she whispered, foolishly wanting him to look at her, to see her as she truly was—a woman, not a girl in boy's clothes.

'And a woman,' he agreed. 'A remarkably lovely young woman—although I shall miss the youth.' He stepped back and said in a louder tone, 'The colour becomes you, Eleanor— in fact, you look every inch a Court lady.'

Eleanor grimaced. 'Perish the thought.'

'Wouldn't you like to go to Court, Eleanor?' Jane asked. 'I would,' she said, her eyes sparkling with the images Court life conjured up. 'I'd love to see the Queen and all the pageantry that surrounds her. It must be so exciting.'

'It appears to be, and if you want to know all about it, who better to ask than your brother,' she remarked, giving William a sideways glance, a mischievous look to remind him of the time he had spent as a Court favourite, receiving a darkly humorous scowl in return. 'As for myself, I have no place there. My clothes may be fashionable and I do savour the pleasures of conversation, which since Elizabeth has come to the throne has so transformed the Court, I believe, but I fear I would show myself awkward in such illustrious company. On account of my origins, my family not being as exalted as some, the doors of Whitehall Palace will remain closed to me.'

'Then you will have to marry a man with a title—an earl or even a duke,' Jane enthused, making an adjustment to the bodice of Eleanor's dress. 'If you do that, your place will be assured among the finest courtiers in the land.'

Aware that William was watching her closely, avoiding his penetrating gaze Eleanor laughed lightly, a soft flush mantling her cheeks. 'I do not think I care for an earl or a duke, Jane. I will be content to live a quiet life with someone who will make me happy.'

'And love,' Anne was quick to say.

Eleanor smiled at her indulgently. 'That would be an added bonus, Anne—and, yes, it would be nice.'

Life at Staxton Hall was comfortable. Dinner was served at eleven in the morning, supper at six. The long dark evenings before bed threw them all together. At supper William was tersely quiet, while his mother and the twins supplied all the conversation. After the meal they would retire to the withdrawing room where they would play cards and chess. With the twins Eleanor found pleasure reading and writing verse. Both Jane and Anne loved music, and Jane, accomplished on the lute, would reach for her instrument and pick out a soothing ballad and sing to them in her clear voice.

Sometimes William would peruse a book Eleanor was reading and they would discuss its content together, but

Eleanor's pulse would quicken at his nearness. His lean, handsome, dark face with its crooked, sardonic smile that was capable of turning her bones to water, his vivid silver-grey eyes that hypnotised her, would bring her under his spell so that she was incapable of using her own intelligent mind.

Everywhere she went in the house she was aware of him. Even when he was off riding about the estate with Godfrey, hunting or hawking for herons around the lake, there was the lingering scent of him, the cologne he used, the brandy he drank. The very essence of William Marston was like an irresistible drug she could not deny but which she kept at bay night and day.

A hint of spring was in the air when William and Eleanor, Anne and Jane set out early one morning to ride to York. After many long weeks of being confined to the house the twins were excited and eager for the trip. With Godfrey and two of William's men in attendance, they were a happy band of travellers that disturbed the quietness of the countryside.

York was a fascinating maze of narrow streets and alleys all jumbled together. As soon as they rode through Monk Bar and began to proceed along Groodramgate, with the majestic Minster towering to the right of them, the crowds, the clamour of church bells, the noise and colour and vitality of the bustling city fascinated Eleanor just as much as it had always done and she felt a lifting of her spirits.

Observing her, William laughed and remarked, 'You look happy, Eleanor.'

'I am,' she replied, looking about her, her eyes shining. 'I love York. I always have. It holds so many happy memories.'

Dodging darting urchins and carts, carriages and drays that rumbled over the cobbled streets, it was difficult staying together. People had to be on their guard, with pickpockets abounding and young women in particular easy prey to villains with evil intentions.

It was a lovely March day with a cloudless sky—not that much of it could be seen with rooftops crowded together and slanting out over the streets, sometimes almost touching in the middle. Each floor of the houses and shops overhung the smaller one below it. In this way space was saved in the increasingly crowded city, but light and air was lost in the lower storeys.

'Oh, wait,' Jane cried excitedly as there was a disturbance among the pedestrians in St Sampson's Square, who stepped aside to make way for a merry travelling group of players in elaborate outfits, colourful and flamboyant. Music was provided by a trio of minstrels who led the way. 'How lively they are.' She laughed delightedly when two of the young men in the group did somersaults in front of their horses. 'And how clever they are. Do you think they are going to perform? I'd love to see them, wouldn't you, Anne?'

'I suspect they have only just arrived in York and will be looking for somewhere to act out their performances—more than likely in the Guildhall or St Anthony's Hall, Jane,' Eleanor told her. 'Come, let's head for The Pavement where there are some splendid shops and we can get some refreshment.'

'Might I suggest we go to the Bull on Coney Street,' William said, beginning to head in that direction. 'We can leave the horses there to feed and rest and proceed on foot.'

After eating a good and wholesome meal they made their way to The Pavement, the decorative fronts of the houses enlivening the street. Here there was the traditional market—the same as in every town all over England. It was both a business enterprise and social occasion, somewhere to purchase a wide variety of goods, meet friends and exchange the latest gossip.

Purchasing materials and the like, browsing among the market stalls and in the shops, buying oranges from a street hawker, then leaving her purchases with one of the men who accompanied them, Eleanor wandered away from the others when she saw a particularly attractive hat furnished with a plume and a jewel attached to the band in a shop window. She leaned forward to get a better look. Seeing other hats which were equally as fetching, she followed the shop window round the side of the building into an alley.

Apart from a man leaning against a wall the alley was deserted. Not in the slightest bit alarmed, she paid no notice and didn't see when he shoved himself away from the wall and slipped behind her. She was about to return to the others when a man's hand came from behind her and an arm circled her waist. With a hand clapped across her mouth, she felt herself being dragged farther along the alley with brutal force to where the man's accomplice waited.

'How is your uncle?' The sibilant hiss of the assailant's voice only added to his air of menace. 'Dead, I hope, otherwise I would have to inform your stepfather that our work at Hollymead was not successful—but taking you back with us to Fryston Hall will more than compensate for that.'

Momentarily stunned, Eleanor could do nothing, and then, realising the threat was real and her senses returning, rage, full blown and frenzied, erupted inside her. The thought that this villainous murderer had set fire to her home, killing her uncle, overwhelmed her and she bit his revolting hand. Her assailant cursed and snatched it away. Taking advantage of the moment, she turned her head and screamed shrilly in his ear, a scream that pierced him like a knife. At once he let go of her.

Her ears filled with her own cries, she did not hear the shout from the entrance of the alley, neither was she aware of the huge hands that snatched her assailant away from her, flinging him in one movement against the wall. Her saviour was

Godfrey. Thank God he had come. She looked towards the end of the alley where William stood outlined against the light. Quickly she stumbled towards him.

William took her arms and peered into her face, his gaze probing hers and finding fear and distress within their depths. Her face was white, having lost every vestige of colour.

'Eleanor—Eleanor?'

Her name spoken in concern and anger rose above the roaring in her ears and she felt herself drawn against William's chest and held in a tight circle.

'Eleanor, thank God I saw you wander off and followed you. Are you hurt?'

She shook her head, glancing over her shoulder at her assailant struggling with Godfrey.

William held her hard against him, feeling her body tremble. 'It's all right,' he soothed, 'it's over. You're safe.'

He looked down the alley to where Godfrey was holding the man who had attacked her, his accomplice having been apprehended by two men William assumed to be parish constables. As Eleanor's trembling lessened he held her away from him, looking at her intently.

'Who are these men, Eleanor? Do you know them?'

She nodded, forcing her shattered senses to work. 'They are the men sent by my stepfather to burn Hollymead. The man who attacked me said he hoped my uncle was dead and he meant to take me back to London—to Fryston Hall. He must have been waiting for me to be by myself—watching me—following me.' She shuddered, aware suddenly of her tingling nerves. She looked down the alley at Godfrey holding her assailant in his massive arms. 'What will happen to them?'

'They set fire to Hollymead and your uncle died as a result. That could be interpreted as murder.'

'And the sentence?'

William shrugged. 'They will be remanded until the Assizes are held when the central judges arrive in York. The Guildhall is used for the hearings, but these men are as guilty as hell and will hang.'

Eleanor shuddered. 'This is terrible, but I'm glad they've been caught.'

Seeing Anne and Jane a few yards away with their escort, William beckoned them over and gave them a brief account of what had happened. Both girls turned their faces to Eleanor.

'Oh, Eleanor,' Anne said, in shock at what William had told them. 'What a dreadful thing to happen. Are you all right?'

'Please don't fuss, Anne. I'm not hurt, just a bit shaken, that's all.'

'Eleanor, go with Anne and Jane to the Bull and wait for me there,' William ordered gently. 'It shouldn't take long to get this sorted out with the constables and make sure these men are locked away.'

'Of course—and then, William, I would like to go to Hollymead. You will take me there, won't you?'

William studied her pale face with a slight frown. Despite her attempt to appear unaffected by the assault to her person, he could tell that she was as tense as a tightly coiled spring. 'Do you have to—after what's just happened to you? Wouldn't you rather return to Staxton Hall?'

As quickly as her mind had filled with fear when she had been attacked, now it cleared, leaving her calm and decisive. 'I want to go. I wish to see for myself that Thomas is managing. I know Walter is due to arrive any day, but I would like to go all the same.'

'Very well,' William conceded, 'but we can't stay long. We must be back at Staxton Hall long before dark.'

'I know.'

* * *

At Hollymead Eleanor saw that Thomas had taken charge of things admirably and was awaiting Walter's arrival with his wife and child from the Netherlands. Already work to restore the part of the house that had been damaged by the fire was underway, with masons and carpenters and a large workforce working to the plan of the master-builder who employed them.

After bundling up some of her possessions that had escaped the fire—clothes, mainly, that, although no longer fashionable and might be a little on the small side, yet could be altered, having put the attack behind her and feeling glad that the two men would get their just punishment, Eleanor, in quiet and re-flective mood, wandered away from Anne and Jane, who were looking over the ruins with interest. It was with a heavy heart that she dwelt on the tragedy that had befallen her uncle—York would be much the poorer without him.

On the edge of a water meadow she stopped and looked at the familiar landscape, her mind picturing the splendour of spring, when the trees would burst into life. William came up behind her.

'Memories?' His voice was quiet, his mood pleasant and attentive.

Eleanor nodded and turned and looked at him, lifting her face to his. The light from the sun added to its gentle beauty and William felt it strike to the very soul of him.

'I was thinking of Uncle John. If I had not run away from Fryston Hall, he would still be alive. The guilt and remorse I feel is terrible and it will be a long time—if ever—that I will be able to live with that.'

'You could not have foreseen the tragedy. It was Atwood who was responsible. Never forget that.'

When she turned and strolled on he walked beside her

with a long, casual stride. They proceeded for several minutes in silence and then Eleanor paused.

'I always came here to play as a child. I belonged here at Hollymead. I had loving, respectable parents who loved me inordinately and let me roam free. I used to sit beneath those trees,' she said, pointing to a group of oaks ahead of her beside a brook, 'and lose myself in daydreams and wishes.'

'And what did you dream and wish for?'

'That I would stay at Hollymead for ever—and like every other little girl I wished that I would be pretty. In spring this meadow is filled with flowers and in summer the scent is intoxicating. It's a lovely place—an ideal place to play and dream.'

'I know,' William murmured.

'You do?'

'This is where you were that day I came to Hollymead and saw you for the first time.'

She looked at him. 'You remember that? How extraordinary.'

He smiled. 'Not really. I remember you were wearing a blue gown the colour of cornflowers adorned with white lace, and you had a daisy crown on your head.'

She laughed lightly, her teeth shining like pearls between her parted lips. 'How observant you were for a fifteen-year-old boy, William. I would sit for hours making daisy chains. Sometimes my mother would help and sometimes my nursemaid. This meadow grows particularly fine daisies with fat, juicy stems—ideal for making daisy chains.'

'You must have been a happy child.'

'I was, but I didn't know anything else so I thought that was the way of things.'

Strolling over to the trees, she sat beside the brook, wrapping her arms round her drawn-up knees and watching the crystal-clear water tumble over its rocky bed in silvery, shimmering, distorted ripples. Sitting beside her, William watched her closely, appreciating the sweet scent of her. Her face was a bright rosy pink and her eyes snapped in a bright tawny blaze in the light of the sun, and he thought he had never seen such a glorious creature in his life.

Several moments passed in silence and then William lifted her hair and stroked the nape of her neck, encouraged when she didn't pull away.

'Tell me, Eleanor, do you still dream?'

'Sometimes.'

'You're trembling.'

'Am I?' She twisted her head round and looked at him, unsmiling. 'That's your fault. In spite of everything I hold against you, you have that effect on me. You know, William, when I saw you at Fryston Hall on Catherine's wedding day, I was determined to hate you. I tried, but for the time we have been together I have seen a different man to the one I had painted in my mind, a man who melted my self-engendered resistance, and I resented that. I wanted to dislike you, but that didn't work either. And then you kissed me, and I no longer knew what to think.'

'It would seem you are confused about me, Mistress Collinwood. I can see your dilemma.'

'Can you?' She believed he could. William Marston had a razor-sharp perception of her deepest fears. 'I have never been so unsure of myself. You see, I don't want to like you. Because of who you are and what you have done I don't want to have anything to do with you, but when I asked for your protection I unwittingly made more problems for myself than I bargained for.'

'And that scares you?'

'Yes, if you must know, yes, it does.'

William watched her, both touched and faintly amused by her confession, and aroused by her nearness. 'Do you fear me, Eleanor?'

'No, not you,' she said quietly, feeling his eyes on her, causing the colour in her cheeks to deepen. 'It's what you might do to me that I'm afraid of.'

As he continued to stroke the nape of her neck, a wonderful languor began to swell inside her, spreading through her with a glorious warm sensation. She knew that very soon her aunt would send for her, so she treasured every moment she had left at Staxton Hall. It didn't seem possible that the feelings she had for William were growing out of all proportion. No matter how hard she tried to fight them, each day they grew stronger and stronger until there was nothing but this joyous moment that dominated her every waking moment.

He let his hand drop and Eleanor watched the shimmering reflections in the water. Again she turned and looked into his eyes. They were narrowed and intent, glowing with need, with warmth. His lips parted, curving in a smile. Pulling her to her feet, he drew her into his arms.

'I should have known what would happen when I agreed to let you ride north with me. You're not a woman a man can ignore. I want you, Eleanor. I've had many women—I cannot deny that, or that I enjoyed each one—but none of them meant anything to me. They were diversions. Would that you were a diversion, too.'

'And Catherine?' she asked, lowering her eyes. 'Was she a diversion, William?'

His eyes darkened. 'No, Catherine was the exception—but she is in the past.' He sighed. 'I never meant for any of this to happen, Eleanor, and I feel I must be honest with you. There's no place in my life for an involvement just now. I have things to take care of, things to achieve, and any kind of attachment could be disastrous, for us both—a distraction for me. I cannot afford that.'

Reaching out, he gently placed a finger under her chin and raised her face to his. His eyes were filled with more than light interest as he admired her lovely face, and when he spoke Eleanor felt that deep, melodious voice wash over her. It caressed her just as his hand caressed.

'I've tried to fight it—to deny it—but you've bewitched me, Eleanor.'

When his arms went around her waist and he clasped her loosely against him, his words caused her some disquiet, but when he peered into her eyes her heart seemed to cease to beat and the languor inside turned into an ache, unendurably sweet. His mouth covered hers, moist, firm, lightly touching at first, then probing and demanding, and, as the ache spread to her bones, sensations burst to life. Sliding her arms about his neck, drowning in these sensations that prolonged the exquisite torture, she wondered how long she could withstand him. When at last he lifted his mouth from hers, Eleanor was trembling with awakened desire.

'William,' she whispered. 'I—'

He interrupted her in a deep, quiet voice. 'I like to hear you say my name and take you in my arms.'

Again his lips covered hers, and he kissed her for a long time, tenderly, carefully, deliberately, holding back the urgent passion that possessed him. It was a restrained kiss, because he exercised the greatest control. Then he raised his head and their eyes met and held—his so light and hers deep and amber, mingling, touching hidden places and already imagining the possibility of a next time. It was like a caress.

'I think we should go back to the others,' he murmured, 'before they come looking for us.'

'We should?'

'It's necessary.' He took her hand. 'Come, before we forget ourselves. We have a long journey ahead of us.'

* * *

The excitement of the day and the long ride had taken it out of them all. They were quite worn out and went to bed as soon as supper was over. Lady Alice, suffering a headache, also went to her chamber.

Eleanor's visit to Hollymead was uppermost in her mind and, wanting to wallow in the memories it had evoked, she was in no such haste to seek her bed. On a sigh she moved to the window and pulled back the heavy curtains and stared out at the night, the memories of her happy childhood surging and washing over her in great waves. The moon was bright in the dark violet sky, shining in untroubled serenity over the land.

'Eleanor.'

There was a movement behind her and the voice that spoke her name was deep, warm and loving. She closed her eyes, feeling the dizzy aura of him, unable to resist it. Wanting to savour the sound of it, she didn't turn, although she could imagine his eyes in the moonlight shining with an expression she would like to think he had given to no woman but her.

She heard him come closer, his footsteps almost soundless on the thick carpet, and then he was directly behind her, so close she could feel the warmth of him on her back. Then his arms snaked around her waist. He pulled her back and she sank into him, unable to resist despite her resolve to withstand his advances. He held her to his chest and buried his head into the curve of her neck, his lips warm, caressing her flesh. Sighing, she began to melt, feeling a languorous magic drift over her.

'Mmm,' he breathed. 'You smell of roses.'

'And you, my lord, smell of horses and fresh air and manly things.'

'Do you mind?' he asked, his teeth gently nibbling her earlobe.

'Not in the slightest,' she gasped, a thrill of excitement tingling along her nerves. 'I like it. It's a pleasant smell.'

'Why are you alone? Where is everyone?'

'In bed. Your mother has a headache and favoured an early night. As for Jane and Anne, they are quite worn out.'

'And you are not?'

She shook her head. 'So much has happened today. I'm tired, but I don't feel like going to bed just yet,' she said softly, covering his hands at her waist with her own. 'I am trying not to think of the attack, to put it from my mind and think of Hollymead instead—to reminisce. Don't you feel like going to bed either?'

'Not yet—at least, not alone.' His arms tightened about her and his voice was husky. 'Do you know—have you the slightest idea how much I want you, Eleanor? Will you not turn round and tell me you feel the same? If you don't, then I will leave you to your reminiscences.'

She turned slowly, shivering slightly, for she felt the full force of his masculinity, his vigour, the strong pull of his magnetism, which she knew was his need for her, wrap itself about her. His face was all shadow and planes in the candles' glow, the cheekbones taut, the lips slightly parted. He was so tall, so handsome. She felt a hollow ache inside as he gazed down at her. She lifted her face and he placed his lips on hers, gently, barely discernible.

Raising his head, he took her head between his hands and splayed his fingers over her cheeks, looking into the liquid depths of her eyes. 'You're incredibly lovely, Eleanor Collingwood. I wonder if you have any idea how lovely you are.'

His voice was soft and melodious. Eleanor stood very still, barely able to breathe, yet she was trembling inside.

'Come to bed with me, Eleanor.'

When he again took her lips, she moaned with pleasure. Did it matter that they weren't wed when his mouth, his hands, his powerful body were demanding things from her that she knew she could give him, things she wanted as badly as he did?

'We can't, William,' she murmured between kisses, which were having a weakening effect on her senses. 'It's not right. Your mother—'

'My mother will know soon enough—if she doesn't already—how things stand between us.'

His mouth closed over hers once more, moulding, caressing, savouring, his tongue invading the dewy softness with hot need. It was a wild, wanton kiss. Heat catapulted through Eleanor, setting her whole body on fire, and cindered every nerve beneath the crushing weight of his passion. She knew her vulnerability and seriously doubted that she could raise a hand to hold him off if she wanted to.

When he released her, he took her hand and led her out of the room and up the wide stairs. She went with him willingly, knowing it was wrong—and yet, she argued with herself, how could it be? She wanted him desperately and just now nothing mattered but that.

Drawing her inside his bedchamber, William closed the door and kissed her again, long and deep, and then with slow deliberation he began to undress her, his burning eyes devouring every inch of her exposed flesh. When she was naked he gathered her up into his arms in an act of possession into which Eleanor found herself snuggling with gratitude and what seemed to be absolute content. She wanted him and it was enough.

His silver-light eyes stared into her very soul, and she was hardly aware of the moment he placed her on the bed. William quickly divested himself of his clothing and stretched alongside her. The firm, hard muscles of his body pressed against hers, and the exploration of his hands on her flesh, gentle and caressing, his lips devouring and tender, had her glowing and purring like a kitten.

A need began to grow inside her as his caresses grew

bolder. It was a hollow feeling that ached to be filled. She felt on the threshold of some great and already overwhelming discovery. She quivered as his fingers stroked the swell of her breasts and continued over her flat belly and on to the curve of her hips and inner thighs and her feminine instinct whispered to her that her body held some incredible surprises in store for her. What he was doing to her was like being imprisoned in a cocoon of dangerous sensuality. She moaned and fought against the tumult of frayed emotions, but no effort of hers could bring about a quieting of her nerves.

William was slow, in no rush to possess her, for, this being her first time, she was innocent and inexperienced and she did not really know what to expect. Trapped beneath the exquisite promise of his aroused body and the persistence of his mouth, Eleanor began to tremble with uncontrollable need, and when he finally entered her William's carefully withheld hunger released itself in a frenzy that demanded that he possess her fully.

Eleanor cried out and so did he, but all around them the people in the great house slept and the lovers were unheard.

Sated and heavy with a contentment she had never believed possible, Eleanor heaved a soft sigh and settled in the sheltering arms of her lover. How wonderful it was to linger in his arms, to watch the flickering firelight wash over their naked bodies still entwined and feel him hold her close, to rest her cheek on his chest and feel his heartbeat, to revel in the warmth of him, the smell of him, and to see his eyes fill with a hungry need as he rolled her on to her back and took possession of her once more, and for a while made her forget everything else.

Later, while she slept in his arms, William lay awake, staring up at the tasselled tester, his mind occupied with how he was to keep this woman who had come to mean so much to him in his house and in his life.

* * *

With the dawn came cold, harsh reality for Eleanor. Leaving the man sleeping amid a tangle of bed covers, his arms above his head and his powerful body stretched out, emotionally spent, she slipped out of William's bed and silently made her way back to her own where she laid down and closed her eyes.

Never had she felt more desolate or more ashamed. What she had done betrayed herself, her upbringing, and worst of all, her parents—and she had betrayed them with the traitor who had betrayed her father, resulting in his execution. She despised herself for it, she despised herself for being so easily tempted and for the unprecedented weakness that had driven her to it. Her weak will and fragile moral fibre had crumbled in the face of William's dangerous appeal. Only a fool without pride or sense would have done what she had done. It was totally inexcusable and she had sunk beyond social and moral redemption.

Later that same morning a messenger arrived at Staxton Hall from Lady Sandford. He brought two messages, one for Lady Alice and one for Eleanor, demanding that she go to Cantly Manor, insisting that her place was with her family. She wrote that Eleanor must inform her of what she intended doing and that when she decided to come she would send men who would escort her to Kensington. She also mentioned that Martin Taverner had been offered a profitable post at Court— thanks to the kindness of the Queen.

'Will you go?' Anne asked when Eleanor told her the contents of the letter. The three of them were in the solar, altering another gown for Eleanor.

Eleanor, who was mechanically going through the motions of carrying on and survival, nodded, ignoring the sudden knot in her chest. William had ridden off with Godfrey after breakfast and didn't know about the letter. The night she had spent in his arms had altered everything. The agony she had felt when she had crept to her room earlier had receded to a dull numbness. All she wanted to do was to leave Staxton Hall and never look back, to forget everything. All her attention must be focused on that, on forgetting that she had ever met William Marston, and that she had been foolish and vulnerable enough to surrender her body to him like a common strumpet.

'In truth, Anne, I think I must. You have all been very kind to me and I am most grateful, but I realise that I cannot remain here indefinitely. Hollymead is no longer my home—I have come to accept that, and I have no wish to return to Fryston Hall.'

'Did you live at Fryston Hall with Catherine?' Anne asked.

'Yes. She was my stepsister.'

'Did you like her?'

'Of course I did. We spent a great deal of time together.'

'It's odd—you think so too, don't you, Jane?—that William didn't spend longer in London before coming here. After all, they were to have been married. He must have missed her—being away from her all that time.'

Eleanor looked from one to the other. 'Catherine married someone else. Didn't you know?'

They stopped sewing and gaped at her. 'What?' Anne asked disbelievingly. 'Oh, poor William. How awful that must have been for him. Why did she do that?'

'I suppose she got tired of waiting,' Jane said. 'She probably thought he was never coming back and she couldn't be expected to wait for ever. But you must know how she felt when William suddenly turned up, Eleanor. Was she overjoyed, upset—or is she so much in love with her new husband that she no longer cares?'

'I—I think Catherine does still care. When William arrived

at Fryston Hall Catherine had only been married for a few hours. It was her wedding day—and, yes, she was greatly affected by William's sudden appearance.'

'Poor William.' Anne sighed, resting her sewing in her lap. 'Little wonder he doesn't speak of her. He must be hurting terribly.'

'He—William—loved her?' Eleanor enquired tentatively.

'Of course he loved her,' Anne told her with all the passion of youth. 'William told us how beautiful she is, how fine and gentle—indeed, none more so. How could he help himself loving her? The worst of it is that I think in his heart he still does.'

Eleanor felt the vicious thrust of foreboding. Anne's words tore into her heart and mind with a rending impact that shocked her. She felt more hurt than she cared to admit. She listened in cold disquiet as Anne went on to sing Catherine's praises, and she found it difficult to equate this loving, caring woman with the Catherine she knew.

'Do you think Catherine will divorce her husband?' Jane asked, threading another length of silk through her needle.

Eleanor shook her head. 'No,' she said quietly. 'Her father would never permit it. Did—either of you ever meet Catherine?' she asked, hating discussing Catherine, but feeling compelled to know all there was to know about how close she had been to William.

'We never did,' Jane said with a note of regret, 'although William used to speak of her all the time when he was home.'

As the two girls continued chatting like two vivacious humming birds, blithely impervious to what she was feeling and the hurtful jealousy scraping at her heart, Eleanor lowered her head over her work, a sick feeling of disappointment welling up within her. She longed to give vent to her own bitter pain. Never had any man appeared so attractive to her, and never had her heart called out so strongly to another.

Was his heart still entwined with Catherine's, she asked herself, and, if so, how could he have taken her, Catherine's stepsister, to his bed? She should have repulsed him, which was what any good, decent, God-fearing young woman would have done. But that wasn't what she had done, she thought with self-revulsion. No, indeed. Instead she had allowed her father's betrayer to kiss and touch her, and worse.

Chapter Seven

The arrival of a second messenger from London later that day brought a letter for William. It was from an associate informing him of matters at Court and other matters that might be of interest to him. The messenger was known to William and, closeted in the privacy of the library, they talked well into the night.

The following morning he brusquely announced to his mother that he was leaving for London that very day.

'What on earth for?' his mother said, alarmed and clearly upset by his sudden decision. 'The roads will be atrocious, as they always are at this time of year. If you must go, then surely the most sensible thing would be for you to wait until spring.'

'I can't wait that long. I have some urgent business to attend to that cannot wait. I shall hire extra men to add to your protection while I'm away.'

'I see. Then, if it is so important, I suppose you had better go. But you will not be away too long, I hope. Staxton Hall has been too long without its master.'

From where she sat, Eleanor watched William in silence. Ever since that letter had come the change in him was immediate and Eleanor could not determine his emotions. There was a new tension in his body, a new tightness about his jaw and a restlessness about his manner. She tried to read his thoughts, trying not to be distracted by the curve of his mouth and softened by the lock of hair falling over his worried brow. What was so urgent that he had to hurry back to London?

She was alone in a small parlour, settled before the fire sewing some buttons on to the bodice of a gown when she heard the door open. She knew it was William and she held her breath as his soft footfalls echoed around her.

'Can you stop that for now?' he asked quietly.

Raising her head, she looked up at him. She studied the terse lines of his face revealed by the firelight. There were dark shadows around his eyes, and the uncompromising lines at the sides of his mouth had not been there when she stole from his room the day before.

His close presence emanated a sense of controlled power straining beneath the surface. Just when she thought that she would not be affected by him he appeared and all her carefully tended illusions were dashed. Why had he sought her out? Why hadn't he just gone away and let her be reconciled to his leaving? Why did he have to prolong her misery?

Setting aside her sewing, she rose and smoothed her skirts, surprised to feel her hands trembling. 'Are you ready to leave?'

He nodded. 'You heard me tell Mother I am to set on extra men to guard the house.'

'Why?'

'To soothe your fears. When I leave you may have need of some convincing protection. Since we've attracted the likes of Frederick Atwood, who knows what could happen? With plenty of guards about, it will add to your safety.'

She inclined her head, playing with a ring on her finger, unable to look at him. She was trying so hard to be calm and composed, but it was not working out that way. 'You still think we are in danger from my stepfather's henchmen?'

'It is possible—although there have been no reports of strangers in the area. However, I don't wish to take any chances. I would have contempt for myself if I did not do my duty towards you and my family,' he said through a twisted smile.

He seemed so sincere. Eleanor could see it in his eyes. He did want her safe, she believed that.

William studied her, relaxing slightly as his gaze caressed her lovely features. She did not seem herself. No doubt she was upset at his leaving. She was a little hesitant, almost as if she wished herself elsewhere.

'Eleanor, I have to go.' Drawing her towards him, he wrapped his arms around her. At first she responded and leaned into him. Then she checked herself and drew back, putting distance between them.

'Will you not have some wine before you go?' she asked, forcing herself to meet his eyes, her own veiled and cautious.

'Time is of the essence.' When she would have moved away, he stayed her by placing his hand on her arm. 'I sense something is the matter. Is it something I have done to offend you?'

Eleanor glanced at him at once. 'No, of course not. Please don't think that.'

'Then what is it? Tell me. Come, Eleanor,' he murmured, his teeth glistening from between his parted lips and his eyes holding a devilish light. 'When I ride away I don't want to remember you with a long face—much rather the lovely smiling one.'

'There is nothing wrong. It—It's just that I'm sorry you are leaving. I—I shall miss you.'

He smiled, touched by the simplicity of her confession and having no reason to read anything else behind it. 'It won't be for long. I'll be back before you've had time to miss me.

What did your aunt have to say in her letter?' he asked. Having been so preoccupied with his own news from London, he had omitted to enquire. His gaze searched hers, but their depths were deliberately shuttered. 'Does she want you to go to her?'

'Yes. She—is concerned and regrets she was not at home when I left Fryston Hall.'

'And?' he asked, studying her closely. 'What will you reply?'

Eleanor lowered her eyes lest he saw the true answer in her eyes. 'I shall give it some thought. Your mother has very kindly told me I am welcome to stay here for as long I wish to—particularly as the roads are not fit to travel just now should I decide to go to Cantly Manor. But won't you tell me why you have to go?' she ventured to ask quietly. 'What is so important that you have to go rushing off to London at a moment's notice?'

Now William's face tightened and shut as if a door had been closed. He turned from her abruptly. 'Please don't ask, Eleanor. It is—of a personal nature.'

Alarm flared in her eyes. 'Personal? William, are you in danger?'

The silence that followed was long and heavy. The firelight cast shadows over his handsome face, making his expression stern. 'I can't say. It's all very complicated, but not beyond me.'

'Then whatever it is that takes you away, I hate it,' she said, suddenly unable to stop herself, the internal war between her mind and her heart escalating to tumultuous proportions.

William looked at her, a flicker of laughter in his eyes. He gave her a penetrating look. 'Now that is what I want to hear—that familiar spirit of defiance I have not heard since you came to Staxton Hall—that bite of temper I saw in you when we first met.'

Eleanor knew he was trying to ease the situation with humour, to make it easier for her, for himself, and she wondered how he would react if he knew that she would soon be following him to London.

Taking her hands in his firm ones, forcing ease into his voice, he said, 'There is someone in London I have to see, Eleanor. Things—happened that I have to put right before I can get on with my life. What happened during those missing years is not over and I have to have the courage to see this through to the end. I have to go. If I didn't do this, I would have contempt for myself.'

Though Eleanor had decided to end their acquaintance, her eyes were suddenly moist because she had no choice, no options. Horribly afraid for him, she lowered her head, not wanting to dull the edge of his courage with her fear and struggling to cauterise her emotions. He mustn't know she was leaving. He wouldn't let her go easily, and never without probing questions. Trying not to think of Catherine, who was like a shadowy, threatening figure hovering on the periphery of her mind, she looked up at him and a faint smile flitted across her lips.

'Then you must do what you have to do, William. And do not be concerned about us here. We are safe enough,' she said at last, hiding the pain she felt in her heart.

They were startled when someone rapped on the door and loudly told William his horse was ready.

William turned to leave.

'William?'

He faced her, his eyes devoid of emotion. For the times she had been close to him he'd let his guard down and revealed the man behind the title and the stern facade, but now, standing before her, he was a stranger, keeping his emotions and thoughts in check. She desperately wanted to know how to reach him, but could think of no way.

'I'm sorry you have to go. Please take care.'

Suddenly there was such intensity in his gaze that Eleanor felt her heartbeat quicken. He snatched her into his arms, breathing deeply of the sweet scent of her.

'I will,' he whispered, his lips against her hair. 'I shall miss you, Eleanor, but I have to go.'

His lips took hers in one final deep and tender kiss and the seductive scent of the sandalwood he always used filled her senses.

Eleanor followed him out of the house, her eyes shadowed by pain. She stood aside as he embraced his mother and sisters and strode to his horse. Godfrey and the messenger were already mounted. A groom cupped hands for his master's boot and William vaulted into the high saddle of his hunter. With a final salute Eleanor watched him ride over the cobbled courtyard and over the drawbridge. Already she felt the suffering of his loss. As suddenly as he had appeared he had fallen out of her life, leaving a jagged, gaping hole in it, and she felt lost and afraid and very much alone once more.

In need of privacy, Eleanor excused herself and went slowly towards the stairs, pausing outside the library before going in to find something to read that would occupy her mind for the next hour until dinner. Idly perusing the many leather-bound volumes on the shelves, but unable to find a book that appealed to her present mood, she decided to abandon the idea.

Passing the desk on which there were inkwells and quills, scrolls and manuscripts, sitting on the top of a pile of papers she saw an open letter. Suspecting it was the letter the messenger had brought yesterday, her curiosity was aroused. It was not in her nature to pry into other people's affairs, but she couldn't resist picking it up, and before she could help herself her eyes were scanning the writing.

There were a lot of things she didn't understand—about

the Court and a ship that had been sighted in the Thames and was due to arrive in London at any time from somewhere she couldn't decipher—but the most interesting and tragic thing that caught her attention was that Henry Wheeler, Catherine's husband, was dead.

It was such a dreadful thing to happen and she was very shocked. Her first thoughts were for Catherine and how devastated she must be to lose her husband after just a few short months of marriage. Reading on, she learned that Henry had drowned, that he had taken a boat late one night from Chelsea to go to Westminster only to meet with tragedy. When his boat collided with another, he was thrown into the river. His body was recovered the next day.

Catherine was a widow. The fact hit her like a thunderbolt. Suddenly everything was clear and her heart was in shreds. She felt as if she was dying by inches. Her face was empty of all expression and there was a terrible blankness in her eyes. Catherine was free to marry again. William knew and had gone tearing off to London to be with her. He had implied he had unfinished business to take care of, something to do with the three years he had been gone, and he had also told her there was someone he had to see.

It was Catherine, she just knew it. What other explanation could there be? The very thought of it devastated her. She never thought she could feel such pain. She couldn't stand it, and her flesh that had quivered when she had been in his arms turned ice cold.

A grey desolation spread over her. Even though she had decided that she would leave Staxton Hall and William for good, and that in all probability she would never see him again, for the brief time she had been in his home she had allowed herself to dream, and his rejection of her diminished her in some irreparable way. She had not asked for this, had not chosen to feel so deeply for him, and she did not know the exact moment when it had happened.

She had not bargained on the bond between William and Catherine. It was still there, pulling at them. What other explanation could there be for him to go rushing off to London when he learned she was free if not Catherine? She knew a dreadful resentment that William had left without telling her that Henry Wheeler had died, as if she were of no more importance than a passing acquaintance. She was shaken momentarily mindless that he could do this to her. It was not just anger she felt, she realised, but humiliation, shame, hurt pride, and an awareness of her own foolish naïvety.

Her jaw tightened, her resilient spirits stretching themselves as they had done once before when she had decided to leave Fryston Hall. Straightening her back, with a new determined gleam in her eyes, and seized with urgency she picked up a quill and wrote to her Aunt Mildred. Only when she was away from anything that was connected with William would she be able to claw back the self-esteem he had stolen from her.

When this was done, she went in search of Lady Alice to inform her of her decision to leave Staxton Hall—that she had decided to wed Martin Taverner she kept to herself.

Lady Alice was sitting near the fire in her chamber, laboriously measuring out different-coloured silken threads to repair a damaged tapestry, while two of her ladies folded linen into a chest. 'So, Eleanor,' she said, looking up at Eleanor, 'you are to leave us.'

'Yes, Lady Alice,' she said with a swift smile.

'We shall be sorry to lose you—especially Jane and Anne. They are going to miss you—we all will. It has been a pleasure having you here.'

To Lady Alice's surprise Eleanor's eyes filled with tears,

but she only smiled and said, 'You have been very kind, and I am going to miss you all.'

Lady Alice frowned, suddenly thoughtful. She felt that the matter that had worried her of late could not be avoided. Her sharp eyes had seen when William and Eleanor had exchanged lingering smiles and complicit looks. How intimate had their relationship become, she asked herself concernedly, and, if so, was there really any harm in it? William was known for a lusty man who, in his youth, had been somewhat wild and for ever attracted by a pretty face, and it was only on his father's death that he had settled down to the more serious matters of soldiering and making sure the estate was well run.

So it was hardly surprising that he was attracted by Eleanor. They were both handsome and free, and despite Eleanor being who she was, none of what had happened had been her fault. Lady Alice had grown fond of the girl and would be as sorry to see her leave as Jane and Anne would be.

'Eleanor—about you and William…'

Eleanor glanced at her sharply, her heart sinking. 'Yes?'

'Forgive me, but I am not blind—or as unsympathetic as you probably think I am. My giddy daughters may walk around with their heads in the air and their eyes blinkered, but it wasn't difficult for me to see that a—a fondness has grown between you and my son.'

Eleanor felt her pointed stare and lowered her eyes as a blush deepened the hue on her cheeks. The fact that Lady Alice was aware of the intimacy between herself and William made it difficult to meet the older woman's gaze and pretend innocence.

'It was no more than a foolish infatuation between two people brought together by circumstance—no more than that.'

Lady Alice nodded, saying no more. So clever were her eyes they could read Eleanor's face, but if she scented an untruth in what Eleanor had said she held her tongue. Eleanor was grateful for her discretion.

'You do realise that William will expect to find you here when he returns.'

'I—I am sure you will explain everything, why I had to leave.'

Lady Alice's lips twisted wryly. 'I'm not at all sure why you are leaving, Eleanor.'

'You will. When William returns to Staxton Hall, everything will be revealed to you.' How would she react when she discovered her beloved son had gone to London to be reconciled with Catherine? Anger stirred inside her. Could he not have spared her, Eleanor, this indignity, and why had her life been transformed into this irretrievable disaster?

Unbeknown to Eleanor, Lady Alice was as informed as she was about the letter the messenger had brought. She knew how things had once stood between William and Catherine Atwood, and that he'd had strong feelings for her. But so much time had elapsed and so many things had happened, which included Catherine's marriage to someone else, she thought it was ended. But when William had told her Catherine's husband had died in a tragic accident and he had left for London immediately, like Eleanor she, too, thought his feelings for Catherine might not be dead after all. Perhaps he had told Eleanor and this was her reason for leaving Staxton Hall.

The hour was late when Eleanor and the men Aunt Matilda had sent to Staxton Hall to escort her eventually reached Cantly Manor. The manor was a veritable honeycomb of a house, with tall chimneys and the walls a mellow, golden stone. It was a big, cold, gloomy house, devoid of life. Both Eleanor and her mother had hated it when they had stayed here before, but then, with Hollymead taken from them, they'd had nowhere else to go.

Confronted by her aunt and feeling weariness spreading throughout her body like a sodden blanket, Eleanor felt her confidence threatening to slip away like grains of sand in an hourglass.

Matilda Sandford was a small, thin woman, heavily gowned in black satin with a rope of pearls around her thin neck. She had never been as beautiful as her sister Marian, but there was an imperious strength in her pale, lined face that Marian had lacked—perhaps if she had possessed some of Matilda's traits, she would never have married Frederick Atwood.

As Eleanor rose from her curtsy and faced her aunt, the older woman seemed to grow taller, haughtier, while Eleanor felt a thrust of baleful envy for Jane and Anne cocooned in warmth and comfort at Staxton Hall.

Sipping warm spiced wine seated in front of a meagre fire, her aunt sat across from her, watching her closely, her body as straight and rigid as a stone statue. Eleanor knew no appeal could reach her. Marriage to her passive, submissive husband had robbed her of compassion, although perhaps she had always been that way, for Eleanor couldn't remember a time when she had been any different.

'Your stepfather should never have allowed you to go all that way to Yorkshire. Hollymead was not your home, Eleanor. Oh, it was a terrible thing that happened—the house burning down like that and resulting in the death of Sir John Collingwood—but it belongs to Sir Walter now.'

'I know, Aunt Matilda. That is why I am here. I could not stay with Lady Alice any longer—although she was very kind and extremely generous.'

'Well, I'm glad you saw sense and realised where your loyalties lie—and you will do well to remember it. Of course, when your mother died I wrote to your stepfather asking him to send you here, but he wrote and told me you were settled at Fryston Hall and that you were a companion for Catherine. I assumed you were happy there.'

Eleanor stared at her. 'You wrote to him?'

'Of course I did. Marian was my dear sister and when she died you should have come to me.'

With hindsight Eleanor wished she had, for then she would not have had to suffer all the indignities her stepfather had heaped on her—and she would never have met William and be suffering this heartache now.

'And Martin?' Aunt Matilda asked. 'You have given marriage to him some thought?'

'I will consent to become his wife,' Eleanor said, swallowing down her reluctance. It seemed the only thing to do. Whether it was the right thing to do was another matter entirely. She was tired by all the struggle and self-examination concerning it.

Immediately a change came over her aunt and a thin smile stretched her lips. 'Eleanor, this is wonderful.' She had expected a long drawn-out battle. By giving in, Eleanor had given her an unexpected gift. 'I am well pleased, as I know Lord Taverner will be.'

Relieved, you mean, Eleanor thought. Relieved that you will not have the disgrace of an unmarried niece living with you and relieved that you will be closely connected to the Taverner family at last. And of course Lord Taverner would be both relieved and delighted.

'I'm happy that you've put aside your whims and fancies and see that marriage to Martin is an excellent match.' Her smile reminded Eleanor of a hoar frost. Privately Matilda had been disconcerted by Eleanor's defiance in the past and was relieved that she had agreed to comply to her wishes, although she was curious as to what had brought about this change of heart in her high-spirited, strong-willed niece.

'I realise my situation is dire, Aunt Matilda, with nothing of my own. I—I will do as you wish and marry Martin—if he still wants me, that is. Whether we will be happy is another matter entirely,' she remarked drily.

'Marriage was never intended to be happy. Fruitful, yes, and we will have to pray that you will succeed in that.'

Eleanor winced at her aunt's plain speaking, but said nothing.

Later, when she was in bed, she felt tears fill her eyes and slant from the corners to her temple and into her hair. For the first time since entering Cantly Manor she allowed herself to think of William.

Had Catherine been ready to receive him with open, possessive arms? Lovely Catherine, elegant and graceful—marriageable and highly suitable for a man like William. Was he with her? Was he kissing Catherine like he had kissed her? The memory only served to remind her of the bleakness of the future that filled her world. William had stolen her heart, but his own had not been his to give. Catherine still had claim on that.

Eleanor forced herself to go over every detail of that one night of blissful passion they had shared. It was like a self-scourging, a deliberate act on her part to try and purge herself of the feelings she had for William. If she was able to make herself accept it, to believe it, to be unconcerned that he had returned to Catherine, she had to wallow in the pain of it—like salt in an open wound that was agonizing, but healing—and then she must learn to suffocate all her feelings for him, not think of him. She must force herself to believe that their embraces had never happened, that everything was the same as before, and she must never compare Martin Taverner with him.

But she knew that the despairing pain she felt would always be there. It might dull with the years, but it would never leave her and she grieved for his loss as though he were dead.

* * *

Lord Taverner and his son were expected at any time. Aunt Matilda was excited by the visit. Eleanor noted her high colour and the way she fidgeted nervously with her handkerchief. Why, she thought, her aunt was like a young girl awaiting her first swain, whereas Eleanor was seated in the window bay shivering convulsively, partly from dread at the expected visitors and mainly because it was bitterly cold in the big gloomy room with its tapestried walls and carved gilded ceiling. She drew her wrap closer about her as the icy chill seemed to penetrate her very bones, and her aunt's presence did not serve to distract her thoughts from her misery.

And suddenly they had arrived. Eleanor rose to meet the guests, forgetful now of the cold and having made up her mind to be calm and reasonable. Lord Taverner preceded his son. He was a man whom Eleanor had no particular liking for. She had seen him bully Martin in the past, and that had not created a favourable opinion of him. He was of medium height and thickset with a balding pate, his face showing all the signs of good living.

Two paces behind his father, Martin was staring at Eleanor owl-eyed, obviously pleased to see her again and enchanted with his bride-to-be.

Lord Taverner beamed at her. He knew Eleanor Collingwood to be a high-spirited girl and that she had a temper—better if she had been more docile, but beggars can't be choosers, he thought. She was not possessed of a particularly submissive nature, a fact of which her aunt was painfully aware, having disobeyed her stepfather's stricture by running away.

'We are delighted you have agreed to Martin's marriage proposal at last, Eleanor. I am looking forward to welcoming you into the Taverner family.'

'I aim to please.'

Lord Taverner laughed loud. 'Not only have you a pretty face, my dear, but a pretty tongue, too. As for pleasing me, you will find it an easy task when you and Martin are wed.'

'As long as her desire to please you is not greater than her desire to please your son,' Matilda ventured, bestowing on her guest one of her rare smiles.

Martin moved to stand in front of Eleanor. His smile was warm. 'I-I am w-well pleased, Eleanor. It's been so l-long since I saw you—at Catherine's wedding, in fact. I never thought y-you'd accept.'

She made to curtsy but Martin caught her hand tightly in his. 'Nay, Eleanor, y-you must not kneel to me. You are t-taller than I remember.'

Seeing his shy smile and hearing his stammer—not quite so pronounced as it had been when she had first known him— she relaxed and returned his smile. His remarkably attractive face, his skin as soft as a girl's, was marred only by the hint of sulkiness about his soft, bow-shaped mouth. 'I have not grown all that much since our last meeting, Martin. You are not tall, but none the less taller than I remember.'

'You are k-kind, Eleanor. Please believe me,' he said earnestly, 'that I have no wish to rush you into anything you w-will regret, but if you will allow me, I-I would like for us to be married very s-soon.'

His father's eye fell on him like a black cloud. Martin's stammer was a curse and just one of the numerous grievances he held against his son, and watching the boy survey his own fingernails in a lazy fashion and buff them against his doublet only added to his anger. He had known for years that Martin was soft and weak and not like other men, and he doubted he would ever take a woman. People would always take advantage of him.

Lord Taverner would rather pass the estate to John, his

other son, who was five years Martin's junior. He had been hankering after a betrothal between Eleanor and Martin for a long time, and although he doubted the marriage would prove fruitful, he would live in hope that his effeminate son would surprise him and prove him wrong. If not, when John eventually wed he would pass the estate to him and his heirs.

When his father fell into conversation with Lady Sandford, Martin drew Eleanor aside. 'I was so happy when I knew you'd come to live at Cantly Manor, Eleanor, and th-that you'd agreed to marry me. We will be happy, I know we will, and you m-must come to Court. It's so exciting—one can't f-fail to be impressed.'

'Aunt Matilda tells me your position at Court has to do with organising entertainments for the Queen.'

Martin grinned, puffing his chest out like a cock pheasant, pleased with himself. 'I assist Lord Robert Dudley—who as you will know is Master of Horse and Ceremonies, which m-means he is asked to organise all manner of entertainments for which the Queen has an insatiable appetite—masques, banquets, jousts, tennis matches, horse races and masquerades, to name but a few. A most delightful programme of entertainments has been planned for the Court season.'

Eleanor noted how eager he had become and an animated gleam glittered in his eyes. He also had a tendency to babble when he became excited, overcoming his stammer. 'You obviously enjoy your work, Martin.'

He smiled affably enough, yet Eleanor found herself mistrusting it—it was a smile that hid something, and that something she felt instinctively would not be to her liking or advantage.

'I'm h-hardly a member of the inner circle, but I d-do like being at Court—as you will, when we are w-wed.'

'And are you still writing your verse, Martin?'

'P-plays, satires, lampoons. They are all the fashion at Court.'

As Eleanor listened to Aunt Matilda and Lord Taverner making plans for her marriage to Martin, in her breast was a leaden weight and yet at the same time she felt a great emptiness, hollow and dragging her down. She was glad of her own detachment, her sense of disorientation, as if she were watching another woman's agony.

There was a foolish refusal to believe what was happening because it was too dreadful to contemplate—too dreadful to consider a life without William in it—that she would never see him again. And so she tried to blank out of her mind that which was unbearable, but must be borne.

Bear it she did, as best she could, but she felt a curious need to see Catherine again, to offer her condolence for her loss— and no matter what had gone before, she did want her step-sister at her wedding. So, three days before her wedding, accompanied by one of her aunt's ladies and a groom, she rode to Chelsea to visit her stepsister, arriving during the afternoon at the house in which Catherine had lived briefly with Henry Wheeler. It was a splendid, well-proportioned mansion, with a gatehouse that commanded the approach to the courtyard, and the River Thames flowing past the bottom of the formal, terraced gardens.

Eleanor dismounted and handed her horse to the groom. Moving towards the steps at the front of the house, on seeing a stable boy leading a horse to the stables at the back of the house, she paused. The huge chestnut hunter with four equal white socks and flowing blond mane and tail she recognised as belonging to Godfrey. There could be no mistake—and if Godfrey was here, then William was sure to be.

Her heart was heavy as she was shown inside the house and taken to a small parlour to await Catherine and, in all probability, William. To her relief Catherine entered the room alone.

Catherine was sorely chafed as to who would come visiting at such an inconvenient time, and she was unable to hide her surprise on seeing Eleanor. Her initial reaction was one of pleasure, but she quickly recollected herself. Her mouth tightened and an icy coldness hardened her eyes. She would like to show her stepsister the door, to send her back from whence she came. It was the snip she deserved.

Her resentment began to rise as her eyes flickered over Eleanor, noting every detail of her crimson gown and jacket, the way she held her head, the stray lock of hair escaping from her hat and the way she fixed her eyes calmly on her, yet Catherine's resentment was marred by the reluctant pride she felt for her stepsister's courage to stand up to her father and leave Fryston Hall.

However, Catherine had not forgotten how Eleanor had taken off with William Marston and that had upset her greatly. Crushing the green monster beneath the heel of her will, she stiffly smiled a greeting and entered into the proper role of mistress of the house, reaching out to embrace her stepsister.

'Eleanor! This is a surprise. I did not expect to see you here. You must stay for refreshment,' she said solicitously.

Eleanor turned and nodded to her companion, who took herself off to the bay window and seated herself in a bright circle of sunlight to give her mistress some privacy.

'I've come to offer my condolences,' Eleanor said with quiet sincerity. 'I should have written and I apologise for not doing so.' False pleasantries were exchanged as they sat sipping spiced wine and nibbling sweetmeats and small pastries, and it didn't take Eleanor long to realise that Catherine, who was as graceful and lovely as Eleanor remembered, didn't want her here. She would make her visit brief. 'Henry was a good man. I was sorry to learn of his death.'

Catherine smiled blandly and shrugged in a matter-of-fact

way. 'Yes. It was tragic. I told him he shouldn't go on the river at that time of night—he was going to Westminster—but he was determined.'

'And now you are a widow.'

Catherine arched her brows. 'I have no intention of being a widow for long.'

Eleanor looked at her, not having noticed when she had first seen her stepsister how flushed her cheeks were—the flush of passion, and the warm light of desire in her eyes, and her clothes looking as if they had been put on in a hurry. This was no grieving widow, but a woman in the full flush of love. An icy shiver travelled down her spine. The thought that William might at that moment be in Catherine's bedchamber, waiting for her visitor to leave, was too much.

'Being married to Henry was a disappointment,' Catherine told her bluntly, 'and not at all what I expected. He was staid, his mind unable to focus on anything other than his business. When I marry again, it will be different.' She relaxed into her chair, looking comfortably smug. 'With my husband who bored me to death now dead, and out of my father's clutches and an extremely rich widow—and a desirable one, I hope— the whole world lies before me and I can have whatever I want. Already I have my sights set on the man I want.'

'I see. H-have you seen William?' Eleanor asked, trying to make the question sound casual, yet unable to keep the hesitation from her voice.

'William?' Catherine studied her stepsister, her eyes as hard and brilliant as gemstones. Eleanor was poised, her expression calm, but in her eyes there lurked a question, a desperate need to know something that was important to her. Catherine's brows rose as a thought struck her. Was Eleanor enamoured of William, even though he had sent Eleanor's father to the block? Just how close had they become on their journey north?

If this was the case, then perhaps there was much to be salvaged of her revenge by letting Eleanor believe she would marry William after all. It didn't matter that she no longer wanted William. The malicious streak in her didn't want Eleanor to have him either. Her lips curled in a slow, knowing smile, a hard gleam lurking in the depths of her narrowed eyes.

'Why do you ask?'

'I-I have not seen him for some time. He is in London and naturally I thought…'

'That he would come here—now that Henry is dead.'

'Yes. After all, you and he were to have been married once.'

Catherine set her goblet down and let her words fall like a dead weight upon her stepsister. 'We were. We still might,' she lied flippantly.

Eleanor felt her heart sink to the very depths of despair. Catherine's mouth curved derisively, her eyes smoky with vindictiveness. She knows, Eleanor thought. She knows why I have come here. Yes, she knew and now she was exulting in it.

'When I recall the angry confrontation between William Marston and your father at your wedding, I think you will meet firm opposition. Your father will not allow it.'

'My father no longer has any say in what I do or who with. As far as I am concerned, when I decide to wed again then I will let nothing stand in my way. He looks remarkably well, by the way— still the same handsome, irresistible William. The two of you must have become well acquainted on your journey to Yorkshire,' Catherine murmured, feeling very much the victor in this game of hearts.

'No, not really, but we did become friends—of a kind.' Eleanor fought the conflict raging within her, and with a soft, wistful smile she said, 'I hope—after all this time that the two of you will be happy together.' Wanting to get out of the house, she stood up. The last thing she wanted was to come face to face with William, to watch him turn those extraordinary silver-grey eyes on her stepsister, to see him smile that lazy, heavy-lidded smile and address her lovingly, with the engaging charm that he exuded in abundance.

'I must go. It is a long ride back to Cantly Manor and I have much to do.'

'Of course, I understand, but are you not going to ask after my father—your stepfather? Since the blow you administered to his head, he has not been the same. He suffers greatly from headaches and memory loss, and his vision is impaired,' Catherine told her, following her to the door.

'You know how I feel about him, Catherine. Whether he is in this life or the hereafter matters little to me. Your father assaulted me, and it was Sir Richard who prevented him harming me further by rendering him senseless.'

Catherine's eyes opened wide. 'Richard? I had no idea. And did he not try to stop you running away?'

'No—quite the opposite, in fact. He was glad to see the back of me and for the life of me I cannot think why.'

Catherine frowned, becoming thoughtful. 'Then that could explain a great deal of what's been happening.'

'Why so?'

'Father doesn't have a mind of his own these days. For weeks after you left he was so ill he refused to leave his bedchamber. All visitors were turned away. A rumour spread that he had been poisoned, and another that he was suffering from the effects of his latest perversion.'

Eleanor looked at her. 'You don't seem to feel any sympathy for your father, Catherine.'

'Why should I? You of all people should know why I don't. He was—and still is—a bully, and I thank God I don't see much of him. One good thing out of my marriage to Henry was that it got me away from him. Of late he's come to rely on Richard and Richard has made it his business to know everything that goes on at Fryston Hall. He behaves as if he already owns it. He's greedy for power and riches and controls everything, even Father, and Father hates losing command. They're constantly having differences of opinion and have begun to grate together like a couple of rough stones on a fast-flowing riverbed.'

'I am astonished. He always seemed invincible.'

'No one is invincible, Eleanor. He can't remember what happened on the morning you left and truly believes it was you who struck the blow. He will never forgive you for it or for running away. I advise you to have a care.'

'He has already exacted his revenge, Catherine, done his worst,' Eleanor uttered fiercely. 'When I left he sent two of his men after me. They set fire to Hollymead—did he tell you that?—and the most dreadful thing of all was that my uncle, John Collingwood, died as a result of it. Your father is not just wicked, Catherine, he is evil, the most evil man I have ever met and I pray to God I never have to set eyes on him again. Ever. He has blood on his hands and he should be brought to account for what he did, but with all his wealth and power behind him he would find some way to wriggle out of it.'

Catherine was surprised by the savagery of Eleanor's words and for a moment there was accord and understanding between them.

'Then you are right to hate him,' she said quietly. 'I can understand that, and I am truly sorry about your uncle.'

Standing in the open doorway, Eleanor pulled on her gloves and turned to her stepsister. She had imagined how she would feel when it was confirmed that Catherine and William were together, but none of her imaginings had produced the icy calm she was experiencing right now, the complete severing of all emotions, the coldness that left her in control.

'How remiss of me. I quite forgot to tell you my news, which, apart from offering my condolences for your loss, is what brings me here today.'

'Oh?'

'Yes.' She forced a smiled to her lips. 'I am to be married.'

Catherine's eyes opened wide, and to Eleanor's surprise she clasped her hand and smiled. 'Really! Congratulations, Eleanor. Do I know the gentleman?'

She nodded. 'It is Martin Taverner—Lord Taverner of Devon's eldest son.'

'I know Martin. He is often seen with Richard about the Court—and you danced with him at my wedding. I hope you'll be very happy.'

'Thank you. I'm sure we will be. The banns have been called and we are to be married in three days' time. You—will be most welcome, Catherine. It is to be a small affair and I would like you to be there if you wish to come.' She smiled hesitantly. 'You could even be my matron of honour. As yet I don't have one—and who more fitting than my stepsister?'

'I—I don't know.'

'Will you think about it?'

'Yes, yes, I will.'

As Eleanor rode back to Cantly Manor, the calmness left her and her face flamed with fury, but it was also wet with tears. She brushed them away angrily. Tears! Tears for William Marston! That man was not worthy of her tears. That William had been at Catherine's home she had no doubt, and she would like to see him drawn and quartered for what he had done to her.

When Catherine returned to her bedchamber, the naked man lying on her bed stirred his big, strong body from its brief slumber and reached out for her. Quickly removing her clothes, Catherine joined him and sighed as he wrapped her in his huge arms.

'Was it an important visitor, my love?'

'No,' she murmured, kissing his blond-furred chest and smoothing her fingers over his skin. 'It was no one—no one of any consequence.'

Eleanor was immediately forgotten. Never had Catherine desired a man as she desired this man. For the first time in her life she wanted a man in her bed and in her life for her own pleasure. She had never stooped so low as to make love to a servant, but this servant was like no other. This blond giant had aroused strange new feelings, feelings she had never experienced before—not even with William, and she would fight tooth and nail to keep him.

Chapter Eight

Just six weeks after coming to Kensington, Eleanor and Martin Taverner were married in the small chapel at Cantly Manor. Two things happened to disrupt Eleanor's carefully held nerves prior to the ceremony, one of them being delight when Catherine arrived to be her matron of honour, and the other not so welcome, for she came with her father, putting Aunt Matilda in a fluster. Eleanor's stepfather had been invited to the wedding, since her aunt, ignorant of the misery he had caused her niece, thought it only right and proper to have her stepfather present, but he had declined the invitation due to ill health.

Eleanor fought her horror at seeing him, smothering the wave of fear and shock that washed over her. For a moment it seemed to her that her eyes must be deceiving her but it was not long before she knew this was no evil dream.

Turning from him she embraced Catherine, saying how pleased she was that she had decided to come.

Catherine smiled awkwardly. 'You were there for me when I married Henry so it was the least I could do.'

When Aunt Matilda drew Catherine aside to instruct her

on her duties—most displeased that she had left her decision to be Eleanor's matron of honour to the last minute, Eleanor found herself alone with her stepfather. He had lost weight and looked unwell. Beneath his eyes were dark circles and his flesh was the colour of dough, but within the eyes themselves there was fire.

Eleanor's proud, disdainful amber eyes met and held his without flinching. She was discovering, agreeably, that now she was face to face with him, the vague terrors that had haunted her since she had last seen him had vanished.

There was a wintry coldness in Frederick's eyes when they rested on her. 'So you are to be wed, Eleanor.'

'That is the reason why everyone is gathered here today.' Considering the turmoil inside her, Eleanor found her voice was curiously calm.

Taken unawares by the sarcastic tone, Frederick gave a short laugh. 'Will you not share a goblet of wine with me before the ceremony?'

'I would rather sup with the devil.'

His eyes narrowed, sparking with anger, and he moved closer to her, fixing her with his penetrating gaze. 'You should not have run away, Eleanor. You have been missed at Fryston Hall.'

'I hope you do not expect me to return the compliment,' she replied coldly.

'Maybe I was somewhat hard on you, but you drove me to it.'

'How dare you tell me it was all my fault? Was it my fault that Hollymead was set alight, killing one of the most gentle men that ever drew breath? That was your doing, not mine— you murderer,' she hissed quietly.

The unexpected word in the silent corner of the room they occupied shocked Frederick into immobility. His upper lip curled back from his teeth. 'Have a care what you accuse me of, Eleanor.'

'Why did you do it? To teach me a lesson because I spurned your advances?'

'Enough,' he snarled, his eyes darting about the room to make sure they were not being overheard. Others were gathered in groups and conversing quietly. 'You forget yourself. Your tongue is as waspish as ever.'

'Then why did you come to my wedding?' she retorted heatedly. 'What do you want of me that you have not already taken and destroyed? First my mother, and then my uncle,' she said, with a sharp pang of anxiety beyond her control, for the subject was still a painful one.

'Be reasonable,' he said through gritted teeth.

'Reasonable? With you? I don't think so. You are not welcome at my wedding, but since you are here and to avoid any unpleasant explanations I suppose you must remain. Excuse me. I have no wish to prolong this interview.'

Before she could turn away, he reached out and gripped her arm, eyeing her narrowly. 'No? Surely this is a most affecting moment—a stepfather and stepdaughter together again after so long an absence.'

'That will do,' she uttered sharply. 'Have you forgotten the sordid circumstances that drove me from you and what happened at Hollymead?'

An ugly smile slid, like a slick of oil, across his features. 'An unfortunate escapade. 'Tis a pity your uncle got hurt.'

'Hurt? You have the audacity to talk about the murder of my uncle as a mere escapade?'

Frederick shrugged contemptuously. 'If you had been more accommodating, Eleanor, that's all it would have been. It was you that turned it into a tragedy.'

'Indeed! And did I ignite the fire that burned my home?'

Shaking her arm free of his grip, she stepped back. 'You should be brought to account for what you did—like the men you sent to carry out your evil deed. Keep away from me and I will try to forget you and that you were ever married to my mother. Shortly I will be a married woman under the protection of my husband and Lord Taverner. You see, I have taken steps to ensure that I shall be left in peace. I am no longer afraid of you.'

Turning her back on him, she walked away with all the dignity she could muster.

To Eleanor's relief her wedding was a very sedate affair, with few guests outside the family and none of the usual frivolities. As a token of their marriage, Martin gave her a ring—a gold band studded with diamonds and emeralds. She was conscious of how cold it was in the chapel, the ivory-silk wedding gown devoid of warmth.

The responses over, hesitantly Martin put his arms around her and kissed her gently on the mouth. His lips were cool and delicate. That was the moment when Eleanor knew that the ice inside her and the frosted rod that was her spine were cold and impenetrable, and there was only one man who was capable of melting it, of reaching her inner self, and would prevent her from responding to this man who was her husband.

The wedding breakfast was an ordeal for her—made a thousand times worse because of her stepfather's presence, which made it difficult to get through. Catherine, looking elegant and very lovely in a lilac dress embroidered with flowers from the palest lilac to the deepest purple and a lilac hood set back on her head to expose her wide forehead, said very little, speaking only when spoken to. Eleanor quietly noticed how her eyes sparkled and there was a glow about her, a bloom she had not seen before. She looked happy, like a woman in love. With William? she wondered, which only intensified her own sorry situation.

When the wedding breakfast was over the married couple left for Lord Taverner's house in Westminster, which he had taken some years before to be close to Whitehall Palace and the Court. It was a large mansion, elaborately ornamented with decorative plaster and stonework and armorial glass. The house was comfortable and richly furnished and the chamber Eleanor was to share with her husband was hot and stuffy and heavily scented with lavender water.

Eleanor was undressed by two chambermaids who fussed around her, divesting her of her wedding finery, tweaking her hair and smoothing out her nightgown until she wanted to scream her irritation. They were to forgo the bedding ceremony, which was often rowdy, with the wedding party playing games as the couple was put to bed, and Eleanor was thankful for it.

The fact that she was no longer a virgin troubled her greatly, and she didn't know how she was going to explain it to Martin. For a young woman embarking on marriage for the first time, virginity was seen as the highest, most blessed state.

The marriage bed had been blessed by Father Webster who had officiated at the ceremony. The chambermaids turned back the bed covers and Eleanor slipped between the sheets, something like terror gripping her heart, and when Martin appeared in his white linen nightshirt and the giggling girls disappeared, she felt her flesh, which still loved and longed for William no matter how hard she struggled against it, shrivel and recoil from him to such an extent that she wanted to jump from the bed and flee. With a sinking heart she watched him advance slowly towards her. His eyes were on her face, his expression one of nervousness as he studied his bride.

'Eleanor, you must f-forgive me.'

She sat up. 'Martin? What is it?'

'I—I cannot share your bed.'

'Oh?' She stared at him, dumbfounded. Her eyes were wide, as if she could not believe what she had just heard, and she didn't know whether to be relieved or insulted. 'You don't find me attractive enough? Is that the reason?'

'No. P-please don't think that. Eleanor, you are the m-most beautiful woman I h-have ever seen, but—but I cannot bed you.'

'Why?' Already it was clear something was very wrong. 'Is there something wrong with you, Martin? Are you ill?' she asked in alarm. 'If so, I will send for the physician. Maybe he can—'

'N-no, Eleanor. I am not ill.'

'But—our marriage?'

'It was a mistake,' he told her brutally.

'A mistake?' she repeated.

He nodded. 'I—I could not resist you—or my f-father's demands on me,' he said, trying to soften the blow, 'and I now realise I should have done so. What we have is a formal arrangement—n-nothing more.'

'Then why did you agree to marry me?'

'I've told you—t-to placate my father.'

The blood burned hotly in Eleanor's cheeks. Angrily she glared at his pale sickeningly pretty face with disgust. 'To placate your father?' she seethed, throwing back the covers and scrambling to her knees. 'And what about me?'

He looked at her pleadingly. 'Please try to understand. All my l-l-life I've tried to be what my f-father wanted me to be—to be the s-son he wanted, and the harder I tried the more d-difficult if became. I—I'm not like other men—although I'm not d-depraved or degenerate. It used to upset me—until I was introduced to the C-Court and saw there were others like me. That was when I r-recognised who I was and accepted it. I s-sincerely hope that you can too.'

'Is your father aware of your—peculiarities?'

Martin blanched at her choice of word. 'He is not ignorant of any matters concerning me.'

'Oh, Martin, how dare you shame me like this. Little wonder your father was prepared to accept me without a dowry—although I know Aunt Matilda has made a generous settlement to compensate for this.'

Martin shrugged. 'It wouldn't have m-mattered, anyway. The f-fact that you have no dowry is amply c-compensated by my own fortune.'

'You do realise I could divorce you for this—or have the marriage annulled?' An annulment, she knew, was out of the question since she was no longer a virgin, but Martin need never know about that now.

He nodded. 'Please don't, Eleanor,' he appealed. 'I know that what I ask of you is most unfair—but—y-you can take a lover, if you like. I would not object—providing you are d-discreet.'

'How very noble of you,' she sneered. It amazed her that he should even suggest such a thing.

'I can see that you're angry—'

'Angry is not the half of it. I'm furious, Martin.' She was fighting for control of her rage.

'You're entitled to be.'

'How dare you? How dare you do this to me? You should have told me from the start.' Suddenly she couldn't bear to look at him a moment longer. 'Get out, Martin,' she uttered with a sudden rush of malice, her voice like steel. 'Get out of my sight.' He looked as if he'd been stung and she saw the stricken expression in his eyes.

He backed away. 'You don't mean that.'

'I mean every word,' she hissed.

'I'm sorry. I'll s-sleep in the d-dressing room tonight. T-tomorrow I'll stay at the Palace. I have rooms there.'

'Yes, do that, and every night after that. Do not show your face in my bedchamber again. Ever.'

Speech was beyond him. He was white and his mouth clamped tight shut.

It wasn't until he'd gone that Eleanor realised he had been on the verge of tears. She regretted her harsh words and was tempted to call him back, but it was too late.

Resting back on her heels, she stared at the closed dressing-room door for a long time. When she could no longer hear Martin's movements she relaxed and fell back against the pillows. She was amazed how surprisingly calm she felt and enormously relieved, when she should be feeling sick with humiliation, hurt pride and failure. No, she thought, pulling the covers over her and snuggling into the soft warmth, she would not miss Martin in her bed.

It was growing dusk when William and Godfrey stood on the quay at Gravesend, gazing at the thicket of ships at anchor in the Thames, a muddle of stout and sturdy oak hulls, tall masts, ropes and elegant ornamental carvings. The redolent aroma of timber, tar and salt filled the air. A thin mist clung to the dark slick of water, its surface swirl dotted with scum and drifting debris. It was half-tide and the smell of the mud was foul. It seemed to cling to their clothes and hair and seep into their skin. The air was damp, the sound of the water lapping against the stones like a living, creeping thing.

Their gazes were fixed on one ship in particular. It rode at anchor away from the other vessels, rolling slightly with the swell. Its decks were noticeably empty. William shivered. A boat was being rowed towards them, the oars digging deep into the water.

'Want taking out?' the oarsman shouted when he drew close, the boat scraping against the stones.

'Yes, to the vessel at anchor out there. The *Resolve.*'

The oarsman glanced at the vessel and shook his head. 'Can't take you there.'

'Why not?'

'There's fever on board. No one's allowed on or off.'

William's eyes met Godfrey's and they stared at each other. Godfrey could feel William's disappointment and frustration. This had come as a dreadful blow. They turned their attention to the oarsman once more.

'Fever?' William said. 'How many dead?'

'A dozen or more. Six at sea and another half a dozen here. The ship's barred from landing.'

'And the captain?'

'Still running things as far as I can make out.'

Thanking him, William and Godfrey turned way.

'We'll have to wait,' Godfrey said quietly. 'Unless you want the fever there's nothing else for it as I can see. Can you think of anything better?'

William's face was grim. 'Atwood. It's time I called on him. Maybe he can be persuaded to part with the answer.'

When Eleanor and Martin came together, keeping up appearances, they were always civil to one another and as the days passed an easy, close camaraderie developed between them. Martin was nothing but courtesy itself, and more than that. He was thoughtful and charming, and Eleanor displayed an attitude that told him she bore him no ill will.

On her first visit to Whitehall Palace to the west of the city to attend her first social gathering, she was overawed by the sumptuous surroundings. The mass of red-brick buildings covered acres of ground on the river front between Charing Cross and Westminster Hall, and was a veritable warren of rooms and a complex maze of passageways and courtyards and beautiful gardens with trees, arbours and seats. In the grounds there were four tennis courts, a bowling green, a cockpit and a tilt yard.

Lord Taverner led the way to the audience chamber, going by way of the magnificent Long Gallery to show Eleanor the beautiful ceiling painted by Holbein, bowing politely to other lords and ladies finely dressed in velvets and furs.

'At least we can be truly thankful that Elizabeth has a fondness for amusement,' Lord Taverner commented laughingly on hearing the jolly music ahead of them. 'Her Court maintains many interesting activities.'

Martin, splendidly attired in a bronze velvet doublet slashed with gold silk and decorated at the cuffs with count less seed pearls, and cream-coloured hose encasing his slender legs, smiled and murmured a small amen.

Dancing was already in progress, the dancers, both male and female, looking like brightly coloured peacocks. The clothes people wore were now more colourful—purple being much in favour—more flamboyant, with a Spanish influence, than in the reign of Mary Tudor and her brother Edward before that.

Lord Taverner immediately excused himself and wove his way carefully through the dancers, intent on liquid refreshment. Goblets of wine were handed around by lackeys and tables had been laden with every kind of delicacy imaginable. Martin eagerly pointed out courtiers of note—Sir Francis Knollys, the elderly William Cecil, who was the Queen's long-time advisor, Lord Robert Dudley, who was clearly enamoured of Elizabeth and hardly left her side—it was whispered he was her lover and the fact that he had a wife tucked conveniently out of the way in the country did not seem to concern him.

On seeing the Queen for the first time in her life, Eleanor couldn't take her eyes off her. She had always been curious about her, wanting to know what she looked like, this Protestant woman who had inherited the throne from her Catholic half-sister, and who excited so many voices in debate.

Queen Elizabeth, with a large capacity for amusement, certainly knew how to enjoy herself, like her father before her. With her red hair and crimson-and-gold gown, the ruff open at the front so as to expose her bosom, and to allow it to rise in gauze wings edged with the finest lace at the back of her head, she moved about the room like a living, vibrant flame, full of confidence and life. Courtiers' eyes followed her and their whispers discussed her.

Her character and personality were as glittering as the jewels about her throat and the rings on her fingers. The imperious woman swirled around the floor with other dancers, her head thrown back and her lips parted in happy laughter as she was handed from one gentleman to the next.

Eleanor presented a pleasing appearance in her finest tightly laced gown of lime-green taffeta embellished with gold thread and falling over her Spanish farthingale in liquid folds to her feet. The bodice and long hanging sleeves were heavily embroidered, and gold edged the small ruff and cuffs encircling her neck and wrists. Jewels and a fluffy white feather were pinned to her green velvet cap that hid the back of her hair, which was plaited behind her head, but the front was visible and attractively curled at the temples, with a central parting.

She looked exquisite and drew the eyes of many curious and admiring gentlemen. The appearance of a fresh female face at Court always attracted attention, and even Lord Taverner's eyes were seen to pass over his new daughter-in-law several times with a puffed-up pride.

Eleanor loved the bustle and brilliance, the colour, the music and the atmosphere, and the raw, pulsing energy that seemed to emanate from the Queen herself and stalk the corridors and galleries of the Palace. With a sudden stirring of excitement and well-being she had not felt in a long time, feeling quite reckless, she smiled at Martin and insisted he dance the lively volta with her.

It was a boisterous dance, considered bold, if not indecent, a dance much favoured by the Queen. It was unusual in that they moved and turned in a close embrace, with Martin's arm around her waist, and a high-leaping step in which their two bodies were pressed together.

Later, when there was a lull in festivities and the Queen had taken to her royal chair and courtiers ate and drank and gossiped among themselves, her eyes were drawn to a man who had just arrived and dropped down on one knee before the Queen. He was fashionably attired in a heavily jewelled outfit of dark blue velvet, the tunic slashed with scarlet, his long, muscular legs encased in fine black silk hose. The Queen gave him her hand and raised him up, smiling at him warmly.

'See how the Queen favours him,' murmured a male courtier standing close to Eleanor.

The gentleman he was speaking to looked in that direction and eyed the newcomer thoughtfully. 'Striking, is he not? Since he has returned from foreign parts, he has quickly become a great favourite of the Queen.' He chuckled low. 'After brazenly seizing a wealthy Spanish galleon in the Caribbean, she is much taken with him—calls him her pirate.'

'And does he seek a high place at Court, do you think, by hanging around the Queen—as do many hundreds of other "true Protestants" loyal to her Majesty?'

'Not him—he is not the sort. Although I hear he got his property back that Queen Mary confiscated.' The courtier sighed. 'It has to be said that every Protestant in England has business with the Queen nowadays—wanting property back and this and that in payment for their efforts to bring Elizabeth to the throne in favour of Mary. Only trouble is, the royal coffers are depleted and Elizabeth has inherited a poor, dispirited and divided country. Little wonder she receives that particular gentleman like a prince when he presented her with a chest of silver ingots and gold coin.'

Having overheard the courtiers' innuendo, Eleanor gazed at the newcomer with renewed interest. And then she became numb, for his stance, the way he held his head and the thick dark hair curling vigorously into his nape she recognised. It was William, but how could it be? For a moment she doubted, but the moment was short lived. It was only a moment, a moment she spent in a daze of emotions—of joy, bewilderment, hopelessness and despair.

And then he swung round to face her and she felt as though she had been struck dead, unable to form any sort of coherent thought. They looked at one another from across the distance that separated them and once more, as though their minds were linked by some invisible thread, their eyes and hearts spoke to one another.

Eleanor's heart had not stopped yearning for him, hungering for him, no matter how savagely she pushed the feelings away. Her female body was not concerned with what went on in her mind, only the physical need to be close to this man. She knew by his expression that he was not as stunned as she was. In fact, he was not at all surprised to see her at Court. Had he known about her marriage all along?

As she moved slowly towards him he watched her, unable to believe this glorious creature was the same young woman he had taken to his home, the same young woman he had taken to his bed. His spirits had been badly bruised by the knowledge that she had left Staxton Hall, and when Godfrey had told him about Eleanor's marriage to Martin Taverner—

'Inasmuch as you intended to wed her yourself,' Godfrey had said, 'I thought you should know,'—the bottom had dropped out of his world.

In the frozen silence that had followed that announcement, white-hot fury, the like of which William had never experienced before consumed him. Hatred and jealousy had sunk their poisonous fangs into his heart and almost destroyed him. Passing before his eyes were visions of a bewitching, tantalising young woman dressed as a youth riding beside him, Eleanor wanting to despise him, but finding she could not, Eleanor lying in his arms, her glorious wealth of honey-gold hair spread over his chest, kissing him, laughing at him and with him.

Why had she done this? Why had she left him to wed another? He despised himself for his stupidity, for trusting her, for wanting her more than any other woman. But as his anger had waned, suddenly nothing seemed important anymore. Not the future, and not even his revenge on the man who had sent him to spend three years in purgatory. Outwardly he seemed the same, his face impassive, but inside everything had begun to crumble, to break up and bleed, draining the life out of him.

When she stood before him, he inclined his head slightly, his indomitable male pride coming to the fore. 'Madam.'

His voice spoke as if to a stranger. Eleanor's throat swelled with pain. His mouth was set in a bitter line, his black brows drawn in a straight bar across his angry eyes, and she saw how resolute his expression was. The harsh light made him look stern and judgemental. His iron-hard determination, his rigid resolution to treat her as no more than a passing acquaintance, tore her to shreds.

'William! I—I trust you are—well,' she murmured, her nervousness making her stammer almost as bad as her husband.

'Please do not concern yourself with my health, Lady

Taverner,' he said coldly, with emphasis in the saying of her new name. 'I would like to be polite and say that marriage suits you, but your eyes tell me it does not.' His gaze slid to her husband standing several paces away.

Eleanor followed his gaze, feeling suddenly cold. Martin was conversing heatedly with Sir Richard Grey, who was lounging indolently against a window that looked out over the Thames. Aware of Eleanor's attention he shoved himself upright, and with all the swagger of his title and privilege sketched a mocking bow, his legs long and narrow in white silk hose.

Eleanor frowned, for her feelings for this particular gentleman were no different from what they had been when he had been a frequent visitor at Fryston Hall—she disliked him intensely. Sir Richard gave Martin an incriminating look, and she wasn't in any doubt about the nature of his feelings for her husband, and having seen how Martin followed Sir Richard around like a love-sick calf, she wasn't in any doubt about Martin's feelings in that regard, either.

Recalling how Martin had showered attention on her months before at Catherine's wedding and how Sir Richard had watched him covetously, seeing her as a threat, she realised at last why Sir Richard Grey had been so eager to see the back of her.

William's eyes flicked over him and he gave no outward sign that he was in any way affected by Richard Grey, but inside his emotions were roiling and seething with ice-cold fury and contempt. If his suspicions that Grey had worked hand in glove with Atwood to dispose of him three years earlier were proven, then he had a score to settle with that particular courtier, but this was neither the time nor the place for a confrontation.

'Your—husband exercises no regard for a lady, and I doubt his wife will be an exception. He is friendly with Sir Richard

Grey I see, a man as devious and greedy as Atwood, a man who lives only for pleasure—and sordid pleasure at that. Your spouse looks put out about something, Eleanor.' He looked down at her and cocked a mocking brow. 'Trouble in paradise, my love?'

She scowled. 'Don't be impertinent, William—and I am not your love.'

'Trouble in marriage is usually found beneath the sheets,' he remarked sarcastically. 'It has not gone unnoticed that your husband keeps the company of—a certain type of gentleman, that he is favoured by them and that his position at Court was granted in a short time.'

Eleanor's features tightened. 'What are you implying, William?'

'It is true that young men who hang about the Court do seem to improve their station in this manner.'

Eleanor was not unaware of his meaning and wished he hadn't spoken of it. Her cheeks turned poppy red and she looked away, deeply embarrassed. 'Please don't speak of Martin in this way. It it isn't polite.'

A roguish grin curled his lips. 'I don't feel like being polite. How well you defend him.'

'Of course I do. He is my husband.'

Placing his finger beneath her chin, William turned her face back to his. 'In name only, I'd wager.' A smile of satisfaction curved his lips when he saw the truth she was too innocent to conceal in her eyes.

'I—I had no idea it would be so difficult.'

'That's too bad, Eleanor. You should have thought of that before you married him.'

William's voice was bitter and it was clear that forgiveness was far from his heart. He wanted nothing to do with her, his attitude said.

He studied her with the casual interest of a man who meets

a woman for the first time, a woman he does not find particularly attractive, he would have her believe, but in his eyes was a darkness, a darkness that concealed his innermost thoughts and his emotions.

Eleanor searched his eyes for something, to see something of the tenderness he had shown her. There must be something, there had to be, but those incredible silver-grey eyes only stared back at her, cold as a block of ice and without emotion and memories of tender kisses and passionate embraces they had shared at Staxton Hall. Determined not to make a fool of herself, with her heart breaking, she lowered her eyes and bobbed a small curtsy.

'Excuse me. My—husband is beckoning.'

William's eyes looked right through her, as if he didn't want to see her, and then he moved on.

Turning slightly, when Eleanor's gaze lighted on Richard Grey she caught a look of intense hatred on his face as he stared at William's retreating back. It was so virulent it stunned her. Then an instant later it was smoothed away and she wondered if it had been her imagination or even a trick of the light.

Having seen Eleanor exchange words with Lord Marston, Martin left his friends and his comfortable vantage point at the refreshment table, where he was able to supply himself with a never-ending amount of wine, and came to her. 'You are acquainted with Lord Marston, Eleanor?'

'You know I am, Martin,' she replied, her tone of voice one she would use to a tiresome child. 'I stayed at his house with his family when I was in Yorkshire. I did tell you.'

'Yes, of c-course. I do remember. Then would it not be p-polite to introduce me?'

'I think not. Lord Marston has left.'

'Then come. The Queen wishes me to present you to her.'

* * *

Tired of dancing and feeling she could stomach no more of the jollities and that she must have some fresh air, making the appropriate excuses Eleanor set her glass down and left quickly. She was not given a second glance by most of the courtiers—it was not uncommon to see someone leave to go outside, away from the closeness of the crowded and over-heated room. The corridor was empty and mercifully cool. Suddenly, to her left, a door, already ajar, was opened farther and a hand shot out and pulled her inside a small room.

'At last,' a voice growled. 'I was beginning to think you'd never leave the revelries.'

Her cheeks aflame with indignation, Eleanor spun round to see William closing the door. 'William!' She stared at him in bewilderment, feeling strange and momentarily tongue-tied. He had clearly been waiting for an opportunity to confront her, but what could he have to say to her that wasn't unfavourable? As he towered over her his face was furious.

'If you have anything further to say about Martin, then you might as well let me have it and have done. If you are annoyed by—'

'Annoyed!' he roared, flinging his arms wide and rest-lessly beginning to pace the wooden floor, his boots resounding loudly. 'God above, Eleanor, annoyed doesn't begin to describe what I am feeling. Will you tell me what in hell's name you were thinking of to marry that—that lame excuse for a man?'

Eleanor paled. 'Have a care what you say, William.'

'Have you no sense? I hadn't been gone from Staxton Hall two minutes before you left. Why in God's name did you do it?'

Her lips tightened. 'Please don't blaspheme. I find it offensive.'

'Blaspheme! Damn it all, Eleanor, you'd make an archbishop blaspheme. What the devil possessed you to marry Martin Taverner of all people?'

His unprovoked attack caught her on the raw. Her face went white but on each cheekbone was a vivid splash of scarlet. Her eyes glittered and narrowed like those of a cat and her anger increased to a madness as explosive as his.

'And why shouldn't I? I have every right to do as I please. Since when did I need your permission to leave your house and return to London?'

'When your uncle placed you under my authority.'

'Your authority? You are not my keeper, William. You never were. My *husband* is. I am no longer your concern.'

Raising his brows slowly, tauntingly at her, a contemptuous curl to his lips, he said, 'Had I a glass I would raise a toast to you. Your beguiling beauty and vulnerability had me fooled and quite undone for a time. When I left you at my home I truly thought you would be there when I returned.'

'What? Waiting for you? You conceited beast. Did you really not stop to ask yourself why I returned to London?'

'Tell me. I would like to know.'

'There were several reasons—the main one being that I loathed myself for being so weak and stupid that I succumbed to your seduction. You of all people! My father's betrayer! I must have taken leave of my senses and you will never know how much I hated myself. Your mother told me I was welcome to stay at Staxton Hall indefinitely, but I could sense her disapproval of me. I considered that under the circumstances and to salvage something of my pride it was best that I left. You also knew Martin wanted to marry me, so it should not have come as such a surprise.'

'Damn you, Eleanor,' he growled, 'it was. I never thought you would do something so stupid. You might as well have sold your soul to the devil when you married him. You know what he is and because of it he will drag you down to his level—the gutter.'

Eleanor drew back in the face of his harsh attack on Martin. 'I—I know he prefers the company of men to that of women—as do many other gentlemen at Court it would seem—but he is kind and generous to me.'

'Like hell he is.' A murderous glint appeared in William's eyes. 'But why the rush to marry him? Why not wait for a better offer?'

'From whom? You? And what could you offer me, William, tell me that? Married to Catherine, it would certainly not be anything decent. Your whore. That's what I would be, and condemned because of it.'

William's face showed his astonishment. 'What the hell are you talking about? And what has Catherine got to do with any of this?'

'Oh, stop it, William,' she flared, beside herself with anger. 'Stop it. Don't pretend you don't know.'

'Believe me, I don't. It would seem you are accusing me of something that is quite beyond me for the moment.'

'Then why don't you tell me the real reason why you left Staxton Hall in such a hurry?'

William's eyes narrowed. His anger that had diminished a moment before resurrected itself and he glowered down at her upturned, furious face. He was not a man to be taken to task about anything, and though he wanted this woman and knew he always would, he was not about to let her throw her weight about like a Billingsgate fishwife.

'I seem to recall telling you that it was personal. When I want to tell you more, I will—though why you should feel it is any concern of yours, I cannot imagine.' His voice was icy and his lean face darkened ominously, as though daring her to question this statement.

'You're right. It doesn't matter to me. Nothing that concerns you matters to me anymore—just as it shouldn't matter to you why I left Staxton Hall to live with Aunt Matilda.'

'You told me you didn't want to live with her, implying that she was a tyrant. What changed?'

'You did. I've given you one good reason why I went to my aunt, and another was when you left me and refused to tell me the true reason. I believed you were an honest man, not a liar and a cheat,' she accused harshly—and though she did but know it, unfairly.

William's hands shot out and gripped her upper arms with such force she swore she would have bruises tomorrow. 'Is that so?' His eyes were slate-grey, his voice cracked with outrage and ugly with menace. 'And what of Martin Taverner? Is he not a liar and a cheat? Did you marry him in good faith, blind to his sexuality—nothing that could be called decent?' he snarled, repeating her own words. 'Or did he reveal all?' Seeing her wince, his expression hardened. 'I thought not. But now you do know and because of your reckless stupidity you have a lifetime of regret—unless, of course, you apply for an annulment.'

'An annulment?' She stared at him in absolute disbelief. 'I cannot believe you said that. Is your memory really that short, William, that you forget it could not be proved that Martin and I have not shared a bed in our entire marriage? It is thanks to you that I am not as pure as driven snow, but used goods. To his credit, Martin was honest with me. To my shame I could not bring myself to be honest with him.'

'And had your husband been so inclined to take you to his bed on your wedding night, he would have known you are too innocent and inexperienced and not clever enough to simulate a virgin's first night. How would you have explained that?'

'Unfamiliar with the kind of world you inhabit, I really have no idea.'

Eleanor wrenched herself free of his grip so furiously she almost fell over. Nevertheless she lifted her head imperiously and William Marston felt the blood flow hot in his veins and the heat of it warm his belly with wanting. She was as dear to him now as she had ever been. When he had first been told that she had married Martin Taverner, the shock of it had hit him right between the eyes like a physical blow. He had thought that with the passing of time he could put her out of his mind, and yet he had come here to Court with no other reason than to see her once more, unable to stay away.

Already he was tired of the tedium and the extremes of Court appearance, but with unfinished business to take care of and not wishing to be too far away from Eleanor, he would not return to Yorkshire just yet.

Eleanor's small chin squared up to him and her eyes, a clear shade of transparent amber, warned him to keep away from her. 'Whatever happens in my marriage is my concern, not yours.'

William watched her spin round in anger and walk blindly away from him, her full skirt swaying defiantly. Opening the door, she turned and looked back at him.

'Be sure to give Catherine my regards, won't you? You deserve each other.'

Before she could pass through the portal the door had slammed shut in her face.

'Eleanor, do you mind explaining to me what you meant by that remark? What has Catherine to do with anything? I cannot understand your foolish reasoning that she is at the bottom of this tangled mystery you seem determined to weave and this temper you are in.'

Eleanor flung herself round to face him, unable to contain what was in her mind, and he was not to know that it had been simmering in her ever since she had read the contents of that letter.

'Temper? Temper, you say?' Moving away from him, she stood in the centre of the room with her back to him, her hands on her hips, her breathing deep and uneven. Then she turned and looked at him, her face expressionless.

William was leaning against the door frame, his arms crossed over his broad chest. His mind and senses were bemused by her, by the way the sun's rays slanting through the window mingled in her bright hair curled at her temples, streaking the copper and gold. He felt a sudden puzzlement as to why all this had happened and why Eleanor had made it so complicated. Who gave a damn about Catherine, for God's sake? Catherine was in the past and meant nothing to either of them.

'Has it not occurred to you what you have done to me?' she flared, glaring at him as he continued to lean casually against the door. His face was blank as he watched her, but in his eyes was a spark that said he was not as calm as he appeared. 'How could you? And how long will it be before the two of you finish what you started all those years ago and get married?'

'Married? What the hell are you talking about?'

She tossed back her head and William was alarmed to see not only anger, but what looked like a mixture of contempt— and was it, could it possibly be anguish?

'I know that now Henry Wheeler is dead you, and Catherine are back together. Why—you couldn't leave Staxton Hall quick enough to be with her, could you, William? In fact, there was something quite distasteful about the way you hurried to her side.'

'What?' Totally bemused, he unfolded his arms and his long lean body rose to its full height.

'You heard. You're not deaf.' She laughed bitterly. 'And there was I, simpleton that I am, thinking you no longer loved her, because if you did you would not have seduced me.'

'That's enough,' William snapped, striding across the floor to stand ominously in front of her. 'First, I did not seduce you and, second, I do not love Catherine, and, if you must know, I never did.'

'No?' she scoffed. Drawing herself up straight, she thrust her chin out and met him eye to eye. 'I do not believe you, for you were giving a fair imitation of it when I called at her home before I married Martin. I know you were there, William, cosily ensconced in her bed. I know. What were you doing—laughing at me—laughing harder together when I'd gone?' Her face was white now, and her eyes seemed huge and much darker in their setting of long, narrowed black lashes.

William shook his head in disbelief, his face showing his astonishment. 'Unless you tell me what all this is about I cannot answer your accusations over what I know nothing about. I don't know where all this is coming from, Eleanor, but it appears to me that you have got things terribly wrong.'

'You would say that. Next you will be telling me you weren't with Catherine when I called.'

'I wasn't.'

'Don't you even attempt to deny it, you—you louse. You were there. I know you were, hiding away in her bed.'

'How?' he demanded. 'How do you know it?'

'Because I saw Godfrey's horse.'

William cocked his brows in bemusement. 'Godfrey's horse?'

'Yes.'

'Where?'

'A stable boy was leading him away.'

'He was?'

'Yes.'

'And because you saw a horse you recognised as belonging to Godfrey, you assumed I was there too.'

'You had to be.'

His face assumed a mixture of amazement and a certain tendency to smile, though the latter did not materialise since the look on her face told him he was swimming in stormy waters. 'I did? Did Catherine say I was there?'

'Well—no,' she replied, beginning to shift uncomfortably, 'but she didn't have to.' William was so self-assured that she was beginning to suspect that things were about to go dreadfully wrong and everything would fall down about her.

'She didn't?'

'No—she—she was—flushed and…' She gave him an exasperated look. 'William! I am not naïve. I—I know what a woman looks like when…'

'She is in the throes of passion?' He laughed softly. 'What a foolish little idiot you have been.'

As the truth finally unfolded in its entire cruelty, Eleanor's heart hammered beneath her ribs. She stared at him, as though having difficulty understanding any of this. 'William, I thought…'

'It makes no difference what you thought. You should have made sure of it before giving yourself in marriage to Martin Taverner—although, believing I was the traitor I have been painted and unable to forgive me for betraying your father, you'd probably have married him anyway. But that aside, because of that one misunderstanding when you imagined I was with Catherine—of which you had no proof—you married Martin Taverner.'

'No, it was more than that. When I asked Catherine if she had seen you, she told me she had, and she led me to believe the two of you would be married.'

William's eyes darkened and his expression became grim. 'Catherine did that?'

Eleanor nodded. 'And I believed her.'

'It was wrong of her to do that. I did see her on one

occasion—briefly. It was a chance encounter. I did not seek her out.' He sighed deeply. 'And because of this you drew the only possible conclusion. Is there anything else?'

'There is a great deal else. You see, before that there was the letter—the letter the messenger brought to Staxton Hall.'

'Ah, yes—the letter. I recall there was a mention of Henry Wheeler's demise, but the main content of the letter was something entirely different. That was the reason why I left Staxton Hall. It had nothing whatsoever to do with Catherine.'

'Then—what was Godfrey's horse doing at Catherine's house?'

William was looking at her with an amusing 'don't you know?' look in his eyes, and then as the truth dawned on her she shook her head as though in disbelief at her own foolishness. The very idea of Godfrey and Catherine was ludicrous. 'Oh! You—you mean Godfrey and Catherine were…?'

Raising his brows, his face creasing in a smile of dry humour, he nodded. ''Tis an unlikely partnership, I agree, but they are besotted with each other—and Godfrey is an experienced ladies' man.' He leaned against the edge of a table and, arms folded, watched her. 'Now we have the matter of Catherine cleared up, I think it's time to take care of the rest.'

'What are you saying?'

'That whatever you have been told and whatever you believe, I did not betray your father.'

Chapter Nine

Eleanor stared at William. She felt as though she'd been felled with one blow. 'But—that was what I was told.'

'By Atwood?'

'Yes.'

His smile was grim. 'One should not believe all one hears, Eleanor. It may create the wrong impression.'

'Are you saying that you had no part in my father's downfall? None whatsoever?'

'I did not betray your father, Eleanor,' he told her with quiet gravity. 'I swear it on my life.'

There was a moment of silence between them. Eleanor felt her resentment fading. Looking into that strong face she felt an uneasy stirring of doubt.

'Your father was a good man,' William continued, 'an honourable man, who was not afraid to stand up for what he thought was right, what he believed in, and I respected him greatly. Contrary to all Atwood told you, we were friends—good friends. What happened was not of my doing—and perhaps if he'd held his tongue and gone about his scheming quietly, he might have kept his head. I would have laid down my own life for him. Please believe that.'

Eleanor took a deep breath, feeling the truth of his words. 'Yes,' she whispered. 'I do believe you. Were you party to the same plot?'

'I had knowledge of it, but refused to take an active part. Unfortunately my innocence was never proven, and because there was an element of doubt my properties were confiscated and my mother and sisters thrown on to the mercy of relatives.'

'And you were banished.'

William's lips twisted with irony. 'No, I wasn't. But no doubt Atwood told you that, too.'

'Yes. What did you mean when—when you confronted my stepfather at Catherine's wedding, when you said he got what he wanted when he married my mother—that he had planned it all along? What you said puzzled me.'

William looked straight ahead, his expression grave. 'It pains me to speak of this and I know it will pain you more. I must tell you things you do not like to hear.'

'How so?'

'Atwood coveted your mother and resented her being married to your father. Somehow he found out that your father was involved in a conspiracy to prevent Mary Tudor marrying Philip of Spain and planted one of his own men among the conspirators—a spy—to play a double game.'

A cold shiver ran down Eleanor's spine. 'Are you saying my stepfather was responsible for the conspiracy being blown wide open—knowing they would all be executed—and then—he—he befriended my mother?'

William nodded. 'I'm afraid that's true.'

'I am truly horrified. I had no idea. So he, my father's own cousin, sent him to his death—although it should not surprise me after what he did to Uncle John. Poor Father. He did not deserve that. You also told my stepfather that he would pay for what he did. I didn't know what you meant by that—but now I do. I realise now that for some perverse reason of his own my stepfather wanted both me and Catherine to think ill of you and, I am ashamed to say, he succeeded—at least where I was concerned. Catherine was not so easily persuaded of your guilt, but then she knew you better than I. Have you spoken to my stepfather since?'

'Not yet, but I intend to.'

'You will find him much changed—he came with Catherine to my wedding and I was shocked by his condition. His deterioration started with the blow to the head Sir Richard gave him. In fact, he's so weak and forgetful that he's had to resign his office as alderman. So if it's vengeance you seek, then you will be wreaking vengeance on an old and ill man.'

'Maybe, but he has the answer to a question that continues to elude me. There is one ghost to be laid and I want an answer. So,' he said, capturing her gaze, 'there we are, Eleanor, and now what's to be done?'

'That's the trouble, William. There is nothing to be done.'

'Nothing? Even now, knowing what you do, you mean to remain married to Martin?'

'It's too late. Martin is my husband until death.'

'Martin Taverner is nothing,' William said with a savagery that surprised Eleanor. 'He is nothing. You are mine, Eleanor, and I mean to have you. I made up my mind that night you spent in my bed, in my arms, that you would never belong to any other man but me. I thank God Taverner is what he is and that he hasn't touched you, because if he had I would have had to kill him.'

'Then why didn't you tell me?' Eleanor cried, her voice rising on a crescendo of terrible pain, unable to believe he was saying this to her now when it was too late. 'You should have told me everything.'

'I should have, I realise that now, but I thought we had time.'

'What happened?'

'The letter—that's what happened. There was a…development…here in London.'

'And you couldn't tell me? Could you not trust in me? I swear that I would never betray your confidence.'

'No,' he said sharply, thinking, 'not after suffering alone for so long'—it would be like sharing his soul. 'When my mother wrote and told me you had come to London, I made up my mind to see you, to talk to you about the future.'

'We have no future, William.'

'And you have no future with that—that catamite. It would seem you are at an impasse, my love. You are mine, Eleanor,' he said with enormous gravity, 'and I mean to have you.'

'Stop it, William,' she whispered wretchedly. 'Don't torture us both like this.'

'I will, when you leave Martin Taverner.'

'There can be no going back, and I swear if you continue like this I will leave London.'

'And go where?'

'Devon, which is where the Taverners live.'

'Then all the more reason for me to speak to him and I shall tell him that you and I are lovers.'

He spoke with the arrogance and certainty that said that it would do her no good to argue. But she would not be dictated to, not by William or anyone else. Her head lifted imperiously and her eyes were a vivid flash of amber in her flushed face. 'You mustn't. Don't you dare.'

'But I do dare. I dare to do anything I like, Eleanor.'

She turned to the door, not wanting to stay to hear more—she could feel her body responding, straining towards him, yearning to give in, to have him enfold her in his strong arms and kiss her into oblivion.

'Go away, William. Go back to Yorkshire and get on with your life—and let me get on with mine. Leave me in peace.'

'Refuse me all you like, but I am not going anywhere. At present I have an apartment here at the Palace. Oh,' he said, leisurely sauntering towards her, 'and if you should think of fleeing to Devon, I will come after you. It's no good fighting me, my love, you should know that by now. I will have you, one way or another.'

Hands clenched, Eleanor strode quickly along the corridor.

'Eleanor! Eleanor, wait. I've been looking for you.'

Hearing her husband's voice, Eleanor stopped and turned round.

Martin hurried towards her, seeing her anger. 'Eleanor? W-what is it? What ails you? What has h-happened to upset you like this?'

'Nothing that concerns you,' she bit back. 'What do you want, Martin?'

'I thought you should know that I shall be s-staying here tonight.'

'Really?'

'You don't mind?'

'Mind? Martin, I don't care,' she cried, enunciating each word.

'But—'

'Do what you like. Go back to your fancy popinjay,' she cried, throwing her hands in the air in exasperation. 'You always do what you want anyway, but do not embarrass me again when I am with you. Ours might not be a love match in any sense of the word, but I am your wife and surely deserve your respect. There was none in the way you flaunted yourself with Richard Grey. Your conduct was disgraceful and not to be borne.' She bitterly resented his unacceptable conduct as much as she resented the triumph she had seen in the Richard Grey's eyes when he had looked at her.

With her eyes spitting fire and her jaw rigid, Martin wondered what on earth had got into her. Reaching out, he placed his hand on her arm, which she snatched away as if he had burned her.

'Don't touch me,' she snarled, her eyes blazing. 'Don't you ever touch me again.'

Without more ado, as if she couldn't bear to look at him, she was about to hurry away, but something in his expression reached out to her, appealed to her and made her pause. In the silence that followed Eleanor felt no longer enraged, but baffled by Martin's passiveness that she now recognised as dignity. On a sigh she went to him and took his hand.

'Martin, I—I know you are infatuated with Sir Richard, but—'

Martin said something about being sorry and she must believe him but he hadn't wanted to hurt her.

She smiled and squeezed his hand. 'I know you didn't.'

'No, Eleanor—please l-listen—I know you w-won't understand, but—'

'I understand perfectly,' she said. 'I've been so naïve. I suppose this has been going on a long time—with Sir Richard.'

Embarrassed he nodded. 'A few months.'

'Then take care, Martin. Stay away from him. He is dangerous. I don't trust him, and I should hate you be hurt.'

'I won't be. P-please don't worry about me.'

Although Eleanor had parted from William in anger, she could not help but take pleasure in knowing he was near. Suddenly she felt a great lightening of her mood and her natural optimism returned. The relief and gladness she felt knowing he did not betray her father was enormous. She was aware of a new sensation in the pit of her agitated stomach. She was honourably married, and even though it was not to the man she wanted, her husband was wealthy and she had lovely clothes and jewels to wear and she had access to the Court and its many pleasures. And tomorrow there was to be jousting to enjoy.

The day dawned bright and Eleanor looked ahead with excitement. When her maid had dressed her in her favourite gold taffeta gown with its high stiff collar enriched with gold lace, she looked in the mirror and was startled, for she looked changed somehow—in fact, she felt different. Her high white forehead and the delicate arched eyebrows looked exactly the same, but there was renewed colour in her cheeks and her eyes and mouth had acquired a softness that had been absent for weeks. Was this the result of seeing William again?

When she arrived at the tilt yard with Martin, jousting had started. The colour and pageantry had her transfixed.

'Is this your first joust?' a stout lady of mature years enquired. When Eleanor nodded, she patted the bench beside her. 'Sit beside me where you can see well. I'm Lady Louisa Durban, and I shall enjoy your company for the time it takes.'

Thanking her effusively, Eleanor sank down, perching on the edge, her eyes wide with wonder as Martin stood with a group of gentlemen discussing the joust.

The Queen and her chattering group of waiting women were already seated in the royal box, Elizabeth in the centre like a dazzling queen bee in her green and gold and ropes of pearls draped around her neck. Eleanor's eyes were drawn back to the lists as there came a roar from the spectators. At either end of the yard two men in armour atop powerful chargers appeared and pulled down their visors on their helmets and took their lances.

'What's happening?' Eleanor asked, seeing several laughing ladies lean forward to give the worthy knights of their choice their colours.

'Lord Robert Dudley is about to sally forth,' Eleanor's companion chuckled. 'Listen how the crowd shouts for him—and that flower in his helmet shows he has the Queen's favour.'

It took skill and good horsemanship to avoid being thrown by a blow from the opponent's lance, even if the blow was softened by the angle and the splintering of the lance. The two opponents thundered towards each other at breakneck speed, lances poised and aimed at the opposing shields.

'They'll kill each other,' Eleanor gasped, hardly able to watch.

'No, they won't, but one of them might be injured when he's knocked off his horse.'

Unconsciously Eleanor held her breath, waiting for the crash of wood on metal, and when it came she gasped out loud and with everyone else shouted with approval when the favourite knight prised his opponent out of the saddle while his horse whinnied wildly and reared back on its haunches.

'Lord Robert Dudley is a worthy knight indeed,' Lady Durban cried, getting to her feet to show her appreciation.

The victor raised his visor and smiled broadly at his adoring public, before looking at the Queen. Elizabeth, obviously delighted with the outcome, stood up and clapped her hands.

And so the afternoon wore on and Eleanor was completely lost in the excitement of it all. When she distinguished a tall knight in brightly polished armour take his helmet from his squire and mount his huge horse, her heart did a somersault. It was William, and he was looking at her. She felt a pleasant warmth. For a second, no more, all the special feelings she held in her heart for this man were revealed as though it were something that was impossible to hide. They looked at each other, neither of them speaking, their eyes locked.

William had seen Eleanor, poised, provocative and glowing with colour, the minute he'd entered the tilt yard. With a spirit of mischief and a desire to tweak Martin Taverner's nose, without more ado he rode up to the barrier in front of the platform where Eleanor was seated. He looked directly at her and smiled lazily.

'Greetings, Lady Taverner,' he said, bowing his dark head. 'Will you not honour me by allowing me to wear your colours?'

He looked devilishly handsome, his dark hair tousled and a roguish gleam in his silver-grey eyes, which gazed only at Eleanor.

She turned poppy red at being singled out so publicly, knowing all eyes were focused on her. She stared at him, not knowing what to do and afraid of doing the wrong thing.

'Come, Eleanor, a token is all I ask. Won't you give a poor knight your favour?'

In confusion, Eleanor turned beseechingly to the lady who had befriended her, seeking her advice.

Lady Durban smiled, her gaze openly sweeping the handsome knight with appreciation, her eyes twinkling with merriment and something akin to lust. 'Do as he asks, Lady Taverner—unless a knight wears your colours already.'

'No—but…'

'Then I would think that lovely scarf around your neck will do nicely,' she suggested.

Entering into the spirit of things, Eleanor, her heart beating fast with excitement, stood up. Placing her scarf on William's proffered lance, she watched it slide slowly down the pole. Taking it and placing it to his nose, he smelled her familiar scent, and then with a smile and a knowing wink and a twinkle in his eye he attached it to his breastplate. Placing his helmet on his head and lowering his visor, he spurred his horse and cantered away.

The Queen herself had watched the touching by-play between the handsome knight of the merry eyes and charming smile and Lady Taverner with amused interest—

and so had Eleanor's husband, but there was no amusement in his expression.

While Eleanor saw nothing wrong with making William Marston her knight in earnest, believing there was nothing improper in this public display of attention to a married woman, that it was all part of the game and not to be taken seriously, Martin, however, was of a different opinion and he did take it seriously.

His eyes narrowed as he looked at the gold streamer that fluttered from Lord Marston's breastplate and then slid to his wife, whose expression was rapt. Lord Marston's opponent was Robert Dudley, which made the joust doubly interesting to the crowd of spectators. The Queen's favourite was tall, but Lord Marston was taller.

Eleanor watched as the opponents lowered their heads and charged at each other. Lances clashed and then there was wood on metal. Both contenders remained in the saddle. They ran the course twice more, fast and furious. Robert Dudley's lance splintered and his squire handed him another. They were both masters of the game but William was the victor.

Amid thundering applause Robert Dudley, his dignity lost, lay sprawled on the ground. On his prancing horse, William Marston removed his helmet to reveal his laughing face.

'That was bad luck for Dudley,' Lady Durban remarked to Eleanor. 'First time I've seen him bested—in front of the Queen too. Your Lord Marston is a champion indeed.'

'He is not my Lord Marston—merely an acquaintance.'

The look Lady Durban gave her told Eleanor she did not believe her for one minute.

William rode towards her, holding her gold scarf. Eleanor rose, reaching out her hand to take it back.

'It brought me luck,' he said. 'May I keep it?'

Eleanor was about to tell him he could when the shadow of her husband appeared behind her.

'I would be obliged if you would return it to my w-wife, sir.'

Eleanor turned to her husband with irritation. Having lost his passiveness Martin set his mouth in a sullen, angry line. 'I don't want it back, Martin,' she told him sharply. 'Lord Marston can keep it.' Turning from her husband's thunderous face, she smiled at William. 'Congratulations, Lord Marston. You did well.'

Behind her Martin paled before he turned his back on her and walked away.

'Oh, dear! Pity your husband isn't jousting, Lady Taverner,' Lady Durban laughed amusedly, 'then they could settle the matter in combat. What an interesting spectacle that would be.'

Eleanor looked at her companion and gave her a conspiratorial smile. 'My husband would be no match for Lord Marston. I doubt he would be brave enough to mount his horse, let alone wield a lance.'

'I said you must be discreet, Eleanor,' Martin said crossly when they were in the carriage taking them home. 'I did not th-think you would flaunt yourself so openly before the entire Court.'

Eleanor could feel her self-control slipping. 'Flaunt? You should know all about that, Martin. It's what you do all the time.'

'You are my w-wife and there is going to be no scandal,' he flared, choosing to ignore her taunt. 'Do you understand that, Eleanor? No scandal. And that means no d-divorce. My father would not allow it. It's going to be a civilised arrangement—whereby you will go to Devon and live as my w-wife should. There's nothing unusual in this,' he said when she shot him a dark look. 'Many gentlemen l-live at Court while their wives live in the country taking care of household m-matters.'

'And children,' Eleanor bit back coldly. 'They take care of children too, Martin. But children are to be denied me—are they not?'

Martin shifted uncomfortably, as he always did when she referred to his preference for the same sex. 'I am w-what I am—I can't help it. But now you are my wife you will do everything p-possible to preserve our—arrangement, and outwardly be a devoted wife to me.'

Having little stomach for argument, Eleanor looked out of the window, unable to see a way out of Martin's 'arrangement' that stretched ahead of her without end.

Frederick Atwood could not still the ache in his head. The pain came and went before it became a pounding agony. Since the blow had been struck by Eleanor before she'd run off to Yorkshire, the headaches were a part of him now and he had grown to accept them—just as he had grown to accept his mistake in making Richard his heir. But that didn't mean he had to like it.

Frederick thought he could ride with the best of them, but his nephew surprised him—greedy parasite that he was, who thought he had a right to take that which would belong to him before his time.

Frederick had come to Chelsea to visit Catherine. He was seated on the terrace with his head leaning against the wooden trellising behind his chair a servant had brought outside for him, when suddenly a shadow appeared between him and the sun. His mind still heavy with sleep—he slept a lot these days—he raised his lids. It took a few seconds for his eyes to focus properly, and when he recognised the man looking down at him his blood turned to iced water.

'Marston!'

'Indeed, Atwood. I thought it high time you and I talked. It wasn't difficult tracking you down.'

Frederick looked round wildly and the empty terrace did nothing to reassure him. He stared at Lord Marston for a moment then, his face pale, his jowls quivering in agitation. With difficulty he rose from his chair.

William watched him struggle to his feet, seeing a man who in the last four months had shrivelled to a man whose strength had been eaten away by bitterness and ill health.

'What do you want, Marston?'

'Do I have to spell it out? I want the name of your conspirator. When you consigned me to hell, you didn't do it alone.'

Anger rose like a hot tide and Frederick asserted himself to support it. 'You're right. Had it been up to me, you would be dead.'

'But it wasn't, was it? And I am the sort that clings to life.' William took a step closer, his eyes cold and unrelenting. 'When I began visiting Catherine at Fryston Hall, it didn't take long for me to see what kind of ruthless swine you were in your dealings with others.'

'Aye, most of them out to cheat me. They deserved everything they got,' Frederick rasped as he made an intense effort to control himself, even to keep his voice from shaking. He chafed beneath Lord Marston's relentless gaze, whose sureness and composure were disquieting.

'And your bullying didn't stop outside your house, that I know. Not content with abusing your wife, you turned your attention to her daughter when she died. You're a lecherous, conniving beast, Atwood.' Here his voice fell a shade quieter, but not so quiet that the quivering wreck of a man in front of him didn't hear the accusations thrown at him.

'I've my own ideas as to why Eleanor ran away from Fryston Hall. She was a frightened young woman and I know what terrified her so much that she was driven out of your house—where, in her desperation following the execution of her husband, her mother had brought her, believing she would be under your protection. Dear God, it was like throwing her to the wolves.'

A sneer twisted Frederick's lips. 'She was a disobedient girl, too stubborn for her own good.'

'Who stood up to you, Atwood, and you didn't like that, did you? When you found her ready to flee, you forcibly tried to prevent her—until your nephew rendered you senseless.'

Frederick stared at William in disbelief, trying to keep his brain clear and cold enough to think. Unfortunately he'd been unable to unravel just what had happened when he'd tried to prevent Eleanor fleeing. He'd been heavily under the influence of liquor, which he'd downed the night before. Even for him the indulgence had been excessive and he had truly believed Eleanor had struck the blow that had knocked him senseless.

'Richard? It was Richard who did that?'

'I think you've been living under a misconception that it was Eleanor—and for his own perverse reason it is to your nephew's advantage that you believe that, but it's time you looked closer to home for the culprit.'

Frederick was shocked by the revelation. He felt sick. A wave of nausea washed over him. 'He wouldn't.'

'Take it from me that is what happened. Like me, Eleanor knows you for the bastard you are. It didn't take me long to know how your mind worked. And so I became a threat—in particular in your dealings with Edgar Collingwood, who was a close friend of mine—as was his wife, Marian, a lady you had coveted for years. In order to get what you wanted, you conjured up a clever plan to get rid of both Edgar and me for good—but when it comes to killing you are a coward, Atwood, so you got some other villain to do the deed. For Edgar it was the Queen's executioner, for me you had other methods.'

Frederick's face flushed and fury blazed from his eyes. 'If

it's vengeance you are seeking—to make me suffer—then do your worst, Marston.'

William looked with scorn at the devil who had so very nearly destroyed his life. 'Suffer? You don't have any real conception of what suffering is, Atwood. Besides, look at you. You're pathetic!' His eyes became piercing, pricking his adversary like barbs. 'I want the name of the man who had me beaten to within an inch of my life and hauled me aboard what could only be described as a death ship. He knew what he was condemning me to and gained pleasure from it. Who was it, Atwood? Your nephew?'

Frederick shook his head and gripped the arm of the chair he had vacated for support. Beads of perspiration had broken out on his forehead. 'No—no, it wasn't him. Now go to hell, Marston,' he hissed, looking away, but not before William had seen something akin to fear shadow his eyes.

William didn't believe him, but it was clear that the fear and agitation inside Atwood was so great that there was no way he would dare betray Sir Richard Grey.

'I think you're afraid to speak out about what you think of your nephew, Atwood, such is the hold he has over you.' A faint, sneering smile twisted his lips. 'It's remarkable how the conscience can be silenced when one is afraid. But worry not. I have other means of finding out, and when I do, the man who hauled me aboard that ship will rue the day he did not kill me instead. As for you—you will go to hell, Atwood. The devil will get his due.'

Eleanor had been married to Martin for one month when she knew she was pregnant. She realised that ever since she had missed her monthly flow that she had put her predicament aside, refusing to believe her suspicions, to allow herself to dwell on it or face up to it, until she was able to cope with it.

It was as if she were trapped in some kind of dilemma and her stunned senses chose to put to the back of her mind the fact that she was carrying William Marston's child and that she had married someone else. And so, in this daze of wretchedness and uncertainty she had blundered into, it was quite devastating—a shocking outcome to one night of indescribably wonderful love.

Thankfully, as yet, she suffered none of the discomforts she had heard about in early pregnancy, apart from enlarged and sore breasts, as if she were being pricked with pins, and already she was having to slacken the laces in her stiff bodice. If she carried on putting on weight at the rate she was doing, she would be as fat as a toad before she gave birth.

What was she to do? What would Martin say? He would say that she was a wanton, a strumpet, carrying the child of one man while married to another, and she could not pretend the child was her husband's since he had never shared her bed.

It wasn't as difficult telling Martin as she had thought. At first shock registered in his face as he tried to take in what she was saying.

'A child? Why did you not tell me b-before?'

'I married you under false pretences, Martin. I was carrying another man's child—though I did not know it at the time.'

Martin looked at her, alarmed, and sat down. 'You are with child! Then you've l-landed us in one hell of an ugly m-mess.'

'No more of an ugly mess than the one you presented to me on our wedding night,' she reminded him sharply.

Martin fell silent, staring at the carpet for several moments, deep in thought. His silence bit keenly into her nerves.

'I have been honest with you, Martin. You are the only person who knows what I have said. It is now your decision what happens to us entirely.'

'It's a c-catastrophe, I admit,' he said at length, 'b-but it need not be a d-disaster.'

'What are you saying?'

'That it could work out to our advantage.'

Suddenly, looking at his animated features, Eleanor felt hope dawn and her despair recede.

Martin smiled delightedly. 'W-we agreed to play a charade so that this marriage would remain untarnished before the w-world. The charade will continue. Y-you say no one else knows so your ch-child will become our child and no one will be any the wiser. My f-father will be well satisfied and cease p-pestering me for an heir. In fact, he will be quite overjoyed.'

'Even though the child is not a Taverner?'

'He'll never know the truth. When you begin to show you will go to D-Devon and await the birth.' He stood up quickly, rubbing his hands in a pleased way. 'Of course the child—be it a boy or a g-girl—must never be told it is not mine. It would c-cause the child great distress if it understands it's a b-bastard and create immense complications.'

'Then we must make sure the child remains in ignorance,' Eleanor whispered, trying not to think of William and how he would react should he ever discover the truth. It was also strange, she thought, that Martin hadn't asked who the real father was.

A glorious June day dawned with dazzling sunlight. It was to be a day filled with entertainment, starting with a sail on the river. When Martin arrived at the house to accompany Eleanor, the despondency and concern over the child had lessened, and when they arrived at the river, she was feeling almost gay again, hopeful of seeing William.

The Thames was seething with activity. With streamers and pennants fluttering in the warm breeze, barges and pleasure boats of every description, filled with courtiers, musicians and sightseers eager to catch a glimpse of the Queen and her lords and ladies, had already taken to the water, making a kaleidoscope of colour.

Martin was in a particularly exuberant mood and Eleanor saw why when she spotted the striking figure of Sir Richard Grey leaning against the rails of the spacious yellow and tan barge they were to occupy. With one hand on his hip, his gaze abstracted, his smile charming as his eyes lighted on Martin, when they shifted to Eleanor he stared with open hostility, and, after giving her a curt nod, he ignored her completely—much to her relief.

'I might have known *he* would be here,' she retorted scathingly. 'You knew he would be, I suppose.'

'But of course.'

'This was to be a day of enjoyment, Martin—for me as well as you. Knowing how I feel about Sir Richard, please don't embarrass me.'

Laughing lightly, Martin took her hand and raised it to his lips gallantly. 'Jealousy b-becomes you, Eleanor,' he remarked, his eyes sparkling with excitement on being in close proximity to his handsome lover, 'but do try to keep it under c-control. Richard is s-sensitive about such things.'

'Richard Grey can go and drown himself in the river for all I care,' Eleanor snapped crossly.

Martin chuckled softly, his face alight with pleasure. 'You are rather hard on him.'

'I find him unbearable—and he obviously feels the same about me.'

'He c-claims you are a bad influence on me.'

'I am your wife, Martin, and expect better.' Turning her back on him, she abruptly dismissed both her husband and Sir Richard Grey from her thoughts. She was determined to ignore her stepfather's nephew and not let him spoil her day. She was enchanted with the whole colourful and vibrant spectacle and she was going to enjoy every minute of it.

As the barge joined the other boats in a flotilla keeping a steady pace with the royal barge, settling among some cushions at the back of the barge, her hair spilling about her head in loose waves of the softest silk, Eleanor just knew it was going to be a peaceful, idyllic day, a day of rest and relaxation that would suit her mood perfectly. Glancing sideways at the water and sipping a goblet of wine a page boy handed to her, she breathed in the smells that wafted from the river. Closing her eyes, she placed the goblet beside her and turned her face up to the sun and let its warmth bathe her face, hearing the gentle splash of the oars and the water lapping at the hull.

Aware that someone had come to sit beside her, half-opening her eyes, she squinted into the sun's glare, seeing the face of a man looking down at her, an incandescent halo around his dark head. Closing her eyes once more, a smile playing on her softly parted lips, she breathed a sigh of deep contentment, knowing William—handsome, magnetic, exuding that fierce sexual allure he always had—was close. Just to be near him was enough.

'William!' she murmured through her slightly parted lips. 'I am astonished. Knowing of your dislike for Court pleasures, I had no idea you would be present.'

'Liar. You knew perfectly well I wouldn't be far away from where you are.'

Her lips quirked in a teasing smile. 'Are you trying to make my husband jealous by any chance?'

'I consider your husband a nonentity, my love, who can be easily got rid of with very little effort.' Settling himself against her on his side, he leaned on one elbow and gazed down at her lovely face. 'I see he is with Richard Grey.'

'I know. I've seen him. No doubt he will monopolise Martin for the entire day. They eat together, drink together—'

'Sleep together?'

Her lips twitched and she giggled softly. 'If it suits Sir Richard's purpose, they will. Apparently he took Martin under his wing when he arrived at Court and he has been there ever since. You must have noticed how Martin constantly strives to please him, to impress him and win his approval, while Sir Richard treats him with a patronising superiority that is often embarrassing to witness.'

'You are extremely observant, Eleanor.'

'When it's under my nose day in and day out, night after night, how can I not be? I sense that man despises all women, that he considers them inferior creatures to be used when necessary and then coldly dismissed.'

William chuckled. 'And your husband?'

'Is of the same opinion. He would like to keep me subdued and in the background.'

'And you refuse to be kept out of sight.'

'Absolutely. I'm liking Court life too much to be banished to the country just yet. For the first time in my life I am enjoying myself as never before and am reluctant to leave it. It's only a temporary state of affairs and I'm sure that in time I shall tire of it and find it all as tedious as you do. I suspect it would suit Richard Grey if I were to disappear and retire to the country. He considers me an intruder, a threat to his friendship with Martin.'

'And does that bother you?' he asked, the whisper coming close to her ear as he smoothed her tumbled hair between them.

'I don't care in the slightest, even though I feel he could happily strangle me every time he looks at me.'

'I'm relieved you don't have the same effect on him as you do on me. Have some more wine,' he said, signalling to a page boy to refill her goblet.

'Are you trying to intoxicate me, Lord Marston, so you can have your wicked way with me?'

He gave a wry smile. 'The thought is tempting, but I wouldn't dream of it.'

'No? Now why don't I believe you? I know you have a yen for me,' she murmured, settling herself more comfortably among the cushions.

'As you have for me, my love,' he whispered.

Eleanor squinted up at him, her rosy lips trembling with gentle humour. 'Don't flatter yourself.'

He smiled a crooked smile, his eyes dark with ardour. 'You're looking exceptionally lovely today,' he said, wanting to lean over and place his lips on hers, to caresses the creamy swell of her breasts rising out of her stiffened bodice.

'I do my best.'

'You had something in mind?'

She smiled provocatively and half-opening her eyes, her gaze settled on his handsome visage. 'I might.'

The strumming of a lute playing a love song drifted by on the same gentle breeze that stirred her hair. She sighed and continued to look up at William. A smile quirked his lips and his eyes shone silver in the bright light of the sun, and she had a feeling he was playing some kind of mischief. People were giving them curious glances, but the sounds coming from the other boats and their own was a shield for what they said to one another.

William tweaked a lock of her hair between his finger and thumb. Warm light softened her features and there was a dreamy, faraway expression in her eyes. Her gown was of saffron silk that made her skin glow like summer cream and lit her hair with a multitude of copper and gold lights. William found it virtually impossible to stop looking at her. He watched her at Court, becoming distracted when her melodious laughter rang out. He found himself captivated by it and the infectious joy and beauty of it. It was music to his ears and it glowed in her magnificent amber eyes.

Eleanor was both exquisite and unforgettable. He realised it as clearly as he realised she was utterly irresistible and felt his bones melt when he saw the soft flush in her cheeks, the gentle curve of her neck, the stubborn tilt of her chin, the way her body swayed when she walked across a room, vibrant and strong. He found himself wanting to kiss her senseless, to feel her melt in his arms, to taste those lips once more. Heat burned in his blood. This was madness. Why was Eleanor different from any other woman he had known? Why did it feel different? Why was he tormenting himself like this when she was his for the taking?

'You have a peculiar look in your eyes, my love,' he murmured, wondering how she would react if she knew the path along which his mind travelled. 'One would think you were in an amorous mood.'

'Perhaps I am,' she murmured, settling herself more comfortably among the cushions.

'Would you like to do something about it? It could be arranged,' he said in suggestive tones.

'Then perhaps you should.' She gazed at him, a challenging look in her eyes.

'And your husband?'

'As long as I am discreet he won't care a fig.'

'He said that to you?'

'Mmm. On our wedding night.'

'And you accepted it?'

She shrugged. 'It's not the normal state of affairs in a marriage, I know, but ours is an unconventional marriage, and since I don't have any kind of feelings for him it really doesn't matter. In fact, when I discovered he was indulging in unmentionable vices with another man, I was relieved.'

'Are you never tempted to pack your bags and leave him?' William asked, brushing a lock of hair from her cheek.

She frowned up at him crossly. 'Please don't start that again, William.'

'I shall carry on until you face up to the fact that you have made the worst mistake of your life and discuss with me how you can get out of it.'

'Sir Richard would love that—you hanging around.'

Sitting up abruptly and draping his arm over his raised knee, William scowled darkly, his anger simmering just beneath the surface. 'To hell with Grey.'

Eleanor laughed lightly. 'Now you're cross, but I refuse to let your grumpiness spoil the day.'

'Eleanor, I will not leave London until you come with me,' he told her boldly. 'I want you to be my wife.'

Eleanor's mouth fell open and she began to laugh derisively. 'Your wife? How can you do this? That you should say this to me now! It's too late for me.'

'It is what I want, what I wanted when I left Staxton Hall and hoped you would be there when I returned.'

'But how can I be your wife when I am someone else's wife? I am not free, William.'

'A divorce.'

'Martin would never consent to a divorce if such a thing were proposed.'

'So you will waste the rest of your life with him?'

'If I must. Part of the marriage service does require the participants to promise "till death us do part." I always abide by my promises.'

They fell silent. William studied her, thinking there was something different about her, that she looked different somehow, her cheeks flushed, rounder. His gaze strayed to the contours of her breasts pushed up from the stiff bodice. They

too seemed rounder, fuller. On the whole she seemed remarkably relaxed and content.

'I have to say marriage suits you,' he remarked harshly.
'You are positively blooming with good health. If I didn't
know better, I would say your marriage bed has proved fruitful.'

His words, spoken with unsuspecting lightness, jolted
Eleanor out of her languor and her eyes snapped open, locking
on to his. For what seemed to be an eternity they remained so,
neither of them moving or scarcely breathing. Although there
was music and laughter and the conversation of the people
around them, there was stillness and silence about them.

William broke the spell. 'You are, aren't you, Eleanor?'

'I am what?' she asked, her heart in her mouth. She had
never been any good at subterfuge.

'With child.'

Swallowing hard, she turned her head away. Quickly
getting to her feet, she stood, holding on to the rail of the barge,
her heart pounding in her chest, feeling the breeze blowing off
the water cooling the heat in her cheeks. William stood beside
her, looking down at her with barely contained anger.

'Has he touched you? I couldn't bear the thought of you
making love to anyone else but me. I went through hell when
I heard you had married. Has that vile excuse for a man touched
you, Eleanor—taken you to his bed? Tell me, damn you.'

She spun her head round and looked at him. 'Martin hasn't
bedded me, if that's what you mean—not once.'

'And you are with child. For God's sake, Eleanor,' he
hissed, keeping his voice low so as not to be overheard by
those within earshot, 'tell me.'

'Yes, yes, William, I am,' she blurted out. 'There, now
I've told you.'

'It's mine, isn't it?' he demanded.

How could she deny it? If she did, he wouldn't believe her.

It had to be his since she hadn't once shared a bed with her husband. She nodded. 'Yes, but you have no rights.'

'Damn you, Eleanor, I have every right. Does he know?' She nodded.

'And?'

'He—he was angry at first—'

'I bet he was.'

'But then he realised that it—it…'

'Might be a blessing in disguise—and keep his father happy, that he has managed to produce an heir, if it's a boy, when everyone doubted he had it in him.' His words dripped with sarcasm and his eyes were hard and uncompromising. 'I'll be damned and in hell first before I let any child of mine be raised by another man—and especially not by a damned catamite. You are mine. You may have married Taverner, but you belong to me. You know that, don't you?' His voice was very angry and very serious. It was not a question, but an order.

Eleanor looked at him, knowing it was true. He was the first man she had known and the only man. He had put his masculine mark on her and she was his until death. He knew it and so did she, but it was futile. Martin was her husband and she could see no way out.

William observed her face was flushed with some emotion. 'What is it?' he demanded to know, his voice harsh with disappointment. He had expected her to comply to his wish that she divorce Martin Taverner, delight, even, that he wanted her for his wife, not what oddly looked like offence. Just as he had thought everything was going to be all right, that she was going to agree on what he hoped for, despite the furore and scandal that would ensue, she had turned truculent and he was damned if he could see why. She was carrying his child. It was right that she should divorce Taverner and marry him.

Eleanor looked ahead at the royal barge and the splash of

the oars as the rowers kept pace to the soft beat of a drum. William said he wanted her for his wife and how easy it would be to agree to all he suggested, to let him take charge of everything and put things right, but why, oh, why did he not tell her he loved her? Why could she not feel he was doing it for her and not the child that had been conceived out of their need for each other?

'As usual, William, in your high-handed belief, you are taking it for granted that I must give up on my marriage and marry you, is that it?' Her voice was flat and empty.

'Is there something wrong with that?' His voice was mocking and his eyes gleamed sardonically, though he was white lipped with anger. 'Am I to have no say on the matter on how my child is raised?'

'What is there to say?' She felt him withdraw from her and his face registered outrage.

'Are you telling me you will stay with him? What the devil for? You don't love him.'

'Very few husbands and wives do, and since we cannot agree, William, I am going to talk to Lady Durban. There is to be a banquet later, followed by a masque and dancing—and even a fireworks display. Will you be there?'

'I have more important things to do that hang about Whitehall,' he ground out.

'Very well. Please excuse me.'

His anger fierce and knife-edged, loving her, hating her, wanting her, sweeping her a shallow bow, he turned his back on her and went to speak to an acquaintance, well away from her.

Chapter Ten

Eleanor was disappointed that William didn't attend the lavish banquet in the Stone Gallery later, where guests could look down upon the river and when darkness fell would watch the fireworks display that was planned. Suddenly the sparkle had gone out of her day.

She found the banquet long and tedious and the masque, heralded by a slow peacocking pavane, dull, and so, tired of watching nymphs, imps and shepherdesses and a temple of gods posing and stepping gracefully to the strain of the music, and in no mood for dancing, she was about to slip away when a page boy brought her a note telling her that, if she would take a turn in the privy garden, she would find a surprise awaiting her. The note was unsigned, but she did not need a signature. Feeling certain that the note was from William, her spirits revived and she hurried outside.

Dusk was falling and the gardens were deserted. Walking quickly along the paths, she gazed about her, looking for William. When the tall, lean figure of Sir Richard Grey suddenly appeared from behind a yew tree, she stopped and stared at him with dismay.

For a moment she was paralysed. 'Sir Richard! You startled me.'

'Forgive me, Lady Taverner. It was not my intention.'

His voice was silky smooth and it sent a chill down Eleanor's spine. 'If you are looking for my husband, I last saw him enjoying the dancing.'

He was watching her, his brown eyes intent, his head tilted slightly to one side. 'I know. On this occasion it is you I wish to see, not Martin.'

Eleanor looked at him coldly. 'You sent me the note.'

He nodded.

'Why?' Her voice was frankly sceptical and impatient.

'Don't be impatient,' he said in a bored voice. 'I thought it was time you and I had a talk.'

'Talk? Really, Sir Richard, I hardly think you and I have anything in common to talk about.'

'You are wrong, we have much in common, you and I. When you married Martin I found it difficult to believe you were the same Eleanor who graced Fryston Hall. Who could have imagined—'

'—that the daughter of a traitor would finish up at the Court of Queen Elizabeth? Neither my stepfather, your uncle, or I, certainly. But here I am. Destiny is a strange thing, is it not, Sir Richard? Please tell me why you have brought me out here. Somehow I don't think it's for a friendly chat.'

Sir Richard did not flinch. His face remained expressionless, though his eyes were hard. 'I will speak plainly. You asked Martin to stay away from me.'

'That's right, I did.'

His lips curled in a sarcastic smile. 'Why? You're hardly likely to suffer a broken heart merely because you sleep alone every night.'

'You're right, I won't.'

Richard Grey was completely at ease as he addressed her in a bell-like voice that held a blend of dislike and reproach. 'I do not have to tell you that Martin's happiness is a first with me. To achieve this, I would do and say anything I wish to make quite sure that you understand me.'

Eleanor lifted her head, her eyes flashing with indignation. 'I do not care for your words, sir. Say what you have to say. I am impatient to go back indoors.'

'Martin and I would like you to go to Devon. We think it would be for the best.'

'What you really mean is that *you* think it would be for the best if I were out of the way.' She smiled thinly. 'I'm afraid not. Before I acquired a taste for life at Court, the idea of leaving London held some appeal for me. But no longer. I'm happy here.'

'That's a pity.'

'Is it?' She tilted her head to one side and looked at him coldly. 'Do you feel jealous of me? Do you feel so threatened by me, a mere woman, that you must put a distance between my husband and me?'

'Not in the slightest. I merely want you out of the way. You—could be forcibly taken down to Devon.'

Colour flooded into her face. 'Do you dare to threaten me?'

'I would not presume. Say rather that I am warning you.'

'Warning me of what, Sir Richard?'

He smiled. 'There are some unhappy people, madam, men and women,' he said, his tone menacing, 'who have paid with their freedom—and some with their lives—for offending me. You should remember that the Taverner estate in Devon is very remote, and unpleasant things can happen in remote places.'

Eleanor paled. 'Martin would never be a party to anything so base, so—so vicious.'

He shrugged. 'Maybe not. He is a gentle soul, is he not? But I would, should you prove difficult.'

Eleanor observed the hard glitter in his eyes and her own snapped as a cold shiver ran down her spine. She repressed a grimace of disgust. 'You would harm me?'

'Believe me, I would not hesitate. But of course there is a way to avoid any unpleasantness. If you were to go to Devon, there would be no reason why you could not take a lover. Martin would have no objection, and neither would I.'

'How dare you! What I do has nothing to do with you.'

'Martin says you would like children.' He looked at her coldly. 'That's unfortunate.'

'It is?'

'Martin is incapable.'

'Is he? And how would you know that?'

'Because he has an aversion to women—in that way, you understand.' A salacious smiled played on his lips. 'Come, Eleanor, you must know all about him by now.'

'Oh, yes, I do know and I understand. But it is not for you to say how Martin and I conduct ourselves in our marriage.'

'It is when Martin's happiness is at stake.'

'Then how do you account for the fact that I am with child?' The divulgence was reckless and the second the words had left her lips Eleanor regretted them, but it was too late to withdraw them. 'Do you really know Martin that well, Sir Richard?' She laughed derisively, tossing her head haughtily, her dominant self-respect springing into life. 'I really do wonder about his taste in friends.'

Sir Richard's eyes narrowed, his lips drawn tight against his teeth, and he glared at her with fierce eyes. 'You lie.'

'I do not, sir. Martin is delighted, naturally. You must ask him. Oh, dear,' she remarked, her eyes dancing with ironical amusement, 'it would seem Martin has made a fool of you— and on his wedding night, too,' she lied uncharacteristically, but because his manner riled her she was unable to resist the jibe. 'I wonder why he didn't tell you—unless, of course, he's afraid of you, afraid of what you'll do.'

His mouth became set in a bitter line, his eyebrows drawn in a straight bar across his furious eyes. There was utter silence. He stared at her and for one brief moment Eleanor sensed his overpowering jealousy and rage. All trace of blandness was wiped from his face and she saw the violence shimmer in every line of his frame. It was then that fear struck her, a fear so profound that she froze when he took a step towards her.

'It was you, wasn't it—you who tempted him, you bitch.'

'I didn't have to. A man is entitled to make love to his wife, is he not?' Her speech was cut short by the sound of a woman's laughter close by. Others had come out to stroll in the gardens before darkness fell. 'Smile, Sir Richard. We are being looked at.'

A flash of cold anger in his eyes, he smiled, but it was a forced smile and he hissed at her between his clenched teeth, 'You think you are clever, don't you, and that you can outwit me. Think again, madam. I shall not forget you.'

Eleanor smiled her sweetest smile, even though she felt her face would crack beneath the effort. 'You are too kind. For my part, I shall make sure I forget you.' And with this parting shot, she walked off, a slender, graceful figure disappearing into the twilight, her saffron silk gown swirling out behind her like a wave.

But despite her outward calm she felt a deep disquiet. As she had turned from Richard Grey, there had been something about his expression that caused her heartbeat to accelerate. Suddenly she was frightened for Martin and she found that fear, in the person of Sir Richard Grey, still went with her. Quickening her steps, she was annoyed to find her legs were beginning to tremble.

She fully intended finding Martin to warn him of the danger, but when she entered the Palace she was thrown off balance when William, in a midnight-blue doublet with a short cloak hanging from his left shoulder, stepped in front of her. His sudden appearance sent everything else from her mind.

'You,' she gasped.

Mocking silver eyes gazed back at her, glinting like hard metal. 'Yes, Eleanor. It is indeed.' Suddenly William's face took on a look of gravity. 'I came to find you because I have some news to impart that concerns you.'

'Oh?'

'Atwood is dead, Eleanor. He hanged himself.'

Everything inside her froze. Although she felt no exultation, overwhelming relief flooded through her, leaving her weak and thankful. 'I am surprised. But why would he take his own life?'

'If that is what he did.'

'What are you saying? That someone killed him?'

'It's possible—and made it look like suicide, although there was no evidence to incriminate anyone. It is widely known that he had many enemies who wished to see him dead.'

'God knows I would not have had him die, but, whatever the truth of it, I cannot feel regret that he is dead. While ever he lived, the threats he made would not go away.' She looked at William, wondering what was going through his mind. 'But what of you? You had a score to settle with him, as I recall.'

He shrugged. 'It is better this way,' he said tonelessly. 'He—or someone else—has saved me the trouble of killing him. He's paid dearly for his villainy.'

'What will you do now? Will you leave London?'

'I intend to, but his death does not mean it is over. There are still matters I have to take care of—one other as evil as Atwood to dispose of.' He looked at her, moving closer, his eyes holding hers. 'There is one other urgent matter to be settled. It would seem you are under my skin, my love, because I could not leave with this thing unresolved between us.'

'William,' she cried, 'how can it be?'

'By God, Eleanor, it can be and you will listen to me,' he said fiercely. When she was about to walk away, his hand shot out and clamped tightly about her lower arm, halting her. 'Do you think I like doing this to you? If it comes to hurting Martin Taverner or denying myself what is rightfully mine, then Taverner can go to hell. He is not the father of the child you are carrying. I am, and I want my child. I will have it no other way.'

'But he cannot be dismissed so lightly or so easily. He is my husband and he will say the child is his. William, where is the proof that it is not?'

'If you think Taverner can get past me to separate me from what is mine, then let me assure you that he will not yet have seen such a fury that I would display should he try.'

Eleanor bent her head in a gesture of absolute despair, her hair falling across her pale face. William moved forward and, lifting her chin, placed his lips gently on hers.

'I'm sorry to be such a brute, my love. Come with me now to my apartment and we will talk sensibly. It is at our disposal and I can guarantee we will not be disturbed.'

She stared at him, her mind empty of all but the thought of William—alone with her in his apartment. A place where no one would intrude—empty of anything other than them.

Taking her hand he quickly led her through the maze of corridors of Whitehall Palace, away from the royal festivities. Courtiers swept by and bowed in their direction, but William paid them no heed.

His apartment looked out on to the river, where crafts of every description sailed to and fro despite the falling darkness.

Eleanor looked around the room they were in, with its gilded furnishings and the high bed with its embroidered crimson-and-gold hangings and valances.

Locking the door and lighting the candles, William turned and faced her, and before she knew it she was in his arms, the long days and weeks of separation finally ended. He touched her face, then cradled her cheek, then he kissed her and there was a trembling deep inside. The smell of him, the taste of his mouth, overwhelmed her. It felt as if the endless weeks of their being apart, weeks of aching loneliness, fell away in the space of mere seconds.

Releasing her, William quickly unfastened his doublet and removed it. Eleanor stood in silent fascination, watching him. He glowed with energy, strength and vigour, his muscles flexing beneath his white lawn shirt, his broad chest covered with dark hair. She could feel the heat of his body close to hers as he stood looking down at her, and her whole being reached out to him, yearned for him to take hold of her in his powerful arms once more and possess her as he had before.

Without words or questions and with the infinite patience of a true lover, slowly and gently he began to undress her, patiently unfastening the lacings on her stiff bodice and removing the wire hoops that supported the skirt of her gown. Then he knelt before her and removed her shoes before rolling her silk stockings down her long legs, sighing over every inch of flesh as it became exposed and placing tantalising kisses here and there, before he laid her back on the bed.

Resting his arms of whipcord strength on either side of her he leaned over her, his wonderful silver eyes caressing every curve of her body, expressing his obvious delight in the gentle curve of her belly where their child was growing.

'You are so beautiful,' he whispered huskily, lowering his body to hers. Her skin tingled as his flesh pressed to hers just as she remembered it. 'You are just as beautiful as I remember—more so now you are with child.' He sighed deeply. 'We have all the time in the world, so let us take advantage of it.'

Reaching up to brush his lips with a kiss, she let her hands slide up over his chest, a finger tracing the line of his strong jaw. His mouth touched hers again, at first demanding, then sweet and achingly tender. She closed her eyes in rapture and her neck arched backwards when she felt his lips on her breasts. They tingled and swelled at his touch, the ripe nipples rising to meet his lips, eager for him. She raised her hands and her fingers slid to the back of his head and gripped the thick cap of his hair with pleasure before one hand stole over his shoulder, halting at the feel of a raised scar on his back. It was a healed wound, and how and when he had acquired it she had no idea, but, reluctant to explore further, she fastened her hand in his hair once more.

Giving herself up to total abandon and revelling in the pleasure he was giving her as his lips kissed the smooth swell of her abdomen, his long, lean fingers holding her waist, pausing now and then to murmur intimate, sensual endearments, she moaned, her emotions soaring even higher, her excitement for what was to happen next uncontrollable, and she wanted him to take her immediately.

When she could bear it no longer, his passion rising to meet hers and fully roused, he pulled her close to the hard, naked heat of him and she felt the rigid thrust as he entered her. Her response was spontaneous and incredibly enveloping, and when she half-opened her eyes to see his face, the passion in his eyes was fierce and frightening. Powerful, conflicting emotions, dammed up for weeks, burst out like a flooded river bursting its banks, gushing forth in a dangerous torrent.

A husky moan escaped her and with her heartbeat throbbing in her ears, her blood flowing through her veins like a liquid flame as he drew out all her suppressed longings that surpassed the first time they had made love, it was far more profound and she could deny him nothing.

Once again he showed her the true meaning of sensuality and passion. What she was doing was dangerous, immoral, even, for was she not committing adultery? And should she not be feeling shame and guilt? And yet William's caressing hands, his mouth devouring her own, his powerful body pressed against hers, gave her no time to consider the sin she was committing, condemned by the church and a crime against her husband.

In the glowing aftermath of their loving they lay for a precious moment in one another's arms. With their limbs entwined they were oblivious to the world outside, only the sound of the river traffic and their breathing disturbing the silence of the room. Turning towards her, William stroked her hair streaming over his shoulder in a mass of contrasting shadows, his lips brushing her warmly flushed cheek.

Eleanor lay as one drugged in his arms, arms that warned her that though he might be gentle and tender, they would never let her go. Rousing herself from the delicious torpor that enfolded her, she sighed, her eyes fluttering open.

William smiled and his rather grave face softened with tenderness. 'I wonder why you fire my blood as no other woman has done, my love. I fear I am quite besotted with desire for you. What is your secret?' he murmured. 'I swear you are a temptress, a witch, out to entrap me.'

Her smile was sublime as she reached up and traced his cheek with the tips of her fingers. 'There is no secret, William. I am neither witch nor temptress. I am myself.'

Taking her hand he placed his lips in the palm of it. 'And a rare creature you are, Eleanor, an incomparable, precious being who has this new life on the way, the woman who is to bear my child—a son, naturally.'

'I'll do my best,' she murmured, laughing softly, 'but you may have to be content with a girl.'

'Or both,' he murmured, nuzzling her ear with his lips.

'Both?' Eleanor became alert. This was something she had not considered.

William laughed, amused by the astonishment that sprang to her eyes. 'Twins, my love. Twins do seem to occur with a frequency in my family that is often quite alarming.'

'They do?'

He nodded, his eyes shining with devilment. 'Not only are Jane and Anne twins, but my mother, also. She has a twin brother—she stayed with him in Pickering when our property was confiscated. He has twin boys and my grandmother was a twin. So you see, my love, it is possible that you too shall have two babies instead of the one.'

Eleanor considered this seriously. She did seem to be putting on weight at an alarming rate—but twins?

'Well—we shall have to wait and see, William, but—two babies? You are pleased?' she asked demurely, trying hard to blank Martin from her mind and what this would do to him and their marriage, for she knew William would never walk away and leave his child or his children and forget them.

'Need you ask? I am delighted—in fact,' he said, leaping out of bed and walking over to a small table by the window and filling two goblets with wine, 'let us drink the health of our child—or two, whatever the case may be.'

Turning back to her, about to hand one of the goblets to her, he froze, unprepared for the stunned expression on her face or the horror that stared out of her eyes. 'Eleanor? Are you not well? What is it?'

'Your—your back?'

A small shiver that had nothing to do with him being naked ran up William's spine, and then, sighing heavily, he placed the goblets back on the table. Wrapping a scarlet velvet robe around his powerful body, he came to sit beside her on the bed. 'It's not a pretty sight, is it?' he murmured, taking her hand.

'But—but what happened to you?' The flesh on his back was a hideous mass of scars and welts caused by a whip. She swallowed hard and, squeezing his hand with both her own, she looked at him. 'William, don't you think it's time you told me exactly where it was you disappeared to for the three years you were absent—and what monstrous cruelties were inflicted on you to cause such disfigurement?'

'I have never spoken about it. Only Godfrey knows the full story. He was part of it.'

'Did you not go to Geneva, which was where many Protestants escaping persecution went?'

He shook his head, a bitter twist to his mouth. 'Geneva! There was no such luxury for me.'

'Then—where did you go?'

'Let's just say I went to foreign parts—through no choice of my own.'

'Why? What do you mean? Are you saying you were banished by the Queen after all?'

'No. By Atwood—not Mary Tudor. One thing I soon realised was that where Atwood leads, there follows a long trail of treachery and disaster.'

'Did you know him well before you met Catherine?'

'No, in fact we had never met. I got to know Catherine when I visited friends in Clerkenwell. They had a daughter, Margaret. Catherine and Margaret were close friends. I approached Atwood to gain his permission to court Catherine. He had no objections—in fact, he was enthusiastic about a union between us.'

'You—fell in love with Catherine?'

He considered her words carefully before he replied. 'I thought I did—at the time. It was later that I began to realise that what I felt for her wasn't love. Catherine was—suitable—eminently suitable to be my wife. We suited each other, yet when we were apart I didn't yearn for her—in fact, there were days when I didn't even think about her. Thoughts of her didn't twist my gut—which is what happens when I am apart from you.'

'What happened to change that?'

As William rested his back against the bed head, his features became set and grim, his eyes hard with remembrance. 'I got to know Atwood for what he really was, and I didn't like what I saw. He was ruthless and would go to any lengths to achieve what he wanted. Anyone who stood in his way was removed—forcibly, if necessary. One of his ventures was to lend money for astronomical interest. An acquaintance of mine borrowed money off him. When Atwood called in the debt and my acquaintance was unable to repay it, Atwood claimed his property.'

'And what happened to your acquaintance?'

'He killed himself, leaving a young wife and three children. I had approached Atwood on his behalf, asking him to reconsider and give him more time to repay the debt. He told me to go to hell.' Bitterness twisted his lips. 'At the time I had no idea how close to hell I was to get. Anyway, that was when our relationship changed and he began to have doubts about my suitability as a son-in-law—especially when I began to question his nefarious, more often than not illegal methods of making money.'

'That doesn't surprise me.'

'When I stepped in and tried to prevent him marrying your mother, knowing how your father despised him, that was the final straw. Atwood knew I was on his back and that I wasn't going to go quietly. The more persistent I became, the more furious he got. One night I was set upon and beaten senseless by a band of ruffians. When I came to—with broken ribs and a broken leg—I soon realised I was a prisoner on a vessel named *George* bound for the Americas.'

Eleanor paled visibly, appalled by what she was hearing. 'And my stepfather was responsible for this—this act of wickedness?'

William nodded his head slowly. 'I could not bear to speak of it before—to remember what it was like when I woke up on that ship from hell.'

'Tell me.' Wrapping a sheet about her, Eleanor tucked her feet beneath her and faced him, waiting for him to speak.

He drew away from her, leaning against the bed head, forcing his mind back to that ship he had wanted to forget. He did not speak at once, but sat for a while, his head bowed, as if meditating. Then he raised his head again with the air of a man who has come to a decision.

'It is a difficult and shocking tale, but no harm can come of you hearing it.' Because of the intrigues of a greedy, ruthless man, he had been abducted, knocked senseless and sent halfway across the world from where, Atwood must have thought, he would never return. The brutality of the men who held him, the conditions under which he was forced to live, would have broken a lesser man. Only his determination, his own iron will, his quick and active mind, his obstinacy, had brought him back to England to confront the man responsible for his misery, to make him pay and to demand answers.

Sensitive to his mood, Eleanor wrapped her warm fingers around his hand and gripped it hard, giving him strength. 'William, I don't want to remind you of your sufferings. It is painful for you to speak of them, I can see that. I only want you to explain a little of what happened so that I can understand.'

Raising his hand, he gently touched her cheek and smiled. 'I can imagine your bewilderment—the questions you must have put to yourself.'

'Then help me to understand.'

Clearing his throat, he shifted slightly, watching her face for her response to what he would tell her. 'Lured by the riches to be had in the New World, Atwood had already commissioned the private vessel, a rover operating out of London, to conduct an independent operation on his behalf. The vessel was well armed, the captain—Lew Paxton his name was well schooled in prize hunting on the high seas—he was also such a fearsome-looking figure that imagination cannot form an idea of a fury from hell to look more frightful. He was large and powerful and bullied his men. He also had a violent temper and a fatal inability to earn the respect of his crew.'

'What was it like? Was the captain cruel to you?'

'Savage and cruel beyond belief. Spawned in evil, he and his men lived to commit their evil. Bloodlust shone in their eyes.'

'But why did he do such terrible things? What possible reason could he have…?'

'Because he enjoyed it. He liked to hurt people, to hear them scream. That was sufficient reason for him.'

William closed his eyes, the sounds and the pictures still in his head. The cries, the endless screams—and then worse. Silence. And then there was the fear that had been in him, and when he was free prevented him from looking back.

'I knew, each time a man was flogged or some other unbearable torture was applied to his body, that I could do nothing. I was powerless—helpless.' He sighed, opening his eyes. 'I prefer not to offend your sensibilities with the details, Eleanor, so I ask you not to press me,' he said quietly, his usually bright eyes dull, his mouth held tight. 'What I will say is that through my severe treatment at Paxton's hands, I had every expectation of each day that dawned being my last. When I left that ship I vowed that one day I would confront the men who put me there.'

'My stepfather?'

'And one other.'

Silent and wide-eyed with horror, Eleanor stared at him as if seeing him for the first time. An immense pity welled up from the bottom of her heart towards this man whose sufferings at last she was beginning to understand.

'Where did you meet Godfrey? Was he on the same ship?'

'No. I met him when we reached South America, when the ship launched a strike against a Spanish vessel close to Maracaibo on the coast of Venezuela. Godfrey, who had left home to become a soldier of fortune when his family fell on hard times, was on that ship. The commencement of these hostilities provided ample employment for every sort of seagoing ruffian. They raided and plundered one another's vessels for goods and hostages—the latter to be held for ransom or used as slaves.'

'Was Godfrey a slave?'

'No. He was employed as a mercenary by the Spaniards and was taken hostage. His obstinacy irritated the captain and he lost no time in punishing this recalcitrant addition to his ship. He also saw Godfrey, because of the sheer size and strength of him, as a challenge—someone to be subdued. The beatings were brutal affairs, personally administered by Paxton, who took delight in thrashing prisoners to within an inch of their lives.'

'Was—was he responsible for what happened to your back?' Eleanor asked in a small voice.

'Yes. At this time life on board ship became a grim struggle for survival. There were internal rivalries and disputes between the captain and crew, and tropical diseases began to take their toll. It was when we were off Panama that a mutiny took place. When the captain was indisposed, eight members of the crew launched an attack.'

'Were you one of them?'

He nodded.

'The leader?'

Again he nodded. 'And Godfrey. When the captain and his second mate became ill, I incited the mutiny and took over command of the vessel. Paxton had his throat cut while he slept—and no,' he said when her eyebrows arched in question, 'I didn't do it.'

'And what happened next?'

'After plundering a Spanish galleon heading for Spain, laden with heavy chests of silver ingots and gold coin stowed amidships we headed for home.' Suddenly he grinned, his teeth gleaming white in his swarthy face. 'The Queen was well pleased when presented with the treasure—not so the Spanish Ambassador who demanded compensation for the plunder on the Spanish vessel, but his protests were ignored.'

'And is that how Godfrey came by his riches?' She laughed when William cocked a quizzical eyebrow. 'The manner in which he flaunts his riches, one cannot help but notice and question as to how he came by them. And he never was your servant, was he, William?'

'Godfrey is his own man, Eleanor, and, contrary to what everyone believes, he is not my servant—oddly, that's the impression he likes to give, which I always find amusing, but that's the way he is. We became close on board ship. Ours is an easy friendship not often met.'

'William, if it was not Catherine that brought you back to London from Staxton Hall, then what was it?'

'A ship called *Resolve*.'

'Why? What does that ship mean to you?'

'When I was beaten and bundled aboard the *George*, Atwood was behind it, that I do know, but I want to know who he paid to do it.'

'And where does the *Resolve* come in to it?'

'The *Resolve* and the *George* sailed together. When I left London for Staxton Hall, I left instructions that I was to be informed as soon as the *Resolve* was sighted in the Thames. The captain of the *Resolve*, I feel sure, knows who took me on board.'

'And if you find out who it was?'

'He'll regret ever being born.'

'Have you any notion as to who it might be?'

His eyes narrowed and glittered. 'I have my suspicions.'

'Will you share them with me?'

'I'd rather wait until I'm certain.'

'Very well,' she said, leaning towards him and brushing his lips with her own. 'And now I must go. I will have been missed. I must have been gone over two hours.'

William's dark brows drew together. 'Go?' A small voice deep inside him began to gnaw at him.

'I have to. Martin is bound to question me about my absence.'

William's face whitened, the rush of furious blood under his skin draining away at the implication of her statement. 'I doubt he will have noticed. Besides, he is no longer important.'

'He is still my husband, William—despite what we have just done. It is a dangerous game we play.'

'This is no game I play, Eleanor.'

She sighed deeply, drawing away from him. 'We must wait.' She was aware that William was not a patient man and that he would not be stopped when his mind was set on something, and he was set on having her and his child, which was what she also wanted more than anything in the world, but she couldn't just leave Martin.

'Wait? Eleanor, stop this, stop it at once.' His voice was a

snarl of jealous outrage. He was a virile man and extremely
masculine. Before he had made love to her she had been untouched and pure, a woman who had never known a lover's
touch, and he was as certain as he could be that Martin
Taverner had not even looked at her with the same desire that
he had—a desire that could melt the bones and the flesh and
cause all coherent thought to take flight.

'God in heaven!' he said, flinging himself off the bed.
'Can't you understand that I want you with me, that I want to
protect you?'

'Who from? Martin? He won't hurt me.' Getting off the
bed, she began struggling into her clothes.

Grudgingly, William went to help her, and when she was
fully clothed he placed his hands on her upper arms and looked
deep into her troubled eyes. 'Eleanor, you are mine,' he said
with great gravity, 'and so is the child you carry. I mean to have
you both. I will not allow what we have to be forced into a
corner that no one must see. I am not a man to accept it.'

'I don't expect you to,' she whispered. 'I am only asking
that you be patient a while longer.'

Cupping her face between his hands, he began to kiss it,
placing his tender lips on her cheeks, her eyelids, her brow,
her mouth. 'You know about desire, Eleanor,' he murmured
huskily, his warm breath mingling with her own. 'I have
shown you, and how much I desire you. What you and Martin
Taverner have has nothing to do with it. Your marriage is ridiculous, an absurdity. He must be told.'

'I know.'

'We will tell him together.'

Before Eleanor could prepare herself for his next onslaught, he had pulled her to him. His mouth fell savagely on
hers, crushing her lips so fiercely she could swear she could
taste blood. Once again she felt the strength of him. Her heart

was pounding, her body pliant, unresisting, straining against him, his breath sweet and warm. Sagging against him, she felt the woman in her respond to his maleness.

William sensed the change in her and his lips softened, moving along her jawline to the fleshy lobe of her ear, which his teeth nibbled gently before his mouth found hers once more.

'You don't want to go back to him, do you, Eleanor?' His arms loosened and he looked down at her passion-filled face. 'To that sham of a marriage?'

She was dazed, her eyes unfocused. 'You know I don't, but for now I have to,' she whispered, drawing away from him. 'We must consider Martin's position in all this. Think how humbling it will be to him if everyone thinks I have left him for you, and that I married him while carrying another man's child. I must show some loyalty. I owe him that at least.'

'I can see it's a difficult moral dilemma for you,' William said drily, 'but in this case I find my loyalties are entirely with you.'

'Please don't try and stop me going back to him, William. We will work it out somehow, I promise.'

He felt some reluctance in letting her go, but he could scarcely keep her with him just now. She would be safe enough, he thought, with a husband who had no mind to bed his wife.

Eleanor's eyes rested on the exposed part of his shoulder for a moment, at the small knot of puckered scar tissue that seemed to have crept up from his back, but she showed no sign of disgust or any further curiosity, nor did she when she pressed herself against him for one last kiss and snaked her arms around him and placed her hands on his back when she bade him goodbye, though William knew she must feel the healed welts beneath his robe with her fingers.

'You're right, you'll have to go back—for now,' he said, brushing her hair out of his face.

'And we will sort this out, won't we, William?'

He didn't answer right away, but bent his head. Eleanor could feel the tension of his body knotted in the joints, rigid in his bones.

'I hadn't thought ever to be jealous of a man like Martin Taverner—a man who has no use for women—for which I thank God,' he whispered at last. 'I wouldn't have thought it possible until I learned that you had married him.' His fingers touched the softness of her cheek. 'One way or another I will get you back, but until I do, the thought of you as that man's wife will be like a worm eating away inside me.'

Eleanor gathered him tight against herself, placing her head against his chest where his heart was beating furiously. 'Then console yourself with the knowledge that because of how he is, he will not touch me, and in that I am protected.'

When she left him she felt as if she were walking on air and a smile would settle on her lips, a smile that told her she loved him—and, oh, yes, love him she did, with her whole heart. This she did not deny.

Martin, in a happy mood as he sauntered along the dim corridors of the Palace, was unprepared for what was about to happen to him when a tall man stepped out of the shadows.

'Traitor,' Richard Grey hissed, feeling for his dagger, smiling unpleasantly, and without uttering another word he swung his fighting arm up in the air. The blade rose in an arc like a bright streak and he plunged it in four heart thrusts.

Chapter Eleven

Unable to find Martin when she returned to the revelries, Eleanor left for home. Having dismissed her maid, she was about to go to bed when a messenger from Whitehall Palace came to inform both her and Lord Taverner that Martin was dead. When the details of the crime were made clear to her, Eleanor was deeply shocked.

That night was one of anguish and weeping. While she had been making love with William, Martin was being stabbed to death. She knew who had done it, that Richard Grey was responsible, and she was appalled by the knowledge that her conversation with that man had brought about her husband's death. Oh, why hadn't she warned him like she'd intended? Why had she allowed William to distract her with his warm lips and strong arms and powerful body?

That short time, that rapturous, insane time had killed not only Martin but William too, for he was as dead to her as Martin. What was it about her that she brought ill luck to those close to her? First there was Uncle John and now Martin. She had killed Martin and her love for William with her wickedness, her wantonness, and she must live with it and suffer the fortunes of the damned until the end of her days, which was no more than she deserved, but in the meantime she must think of her child and find some way to live with what she had done.

She blamed herself for what had happened, blamed herself for telling Richard Grey about the child, for taunting him and wrongly letting him believe the child was Martin's. The way Martin had died—stabbed repeatedly by his lover in a dark corner of Whitehall Palace—filled her with horror and remorse. Jealousy may have led Sir Richard astray but, apart from being besotted by the man wielding the knife, Martin had done no wrong.

The following day, one by one visitors arrived at the house, their lips expressing their sympathy for her loss. Lord Taverner accepted Martin's death calmly, seemingly unmoved by the news that his eldest son had been murdered, and it was this callousness that so embittered Eleanor, for she genuinely mourned her young husband. She missed his gentleness, his friendship and the brightness of him. Her sorrow defied release. It hid itself in a hollow place in her heart. And so, stunned and enclosed in a curtain of shock she kept to her room, save for the occasional trips downstairs to eat with Lord Taverner.

The questions had started as a hunt for the murderer began. Eleanor knew the culprit, but she did not have the courage to point the finger publicly at Sir Richard Grey, and, according to her father-in-law, Sir Richard had left the Court, shocked and grief-stricken by Martin's death.

Eleanor pushed away her dinner, feeling sickly as she toyed with the greasy lamb on her plate.

Lord Taverner looked across the table at her, his eyes narrowed and steady. Almost idly he asked, 'Is there something wrong with the food?'

Though her insides were trembling, Eleanor knew that the time to tell her father-in-law about the child had arrived. The longer she waited, the more pressure would build and the more difficult it would be.

'No, the food is as delicious as always—only—I'm not hungry—in fact I am feeling somewhat queasy. Lord Taverner—I—I think you should know that I am with child.' She spoke plainly for there was no other way to tell him. That she had been able to do it surprised even her. But it was said now and so much the better.

Lord Taverner began to smile, a smile that was a mixture of appalled disbelief and hideous amusement. Pushing back his chair, he stood up and walked round the table towards her, his eyes never leaving her face.

'Whose is it?' He smiled thinly. 'Who's the father? Because if you intend passing it off as my son's you can think again. Do you take me for an idiot—when the world and its neighbours know the two of you rarely occupied the same house, never mind slept in the same bedchamber?'

'I am sorry,' she whispered. He was furious, of course, and she didn't blame him.

'Did he know?' he asked her harshly, adding emphasis to his sternest countenance to the question that was more like a command.

'Yes, I told him.'

'And?'

'He—he was prepared to accept the child—to bring it up as his own,' Eleanor answered lamely. 'At first he was angry, of course, but the more he thought about it, the more excited he became.'

'Like hell he was,' her father-in-law erupted, his face flamed with anger. When he next spoke his voice was low and horribly calm. 'And did he think I would be so besotted at the prospect of his producing a child—when all the odds were stacked against it—considering his aversion to your sex—that I would not find out the truth—that I would be none the wiser when I looked into my grandchild's face? I have another son who is not so bad for my health who will inherit the Taverner estate, not your bastard, madam.'

Eleanor's face drained. Gripping her hands together in her lap, she sat mute and unmoving as his harsh words whipped her.

Lord Taverner moved closer, his eyes black pinpoints boring into hers. 'So you are to bear the child of a man who used you for his own convenience and then deserted you, a man who spiked you and then spurned you, and you thought to foist his leavings on to my son.' He laughed mockingly. 'What other way is there for a woman alone with a bastard— prey to a pitiless society.'

Eleanor bowed her head before his hard, condemning face. He was right. Society believed that the sin was all the woman's fault, that the blame for her conduct was all hers, that she had brought it on herself and the child.

'It wasn't like that. I swear it wasn't. I didn't know myself until after we were wed. Had I known, I would never have married Martin.'

'But you agreed to go along with this—this charade?'

She nodded.

'I was suspicious from the beginning. Little wonder your aunt wanted to get you married off—and who better than to Martin, too simple minded to notice.' Every trace of emotion left his face. When he next spoke his voice was as cold and as devoid of feeling as a wind blowing over an empty landscape. 'I want you out of my house. Pack your bags and get out. I shall lock the door as soon as you have gone. That is my final word.'

He turned his back on her and not until the door had

thudded closed did Eleanor let out her breath. The silence became a living shroud. The problem of what she would do, where she would go, was a sad and frightening burden.

The day was hot and the Palace stuffy. William went outside, hoping the fresh air would dispel his headache, which had been with him on waking. As the day progressed it became worse. Feeling restless, he rode to Chelsea to see Godfrey, where he had been staying with Catherine ever since they had become enamoured of each other.

Despite his infernal headache, which showed no sign of letting up, a slight smile quirked his lips. Who would have thought it? Godfrey and Catherine—Catherine with her often spiteful, manipulating ways. Godfrey had laughed uproariously when William had shown an interest in his affair with his new love, saying they bothered him not at all, that he'd looked beyond that, that Catherine was beautiful, proud and stubborn beyond belief, but she was also vulnerable and wounded, having suffered much under her father's rule, which she tried to hide, but he could see it in her eyes.

William had cocked a sardonic brow at his friend as he waxed lyrical. Wounded? Vulnerable? He wondered how these creditable traits of Catherine's had escaped him, although when he'd first met her he'd admired her intelligence and her honesty, and if at times she had seemed petulant and sullen, he had believed that might have had something to do with her father and that marriage would dispel her disagreeable moods.

The previous day had found him at Gravesend to see the captain of the ship *Resolve*, his enquiries having revealed that the fever had abated on the vessel with no further deaths for two weeks. Believing the danger past, he had gone on board. The one thing that had kept him alive during those dark days on board the *George* had been revenge. Someone must pay.

The name of Atwood's accomplice the captain of *Resolve* had made known to him for a price—a price worth paying, for the captain had confirmed his own suspicion that the man who had hired men to beat him to a pulp was Richard Grey.

The journey to Chelsea was arduous. There seemed to be too many people, too much traffic, too much dust, and the noise of the streets was deafening. Sweat soaked his body and the heat drained his energy, making it difficult for him to breath. Three times he had to stop to overcome a wave of dizziness. He had not eaten—the thought of food made him nauseous—and his headache was worse, blinding.

By the time he reached the house in Chelsea he could hardly stay in the saddle. His strength was gone and he felt as weak and helpless as a babe. There was no use pretending about it. He'd got the fever. The door opened and, sliding off his horse, he collapsed on to the hall floor. Dimly he heard someone shriek for help and the next thing a pair of massive arms hoisted him up and carried him upstairs and laid him on a bed.

In a moment free from delirium, he stared into Godfrey's worried face. 'That damned ship,' he gasped, licking his dry lips. 'The fever—I thought it had gone.'

'You were a fool to venture on board,' Godfrey growled with harsh reproach. 'I told you to wait, but you always were the impatient one.'

'It's infectious. You might catch it—and Catherine. Keep out, Godfrey, and let it run its course.'

'If it's the fever, I'll take care of you, so lie still.'

'Eleanor,' William said, his voice thick and hoarse, the words slurring one over the other, 'don't tell her—she mustn't know, not yet.'

'And you mustn't fret,' a worried-looking Catherine said, flanking Godfrey.

William glared at her, his eyes red and glittering. 'What are you doing here? Godfrey—for God's sake, get her out.'

Godfrey turned to her with concern. 'He's right, Catherine. Go and get him some tea and herbs—whatever you give for a fever—and send the servants home until it's safe for them to return.' When she'd gone, he turned back to his friend. 'You'll get well. You've suffered worse.'

William closed his heavy lids. Yes, he'd suffered worse, much worse, and he'd recovered, he'd overcome and he would overcome this time. But then he might not. Immediately his eyes flew open and he gripped Godfrey's hand.

'If I don't pull through,' he gasped, 'promise me you will take care of Eleanor—take her to Staxton Hall—where she belongs. Promise me.'

'I promise. Now rest, William. Rest. You'll feel better after a good night's sleep.'

William's mind tumbled in an eddy of confusion. A vision of Eleanor drifted into his shadowy world—Eleanor, lovely, beautiful Eleanor. His feverish mind raged in delirium, wandering restlessly through a haze of shifting shade, of days and nights darkly shrouded. The intense fire holding his mind and body in a sweltering heat made him toss and turn and fling off the heavy covers that held him down.

At times he felt someone lift his head and force cold water through his parched lips, commanding him to drink, and in his ravings broken and abusive words spilled from his lips. When the effort of swallowing proved too much, his head would fall back on to the pillows.

Coming awake in the dimly lit room, his body felt weak and helpless, and when he tried to raise his arm it felt like a lead weight. Roused to awareness, the first thing he saw when he opened his eyes was Godfrey bending over him.

William moved his lips and the hoarse croak bore no resemblance to his voice. 'How long have I...?'

'Five days,' Godfrey told him, thankful to see William's eyes were clear and no longer bloodshot with fever. With his black hair stuck to his damp forehead, he was pale as wax and two deep grey shadows ran from his nostrils down to the corners of his mouth, but he had pulled through, even though it had been touch and go for a time and Godfrey had thought he might not make it. 'Thank God the fever's left you.'

'You've been very sick,' Catherine said, coming into the room with a bowl and some cloths draped over her arm.

'I must have been.' Reality gradually came to stay and yet William's mind was a tangle of confusion and he could make no sense of what had happened. 'I can't remember a damned thing—apart from leaving Whitehall and collapsing here at your house.'

'So you won't remember abusing me every time I tried to make you drink,' Godfrey accused with a touch of humour.

'Really?' William said, his eyebrow tilted sardonically and his mouth curved in a disbelieving smile. 'Was it bad?'

'In your delirium you certainly had a most ungentlemanly turn of phrase,' Godfrey chuckled, casually draping an arm over Catherine's shoulders.

'And if you hadn't been at death's door, I would have been thoroughly entertained,' she laughed.

William frowned, looking concernedly at them both. 'I hope I haven't exposed either of you to the fever. I asked you to stay away from me, Catherine. Clearly you ignored my request.'

'You were in no position to object—and Godfrey got tired of trying to keep me out. Now don't try to speak anymore—you'll tire yourself.'

Godfrey held a goblet of water to his lips. The cool water was welcome and made him feel a little better.

'Eleanor! I have to see her.'

Godfrey shook his head. 'Patience, William. You will do yourself no good in trying to rush things. You have to get your strength back and be completely free of the fever. For the time being you must stay here. It wouldn't do to infect her—not in her condition now, would it?'

'You're right, I suppose,' he grumbled, 'but don't expect me to be staying too long. I have things to do that can't wait.'

William's head fell back on the pillows. What Godfrey said made sense so he would have to bide his time, but he prayed Eleanor was all right and that she didn't think he'd abandoned her.

He drifted back into sleep, thinking of Eleanor and how she must be suffering. His own heart had always been moved by suffering and he longed for the time when he could go to her and comfort her. He realised now how much he loved her, that he had loved Eleanor Collingwood almost from the first moment he saw her. His heart and every loving instinct told him he should rise up from his bed and go to her and help her through her anguish, to hold her in his arms and shield her from the pain and sadness, but his common sense told him Godfrey was right and he must wait until he was completely free of the fever.

In a heavy black satin gown Lady Matilda Sandford stood before the window in the solar on the first floor of Cantly Manor. It was a bright afternoon in July and she was watching her niece's luggage being unloaded from Lord Taverner's carriage in the courtyard below. Turning, she looked at the aforesaid girl, feeling a resentment twisting and turning inside her. Resentment against Eleanor who, after all she had done for her, had thrown gratitude back in her face, and resentment against the girl who had so embarrassingly prevailed upon her generosity and her kindness.

The girl Lady Sandford had arranged to wed one of the most eligible young men at the Court of Queen Elizabeth had brought this hideous shame in the shape of a bastard child back to her house—and worse, she had caused enmity between herself and Lord Taverner. She could hardly bring herself to speak lest she spewed forth a torrent of bile.

'I have no doubt you feel yourself ill used, Eleanor, but you could not be more wrong. Your immoral conduct has been inexcusable and you have brought disgrace on Lord Taverner's good name and my own. You have shamed me and your dead husband with your adulterous indiscretion and your uncontrollable desires for another man.'

Eleanor listened to the blistering tirade as her aunt went on to list others she had shamed, adding to her lingering guilt, dwelling on what she had let another man do to her and blaming her for obliging, and that whoever he was he had not wanted her, only her body, otherwise he would have married her. Eleanor realised she might be right, for not once had William told her he loved her, and nor had he enquired after her.

'Go straight to your room and do not come out until I give you permission. I don't want to see your face again today.'

Leaving the solar, Eleanor felt a sharp stab of pain around her heart. She hadn't expected support from her aunt, whose whole life revolved around pleasing Lord Taverner, but she might at least have shown some compassion. Filled with misery, she went swiftly to her bedchamber. Once inside, she hurled herself full length across the bed and burst into tears, feeling ashamed and at fault—and almost beyond salvation.

Eleanor often wondered how she got through the following days leading into weeks, for her emotions were in turmoil and her spirit low. Aunt Matilda rarely spoke to her, and when she did Eleanor had come to expect only stinging taunts and contemptuous looks and wished she would leave her alone altogether.

The warm and sunny weather agreed with her and she made the effort to walk in the garden at Cantly Manor every day. She wandered along the paths, through flower-filled enclosures, where birds warbled merrily and bees and butterflies flitted from one glorious bloom to another, and in a cloud of white, gold and red and black, settling and drowsily moving in the fragile warmth, but she saw none of it.

There was no word from William. Why did he not come? she asked herself in anguish. She told herself there must be some good reason, but what reason could a man have that would keep him from the woman he must have some kind of feelings for and his unborn child, when she needed him so?

Was he ill? Perhaps he was injured. Eleanor could feel a tide of suffering rise in her in despairing pain, which she did her best to subdue, for it was too unbearable to dwell upon. She would have gone to him but she was in mourning and it wouldn't be proper—not that she cared about proprieties when William might be ill. But if he were, she clung to the conviction that Godfrey would have come to tell her.

Martin's death still continued to haunt her, and as far as she was aware his murderer had not been caught.

One afternoon she was summoned to her aunt's presence. Visitors had arrived and had requested to see her. Eleanor made her way to the solar, reluctant to face anyone at present. Until now she had remained virtually secluded within Cantly Manor, hating the hostility lodged within its walls, yet needing its security and privacy more so now it was no longer possible to conceal her pregnancy.

Her aunt was standing in the centre of the room with the visitors, a man and a woman.

'You wish to see me, Aunt?'

The man and the woman turned together, and when Eleanor saw it was William and Catherine her knees almost buckled beneath her. Her heart gave a leap and missed a beat, then began to thump madly as her eyes became locked on William's, and they looked at one another as though their minds were linked by some invisible thread. It was his face, the face she knew by heart. It was the same, but now there were a few shallow lines around his eyes and mouth, and his cheekbones were sharper beneath the skin.

Her heart had been filled with angry recriminations and rancour, for she had not understood why he had not come to see her, or even been aware of what had kept him away. But her flesh had not stopped wanting him, needing him, loving him. Dragging air into her constricted lungs, she stared blindly. He was here now, so he must care for her after all.

He had been standing with his back partially to her when she entered, impatiently slapping his thigh with his leather gloves while he gazed out of the window to the courtyard below. Attired entirely in dark green, the only relief a small white collar, his broad shoulders were squared, his jaw set, and even in this pensive pose he seemed to emanate the restrained power and unyielding authority she associated with him.

William's gaze became riveted on Eleanor the instant she stepped into the room and the sight of her had the devastating impact of a punch in the chest. This woman who was dressed in sombre black was Eleanor, his love, the woman who had so recently become a wife and was now a widow. The child was showing and never had she looked so radiantly beautiful or so serene, but there was a raw desolation in her lovely eyes. The light that had been put there by their loving and what was between them was gone completely.

Unperturbed by the disapproving look Lady Sandford gave

him, he went directly to Eleanor and took her hands, his gaze searching her face. The ecstasy he had experienced on the day he had last seen her was still a marvel to him, for he had thought he knew all there was to know about passion, but he had not, not until Eleanor. Now he wanted nothing more than to drag her into his arms and hold her close, but with Lady Sandford's hawk eyes fixed on him he was forced to control every muscle in his body, tightening, straining to endure the torture of Eleanor's nearness.

'I hope you did not think I was avoiding you,' he said softly. 'I called at Lord Taverner's house in Westminster to see you as soon as I heard about what had happened to your husband, but I was told you were not receiving visitors.'

'No—I my father-in-law thought I was not up to it.' William was looking at her intently and his magnetic eyes stirred her painfully.

'I can understand that. I trust you are suffering no ill effects from the tragedy?'

'No—although I cannot deny that Martin's death came as a dreadful blow,' she answered, trying to ignore the warmth tingling up her arms as he kept hold of her hands a moment longer before releasing them.

'You've had a great shock, but you are in good health and strong. All will be well, you'll see.'

Eleanor almost melted beneath the aching gentleness in his compelling eyes. 'Do—do you know who killed Martin? Have you heard?' she asked on an eager, hopeful note.

'No, although speculation is rife. It's a true mystery and people revel in mysteries. When they cannot find solutions they fabricate them, and there are all kinds of stories being bandied about. But come, Eleanor, it's not good for you or the baby to dwell on such dark thoughts. Your mind should be on such matters as layettes and cradles and that kind of thing.'

Eleanor smiled up at him. William's arrival was like a glimmer of light in a dark world. 'I know, but when I think of the manner of Martin's death, it's no easy matter. I—I see you have met my aunt, Lady Sandford.'

'Indeed. Thank you for receiving us, Lady Sandford,' he said with a slight inclination of his head. 'It was extraordinarily gracious of you.'

Lady Sandford stepped forward. 'You are very welcome.' She turned away, signalling to a servant to bring refreshments. 'I have told Lord Marston what a pleasure it is to meet him at last and thanked him for taking such good care of you when you were in Yorkshire.' Her eyes held Eleanor's. Lord Marston's unhidden interest in her niece positively invited questions, and the idea had already formed in her mind that this illustrious lord might well be the father of Eleanor's child, but good manners forbade her to voice the question outright.

'I am also pleased to meet your stepsister at last,' she said, turning to the young woman who accompanied Lord Marston. 'It would appear she is quite concerned about you, Eleanor.'

Eleanor was moved when Catherine came and took her hand and kissed her on the cheek with what seemed like affection.

'I am here to offer my condolences, Eleanor—rather belated, I know, but I have only recently become aware of your loss.'

'It was good of you to come, Catherine,' Eleanor remarked, instantly establishing a familiarity that had not existed between them for a long time, not even at her wedding to Martin, when Catherine's attitude had been remote and cool.

'Sometimes it takes a tragedy such as this to make one realise what is happening. It's a dreadful business. How are you feeling?' Catherine enquired, a smile on her carmine-painted lips, her gaze raking Eleanor's figure from her gauze cap to the hem of her blue taffeta gown. 'In full bloom, I see.'

Eleanor stared at her in amazement. Perhaps it was because

she was so used to Catherine's peevishness in the past that her
sudden affability was unexpected enough to pierce her ab-
straction. It was the first time her stepsister had spoken kindly
to her in a long time and she was pleasantly warmed by the
friendliness of her greeting, but she remained wary. It was
over two months since she had seen Catherine and she still
hadn't forgiven her for working her mischief, for implying
that she and William were together. Martin might still be alive
if Catherine had been honest with her. She wondered if she
and Godfrey were still lovers—if so, could this be the reason
for this change in her?

'I—I am as well as I can be, Catherine. I thank you for asking,'
she replied, trying not to look at the tall, perfectly built man who
stood watching her with expressionless, glittering eyes.

'As soon as I heard, I was concerned about you— we both
were,' Catherine said, turning briefly to include William in her
statement. 'Having lost my own dear Henry after such a short
time of marriage, I know exactly how devastated you must be
feeling, which is why I would like you to come and stay with
me in Chelsea I have suggested it to Lady Sandford and she
is willing to agree—if it's what you want, naturally. You must
be taken care of.'

'I hope you are not implying that I am incapable of taking
care of my niece, Lady Wheeler,' Lady Sandford remarked
stiffly, looking extremely disgruntled that her efforts to look
after Eleanor might be criticised. 'Since her mother's—my
own dear sister's—demise, I have done my best to do what
she would have done for Eleanor.'

Catherine started at the sound of the imperious voice. 'Why,
no, I was implying no such thing,' she said, quick to cover up
any offence she might have given and tactfully going on to say,
'but I thought, being so recently widowed myself, you understand, that we could be of help and comfort to each other.'

Meeting her aunt's cold eyes, Eleanor was as aware as she was that their relationship was anything but close. 'Aunt Matilda could not have done more for me,' she murmured, hearing the irony of her words.

'And now it's my turn. Please say you will come, Eleanor.'

'Catherine—forgive me—but I am bewildered. Since when did you care about how I was feeling?'

'I am trying very hard to do the right thing.' Drawing Eleanor aside, on a softer note that only Eleanor could hear, she said, 'William wants you to come to Chelsea. You must come, Eleanor, you have to.'

Eleanor looked at her aunt. 'Are you in agreement, Aunt Matilda?'

Lady Sandford's eyes grew piercing. 'The choice is yours, Eleanor. When you married Martin Taverner I recognised then that I no longer had any authority over you. Now you are a widow, you may do exactly as you please. However,' she said, speaking to Catherine, 'I trust you will take care of her. With a child on the way—and Lord Taverner having announced to the world that his son had no part in its conception—there will be one almighty scandal when it is born.'

'Then we will shoulder the scandal together and live it down,' William uttered firmly, shrugging indifferently as he took a stand beside Eleanor. 'Gossip doesn't matter to me, and since it does to you, Lady Sandford, I would advise you to accept it. You see, the child Eleanor is to bear is mine and I intend to marry her as soon as it can be arranged. Naturally it will be a quiet affair, attended by just close family and friends.'

Turning from the shocked expression on Aunt Matilda's face and the all-knowing look on Catherine's, Eleanor stared at him. His firm conviction that she would marry him, that she had no choice except to marry him, was more than she could bear just then.

'You must let me choose, William, let me decide.' Her voice held no intonation. Total control was all she could bear. To allow any emotion through would break the dam of her tears. Dignity was a kind of refuge.

At that moment the refreshments were brought in, creating a welcome diversion for Eleanor.

'William, will you walk with me along the gallery. I—think we should talk.'

'Of course. Lady Sandford, please excuse us.'

The long gallery overlooking the immaculate gardens was quiet. Walking slowly along its length, William fell into step beside Eleanor. After a moment he stopped and, taking her arms, turned her to face him. He did not care for the strange expression on her face. He could not as yet describe it or what it meant, but he did not care for it. He smiled in an attempt to lighten her mood and lifted his arms to draw her into his embrace, but she edged away from him.

'Eleanor, what's the matter?' he demanded, his voice harsh with his disappointment. He had expected relief, delight, not what strangely looked like offence. Just when he thought everything was going to be all right, that she would agree on what they both hoped for, now that she was free, she had turned truculent.

'Where have you been? Why did you not come? It's weeks since Martin was killed and not a word from you. What was I to think?' With her heart filled with angry recrimination, her voice was as anguished now as it had been when she had asked the question of herself when she had been told about Martin.

William blanched. 'I'm sorry. I told you I did call, the day after, but I was informed you were too grief-stricken to receive visitors. I should have tried harder to see you, I know that now, but circumstances beyond my control made it impossible. Come, Eleanor, calm your anger and let us discuss what we are to do next.'

Eleanor stood before him, the look in her eyes telling him she was her own woman and if he thought he could bully her into doing his will then he could think again. 'Discuss? Has it not occurred to you that I might appreciate being asked to marry you? Am I to have no say in the matter—an important matter that will affect my whole life?'

William looked amazed. 'What is there to say?'

'William, a lot has happened to me since we last saw each other. I have suffered most cruelly. I have been a widow for so short a time and I cannot possibly marry you—not now. There has to be a decent period of mourning, and I need time.' Her unrelenting distress was evident in her tone.

'I am not so insensitive not to know what you have been through, which is why I have given you time to come to terms with all that's happened.'

'I haven't—not yet. It's too soon—and—and I don't think I will ever be able to come to terms with what I've done.'

William stared at her, his anger fierce and knife-edged. 'Done? What are you talking about? Anyone would think it was you who killed Martin Taverner.'

'It might just as well have been me,' she flared, the expression in her eyes savage. 'I killed him just as surely as if I'd wielded the knife. The wounds of Martin's death and the awful manner of it are still wide open—it's like Uncle John all over again. God knows I have wrestled with my mind, with my guilt, but the memory of it will not go away. I killed Martin—we both killed him. How can we possibly live together in harmony with the ghost of the man we have killed between us?'

'What are you saying, Eleanor? For God's sake, tell me.'

'That last time we were together at Whitehall Palace, when you saw me coming in from the garden, I had been with Richard Grey. He—he was offensive, saying he wanted me out of the way and that Martin was going to send me to live in Devon.'

William looked at her incredulously. 'He what?'

'I think Richard Grey wanted me as far away from Martin as was possible.'

'And you didn't think this meeting with Richard Grey important enough to tell me?'

'I should have, I know, and it would have made a world of difference if I had. I realise that now because we could have warned Martin. I taunted Sir Richard—which was quite wrong of me, I know, but I was angry. I—I told him about the baby and implied Martin was the father. He was furious jealous, the kind of jealousy a lover feels when his partner has been unfaithful.'

'Now that I can understand,' William remarked scathingly, still unable to understand Eleanor's hasty marriage to Martin Taverner and how furious and devastated he had felt on finding out.

'I saw murder in his eyes,' Eleanor whispered fiercely, her face ashen, 'and I knew I must find Martin, to warn him, but when I saw you and you told me about my stepfather's death, everything else ceased to exist. After that I should have resisted you. I had a premonition of what would happen and I should have looked for Martin.'

Her eyes were tortured and she reeled with what looked like such pain that William took her arms to hold her still. Had she been bottling all this inside her since Martin had been killed? He cursed himself for his stupidity, for his neglect of her. He should have insisted on seeing her when Lord Taverner turned him away from his house. He had intended trying again, and but for that damned fever that had laid him low he would have.

'Eleanor, are you saying it was Richard Grey who murdered Martin?'

She nodded.

'But you didn't see him do it, did you?'

'I didn't have to. I know it was him. I am certain of it. Where is he now?'

'As far as I know, he left Court soon after the murder.'

'So nobody thought to question him?'

'Why should they? He was not a suspect.'

'Considering his relationship to Martin, he should have been.'

'Eleanor, you must stop this. It will do you no good.'

'But he did do it,' she cried, 'I know he did and he must be brought to account. He cannot be allowed to get away with it.'

William's expression was grave. Taking her hands, he drew her down on to a window seat and sat facing her. 'Eleanor,' he said with sudden, profound emotion thickening his voice, 'from my own encounters with Richard Grey, I know full well that he is capable of murder, so you don't have to try to convince me of that.'

Eleanor saw what she thought was conflict in his face. A decisive, almost ruthless part of his nature seemed to be warring inside him with something immeasurably more vulnerable. 'You do?' Her voice was a little shaky and caught in her throat.

He nodded, holding her gaze with his own. 'It was Grey who put me on that ship. That I now know for certain.'

She stared at him in amazement. She could not doubt his accusation, for had she not some claim of her own to make? 'Oh, William—I—I had no idea. You told me my stepfather was behind it and one other, but I did not imagine it was Sir Richard Grey.'

'Atwood employed his nephew to do his dirty work. Losing both his parents at an early age, Richard Grey found a niche for himself at Fryston Hall. Greedy, grasping and calculating he was—just like his uncle—weaned on violence and often murder. When I appeared on the scene, gaining Atwood's friendship—or what passed for friendship at the time—Grey was so irritated that his thoughts became entrapped in the resentment he felt for me.'

William grimaced. 'He had no special licence to that emotion, however, for I suffered from like emotions. I can imagine his willingness to do his uncle's bidding when he asked him to get rid of me—to dispose of me somewhere that there wouldn't be a hope in hell of me coming back, ever—leaving everyone to think I had been a part of the plot that damned your father and had been banished.'

Eleanor's brow puckered in a puzzled frown. 'If—if my stepfather wanted to be rid of you as much as that, why go to all that trouble of sending you to the Americas? Why did he not kill you and have done with it? That would have been one sure way of getting rid of you for good.'

'You stepfather would have, but Grey was a different matter. Beneath the skin Richard Grey is as cruel as Captain Paxton was. He knew perfectly well what he was doing when he abandoned me to Paxton.'

'How do you know it was Richard Grey, William? Did my stepfather tell you?'

'No. At the end he was too afraid of Grey to inform on him. Do you recall me telling you about the other ship that accompanied the *George* to America?'

She nodded expectantly.

'I spoke with the captain, and he confirmed my suspicions. It was Grey who had me beaten and bundled on to that ship—and he paid Paxton a handsome price to do it.'

'I see. What will you do now?'

'Make Richard Grey regret the day he agreed to help Atwood dispose of me.'

'And if he murdered Martin?'

'I will notify Lord Taverner of what you have told me and he will have him sent to the Tower for questioning. It is my intention to see to it right away. I want to leave for Yorkshire while you are able to travel.' He grinned, his gaze travelling to her swollen abdomen. 'At the rate you are expanding, my love, I think you are to give birth to an elephant or triplets.'

Relieved that he had introduced a lightness into the conversation, Eleanor's expression was one of mock-horror and she laughed softly. 'I sincerely hope not. One baby at a time is quite sufficient.'

Taking her hands and drawing her to her feet, William placed a gentle kiss on her forehead. 'We'll talk about this later. Just now I'm more concerned with getting you to Chelsea and settled in.'

'And Catherine?'

'Catherine will surprise you. She's genuinely looking forward to having you stay with her. Godfrey has had a strange affect on her. She is a changed person, as you'll see for yourself.' He looked at her gently, but there was no wavering in him. 'Eleanor, there is something I want you to understand. Never, not even in my weakest moments, have I considered letting you go.'

Tipping her chin up, he forced her troubled gaze to meet his implacable one. 'It's as impossible to put you out of my mind as it is to stop breathing. I want you with an intensity that seeps into the very deepest part of me. I want you, all of you, all of the time. I want to feel the smooth naked flesh of you, your slender waist, hip and thigh, which I can only imagine beneath your gown, the lift of your peaked breasts, which are round and full beneath your bodice.'

A little smile tweaked her lips. 'That snaps of greed to me, my lord.'

'Ah, but my greedy mind isn't alone, for I want more than the physical act of loving, I want your friendship, your companionship, to know your innermost thoughts. You asked for time. I cannot give it to you. You have to face the inevitability of our marriage, because you have a child to consider—my child—and that child will not be born out of wedlock. I assure you the marriage is going to take place. You must realise there is no going back, that there is no escaping what is to happen. Accept it. What have you to say?'

His voice was firm and Eleanor hated his words. Accept it! She really didn't have any choice. She turned away, not daring to look at him, and she knew she would have to submit to his decision and his authority. Placing his hands on her shoulders, he turned her round to face him. His lips touched her cheek, his free hand moving about her waist possessively. She wanted to push him away, to argue with him, but when she felt the strength of his muscles as he held her tightly and his lips closed over hers as he gathered her to him, there really was nothing more to say.

Chapter Twelve

The water of the River Thames moved gently past without a ripple, with swans floating on its glassy surface. The day was pleasantly warm, the sky blue and giving an added beauty to the river. Boats went back and forth, their oars, dipping and rising in unison, dripping water.

Eleanor strolled along the embankment with Catherine in companionable silence, each content to be in the other's company after so many years of discord, which they had both agreed to put behind them.

'Eleanor, I'm sorry about the things I said to you that day you visited me,' Catherine murmured, sighing ruefully.

Eleanor gave her a look of reproach. 'I thought we'd agreed to put all that behind us, Catherine.'

'I know, but I just want to say this. I didn't make you very welcome, and I apologise for that. I was ill mannered and extremely rude. I let—no, I made you believe William and I were—well, you know…and I really shouldn't have. It's plagued me ever since, for I know that it was my fault that you went and married Martin Taverner—and because of that I am responsible for the dreadful chain of events that followed.'

'I agree. It really was quite wrong of you to make me believe that you and William were back together,' Eleanor said, speaking softly and without rancour. 'But it is over now, so there is no point in resurrecting something that is painful to us both.'

'I know, it's just that I was terribly hurt when William went away, and when he came back and I was married to Henry, I didn't want him to notice you, to look at you, as he had once looked at me. I'm sorry,' she said awkwardly, finally glancing across at her. 'Things were intolerable for you at Fryston Hall, I knew that, and I carry a heavy burden of guilt at not defending you or supporting you when you most needed it. Can we be friends?'

'Friends and sisters,' Eleanor said, smiling her forgiveness and reaching out her hand. Catherine took it in her own and tucked it in the crook of her arm.

'Thank you. That means a lot to me. This is a new beginning for both of us, no matter what happens in the future, we will stay in touch. When we are apart we will write to each other.'

'Yes, we will, and you must come to Staxton Hall to stay. Tell me about you and Godfrey, Catherine. I was most surprised when William told me how close you've become—lovers, in fact,' she said, giving Catherine a knowing, approving look.

Catherine sighed and looked wistfully into the distance, a happy smile playing on her lips. 'We became lovers almost immediately. Godfrey! I've never met anyone quite like him. He makes me feel so alive and reckless and I don't care. For the first time in my life I have met someone I want to be with always, a man I want so much it makes me ache—someone who loves me for myself. He may not be from noble stock or fabulously rich—although I do believe he came back from the Americas with his own booty,' she remarked laughingly, her eyes twinkling merrily, 'but he will do for me.'

'I doubt your father would have approved of him.'

'I know that. We both know how my father liked to live in the style as grandiose as the royal Court itself, but he is dead and such things are beyond my consideration.'

'How did his death affect you, Catherine? Were you saddened by it?'

Catherine's lips curled in a bitter smile. 'I can't say that I was affected by it—more the manner of it. That he could hang himself surprised me, but I was not stricken by grief, if that's what you are asking. As you know, he never behaved like a father to me. I had hoped for some degree of affection as I was growing up, but received none at his hands—which instilled an unforgivable bitterness in me. Love was a rare commodity when I was a child.'

'I don't think your father knew how to love.'

'No. He surprised me when I married Henry, that lavish banquet and everything, but after that there was nothing. Your leaving didn't help.' She smiled. 'He didn't get over that—in fact, I would say it was the death of him.'

'I hope not. I certainly didn't intend it to be. I was merely looking out for myself.'

'Of course you were and I don't blame you, but things began going downhill after that. His business associates and fellow aldermen began to avoid him. No longer popular, he lost money—and his dream of ever becoming Lord Mayor of London crumbled to nothing. He must have been very disturbed to do what he did. But none of that matters to me anymore. I'm looking forward to a new and better life with Godfrey.'

Eleanor looked at her, glad that they were able to talk like friends at last. 'I am surprised. There was a time when these things were as important to you as they were to your father.'

'True, but Godfrey has taught me much—such as having understanding and consideration for others. Nothing matters as long as I have him and we are together. I have all I want.'

'And will you marry him?'

'I hope so, but for now we are happy as we are.' Catherine glanced at her stepsister enquiringly. Since Eleanor had come to Chelsea, Catherine had noted how withdrawn she was. Clearly something preyed on her mind and she suspected that that something had much to do with William. 'But what about you and William? I expect you will marry quite soon.'

Eleanor smiled and looked down at her swollen abdomen, feeling the child move vigorously—in fact, it was never still. 'I think we'd better,' she laughed, 'otherwise this little one will be born illegitimate, and that would never do.'

'But you do love William?'

'Absolutely,' she answered quietly, honestly. 'He is my life. I'm—I'm just not sure…'

Catherine heard the catch in her voice and looked at her with concern. 'What? If he loves you?'

'Yes.' Her face became expressionless and Catherine observed a deep sadness in her eyes. 'He—he hasn't said—and then he stayed away when I most needed him—when Martin was killed and I suffered so much. Why did he do it? If he loved me, he would have come to see me—wouldn't he?'

'Eleanor, he couldn't. How could he when he was so ill?'

Eleanor came to an abrupt halt, her eyes suddenly alert. 'Ill?' A wave of anguish broke through her. Her face was carved into a pale mask and her amber eyes were huge and unblinking. There was a dreadful silence, then, 'How ill? Catherine, what are you talking about?'

'William contracted a fever, Eleanor—after going on board a ship where it had been rife for weeks, Godfrey told me. He was laid low for a long time. It was touch and go for a while and we really thought he might not recover. When he did get better, he couldn't go to you for fear that you might become infected.'

Catherine's words tore into her brain with a rending impact that fairly staggered her. 'But why was I not told? It should not have been kept from me.'

'It's supposed to be a secret. He didn't want to worry you, so he's going to be very angry with me for telling you.'

'Not half as angry as I will be when I speak to him.'

Her frenzied thoughts must have shown in her face, for Catherine looked at her worriedly.

'Are you all right?' she asked.

Eleanor was incensed. 'There's nothing wrong with me that a confrontation with William Marston won't put right. Where is he, Catherine? I must see him.'

'I believe he's with Godfrey, preparing to leave shortly for Whitehall before dark. But don't worry. He won't go without seeing you.'

'No, he will not. Excuse me Catherine. I have a few choice words to say to him that will not wait.'

Blind to everything but her intention to find William and give him a piece of her mind, she stormed into the stable. With her hands plunked on her hips, she paused to allow her eyes a moment to adjust to the gloom. William and Godfrey were saddling their horses, William squatting down as he examined his mount's hoof.

On seeing Eleanor in her angry stance, his long, lean, handsome body uncurled to its full height. Eleanor felt her heart contract with pain and tremors of it seemed to flow into every part of her body. The internal war between her heart and her mind escalated to tumultuous proportions as she absorbed the strength and the power of him. She loved this man so much, more than anything she had known, and without him she would wither and die, but she was not about to become distracted by that crooked, wicked smile he was giving her now that made her legs go weak.

'Eleanor! I was just coming to find you.'

'I've saved you the trouble.'

One brow raised in arrogant enquiry, William tightened the girth on his horse, looking not only casual but supremely unconcerned. 'I'm about to leave for Whitehall. I want to be there before dark.'

'This won't take a moment.'

'Hell's teeth! What the devil's happened?'

'As if you didn't know,' she burst out furiously, and then, with a superhuman effort, she took control of her rampaging ire. Lifting her chin, she looked straight into his enigmatic silver-grey eyes, but he seemed unaffected as he casually rested his arms on his horse's back and fixed his steady gaze on her face.

William waited for her to tell him why she was here in such a temper, noting a soft flush beneath the fine creamy smoothness of her skin. 'May I ask the reason for this temper you are in?' he asked unwisely when she failed to speak.

'Temper? Temper, you say?' she flared, feeling her control slide once more into fury. Moving to stand at the other side of his horse, she glowered at him across its back, before looking sideways at Godfrey. 'Be so good as to leave us, Godfrey. There is something I have to say to your good friend that might offend your ears.'

Throwing his hands in the air and laughing deeply with outright amusement, shaking his head in bemusement, Godfrey left them alone.

'So,' she said scornfully when they were alone, giving him a haughty stare, 'you have been ill, William—close to death's door, I hear, and you wanted it kept from me. How could you? How could you do that? Am I or am I not to be your wife, the woman you are to share things with? Did you really think I wouldn't want to know—that I didn't want to know everything there is to know about you?'

'You had enough troubles of your own to contend with at the time. I didn't want to add to them. But if it's any consolation, I felt a great deal of concern for you.'

'Concern?' His infuriating calm made Eleanor long to kick him in the shin. 'Guilt more like. Guilt for getting me with child.'

He cocked an amused brow. 'It does takes two.'

Eleanor's amber eyes blazed at him across the horse's back. 'I do know that. In my foolish, gullible disbelief, I thought you wanted me—it was that same stupid streak of naïvety that led me to sacrifice my virginity and my pride to you. I let myself believe that you wanted me, that you loved me.'

'I'm going to marry you, aren't I?' he drawled.

'You proposed—no, of course you didn't—you *told* me we were going to be married, not because you cannot live with me or you worship the ground I walk on, not because I make the blood sing in your veins when we are together. I now know you are doing it out of pity and guilt and responsibility—and, yes, obligation—and for a hundred other reasons, but not the one that matters to me.'

'Which is?' He was watching her closely.

'That you love me—or would even want to marry me if it were not for the child.'

'Really? Then it was very bad of me to put it like that. But when you told me you were pregnant, I had no doubt you would marry me.'

'You didn't have to doubt,' she snarled. 'You see, I am a complete and utter fool when it comes to you.'

Laughing lightly, William sauntered round the horse to stand in front of her, towering over her. 'I expected you to be angry and upset when you found out about my illness, but I hadn't expected it to begin with the angry aggression of a duel,' he said, chuckling softly, seeming to be amused by her ire, which infuriated Eleanor even more. 'I would have preferred sympathy and concern and enquiries as to how I am feeling now.'

'Of all the arrogant, selfish beasts!' she burst out angrily.

She was magnificent, even when she was being defiant, William thought, as he looked at her, wisps of hair caressing her cheek and the rest of it bouncing about as her head bobbed in her anger. Her lips were soft and sensuous, her eyes a clear and sparkling shade of deep amber, fringed by thick, black lashes. Courageous, proud, impertinent, adorable, beautiful in the undisguised fullness of impending motherhood—yes, she was all of these and he fully intended that she would be his. This delectable woman, whose stormy eyes were spitting fire, would be his wife, grace his house and bear his children, and pit her will against his whenever she saw fit.

'Eleanor, you know how I feel about you.'

'No, William, I don't how you feel. That's just it.'

'Why? I've told you often enough.'

'Really?' she scoffed. 'Then my ears must be going deaf, because I have failed to hear you.'

'Eleanor, I want to look after you, take care of you and know that you are safe—in my home, as my wife and the mother of my children. Dear Lord, you act as though I'd offered you some insult instead of an honourable proposal of marriage.'

'Honourable?' She gasped. 'Why, your arrogance stupefies me—your stubborn belief that you are right, and that you only have to snap your fingers and I will do your bidding without murmur or complaint.'

'Are you trying to tell me you don't want to marry me? You are to bear my child, don't forget.'

'How could I forget? Look at me. I'm as fat as a cow already and I'm only halfway through my pregnancy.'

William's lips curled in a roguish grin and his eyes twinkled with mischief. 'I'm very partial to cows.'

His propensity to make a joke of it only served to increase her ire. 'That's beside the point, William—and don't be flippant. *You* decided, not me.'

Even as she continued to berate him, William's mind and senses were bemused by the way the sunlight penetrated the wooden slats at the windows and tangled in her bright hair, streaking the copper and gold with silver light that gave it a halo affect. It curled vigorously over her shoulders, twisting and tumbling to her thickening waist.

Closing the distance between them, he reached out and gently tucked a strand of hair behind her ear and, tenderly cupping her chin in his hand, looked deep into her stormy eyes. His brows pulled together as an astonishing realisation struck him, for, despite her magnificent show of courage, Eleanor was apparently on the brink of tears.

'Why are you behaving like this, Eleanor? I was ill and now I am well. Why are you cavilling over a trifle?'

'Oh, you—you insensitive, insufferable, heartless man,' she cried, pounding his chest with her fists in frustration. 'I do not consider you being so ill that you almost expired a trifle,' she said, wanting to close her eyes against the scalding tears that threatened, but keeping them open and looking at him through a bleary haze, aware of his closeness and feeling her weak woman's body straining towards him. 'When you didn't come to Cantly Manor, I truly believed you didn't care enough—for me, when all the time—you were… You might have been dying. How do you think that makes me feel? I could not have borne it if you had died.'

With sudden, heartbreaking clarity, the seriousness of his illness and the fact that she might never have seen him again, that she might have lost him when he had come to mean everything to her, was overwhelming and the tears flooded from her eyes.

William's expression softened and in it was his desperate need to help this self-willed woman. Tenderness burst inside him and, unable to watch her torture herself any longer, he pulled her into his arms.

'I am sorry, my love. Based on the things you have accused me of, I know perfectly well that I am guilty of all of them and deserve your chastisement. I am fully conscious of the true depth of my failing to consider your wishes in all matters concerning us. Where my illness is concerned, I truly did not want to worry you with anything that might have distressed both you and the child. But, throughout my ordeal, my thoughts were entirely of you. You must believe that.'

'They were?' she asked, finding it difficult to be convinced.

'I am not marrying you for the sake of duty or because I feel obligated.'

'Then tell me why? I need to know,' she whispered. Her body became still in his arms, her cheek resting against his chest as she waited, not breathing, anticipating his next words.

Tightening his arms around her, William placed his lips on the top of her head. 'It's because I love you,' he said fiercely. 'I love you more than life,' he whispered softly, burying his face in her hair. 'You called me heartless, and you were right. You see, my love, I didn't know I had one, until I met you, and even then I didn't recognise what it was feeling. You are a light in my life and my body and my soul craves for you. Without you I will cease to live.'

Eleanor turned her tear-streaked face up to his, her eyes shining with all the love that was in her heart. 'I could have lost you.'

'Don't, Eleanor, don't cry. It would take more than a fever to get rid of me.'

'I do love you, William. I love you so very much.'

'And you will marry me—and have my baby?'

'Gladly.' She smiled through her tears and laid the palm of her hand against him cheek. 'Thank you for asking.'

Fryston Hall had an air of the sinister about it. Having been shuttered and the servants dismissed on Frederick Atwood's death, it was strangely silent, almost like a tomb. Sir Richard Grey had inherited his uncle's estate, but he had no wish to live in the house and according to Catherine, intended selling it.

Eleanor shuddered. She had agreed to accompany Catherine to collect some of her father's things, since Catherine hadn't wanted to come alone. Godfrey was tied up with William on some important business at Whitehall. The sombre atmosphere preyed on Eleanor more than she cared to admit, but Catherine seemed to be above fears of this kind. Even the driver of the coach preferred to remain outside rather than enter this gloomy old house in Bishopsgate.

'There are a few things I have to do in Father's rooms, Eleanor—and some things I would like to take back with me. Would you like to help?'

'If you don't mind, Catherine, I'd rather not. I'll wait here until you've finished.'

'I understand. I'll try not to be long.'

Eleanor watched her hurry away before looking around her. Lifting her skirts, she slowly climbed the stairs, the walls on either side hung with tapestries. Wandering through the familiar labyrinth of passages and rooms, she did not linger in any one place, for everywhere she looked was a painful reminder of Frederick Atwood and all she had suffered within these cold stone walls.

She walked past the stairs that led to an upper storey and

into the great hall where only months earlier they had cele-brated Catherine's marriage to Henry Wheeler. Looking around the eerily quiet, empty room, it was impossible to believe that all that merrymaking had taken place here. How much had happened since that day when her entire life had changed.

'Catherine?' she called. There was no answer. She must be too far away to hear her, she reasoned.

Going back to the stairs and climbing to the next floor, she looked around, but there was no sign of her stepsister. When she was about to go back downstairs, on hearing slow and measured footsteps she paused and looked ahead, wondering who it could be since Catherine must be in another part of the house. Her eye was caught by a tall figure advancing slowly towards her down the gallery. It was a man dressed in black and as he came closer, she felt the blood run cold in her veins, while her mind raced feverishly.

It was Robert Grey. She felt the sweat standing out on her brow and the blood drain from her face. He was like a sombre ghost haunting this old unwelcoming dwelling. She watched him warily as he halted close before her.

Confronted by Eleanor in her shimmering lime-green dress, Sir Richard stopped several feet in front of her. His nostrils flared and his eyes sparked suddenly as they slid down her neck, following the outline of her low, square-cut bodiced gown, where her perfect ripening contours were clearly defined by the soft silken material.

'I see you really are breeding like a bitch, Lady Taverner,' he jeered, arrogant in his demeanour, confident with Eleanor alone. 'Soon you'll be parading your belly about the Court for all to see and speculate on who the father might be. There are several who will take some convincing that it is your husband's child you carry, and that it is not some other man's by-blow.'

Eleanor stiffened, clasping her hands at her waist as if to

protect the child. Knowing she was alone with Sir Richard and how dangerous he could be, she fought to stop herself trembling and to hold on to her self-control. 'What are you doing here?' she asked.

'I might ask the same of you.'

'I should have remembered that as your uncle's heir this is now your home, if you want it to be, although Catherine believes you intend to sell it.'

'With my uncle's death I have become a man of some substance, power and circumstance,' Sir Richard stated. His smile was cold. 'I intend to enjoy all of it.'

'And all thanks to my stepfather.'

'Indeed. I have acquired many things—and I might or might not sell Fryston Hall. As yet I haven't made up my mind.'

'Then if you decide to live here, I hope it gives you more joy than it gave me. It hasn't taken you long to move in, or perhaps it's provided you with the perfect hideaway if you are lying low.' Her voice was harsh and meaningful and Richard Grey knew perfectly well to what she referred, even if he pretended otherwise.

'You speak in riddles, Lady Taverner. Won't you explain what you are talking about?'

'Martin.' She took a step closer, looking him straight in the eyes, trying not to show her fear of him. 'I know it was you who killed him. Who else would want to? Who else had reason to want to end his life—and in so brutal a manner? It was quite shocking and Martin did not deserve to die that way, if at all.'

'You know nothing,' Sir Richard uttered scornfully. 'Martin had no reason to be afraid of me, he knew that.'

'That doesn't mean to say you didn't kill him.'

'What did you imagine I would do when you triumphantly announced that the child you are carrying was Martin's? That

I would simply ignore it and carry on?' As he spoke and the words came pouring out, his features grew ugly and contorted with the anger and wild hatred that had been festering inside him ever since this woman had thrown Martin's child in his face. 'He tried to make a fool of me—you both did. What did he expect I would do? Did Martin honestly expect me to ignore the fact that he had betrayed me?'

'With his wife,' Eleanor pointed out coldly. 'But no matter what I told you that day at Whitehall, he did not betray you. For the short time we were man and wife, he never once shared my bed or even attempted to. So you see, Sir Richard, the child isn't Martin's. He remained faithful to you right to the end. Now, how does it feel, knowing you killed your lover for nothing? I did imply that the child was his. I should not have done, I realise that now, and I deeply regret doing so in so much as he is dead because of it. Sadly, I cannot retract what I said.'

A deadly smile twisted Sir Richard's features and his voice became dangerously soft. 'You're right. Martin would still be alive today if you had you not made your mischief, Lady Taverner, so the blame lies with you also and you must carry the guilt of it.'

'I shall—to my grave. But you were the one who wielded the knife. If you had truly cared for Martin, you would not have killed him. You won't get away with it,' she said, struggling to keep her voice even, wishing Catherine would appear. She turned back towards the stairs. 'Good day to you.'

'Not just yet.' He strolled arrogantly forwards and, reaching out, grabbed her arm and pulled her back. 'I am not done with you,' he hissed, spinning her round to face him and holding her in a vice-like grip. 'A face such as yours, so fine and fragile, would not bear well under a fist, Lady Taverner.'

Eleanor shuddered at the callow crudeness of his threat.

Struggling within his hold, she opened her mouth and screamed as loud as she could.

'Let her go,' a voice thundered.

It was William, sword raised, bounding up the stairs.

'William, thank God!' Eleanor shrieked. 'Help me.' She kicked and struggled, trying to get her attacker to let her go, but he was massively strong.

'God damn you, Grey!' William shouted, striding towards them.

Sir Richard released Eleanor and fell back, drawing his own sword. William circled him. The surge of anger that had engulfed him when he had seen Eleanor in his murderous grasp was replaced by a blackness of spirit.

'So, Marston,' Sir Richard sneered, 'you appear like a ghost from the past. You should have died on board that ship. I paid Paxton enough money to see to it.'

'And he paid with his life for his treachery,' William snarled. 'As you will—when the Queen's men get here to arrest you for the murder of Martin Taverner. When Atwood hanged himself, you must have thought it was your lucky day. Things turned out for you very well. Pity you will not live long enough to enjoy your inheritance.'

Madness flamed in Sir Richard's eyes. 'My uncle did not hang himself. When he ordered me to get rid of you he wanted you dead, but I had my own idea of how you would be disposed of.'

'Which failed. I came back. Did Atwood give you a hard time over it when he realised you had failed him? Was his wrath so severe that he threatened to disinherit you, so you killed him and made it look like he took his own life?' Sir Richard's nostrils flared and William saw he had hit upon the truth. 'Predictable as always,' he scoffed, 'you are well and truly caught.'

All Sir Richard's pent-up anger and resentment that he continued to feel for his uncle blazed in his eyes, and the image of him kicking his life away at the end of the rope was a pleasing one. 'He wanted to kill me, but I killed him instead—as I will now kill you, Marston,' he snarled, raising his sword.

Chilled and sickened to the bone, William launched the attack with all his considerable skill, thrusting and cutting with a determination and expertise that astounded Eleanor, who had fallen back so as not to be caught up in the fight.

Sir Richard exhaled sharply as he fell back against the wall. William drew back his fist and slammed it into Sir Richard's jaw. His head jerked back and he released his hold on his sword. Shaking his head, with a roar he then launched himself at William, who met the assault with a rain of blows to the other man's face and chest, knocking him to the floor. It became a mêlée of flailing arms and legs, but, being possessed of a heavier build and above-average strength, William had the advantage.

Eleanor, her heart in her mouth, watched them rolling over and over. Then she heard a disturbance below. Someone was thundering on the door, which crashed open beneath the onslaught. There were raised voices, the clattering of boots and feet pounding up the stairs. Suddenly the house seemed to be full of men wielding swords. Godfrey was in front and, seeing his friend on the floor, with a loud growl he went and separated the two combatants and hauled a badly beaten and gasping Richard Grey to his feet.

Wiping blood from a slight wound on his forehead with his sleeve, William confronted Atwood's nephew with hatred in every line of his body. 'I swore revenge for what you did to me. For too long you have escaped justice and escaped your fate, but no longer. When you killed Martin Taverner in cold blood, you went too far.' He looked at the men gathering round. 'Take him away.'

Not to be defeated so easily, feeling Godfrey's grasp slacken, the captive seized on the opportunity to escape down a narrow flight of stairs at the back of him. William's eyes settled on the departing Sir Richard with cold fury tearing through every pore of his body. Like a panther he shot after him, spurred on by the image of Sir Richard's rough handling of Eleanor earlier. Sir Richard had reached the bottom of the stairs when all at once he staggered and fell under William's weight as he hurled himself at him.

Hardly able to believe the evidence of her eyes, Eleanor watched in astonishment as William threw himself on Sir Richard and once again the two men rolled on the floor, locked in a desperate struggle. Sir Richard fought, moreover, with all the fury and desperation of a man cornered. He uttered inarticulate cries of rage as William's fist not for the first time slammed into his jaw, before Godfrey stepped in and brought him to his feet, struggling and gasping.

'Nice work. Bind his wrists,' William gasped as men came to his aid. 'Cease struggling, Grey. You cannot escape. Take him out.'

Even firmly in the grip of the strong men, Sir Richard continued to fight like a demon. He was white-faced and foaming with rage, his eyes, filled with madness, glaring murderously at William, as he was dragged out of the house.

William crossed to Eleanor. He stared down at her, his gaze probing hers and finding fear and distress within their depths. Reaching out he gathered her in his arms as she came to him and softly cried her relief against his chest, becoming more intense as the stress of the last hour was released and her fears put to rest. William kissed her head and lovingly brushed a silken tress from her cheeks.

'It's all right now. The worst is over,' he murmured with a tender smile.'

'Thank goodness Godfrey and those men came in time,' Eleanor whispered brokenly against his chest. Trembling with relief, she clung to him, wetting his doublet with her tears and she felt his lips on her hair and the gentle stroking of his hand as he held her close. 'Where will they take him?'

'To the Tower for questioning.'

'He confessed to killing my stepfather and Martin. Will—will he be executed?'

'I expect he will, which is no more that he deserves.'

When Eleanor quieted, she looked up at William's anxious face and smiled. 'I'm sorry. I was afraid for you. I thank God my baby will not grow up without a father.' Her heart wrenched at the sight of the bruises and cuts on his handsome face. They were a brutal reminder of what he had been through. She forgot her own discomforts in witnessing his. Tenderly she touched a raw spot at the side of his jaw, her expression one of deep concern. 'I think you should let the physician take a look at you.'

William took her hands in his. 'Don't be alarmed by my appearance. The bruises are superficial and will fade soon enough. I'll live.' Looking around him, he shuddered. 'Dear Lord, how I hate this place. Come, let's get out.'

'How did you know to come here?' Eleanor enquired, going with him to the door.

'I knew this would be where Grey was hiding. What I didn't expect was that I would find you here.' He paused and glanced at her. 'Why are you here, Eleanor? I would have thought Fryston Hall to be the last place you would be.'

'I came with Catherine. She had some things of her father's to collect and she didn't want to come by herself. I wonder where she is.'

'Here,' said a voice beside her.

Eleanor turned and saw her stepsister and smiled with relief. 'Catherine! Thank goodness. Where have you been?'

'In Father's rooms, looking through his things. There is far too much to take back with me today. I really must arrange to have them removed. Although what I will do with them I really don't know. What was the commotion all about, by the way?'

Eleanor and William looked at each other simultaneously and smiled.

'I'll tell you on the way back,' Eleanor said, laughing and linking her arm through Catherine's. 'Come, let's go home.'

Eleanor and William were married very quietly in the small chapel in Catherine's house in Chelsea. It was festooned with garlands of flowers, the heady scent of honeysuckle and lavender so intoxicating it made Eleanor's head swim.

William was already inside the chapel when Eleanor arrived with Catherine. She paused in the doorway to look at him. Resplendent in a doublet of midnight-blue velvet and a small white lace collar, he was standing with Godfrey, his head leaning to his as they exchanged words. Eleanor knew the moment he became aware of her presence. His words died on his lips and he turned his head to look at his bride.

Her snow-white satin dress was ornamented with tiny pears, the sleeves ending at her elbows edged with deep lace. Her hair hung free down her back, her honey-gold tresses tumbling to her waist.

Striding towards her, William took her hand and drew her to him, unable to define the mixed emotions he felt as he looked at her. She was beautiful, utterly lovely, his bride.

'Eleanor, you dazzle me.'

Eleanor felt herself blushing under his intense regard and her own eyes never faltered in returning his gaze. 'I wish my mother and father were here this day to see me wed to the man I love so dearly,' she whispered, unable to believe her happiness.

'I believe they would be well pleased, Eleanor. You must

have thought fate struck you a harsh blow when your father died, but things have a way of coming right. I would not have asked you to be my wife if I did not think I was capable of making you happy.'

'How I wish it was for the first time.'

'You yourself decreed our parting. I hated what you did for a while, but then I saw why you did what you did. I shall love you till I die. So come, my love, and marry me.'

The ceremony took hardly a moment in time. Plighting their troth, they both felt the solemnity of the priest's final blessings, which faded away in a final amen. Eleanor raised her eyes, eyes shimmering with tears in orbs of amber and laced with love and hope for the future she would have with this man who was now her husband.

William's strong hands closed on her arms and with his throat tight with emotion almost too great to be borne, he murmured, 'Kiss me, Eleanor.'

She raised her mouth blindly for him to place his lips on hers, then, after he pulled her hand through his arm, they turned from the altar and together walked out of the chapel, while Catherine and Godfrey, arms entwined, looked on, envisioning their own wedding day in the near future.

By tacit consent, the newly-weds stayed with Catherine and Godfrey for a few days before setting out on the long journey to Yorkshire. The parting for William and Godfrey was a difficult one, having been through much together, but Godfrey, intending to take Catherine to his native Glasgow, promised they would call at Staxton Hall when they travelled north.

If William's family had expected him to bring Catherine home to Staxton Hall as his bride, they hid their surprise and rejoiced in his marriage to Eleanor.

Lady Alice kissed them both when William took his bride on his arm and presented her as his wife, daring his mother to dispute him or disparage Eleanor in any way for being so far on with child when they had only been wed three weeks.

'I am delighted for you both,' Alice said. 'This is indeed a joyous time for all of us—and I see there are more surprises on the way.' She raised her eyebrows slightly at Eleanor's advanced pregnancy but asked no awkward questions, being content to await the birth in anticipation of an easy delivery and a healthy child.

They were an impressive couple—William as handsome and proud as a man should be, and Eleanor as beautiful and content as a woman could be.

Eleanor settled into life at Staxton Hall with ease. With the two men who had set fire to Hollymead and attacked her in York executed for their crime and Sir Richard Grey having met his end on the block, she felt that life as she had known it at Fryston Hall was over for good. William's mother and his sisters fussed over her and watched her constantly; when she jokingly complained, they laughingly told her that she'd better make the most of it, since they were leaving Staxton Hall to take up residence in Alice's brother's house in Pickering when the baby was born.

For William, life with Eleanor was everything he ever hoped it could be, and more. A surge of tenderness and profound pride swept through him at her sweetness and her candour, and she filled him with joyous contentment. She was a rare woman and everything he had ever wanted. He loved her, all of her—her intelligence, her sensitivity, her gentle, passionate nature, but most of all he loved her courage, the kind of courage that had enabled her to confront adversity time after time.

Without it she would not have left Fryston Hall, and she would have been lost to him.

Eleanor's labour began suddenly and fiercely in the first week of November. Contractions gripped her body and, after a moment's panic, she was struck with the enormity of the situation.

'It's too soon,' she cried, panicking as another pain gripped her. 'The child is not yet due.'

Coming into the room, William's mother calmly assessed the situation and ordered Eleanor to be taken to her room. 'It's not unusual. The child is obviously in a hurry to see the world.'

With dawning alarm William gathered Eleanor into his arms and mounted the stairs and carried his tender burden to their room. Everything was blotted from her mind, the centre of her being focussing only on getting the baby out as soon as possible.

As the pain assaulted her in a continuous wave, with the birth of the child the relief was enormous, but short lived, for quickly there was another agonising pain and Eleanor's second child was born. Twins. A boy and a girl.

Later, holding her babies—small and as soft and light as thistledown—she looked sleepily at William, who had come in to the bedchamber and was leaning over her. 'We have two babies,' she whispered, 'just like you said we might. Two beautiful, perfectly formed babies.'

Settling himself beside her on the bed and taking the boy in his arms, Eleanor smiled through her tears of happiness as he looked proudly down into the tiny, wrinkled face of his son.

'Are you pleased with our children, William?'

His eyes glittering with unsuppressed pride and joy, William smoothed the curls off her cheek stained with a rosy blush. His sensual lips quirked in a half-smile. 'Pleased is an understatement. A boy and a girl—how wonderful is that? They are beautiful. Just like their mother,' he said, his voice raw from the emotion of the past twelve hours.

Knowing how hazardous childbirth could often be, William had lived the horrors of the things that could go wrong. Leaning forward he covered her mouth with his own, the gentle kiss eloquent of the profound love he felt for her, and relief that her ordeal was over and she was well.

'Thank you, my darling,' he breathed against her lips.

Settling her cheek against the tiny head in her arms, she closed her eyes and whispered, 'You're welcome.'

* * * * *

On sale 2nd May 2008

A RECKLESS BEAUTY
by Kasey Michaels

A rebellious innocent

Fanny Beckett has adored her adopted brother forever –
where he goes, she follows. But when she pursues him into
battle, Fanny finds herself not only in the line of fire but
also in the embrace of a handsome stranger!

A jaded lord

Valentine Clement, Earl of Brede, has seen enough
of fighting to know that there is no adventure to be found at
Waterloo. The moment he sees the reckless beauty, he is
duty-bound to save her. Although with such a woman, it
may well be his lordship who is in need of protection…

Available at WHSmith, Tesco, ASDA, and all good bookshops
www.millsandboon.co.uk

0408/04a

MILLS & BOON

Historical

On sale 2nd May 2008

THE LAST RAKE IN LONDON
by Nicola Cornick

Under a blaze of chandeliers, in London's most fashionable
club, Jack Kestrel is waiting. He hasn't come to enjoy the rich at
play, he's there to uphold his family name. But first he
has to get past the ice-cool owner, the beautiful Sally Bowes…
and the wicked glint in his eyes promises Jack will take
care of satisfying Sally's *every* need!

Regency

THE OUTRAGEOUS LADY FELSHAM
by Louise Allen

Belinda, Lady Felsham, plans to enjoy herself. She suspects that
the breathtakingly handsome Major Ashe Reynard is exactly
what she needs. Society is just waiting for them to make a slip!
Still, the outrageous couple embark on an affair – and Belinda
becomes increasingly confused. She has no desire to marry,
but Ashe is a man she cannot live without…

Available at WHSmith, Tesco, ASDA, and all good bookshops
www.millsandboon.co.uk

0408/04b

MILLS & BOON

Historical

On sale 2nd May 2008

AN UNCONVENTIONAL MISS
by Dorothy Elbury

Miss Jessica Beresford is headstrong, impetuous and poorly
dowered. Benedict Ashcroft, Earl of Wyvern, knows he should
steer well clear of her, however dazzling her beauty. He cannot
dally with such an unconventional miss…can he?

THE WARRIOR'S TOUCH
by Michelle Willingham

When Connor MacEgan's hands are crushed, he may
never wield a sword – or touch a woman – again. Aileen
holds a secret that could break their hearts long after
she has mended his hands…

THE SCOUNDREL
by Lisa Plumley

Brawny blacksmith Daniel McCabe is not the marrying
kind. He likes his freedom just fine, and no lady is going to
change *that!* But an unexpected delivery will make the
bachelor rethink his roguish ways.

Available at WHSmith, Tesco, ASDA, and all good bookshops
www.millsandboon.co.uk

0408/05a

MILLS & BOON
BY REQUEST
3
NOVELS ONLY
£4.99

**On sale
2nd May 2008**

In May 2008 Mills
& Boon present two
bestselling collections,
each featuring
fabulous romances by
favourite authors…

His Bride on His Terms

Featuring

His Bid for a Bride by Carole Mortimer
His Inherited Bride by Jacqueline Baird
His Forbidden Bride by Sara Craven

Available at WHSmith, Tesco, ASDA, and all good bookshops
www.millsandboon.co.uk

0408/05b

**On sale
2nd May 2008**

MILLS & BOON
BY REQUEST
3
NOVELS ONLY
£4.99

Don't miss
out on these
fabulous
stories!

High Society Weddings

Featuring

The Tycoon Prince by Barbara McMahon
The Ordinary Princess by Liz Fielding
Princess in the Outback by Barbara Hannay

*Available at WHSmith, Tesco, ASDA, and all good bookshops
www.millsandboon.co.uk*

*A delicious addition to the
Moreland family novels!*

Gloucestershire, 1878

Ever since Anna Holcombe refused his proposal, Reed
Moreland has been unable to set foot in the home that
was the backdrop to their romance – Winterset.

But when Reed has dreams about Anna being in danger,
he heads back to Winterset, determined to protect the
woman he still loves. Once again passion flares between
them, but the murder of a servant girl draws them deep
into deadly legends of Winterset…and a destiny neither
Anna nor Reed can escape.

Available 18th April 2008

www.millsandboon.co.uk

Celebrate 100 years of pure reading pleasure with Mills & Boon®

To mark our centenary, each month we're publishing a special 100th Birthday Edition. These celebratory editions are packed with extra features and include a FREE bonus story.

Plus, starting in February you'll have the chance to enter a fabulous monthly prize draw. See 100th Birthday Edition books for details.

Now that's worth celebrating!

15th February 2008

Raintree: Inferno by Linda Howard
Includes FREE bonus story Loving Evangeline
A double dose of Linda Howard's heady mix of passion and adventure

4th April 2008

The Guardian's Forbidden Mistress by Miranda Lee
Includes FREE bonus story The Magnate's Mistress
Two glamorous and sensual reads from favourite author Miranda Lee!

2nd May 2008

The Last Rake in London by Nicola Cornick
Includes FREE bonus story The Notorious Lord
Lose yourself in two tales of high society and rakish seduction!

Look for Mills & Boon 100th Birthday Editions at your favourite bookseller or visit
www.millsandboon.co.uk

2 FREE

BOOKS AND A SURPRISE GIFT!

We would like to take this opportunity to thank you for reading this Mills & Boon® book by offering you the chance to take TWO more specially selected titles from the Historical series absolutely FREE! We're also making this offer to introduce you to the benefits of the Mills & Boon® Reader Service™—

- ★ **FREE home delivery**
- ★ **FREE gifts and competitions**
- ★ **FREE monthly Newsletter**
- ★ **Exclusive Reader Service offers**
- ★ **Books available before they're in the shops**

Accepting these FREE books and gift places you under no obligation to buy, you may cancel at any time, even after receiving your free shipment. Simply complete your details below and return the entire page to the address below. You don't even need a stamp!

YES! Please send me 2 free Historical books and a surprise gift. I understand that unless you hear from me. I will receive 4 superb new titles every month for just £3.69 each, postage and packing free. I am under no obligation to purchase any books and may cancel my subscription at any time. The free books and gift will be mine to keep in any case.

H8ZED

Ms/Mrs/Miss/Mr ....Initials ....

BLOCK CAPITALS PLEASE

Surname ....

Address ....

....

....Postcode................................

Send this whole page to:
UK: FREEPOST CN81, Croydon, CR9 3WZ

Offer valid in UK only and is not available to current Mills & Boon® Reader Service™ subscribers to this series. Overseas and Eire please write for detailsand readers in Southern Africa write to Box 3010, Pinegowie, 2123 RSA. We reserve the right to refuse an application and applicants must be aged 18 years or over. Only one application per household. Terms and prices subject to change without notice. Offer expires 30th June 2008. As a result of this application, you may receive offers from Harlequin Mills & Boon and other carefully selected companies. If you would prefer not to share in this opportunity please write to The Data Manager, PO Box 676, Richmond, TW9 1WU.

Mills & Boon® is a registered trademark owned by Harlequin Mills & Boon Limited.
The Mills & Boon® Reader Service™ is being used as a trademark.